THE VERY AIR

Also by Douglas Bauer

PRAIRIE CITY, IOWA (NONFICTION)

DEXTERITY (A NOVEL)

THE VERY AIR

A Novel

DOUGLAS BAUER

❖ ❖ ❖

William Morrow and Company, Inc.
New York

Library of Congress Cataloging-in-Publication Data

Bauer, Douglas.
      The very air : a novel / Douglas Bauer.
            p.   cm.
      ISBN 0-688-09460-0
      1. Texas—History—Fiction.   I. Title.
PS3552.A8358V46   1993
813'.54—dc20   93-47253
                                                CIP

Printed in the United States of America

First Edition

1 2 3 4 5 6 7 8 9 10

BOOK DESIGN BY BARBARA BACHMAN

For   Sue

❖   ❖   ❖

A c k n o w l e d g m e n t s

I want to thank the National Endowment for the Arts for a grant that helped support the writing of this novel.

In addition, I'm deeply grateful to the people of Del Rio, Texas, most especially Bess Bradley, Carmen Fuentes, Janet Weber, Zina Worley, Dan Bus, and the staff at the Val Verde County Library.

I owe great debts to John Wheat and others at the Barker Center for Texas History at the University of Texas in Austin; I owe extraordinary ones to Gene Fowler, Durrell Roth, and Bill Crawford, who generously shared their enthusiasm for and tremendous knowledge of the particular history from which this fiction was made. I also want to mention Gerald Carson and his book, *The Roguish World of Dr. Brinkley*, which supplied some essential factual groundwork.

Many others offered help and advice, including Rachel Maurer, Dr. George Oetting, Dallas Turner, Dr. George Ritcher, and Dr. Taylor Floyd. And in Houston, George Werner's information regarding train travel was invaluable.

Finally, I am fortunate indeed to be the beneficiary of the wisdom and the energy of my editor, Maria Guarnaschelli, and my agent, Al Lowman.

"Now Faith is the substance of things hoped for, the evidence of things not seen."

— HEBREWS 11 : 1

❖ ❖ ❖

"Illusions need not necessarily be false."

— SIGMUND FREUD,
The Future of an Illusion

BOOK ONE

◆ ◆ ◆

1905

C h a p t e r

‖

On the twenty-third of April, in 1905, Luther Mathias's mother came into their house and sat down at the table and began to laugh hysterically. Her name was Sarah Jane. She was a short, thin woman who had once been almost plump. Her face was permanently raw from the weather of the Panhandle—winds of fierce heat and winds of fierce chill—and it was deeply lined from the strain of her life on a tiny livestock farm five miles from Cliffside, Texas. She was twenty-six years old and had been very beautiful, but she now looked twice her age and her sunken face was set in a misrepresentative meanness. She and Luther lived alone for months at a time. Her husband, Aubrey, Luther's father, bunked for much of the year on a huge cattle ranch near the Oklahoma border where he worked as handyman and keeper of the stock. On this day, she'd come inside from an unusual late-spring blizzard after feeding the horses, which were by equine standards almost as thin as she was. There was frost in her eyebrows and lashes. It was shortly after sundown.

At first, her laughter was nearly silent. Her upper body simply shook. Luther, who was ten years old, watched her from across the room and saw it as the same violent shivering she'd been suffering for weeks. But then sounds—a cackling, really—began to issue from her throat. They built in pitch and strength. Her shaking turned convulsive. This was behavior he hadn't seen before. He'd watched her shake and often heard her muttering argumentatively with something he himself could not see that followed her back and forth between their two rooms. He'd grown used to the shaking and, in a way, the muttering enthralled him. But this laughter was new and he was frightened by its wildness.

"Cliffside!" his mother shrieked and her laughter grew still stronger. "Cliff!" she shouted. "Side!" She lowered her eyes. Her giggle was coquettish. "Truly, that is the most amusing thing in my memory." The frost had melted and was running down her face. Her look was dispersed, falling no more or less on Luther than on his bed in the corner or the wood stove beside it. She laughed. Then her eyes appeared to focus and define for an instant a space in the room between Luther and the stove. She said to the space, "Y'all shoulda told me that your name was Cliff Side." She fell back in her chair and directed her laughter to a low ceiling beam. She flopped about in the chair like a merry epileptic. Then she grew quiet, now and then shouting "Cliff! Side!" with the same antic force. Her son stood where he was, his fear paralytic, watching the cords in her throat flex and loosen when she swallowed.

After a length of time he realized the room was getting cold. He walked to the stove and fed it some wood. He stood close to it, taking its heat. The sounds in his life were the stove's burning wood and the high-whistling wind. His mother had been still in her chair for a while. She had not changed her position. Her head remained tilted to the ceiling. With reluctance he moved away from the safe heat of the stove. When he reached her side he saw that her eyes were closed. "Mama?" he said.

Luther Mathias was a highly intelligent child in most any way that intelligence might be measured. He read avidly in school and at home he read the Bible for its melodrama, for the hyperbole of violence and magic and abundant reward that marks the best children's stories. With animals, he had a veterinary sensitivity that could be called empathic. Beneath all this, his common sense was preternatural. So he had understood, though his impulse was otherwise, that he should wait until morning, when the sky was light and the blizzard might be finished, before riding into Cliffside to get word to his father that his mother was dead.

He rode toward the dawn. Cliffside was three miles east and two miles south of their farm. Three hundred seventy-five people lived in the settlement. Amarillo was fifteen miles farther east.

The snow, which had ended, had spread itself over the terrain as though purposely troweled. The astonishing flatness of the Panhandle allowed the lifting sun no coyness, no veiling treeline, no hillocky sweep behind which to rise in a diffuse, majestic tease. It simply broke the line of the horizon, an obvious orange curve that was blinding and uncomplicated, and started up into the sky. It was a sunrise altogether without mystery. Or it was mystery itself, depending on your attitude toward subtlety and nuance.

He was not yet sorrowful. His mind was filled instead with his responsibility and his heart with the unsettling strangeness of the previous night. He kept hearing as he rode his mother's frantic laughter. He tried vainly to place its fierceness within the history of her diffidence. He was, of course, a boy, and understood nothing of the epidemic madness among women of these times who lived in isolation and listened to the wind.

He was hearing, too, the last words she'd spoken as she had lain in his bed. For she had not been dead when he had whispered, "Mama?" She'd opened her eyes to his voice. They were thickly glazed, as though a clear gel covered them. Taking her hand, he'd helped her to stand. The temperature of her skin would have alarmed someone older. But she had been carrying the fever undiminished for a month and he'd gotten used to the heat of his mother's skin. His will had gradually made the sensation reassuring. It had become a source of warmth to him, sustenant like the wood stove's.

She'd walked across the room and lain down in his bed. She still wore her coat. She was shaking once more, but not with any laughter. Then she'd opened her eyes again and said in a soft whine, "I will. I promise y'all I'll go directly, just as soon as y'all close up that hole in your belly." She'd again been speaking to the space. She'd stared at it a moment, she'd seemed to her son to be listening to an answer, and finally said without emotion, "Y'all are a horse's ass of the first water." Then she'd closed her eyes. He had never heard anything remotely close to profanity from his mother's lips.

He had seen animals die. He had watched a mare, whose tongue was paste-covered and swollen thick as a shoe, as its life went out of it and so he had learned that at the moment death arrives there is the sensation not of loss but of increased presence. And because he was a child, he held no condescending assumption that witnessing a human death differed in the least from watching an animal's. So when the room had suddenly felt crowded and its air close and busy, he'd known that his mother was no longer simply sleeping. At some point later on in the night he'd touched her face and was reminded that her skin hadn't always been on fire.

He reached Cliffside (*Cliff! Side!* he heard her shout, as he read the depot sign) and, as his father had told him he would in an emergency, Luther found the telegraph operator inside, seated at a desk. He was young and baby-faced and was filled with self-importance in his role as the person who linked Cliffside with the world. He had grown a failed goatee in an attempt to look older. Luther took off his cap and reached inside his coat for the piece of paper with his father's address on it.

He gave the paper to the operator and told him to send a telegram that said, "Mama is dead." The telegraph operator nodded. Luther stood patiently. He glanced around the tiny room with its single wooden bench. The telegraph operator stroked his pathetic goatee. He studied his soft, white hands and his clean fingernails. Behind his front of self-importance, he was a foolish young man who lived with his mother. He was barely more than an apprentice at his job and he'd had no experience in handling a matter so delicate as this. Finally, he found the courage to inform the boy what the telegram would cost.

Luther had forgotten that his father had told him a telegram required money. He had none with him and when the operator asked for some he was confused. He sat down on the floor. There was no whimpering buildup whatsoever; his crying was full from the moment of first utterance. He sent up a wail of extreme, lunatic grief. People in the general store next door looked up. The operator hurried around from behind his desk and squatted down beside Luther. When he finally got him calm he assured him his telegram would be dispatched free of cost.

After the word was sent off, the operator asked Luther where he would go and who was there to watch him.

He said, "Back home, I reckon, to sit with my mama."

The telegraph operator knew that at least three days might pass before the boy's father could return. He asked if there were friends or relatives in Cliffside.

Luther shook his head. "Gramma's yonder, outside Amarillo," he said. "But she's always hated Mama." This was untrue. His grandmother had died two years ago, but he'd forgotten that she had. He'd been brainwashed in a fashion and was offering as truth what he'd heard his mother scream repeatedly in the last months of her life.

The operator wondered if there were neighbors on farms who might be alerted, but he didn't ask. He was stopped by the boy's change of mood, which had all at once become sullen and uncooperative. It was as though he were saying that he'd been in charge of himself long enough through all this. It was now someone else's turn and, having gotten no help himself, he was not about to offer any. So the operator did the only thing he knew to do. He took young Luther home with him and gave him to his mother.

Then, as now, there was a requisite strain of low social malice in small-town life that was fed by scandal as fire is fed by air. Citizens listened to rumors, which they improved and passed along, and they reached condemning verdicts on matters about which their knowledge was slender at best. But on the other hand, when they were presented with true misfortune, the wish to help swept through and took hold of the people. It was a deep and involuntary fervor. They simply couldn't help themselves. They were no more able to keep from doing good than they could check their impulse to spread some lively gossip.

And so the telegraph operator's widowed mother first told her pastor at the Cliffside Baptist Church about the young boy who'd come to send the tragic telegram. Then she told her sister, whose husband was the mayor. By nightfall, everything logistical, spiritual, and practical had been seen to and Luther sat at a table in the telegraph operator's mother's huge kitchen, surrounded by women from the town who would stay with him in shifts until his father arrived. He had just finished a wedge of heavily cinnamoned apple pie in a lake of cream and his smile was almost sly with the contentment of an appetite at last satisfied. His mother lay in a coffin in the town mortician's parlor. The expression on her face was not unlike her son's.

Aubrey Mathias was a deeply stupid man, but he was not at all a mean one. His regularly leaving a woman and a child to care for themselves on the desolate plains was a common circumstance that required no explanation. Not even his wife had consciously felt it as neglectful. Like everyone else, she'd accepted it as an ordinary practice among unskilled men who knew at most a few ways to earn money with their hands and who went where they could for marginal wages.

It followed, then, that when he stepped up onto the porch of the telegraph operator's mother's house, he was welcomed with warmth and unqualified sympathy by the operator's mother and two of her friends. The operator's mother asked him to come in and sit down while she went to fetch his son, who was reading upstairs. Aubrey watched her walk across the room. She was an extremely buxom woman who moved in a careering, sway-backed way that made it appear her ample breasts were pulling her along. Watching her, Aubrey had to smile, and then, despite the terms of the occasion, he felt a wave of lust sweep over him. However comical her breasts made her appear, they were breasts after all, enormous ones in fact, and he had been away from women for more than three months. He shifted, uncomfortable in his chair. He was very tall and, because they'd been broken so often in the course of his work, the bones of his arms and legs had strangely irregular though natural-seeming planes, like the curved and knotted limbs of a tree. He looked awkward and out of place inside a house, in the way a tree would.

While he waited, the operator's mother's friends hurried to get him coffee and pound cake. In the kitchen they moved around each other in the graceful weaving pattern of an instinctive minuet. They kept severely erect postures. Their corsets and their stiff, high-collared dresses saw to that. But they were loose inside themselves and flustered with excitement as they fixed the man his snack. This, after all, was the moment they'd been waiting for.

When Luther came down the stairs, tucked under the arm of the operator's mother, he saw his father set his coffee and his cake down and stand to greet him, and a powerful disappointment came over him. These past two days had been for him a lovely dream of attention and care and they had reminded him that he was a child with a child's right to be utterly resourceless. Now, seeing his father, he knew instinctively that he must take charge again, at least of himself, in some altered way in some altered life that he could not imagine. He felt a sense of loss more precise and more relevant than anything to do with his mother's death.

His father got down on one knee and placed an arm on his shoulder. He looked him in the eye and said softly, "How y'all been makin' out, son?"

Luther nodded and waited until he was fairly certain he had found his adult disposition. "Good enough, I reckon," he said. "How *you* been makin' out, Papa?"

"Oh, dear Lord," said the operator's mother, turning to her friends in the doorway of the kitchen. "This boy's courage is well past ordinary."

He was at first simply curious at his mother's funeral and kept turning his head this way and that to catch the gestures of the ceremony. He could hardly be expected to feel the fear of inexperience in the vicinity of death. He had, after all, pulled a chair to his mother's bedside and leaned close to receive her heat. He'd sat with her then and felt the heat leaving her. He'd heard the wind stop at the darkest hour of night and had had to listen to an extraordinary stillness. His mother dead. Then the wind. Imagine the depth and the timbre of that stillness! ·

Staring at his mother as she lay in the coffin, he was fascinated by the way she'd been made to look. Her face was masked in primary colors from the mortician's palette. She was heavily powdered and her lips were touched with a zest-implying red. It would be nice to be able to say that her look of pinched exhaustion had fallen away, that an allusion to her youth and beauty had resurfaced. But she appeared, if anything, even older in her coffin and, with her face so crudely rouged, looked like an aged harlot.

He might not have recognized her, except for her mouth. Its sly hint of a smile was the same one he'd watched her lips form in the hour she was dying. The mortician had been pleased to see this smile. It seemed to him to suggest that she had glimpsed her reward as she'd exhaled her final breath. With his makeup, he often tried to draw just this expression and he could never get it right.

It was not until the end of the service at the Cliffside Baptist

Church that Luther was once again seized. Sitting with his father, waiting for a signal of what to do next, he watched the telegraph operator and his mother pass the coffin. The woman turned and came to him. She leaned down and put her arms around him and her voluminous bosom pillowed him in her scent. Luther pushed his face into it and then his crying came. The operator's mother held him for as long as she could, which was not very long, for her position was awkward and a strain on her back. When she straightened up, she looked down at him and said through her tears, "Y'all are the bravest little man in Texas."

He nodded, crying freely. Now he sensed all of life pressing against his face, as the telegraph operator's mother's bosom had. But life had no pleasant scent and was not especially soft. Its effect, in fact, was more like suffocation.

Luther replied at last, "I know I am." He had turned his head and spoke this statement to his father. Through his wailing he managed to get an edge of dry defiance into it.

They rode back home on his father's horse. His own horse walked behind them. Its reins were tied to his father's saddle. It carried his mother in her coffin, strapped down on its back in a careful arrangement of ropes and cinches. She'd be buried at home. Although Aubrey was rarely there to tend it, he thought of the sad little farm as the home place and had determined that his wife should be there always. As he'd tied the coffin down, he had said, mostly to himself, mostly just thinking out loud, that he hoped the ground behind the barn was not frozen.

The day was chilly but warmer than it had been. The sky was overcast, which is to say, beneath a northern Panhandle sky, that the whole world was. Luther sat forward in the saddle, his father behind him. He'd been allowed to stay in the pew and cry for a much longer time than he might have expected. But finally his father had squeezed his knee and said, "That'll do."

As he rode, his mind worried the picture of his mother's body loose in her coffin. He imagined her sliding and flopping around as she had in the chair the night he'd watched her die. His father's arms reached around him to keep a loose grip on the reins. Luther felt safely enveloped by, tucked into, his father. It was a sensation unique in his memory.

Holding him in this unavoidable hug, his father began to speak. Luther felt the strength of Aubrey's breath on his ear. He heard his father explain that he would soon be returning to the huge cattle ranch near the Oklahoma border. That he'd thought long and hard about it and had come to realize there was simply no way he could care for Luther now. He couldn't bring him to the ranch near the Oklahoma border. He couldn't leave him at home, alone without a mother. So he had sent a telegram to Luther's aunt and uncle and asked if they'd agree to take over his raising. He said he hadn't yet heard back, but that that was not unusual, since they collected their mail only now and then.

Luther asked, "Aunt and Uncle which?"

"Aunt June and Uncle Ray," his father said. "Who else would I mean? She's my one sister."

Luther said nothing for some moments. He tried to see himself in the future his father was describing. He tried to see his aunt and uncle and the place where he might soon be living. But none of this came to him, for his aunt and uncle were virtual strangers to him and he'd never visited their home, since, in fact, they didn't have one. Finally, he was able to summon the single piece of information about them he remembered. He asked, "Do they still got that Wild West medicine show?"

His father said they did, although he believed he remembered they'd recently changed it somehow. He said, "You remember how you like Aunt June."

Luther had no idea whether he liked his Aunt June or not. His mind at her mention flashed with impressions of a gigantic and brightly colored wagon, and his ear remembered faintly a kind of giggling music. But only dimly, deep within these impressions, stood the figure of Aunt June. In young Luther's mind she was a shy and mannish figure and that was all he recollected. So, to his father's assurance, "You remember how you like Aunt June," he might honestly have answered, "I do?" or "No, I don't," without intending any argument. But instead, he said, "I reckon," and let it go at that. And though Aubrey, to his credit, was alert for the response, he was not remotely keen enough to hear its hedge of compromise.

*   *   *

Waiting at the table for his aunt and uncle to arrive, he drank a cup of coffee and tried to read his Bible. It lay open to the book of Judges, the tale of Jephthah, son of a harlot, who vowed his only daughter into lifelong virginity if God would help him slay the Ammonites. It was one of his favorite stories, all war and innuendo and a dickering Lord who set terms of the most imaginative usury and doubled His interest at the hint of a late payment. Yet Luther's mind wandered from its verses. He felt aimless and lonely and longed to be in school.

He felt, too, a mix of fear and curiosity about his aunt and uncle and his mind worked to clarify his sense of who they were. He tried to remember the last time he'd seen them, but his child's idea of chronology served him badly. He felt sure it had been a long while since they'd visited, but that was the best he could do. He held only the memory of their wagon as the largest in the world and as ablaze with reds and yellows.

His father had left the day before to return to the ranch near the Oklahoma border. He'd looked around the room and patted the back of Luther's head. He'd asked him, "Y'all got everything you need?" Luther had nodded and said that he had everything. Neither had the slightest sense of what that might be.

He'd walked outside with his father, who'd mounted his horse and, as he'd ridden away, asked him to visit when he could. He'd told him again to mind his Aunt June.

Now Luther got up from the table and left the house and walked out behind the barn to visit his mother's grave. He was not so much conscious of saying farewell as of wishing some company while he waited to be claimed. He and his father had begun the grave as soon as they'd returned from Cliffside and the digging had gone quickly. It had been a mild winter, the spring snowstorm notwithstanding, and their shovels had easily sliced the firm unfrozen earth, bringing up thick, neat plates of soil. Luther was tall and strong for his age and his contribution to the work had been measurable. When they'd finished, Luther had paused, breathless with fatigue and with a formative mixture of loneliness and anger. Yet he'd also thought that the rectangle of returned earth covering the coffin looked lovely, like a garden. Seeing it as such he'd felt for an instant a farmer's seasonal excitement.

But standing now before the grave, it no longer seemed like a spot the sun could help. It no longer appeared to him like a garden. He looked up at the sky. The day was bright and shadeless and the world seemed lighted in crisply edged colors, even the variegated grays of the farm. He tried to remember his mother as she had been, a devoted and monotonously sober woman whose way of showing her son that she loved him was by doing nothing to suggest that she did not. He wanted to remember her as common and colorless but his memory was blocked by the dramatic final days. By the unfathomable fact that she lay dead in a box in a hole he'd helped to dig. And before that, by her behavior as she was dying. Her madness had often frightened him during those months but as it happened she had never turned it on him. Indeed, she'd ignored him for the many busy adversaries who'd competed for her temper. He'd been a faceless witness to his mother's dementia and whenever he could feel that his safety was not threatened, he'd found her performances in a real sense thrilling.

Now, all the strangeness in his life settled on his yearning to be about his day at school. He began a dry sobbing. When he'd asked his father where he would go to school now, he'd received a blank stare in reply. It was clear that this detail had not occurred to Aubrey, who himself had left school after the third grade and whose few years of study had been so irrelevant to his life, he had no notion of learning's place in anyone else's. So in answer to the question, Aubrey had finally answered, "I reckon your Aunt June'll figure out what's right."

As Luther left his mother's grave and started back toward the house, he heard the inimitable sounds of hoofs and wagon-jangling coming toward him from the sun. He turned and looked toward them, his hand shielding his eyes.

Pulling the wagon was a team of work horses, bred to a thick and brutish inelegance, yet so well groomed they seemed a pair of dandies. They drew quite close to Luther, leading the wagon through a wide sweep before they came to a stop. He could barely make out Aunt June and Uncle Ray on the seat beneath a lip of roof. One of the horses snorted, releasing his breath in a gust that rattled the loose flesh around his mouth; the other immediately shat.

Memory's magnification of the size and scale of things is as absolute as a law of nature. And if young Luther, squinting up at his future, had been seeing what he saw under normal circumstances, he'd have felt greatly disappointed. He'd have recognized at once that this was not, as he'd remembered it, the world's largest wagon, though it was true that it was covered in reds and yellows. But the wagon was obviously old and broken down, and, despite their groomed flamboyance, so were the horses; the sway of their backs was alarming and comical.

But these were not simple moments in Luther's life. He looked at the wagon and the couple on its seat with a freshly orphaned need for hope and his survivor's heart willed a splendor to the scene. To him, the wagon's festive colors were almost bellicose. Every inch of it seemed filigreed, as though a tatooist had been asked to try his art on its surfaces. Banners ran the length of both sides. Above them arced the words RAYMOND C. WHITE'S MEDICAL COMPOUND. His eyes saw the horses and the wagon as majestic, as though they'd come to him not across the plains but down from Heaven.

He waited, seized with shyness and with that fear that leaves us dumb in the face of the majestic. He watched his aunt climb down from one side of the wagon. He saw that she was tall and big-boned and looked like his father. When she reached him she patted the back of his head, as his father had. Her rough wool coat had that strangely sweet smell of horse all through it, a smell Luther loved. She said nothing at all. She'd inherited, too, with her brother's height and bones, the family's conversational dimension. But her smile was large and this was hers alone.

Then, from the wagon, his uncle erupted with laughter. Still smiling, Luther's aunt picked it up. Luther looked at his aunt and up to his uncle. Some thirty seconds had passed since their arrival and not a word had yet been spoken. There'd been his aunt's smiling silence and now the two of them were offering him this deeply amused duet.

He watched his uncle stepping down. He was his wife's physical opposite; short against her height; red-faced against her fairness; against her thinness an emphatic corpulence. Their mismatch was so complete it appeared a strategy.

As Luther's uncle came toward him, his laughter altered into something smoother. He tipped his hat, revealing his bald head.

One could imagine this man and woman, young and lonely, meeting for the first time and realizing instantly the smiles and the attention they would draw as a pair, where neither individually had drawn much more than tolerance. One could imagine them looking at each other across stacks of wheat at a barn dance in West Texas and thinking separately, "Oh, I think so," and "Oh, what fun!" For alone, she was a tall, silent woman whose wish to convey pleasure was in need of a medium. He was a man seeking sanction for his manner beyond the cliché of the jolly fat man's propensities. But together, if their self-consciousness was light, if they could laugh at themselves, then their merriment was virtually ensured.

Luther's uncle reached him and extended his hand. It was tiny and pudgy but he offered it with gusto. Then he took off Luther's cap and ran his fingers roughly through his hair. He was clearly laughing still but it had now become soundless. He had shown Luther three ways of laughter in less than a minute. He would show him many more.

Finally, Luther smiled at his uncle and then at his aunt. His spirits had had a long way to travel to get even to a smile and it was for the moment the best he could do.

His uncle seemed to understand and judge it good enough. He winked at his wife and then he winked at Luther. At last there were words. He said, "June, life is but a series of ironifications. Yesterday, we cried when the old dog died and we had to throw him out. And here today we come across this boy, standing in the wilderness with hat in hand, who looks like he'll just exactly fill the dog's spot in the wagon and who no doubt eats much less."

"Ray, Ray," his wife said. The tone of her scolding was the voice of love itself.

Then the curtain behind the wagon's seat was pulled back and a boy's head peered out into the day. Looking up, Luther judged the boy to be his age or slightly older. The boy blinked his eyes, a mole's weak squint. His face was round and vacant. The blankness it expressed could be described as prodigal.

"Ray Junior!" Luther's uncle cried. "This here's your cousin Luther! Your uncle Aubrey's boy!"

"Oh," the boy said, as though his father had informed him that the sun was in the sky.

2

And so, with his uncle and his aunt and his cousin, Ray White, Jr., Luther journeyed in the wagon selling Raymond C. White's Medical Compound. They traveled through northern Texas, Oklahoma, and western Arkansas. For the months of spring and summer, and some early days of fall, they slept in the wagon, or beneath it or beside it. When they'd stopped for the day, they caught catfish from creeks and bullfrogs from their banks. After they'd taken all the fish they needed, they waded into the water for long, cooling baths. Ray White floated on his back and spouted water as he whistled, his stomach protuberant like a swollen milk-white island. His penis bobbed and floated, the island's tiny outcropping. June attempted to enter the water unnoticed and wrap the creek around her like a cape. But more often than not she stumbled in, grunting and splashing, and when Luther looked toward the noise he caught a glimpse of his aunt as she turned away. Her body from behind was classically columnar. The cheeks of her buttocks were firm and concave.

The family moved to an intricate map in Ray White's head. It was drawn and redrawn, not with the conventional notions of efficiency, but with a prescient sense of the towns that would welcome them and a memory of those that would welcome their return. When the weather turned, no matter where they were, they headed for the nearest town that had rentable rooms and a school for the boys.

Ray White found jobs selling dry goods, or women's hats, or general merchandise. He wished to keep himself in touch with his skills without working them too strenuously. He floated through the days, garrulous and charming to the women of the town, strange and sissified to the local men, who laughed behind his back at his graceful walk and his inflated speech.

June imposed an order on their rented rooms. Unlike Luther's mother, unlike the thousands of women of her time driven mad by lives of neglect and solitude, June had found a life that left her rarely alone and never neglected. She perceived herself uniquely fortunate in this regard. She experienced solitude as something rich and thick and sensually abundant. Often, alone in the late morning, she would burst into song. She sang "Columbia, the Gem of the Ocean." She sang the Stephen Foster songs that Ray White liked to play on his banjo. She sang "Oh Susannah" and "Away Down South." She sang badly. But when she was alone her screech was lusty. Hearing herself, she would stop and laugh uproariously, something, like singing, she could not do in public without her husband's prompting. Solitude inspired her laughter as, at the end, it had inspired Luther's mother's. But the difference in their inspirations was complete and the difference in the sounds of their laughter was as that between the dawn-notes of a bird and the coyote's nightly howl. Her pleasure sometimes lasted for as long as two months before she felt her restlessness stirring.

To his teachers, Luther was viewed each autumn as a kind of offered miracle. He simply appeared in the doorway with his cousin, three or four weeks into the term. The first few times he arrived in this fashion he was rendered nearly mute by shyness. But he began to understand, and then to savor, the fluster of attention his entrances caused. The dead-blank faces of the students wrinkling suddenly to life. The teacher's initial confusion and then her careful welcome. The source of Luther's pleasure was the same as his uncle's delight whenever he drove the clanging wagon down a quiet main street and caught an unsuspecting town off guard.

Once settled in the schoolroom, Luther became instantly preeminent. Introduced to Latin and geometry, he made the most of meeting them. When the students made a circle for an hour of oral reading, Luther recited with a lovely and confident inflection that was the aural equivalent of an index finger beckoning a listener to come closer. Some of this cadence in his voice was the Bible's, the meter of its verses. And some of it was a rendition of the lilt in Ray White's words when he drew the people close to sell them his compound. A few times each term, Luther yielded to the urge to abandon the story he was reading for the more interesting one forming in his head. He read fluently and was far ahead of most of the students struggling to follow. Many of them had no idea, when he began to improvise, that they were hearing something that was not in their readers. His teachers were enchanted, so thankful for his nimble mind among a roomful of clodheads who breathed through their mouths and spoke through their noses that they usually let him finish what he'd started.

In every way, Ray White, Jr., suffered by comparison. He was six months Luther's elder and his overwhelming attribute was a lack of curiosity so complete that it bordered on the original. He had inherited only the unfortunate features of his parents. His father's obesity, his mother's public inexpressiveness. His father's impracticality, his mother's clumsiness. One might rightly regard this as genetic doom. Yet the boy lived oblivious inside a self-absorption, and who's to say this, too, was not some whimsical yield of the genes in combination? Consequently, he had no vision of himself as sadly lacking. He was not a delinquent child, for delinquency requires some sort of inquisitive spirit. He was not complainant, for the impulse to complain requires the view that life is not providing what it should. He was, wherever he was, simply present, with his relentless lack of interest in the world beyond the reach of his arm.

In early spring, Luther and Ray Junior were taken from school to assist the preparations for their season on the road. Luther and his teachers parted with the pain of lovers being forcibly separated. Luther shuffled silently through his chores and stayed to himself. He read and reread the book his teacher had inevitably given him in farewell. But after a week his mood would begin to lift. He helped his aunt make the wagon ready. He rehearsed with his uncle and his cousin the season's dramatic skits, which Ray White had ordered over the winter from the catalog of J. J. Lipanzer and Son Publishers in Chicago. Before Luther had joined the family, his uncle had been limited in his selection by June's refusal to participate and by the narrow range of supporting roles that might be right for Ray White, Jr., since there were only so many skits that featured trees or boulders.

By the time they were ready to mix the season's first compound, Luther's memory of the schoolroom was imprecise. Eagerly, he set the washtubs in a row and filled them with rainwater. He helped his aunt add the Epsom salts, the licorice powder, the burnt sugar, the cake coloring, the Black-Draught laxative. Then he watched his uncle measure and pour in the alcohol. Ray White's face was always solemn for this ritual, notably so, since it rarely was otherwise. One might have assumed he was mimicking seriousness but in fact his face showed the truth of his mood. He brought his full concentration to the procedure, for he saw the fate of his family's well-being in the proper mixture of the various ingredients. His was not the eerie sorcery of the witch at the cauldron. Instead, his concern was the chef's for the taste, for he'd concluded in his time that if his compound hit the throat with an exact medicinal bitterness, customers would feel satisfied they'd gotten what they paid for.

When he'd finished, he dipped a tin cup into the tub. He swirled the liquid. He brought the cup to his nose and snorted, then took a swig and gargled loudly before swallowing. His sounds were as crude as an oenologist's. Then he looked around and said, "I believe, my Junie Moon, and my handsome son, and my keen young nephew, that this compound assures us of a season we'll recall in the future with a fondness for work that was abundantly rewarded." Said that, or something close to it. In any event, he was ready.

Then he drew them all a cup of the compound. Their initial sips were cautious, for it seemed every season to find new passages and hollows inside the body where it pooled and burned. Next, Ray White toasted the months ahead. They drank in celebration, and in Luther's case, at first, with the belief that the compound did what Ray White claimed. Flushed you out. Set you up. Performed a thorough spring cleaning on that sacred house, your body.

This was the pattern of Luther's life from the age of ten until he was seventeen. And his attitude toward it, which began as terror and excitement in response to its waywardness, quickly turned to love and settled in, after doubts, as a loyal engagement with its daily rhythms; in other words, love matured.

Most of all, he loved performing the skits, which were staged beside the wagon. A canvas backdrop, trees painted on one side, desert on the other, was hung along the wagon's length. Luther played a sick boy expiring of consumption. He played a brave lad who eluded a band of starving wolves (their howls from the throat of Ray White, Jr., who sat inside the wagon) to deliver a letter of love to a heartsick shepherd. In his favorite role, he played a young scout at the Alamo walls who took a Mexican bullet intended for Jim Bowie. He died often and increasingly well. He learned to milk a child's death throes with spasms and moans and the wild rolling of the eyes that asked why, oh, why was the world getting dark? He worked to perfect his roles, and what he loved most about acting with his uncle was the giddy sense of emotional permission. There was no such thing as a scream too piercing, no such thing as a gesture too broad. No matter the flamboyance he brought to his scenes, he found to his delight he was allowed even more. "When you're acting for the rubes," his uncle advised, "imagine the most you can put into it and then double it, twice."

Every night, at a point in the skit when the drama was cresting and the tension was high, his uncle would pause and step forward, out of one character and instantly into another. Then he'd begin his monologue on behalf of the compound. His audience made this shift with him eagerly. Who can say why? Perhaps they enjoyed a kind of combat that went on while they were listening: I dare you to persuade me that I should buy your compound. Perhaps they knew prophetically that commercials offer at least as much as the insipidities they bracket.

With Luther and his cousin moving through the crowd carrying bottles of the compound in straw baskets, Ray White began to sell. He thanked them all for coming and showed his thanks by playing two Stephen Foster tunes on his banjo. He told a few jokes. He told them the story of the attractive Quaker widow named Mercy, and her lascivious minister who prayed to his Lord to, "Have Mercy on *me*."

Then he asked if by chance there was anyone out there whose teeth and gums hurt. If anyone's kidneys were a cause of some distress. He asked if constipation was an unrelieved plague. He asked them, that is, what he already knew: That someone's did; that someone's were; that it *was* a plague and more. In the country at this time, everyone's teeth throbbed, everyone's kidneys cramped. Everyone's belly was bloated with gas. These were features of the body's performance as predictable as hunger and fatigue. Yet people tended to suffer them privately, so that Ray White's diagnoses seemed to them impressively individual.

Next, he described the compound's secret mix of herbs, passed on to him by a Shawnee Indian he'd befriended at the reservation school in Altus, Oklahoma. He said, "Certainly, we all know the incalculational wisdom that the red man possesses in medicinal matters." Some people nodded that they certainly did. Ray White described a time when, as a boy, he'd been sick, near death, and how his friend with his herbs had nursed him back to health. He said he'd sworn a Shawnee oath, certified with blood from a cut in the crown of the head, that he'd hold the ingredients secret.

As he spoke this, he leaned forward, as though taking a deep bow, and took off his derby while June stepped next to him and held a lantern close. It lit the raised white scar toward the front of his bald dome, the lasting signature of the day he'd been knocked unconscious when he'd slipped on a rock in a creek near Abilene while trying to mount June from behind.

When June put a light on the scar, people moved forward to get a better look, and Luther wove among them, carrying his basket. He was still afloat on the energy of his performance and he moved with a feeling of regality.

Still stooped over and talking to his shoes, Ray White explained the Shawnee ritual. How you clipped and shaved each other's hair to clear a long bald spot. "As you can see," he shouted, "my head would no longer require the initial step!" How the Shawnee made his cut in your head, then you made yours in his. How you rubbed your heads against each other's to mix the blood and seal the oath. He wiggled his head in the lantern's light.

Always at this moment, Luther saw a few, and often many, in the crowd nod their heads while their lips formed a quite particular smile. It was a smile that contained elements both of sorrow and of wonder, and Ray White had taught him that whenever it appeared, it meant the people had forgotten that they'd come for mere amusement and had begun to believe what Ray White was saying.

Ray White stood straight again and said that though he could not reveal the secret of the herbs, he *could* pass on their amazing healing powers. He said it would be small, would be mean of him not to share

their benefits and that, besides, both his God and that of the Shaw-
nees would have seen to him long ago if he'd kept them for his own.

Then he held up the compound in its dark brown bottle and stared
at it through an especially long silence. He seemed entranced.
Watching him, the people began to grow self-conscious. There were
uneasy giggles. Should they leave? Should they stay? Should someone say something?

At last, now grave and dignified, he turned to them again. He said
the compound could ease the throbbing of teeth and gums. He said
that it could soothe their kidneys' pain and end their constipation.
After each declaration he whispered, "Yes, it will," answering himself like his own gospel chorus. A syncopation clarified, which people
didn't realize they were keeping time to. A few of them actually
began to tap their feet.

"It will cure dyspepsia. *Yes it will.* It quiets female complaints."

Then a man at the back stepped forward and shouted to Ray
White, "Your besetting sin, my friend, is your undue modesty! I
bought a bottle of your compound last spring. From that day till this
I've had no more liver trouble and my scrofula is a memory. I've
come all the way from Lubbock to get more compound this year."
He waved a fan of dollar bills. "A bottle—no—*two* bottles, please."

And folks began to buy.

This was an age of vulnerable boredom. Life in America at the turn
of the century was extremely confined. Contrary to the romance
we've embraced, we were not a nation of large-hearted explorers
who sang and sweated and belched our way across the wilderness,
pausing to thank God as the sun fell in the west. Those who strayed
and wandered were the eccentrics and the malcontents who couldn't
find their niche. It is they we have to thank for the clearing of the
continent. But most of the people stayed close to the house. They did
their work and they made their meals and they said their prayers,
alone or in pairs or among a tiny group they saw day after day. It was
inevitable, then, that they'd grow sick of themselves and sick of each
other and sick of the limits of their small, hard lives. So it's no
surprise that Ray White's patent absurdities would win the people's
affection and after that their trust. He came into town from somewhere beyond, arriving suddenly with energy and flourish. He gave
them entertainment that was far beyond the ordinary. Somehow, he

seemed both safe and strange, and that usually proved an irresistible combination.

And there was something more. When these peoples' mothers and fathers had been aided by doctors, they'd received treatments of astonishing violence. They were blistered with poultices. With purgatives and emetics, they were induced to shit and vomit while doubled up in pain. When they'd complained of high fevers, their skins had been lanced, the cuts then spread with cream and sugar to make them even more appetizing to the leeches. Christian young men with the wish to serve humankind sat in medical academy classrooms studying the theories that led them to these acts.

Many of the people who came to hear Ray White had also survived the cures of violence and they had had enough. They'd learned to place their faith in their own common sense, which told them that the first step was to make less pain, not more. Among themselves, as though exchanging recipes, they traded the ingredients of old family treatments.

But to his credit, there was also power and allure in Ray White's oratory, which lay, at bottom, in his love of performing and in the way he'd learned to use his lifelong sense of exile.

Within this life of lyric nomadism, whatever changes took place were small and easily absorbed. When their route made it possible, Luther visited his father on the huge cattle ranch. It seemed to him, on each occasion, that his father had aged a great deal, that his voice had become increasingly hoarse, that the planes of his bones had grown even more irregular. In part, Luther was right. But he was also unconsciously measuring his father against his uncle Ray, and the prankster's spirit is one of formidable immaturity.

One night, weaving among the people with his basket of the compound, Luther listened as usual to his uncle's monologue. He'd learned to use without thinking the steady tempo of the pitch as a pulse that measured his own movements through the crowd. But because his uncle's words were comfortably familiar, he'd come to give them only a portion of his attention and on this evening he was letting them pass unheard when they suddenly began to ring with dissonance.

Luther stopped and put his basket down. He began for the first time in months to listen hard. He heard Ray White saying that the scar atop his head had resulted from a brush with death while climbing mountains in Nepal. A noble Nepalese had found him where he'd fallen, dazed and cut and bruised, and nursed him with the formula contained now in the compound. In reaction, Luther looked around and searched the faces nearest him. He sought in someone else's expression the same bewilderment he was feeling himself, a puzzled look that would confirm that this was *not* the story; this was not how his uncle had acquired his scar.

For more than a week, Luther heard the new story. Throughout the time, he kept his private counsel. He moved moodily about his chores and performed the skits distractedly. In the middle of the show in Dimple, Texas, he forgot who he was playing, turning to take the Bowie bullet in his heart at the very moment he was supposed to hand the letter to the love-besotted shepherd.

One morning, his aunt asked him if he were ill and felt his forehead. In a churlish voice, he denied that he was. She asked him again the following day and got no reply at all.

"Luther's out of sorts," June said to Ray White. "He don't have a fever but he's been brooding unusually and he don't seem too much interested."

Ray White lifted his eyes to Luther, who was sitting out of earshot on the front seat of the wagon and staring out at the horizon. "Interested in what?" he asked.

"In anything," June said. In silence, the two of them observed the boy. Neither had an idea what was on his mind, since, to them, there was nothing elusive or fragile in the philosophy of their work. So far as they were concerned, Ray White's changing of his story was an experimental tinkering, neither more nor less considered, neither more nor less fraught, than substituting one banjo tune for another from Stephen Foster's *Songs of the Sable Harmonists*.

After a moment, Ray White smiled. He said, "Ah, I think I know what's troubling the lad." Speaking this, he affected a brogue.

"What?" asked June.

"His age."

"His age?" asked June.

"He's almost thirteen," Ray White said. He opened his arms, as though to say, Don't you see? He said, "It's the time in his life when that *sweetest* of desires comes sweeping over a boy." He moved close to his wife. He reached beneath her petticoats and placed his hand on her shin.

June smiled. "You think?"

"Indeed, I do. There's a sense of frustration he feels at this time." His hand moved up along June's calf toward her knee. "And he's liable to feel it at the drop of a hat, towards most anything."

June smiled at the brush of Ray White's hand along her leg. Wherever he touched her, it was nearly as though she were feeling her own hand on her skin, had she been able to give her own hand such permission. She said at last, "And probably the reason there's been no like display from Ray Junior is because of his unusually even temperament."

"*Unusually* even," Ray White nodded.

And so it was that, over those days, Luther was forced to recognize that his uncle told lies. Until then, against all the casual evidence surrounding him, he'd unthinkingly assumed, for instance, that Uncle Ray must have added the Shawnee's secret herbs when none of them was looking. But now the Shawnee herbs were root meats from Nepal. He was, as Ray White said, nearly thirteen at this time and was just beginning to have a conscious view of life, to consider people and events below their surfaces.

He waited one morning for his uncle to finish shaving. They were camped by a stream near De Queen, Arkansas. The day was bright and hot and the slant of the light seemed nearly horizontal. Since sunrise, Ray White had been unable to stop inventing tasteless jokes in Negro dialect inspired by the name of the nearby town. "If you duh' queen, den' who be duh' king?" That sort of thing. Even June had asked him to be quiet, for the simple reason that the jokes were not funny. "I'm trying, Junie Moon," he said, laughing. "I swear, I'm trying." Then he'd think of another one.

Luther climbed up into the back of the wagon and sat down next to his uncle. He was trembling, but he was not entirely fearful. He was trembling, too, from a vague sense of intrigue that had deepened with the days, from a certainty that some scheme, some grid of life, was about to be explained.

His uncle handed him a cup of coffee. They stared out at the morning and its planar stream of light. Ray White asked if he had fed and groomed the horses. Luther sipped his coffee and said that he had.

Then he asked his uncle why he had changed the story of how he'd gotten his scar. And why the compound's secret ingredients had changed.

Ray White turned and smiled. His surprise was honest. "I guess that's right," he said. "I guess this is the first time I've changed the pitch since you've been with us."

"Yeah," Luther said. "I reckon it is."

"Don't say *reckon,* Luther. Remember, *rubes* say *reckon.*" Ray White sipped his coffee. He held to certain ideas about the use of the language and only his wife escaped his rigid rules. To her, he applied a special syllogism: June said *ain't* and she said *reckon,* yet he worshipped June, his love for her was measureless. Since he could never love a rube, June was not a rube.

"But to your question," he said. "I suppose I changed it mostly just because I was getting weary of that same old Shawnee story." He turned to Luther and winked. "Weren't you?"

Luther shrugged his shoulders.

"Yet I am damned," Ray White said, "if I can seem to improve on it." He laughed. "But I *do* see why it works. The yokels understand if you talk about a Shawnee. But for all they know, Nepal is somewhere down there beside Louisiana."

"Where is it?" Luther asked.

His uncle's face went blank.

"Where is Nepal?" he asked again.

"It's in Italy," Ray White said finally.

Luther nodded. He continued to look out from the rear of the wagon. He swung his legs back and forth. They were getting very long. He would have his father's and his Aunt June's height and he was beginning to resemble them facially as well.

He said, "The compound don't do much of anything, does it? I mean, any good, extraordinarily?"

Ray White placed his hand on Luther's thigh and patted it gently. He looked at his nephew. His smile was prideful. He was the bittersweetly wise adult, welcoming the boy into the first realm of manhood. He said, "A person forgets, young Luther. . . . After he's worked things out for himself, he gets accustomed to them. So I apologize. I've been neglectful in my responsibilities to you." He nodded. "Does the compound do any good? Well, I suppose that depends on what you mean when you say *good*."

Luther thought a second. "I mean, just, it don't help anyone especially."

Ray White raised his hands to his cheeks and ran them over their freshly shaved smoothness. He said, "The first medicine I ever sold was something we called Garland's Magical Corn Salve. I say *we*. I was working for the Garland brothers. They had shows throughout the country. Hundreds of them. And every one of them identical. Their play scripts were identical. Their music. That's when I first played the banjo for the public. Their wagons, their teams of white horses, everything. They made all their employees dress in formal Prince Albert frock coats, so we would all look dignified. We wore pin-striped trousers and gray dress vests. They had us wear pearl-gray spats over our shoes. If the Garlands got a report that you weren't wearing your formal suit, they fined you two dollars. They were geniuses, that's clear, because they understood how uniformity guaranteed complete control. When the rubes saw a Garland brothers show come into town, their eyes got big as silver dollars. They'd never seen such elegance and, simply put, they were humbled in its presence. So it was easy to get them to buy the corn salve. They felt stupid already in the face of all that elegance and they'd've only felt more stupid if they hadn't done what we told them. They felt, now that I think about it again, they felt obliged.

"We told them the salve would make the corns on their feet disappear. We explained how you soaked your feet in water, then rubbed the corns with the little cakes of salve." Ray White turned again to look at Luther. "You know what the magical corn salve was?"

"What?"

"Oxydol laundry soap we boiled until it jelled. Then after it was cool we cut it all up into little wedges. The Garlands had an exact recipe for all this, for just how long to boil it and how big to make the wedges." He smiled again, to himself this time. "But you know what else?"

Luther looked at his uncle and waited.

"It worked. And the reason it worked is that most of the corns weren't corns at all. They were just dirt calluses people get when they go barefoot and don't wash their feet. Which gets back to what you mean when you ask if something does any good. And I would answer by saying that if you tell somebody he's got dirty feet and he ought to wash them, you've insulted him. But if he says his dirty feet are corns and you say, 'Here's this salve that will make them go away,' then you've cured him."

Ray White paused. He glanced at Luther. Among the arrows of skill in his salesman's quiver was the unerring sense of when to pause and let his words continue working.

When he spoke again, he offered his belief that medicine was a funny thing. He said that it was obvious to him after all these years that the one necessary ingredient in any medicine was the mind's belief in it. And if that were so, he felt it was his duty to make sure, in his pitch, that the compound contained an ample dose of that belief. "When all's said and done," he said, "it might be true that the compound's not worth much. It might even be true that it's worthless. But if it's worthless, it is also harmless. And that's the most important thing to keep in mind: worthless is one thing and harmful's something else."

He next asked Luther to think about the pleasure their show gave. He cited as evidence the sound of laughter. He spoke of crowds of people whose faces were so tightly pinched at the beginning of a show there was reason to suspect they would soon be trying laughter for the first time in their lives. He listed a dozen towns they had revisited that season. He reminded Luther how the wagon's arrival had set loose the excuse for a general silliness, one that seemed to him as welcomed as rain in a drought.

Then he fell silent again.

Luther took a cold sip of coffee. He said, "But what about your growing up on the Shawnee reservation?"

Ray White asked, "What about it?"

"Y'all didn't, then?"

Again, Ray White smiled. He said, "Another reason this country is great is that if the history you've been handed doesn't suit your purpose, you're free to proceed and get another one."

Luther frowned, considering this.

"I believe that's so," Ray White continued. "I truly do. I believe it's openly implied in our U.S. Constitution." He nodded his head. "And now, handsome Luther, we must get us to De Queen." His face lifted. Another tasteless dialect joke flitted through his mind. He held it for an instant and then let it pass. He said, "I've enjoyed this conversation. I have in fact enjoyed it keenly. I hadn't thought about those days with the Garland brothers' shows for some time." He sighed. "Such elegance, truly. Come here and let me show you the coat and the pin-striped trousers I wore. I have them in my trunk." He pushed himself forward and dropped lightly to the ground. He pulled his vest straight and again winked at his nephew. "But we have us our own little world of elegance right here, don't we?"

So the sale of the compound continued steadily. The Pure Food and Drug Act had recently been passed but the sternness of its warnings regarding patent remedies altered no curative philosophies among the people of the plains. And all the while, as they moved from town to town, the unity of Ray White's family grew to a complementariness that a modern social worker might use as a model. Each of its members received what was needed from the life as it was led: love; laughter; a full, day's-end exhaustion. Life went on this way for nearly four more years, and who can say how long it might have continued if June hadn't died?

*J*une began to cough in early September, on the morning after a sudden storm had caught them packing the show to leave the town of Tulip, Texas. Their plan, after Tulip, was to follow the Red River west and play five or six more towns in the last weeks of the season. Dressed unprepared in long summer skirts, June was shutting up the wagon when the night skies opened. She was soaked through in a minute and continued to work as the ground became red mud. The sodden weight of her petticoats slowed her movements considerably.

For two weeks after the rain, all of West Texas lay beneath a tent of cold and grayness. As he heard his wife's coughing persist, Ray White repeated again and again that he'd rarely known such weather at this time of the year. It became almost their exclusive conversation: June coughed and Ray lamented the bone-chilling gloom.

They broke off their course with no other plan than to get out from beneath the prevailing skies. Ray looked overhead for some indication of the direction he should take. He saw that his luck appeared as good or as bad in any one of them. He headed them south for two days. Their season had been unusually successful and, so near its end, they resisted letting go of it. They both felt this reluctance and agreed with each other that they should combine their search for sun with some shows along the way. But they were feeling, too, that June's need to get inside was becoming critical. Each of them kept this latter feeling private, for to openly acknowledge it would have been to admit alarm into their life. They stopped, at June's insistence, to play a show in Shamrock. They played another in Quail. June stayed in the wagon and tied a bandanna, bandit-style, over her face to muffle her coughing. She was not, in her condition, an endorsement for the compound.

There was no sun to the south or, after three days heading west, in that direction, either. So Ray White turned north toward the Red River again. If traced, a kind of heedless panic would have been suggested by the pattern of their route through the prairie grasses. June's coughing fits grew in their length and ferocity. In the midst of one, she pulled a muscle in her ribs. The gloom inside the wagon began to thicken like the sky's. Once, taking his aunt's hand to help her down, Luther felt the heat of her fever on her skin. The shock of recognition sent his mind back to a time he'd all but lost connection to. He was suddenly filled with a series of emotions that competed for preeminence. Briefly, a not unpleasant nostalgia was among them, but it was quickly overwhelmed by a sickening fear. In that moment Luther understood that life sometimes pauses and perversely doubles back on itself. He guided his aunt toward the rear of the wagon.

Ray White gave up his search for the sun near Pampa. From the wagon they could see, across an infinite flatness, the squat broken skyline of the town some miles away. He drove them toward it. They found rooms for rent on the quieter street of a central intersection above Charles Cook and Son's furniture store. As they helped her up the outside stairs, June leaned to one side, favoring her injured rib. Luther envisioned her backbone curling. He was not directly reminded by this of his father's ever more radically warping bones, yet as June grew worse she'd begun to resemble her brother more and more. It was as though she'd needed all her health to give off what was feminine and softening in her. Luther *did* see this, her steady devolution toward a crude and haggard maleness. But he convinced himself that it was a hopeful sign, for it seemed to him the opposite of the turn his mother had taken. He remembered the remoteness of her feverish incoherence. In contrast, the sense of life inside his aunt now seemed more plain and undefended.

There'd been times in Ray White's life when his show had been forced to leave a town because the local physician had complained of it to the sheriff. Because of this prejudice, he did not tell the doctor he found in Pampa that he sold medical compound from the back of a wagon. The doctor was a jowly man in a wrinkled suit. When he entered their rooms, Ray White noticed that the toes of his boots were badly scuffed and covered with dust. His appearance offended Ray White. He suspected that the doctor viewed the family as transients and that he dressed with neatness and respect and wiped the dust from his boots when he called on his regular patients.

The doctor gave June sulfa pills. He urged Ray White to keep cool cloths on her face and to make her drink tea. He asked how long she'd been coughing.

"A few weeks," Ray White said.

"And how long she been coughing up that blood?" The doctor pulled absently at the bristly clumps of gray hairs growing from his ears.

Ray White watched this with disgust. Then he said he didn't know she had been, which was true. In the grip of a denying stoicism, June had managed to hide her blood-threaded phlegm from all of them.

At his uncle's insistence, Luther and Ray Junior began classes at the local high school. They went off every morning, quietly closing the apartment's outside door. They were unfailingly greeted by a bright morning sun. As if to mock them all, the sky had cleared the day they'd reached Pampa. The sound of June's coughing followed them down the stairs.

The lessons of the schoolroom floated unexamined past Luther's eyes. He felt a dreadful precariousness inside him. There was nothing familiar in the days he was living. In their rooms, where there had always been sustained and boisterous sound, the quiet in the air was a humidity. His Uncle Ray moved about on tiptoes with his ear cocked toward the bedroom. He and Luther and Ray Junior spoke in near whispers.

As he sat at his school desk, Luther thought more and more of his mother's last night of maniacal laughter. He felt, in remembering it, that it had expressed a statement she'd been desperate to deliver. And it seemed to him there was something of that same need in his Aunt June's coughing. Though he still told himself that she was not dying, the dolor of his memory was insisting otherwise. It caused him to hear once again the stillness that had enfolded him the night his mother, and then the wind, had died.

For the only time in their lives, Luther and Ray Junior began to share a disposition. As Luther turned inward and slow and apparently inattentive, Ray Junior's increasing anxiety gave him an energy that made him almost animated. Their temperaments fell and rose respectively and met in a mutually soothing accident of instinctive understanding. They said very little and whatever they said was more than what was needed. In classes, their eyes rose from their texts and found each other's. One morning, at the end of their second week in Pampa, after a night during which the disheveled doctor had again been called and they'd listened for hours to June's sustained and complicated hacking, their looks locked and each of them watched the other's eyes fill with tears.

Do these instances of improbable harmony suggest that for every hardship God imposes, He includes some small and unexpected compensation? Or do they show, instead, His need to prove that He can manipulate us wholly, sending us when weakened into the most unlikely alliances?

It was after school on a Thursday when Luther climbed the stairs to the apartment and sensed as he ascended a change he couldn't specify. He was alone. Ray Junior, on a whim, had decided to stay after school and talk to the football coach. He was interested to see if he might have the makings of a center.

"I been watchin'," he'd said to Luther. "It looks to me like the center ain't asked to move but straight ahead. And I think that I would enjoy hittin' people."

Luther reached the top of the stairs and opened the door. He walked into the room and wiped the sweat from his face with the sleeve of his shirt. He virtually sniffed the air. He realized then that he'd not heard his Aunt June's coughing. He held his breath and listened for it now. He glanced toward the bedroom and saw that its door was opened and its bed was empty. As a last, supreme defiance, his heart rose to the idea that June was miraculously well and was up and out of bed. His look flew around in search of her.

He saw his Uncle Ray at the far end of the sitting room, erect in a chair in a corner by the opened windows. The afternoon light shone on one side of his face, the other side made featureless by the room's deep shade. He was dressed in a way that Luther didn't recognize. But as his eyes focused he could see that his uncle was wearing the Prince Albert frock coat and pin-striped trousers from his days with the Garland brothers. He sat with an alert and formal posture, his short legs crossed. He wore pearl-gray spats over his shoes. And it was this, the strangeness of Ray White in costume, that easily defeated Luther's effort at denial.

He saw his uncle raise his hand and beckon him. He walked into the room and sat down on the other chair, which was made of wicker and creaked loudly as it took his weight.

Ray White's eyes moved busily over Luther's face. It was as though his look were seeking an angle it could hold, a kind of purchase. It was Luther's impulse to cooperate. He held himself entirely still.

"Where's Ray Junior?"

"He'll be along," Luther said. He saw that his uncle was sweating profusely. "He's asking the football coach could he maybe join the team."

"The football team?" Ray White said. His look let go. He reached for a bottle of whiskey on the table. He poured some into a glass and took a sip. He shook his head and dabbed his forehead with the red bandanna he held in his hand. "My Lord. Poor Ray Junior. What might he be suited for but to be the football itself?" He let this awkward sentence out slowly and though his pronunciation labored he got each word.

Luther had never heard his uncle hint at disappointment in Ray Junior, so his sigh of mild scorn sounded ragged with contempt. "He only wants to be the center. He could maybe be the center."

Ray White nodded. He took a drink of whiskey and cleared his throat. He said, "Your aunt took a profound turn for the worse just after you boys left for school. Her coughing got lower and . . . " He waved his hand. " . . . hollow. It wasn't so much coughing as a voice almost."

Luther began to nod with what might have appeared an inappropriate exuberance. But Ray White's description was so close to what Luther believed he had heard in June's coughing that he felt a pride that their perceptions were the same; that the way he practiced grief was correct and adult.

"I got that doctor up here again." Ray White shook his head. "I have to say that I wish I'd have found us another one. I detested the idea of that son of a bitch walking in here. Not even bothering with the details of his appearance." He drank from his glass. He said, "But coughing as she was, there was no time to find someone else." Saying that, new pain crossed his face. "No," he said, "I suspect that's wrong. I suspect that I knew even then that it was too late." He nodded. "Yes, even as I was dressing, I already knew that. So I *should* have taken the time to find someone with a measure of elegance and dignity."

Luther watched his uncle dab at his eyes with the bandanna. "But at least I can report that when I walked into that doctor's office this time, his eyes got big as flapjacks." Ray White nodded and straightened his gray formal vest. Luther understood then what his uncle had meant when he spoke of getting dressed; that he'd put on his Garland brothers suit for his trip to get the doctor. Ray White said, "This time, I impressed him right through to his gizzard."

He turned and stared out the window. Luther did the same. They heard the passing of wagons on the street below. They heard two men's voices exchanging greetings, saying extremely obscene things in a mellifluous manner.

Ray White asked, his voice vacant, "How were your lessons today?"

Luther blinked and frowned. "To be truthful, I ain't paid—"

"I *haven't*," Ray White interrupted. "I haven't paid. Impressive speech is your friendliest ally and your best weapon, Luther." He leaned forward and filled his empty glass. He wiped his face. His winged collar was soaked with sweat. He said, "After I came back from the doctor's office, while I was sitting with your Aunt June and waiting for him to come, do you know that she asked me for a glass of the compound?" His words had become more slurred and now he seemed to Luther to be speaking to himself. "She *was* delirious. And when she asked me for it, my first thought was that she was trying to ease my concern. It would be like her to think to do that." Again he cleared his throat. "But then she asked for it again. She coughed up an awful portion of blood and she repeated for me to get her some of the compound. She had a pleading manner when she said it the second time. I have sat here since late this morning, asking myself if she meant it. I have asked myself, was she joking, right up to the end? Or was she not? I would say she was, but when she asked the final time for the compound, her eyes, I swear, got clear and focused and her mind seemed to do likewise. You know how she does, how she'll train her lovely eye on you and then talk to you with it.''

Luther wanted to shake his head. He had never felt his aunt talking to him with her eye. She had talked to him fully and squarely and never, as he'd experienced it, with any partial aspect of herself.

Ray White said, "And then I began to think, if she did want the compound at the end, is that actually a tribute, in a most ironical way? Should I be glad of it? Or is it the worst thing I could ever hope for? My wife . . . departs, leaving me with the sense that I have delusioned even *her.*''

Luther sensed that his uncle was not expecting or wishing him to speak. And the only thing he could think to ask Ray White was whether he *had* given June the compound. His uncle's account sounded unfinished and Luther saw this as a sign of how badly he was shaken. He never let go of a story before giving its moral and underscoring it to excess.

The sound of horses on the street came up to them. Luther sneaked glimpses of his uncle, who continued to look toward the window and who seemed to him a stranger. He understood that Ray White's behavior was issuing from drunkenness and mourning, but Luther had never seen him other than cheerful when drunk. He had never seen him more than fleetingly sad.

Luther's long young legs felt in need of stretching but he believed that if he rose he would break this mood, which only his uncle had the right to do. In the quiet, he began to imagine his aunt's dying. He wondered if her coughing had turned finally into laughter. He wondered if she had thrashed about in her bed. He wondered if she'd spoken *true* nonsense at the end, not merely this simple confusion about the compound. He realized that of course he couldn't ask his uncle any of this now. But as he imagined beyond these coming days to the time when he *could,* a fresh and certain warmth came into him. Suddenly he sensed the even fuller sympathy that would mark his life with his uncle from now on. He saw, in fact, that it had already begun. He had never had the chance to draw for anyone the picture of his mother's death. No one had ever thought to ask him what had happened or how it had been. And now it was clear that his uncle was the one with whom he'd be able to compare experiences. The two of them would describe for each other that moment in the death room when the *air* begins to breathe. They would share their versions of the precise sounds of loss!

He wondered how his aunt would look in her coffin and he hoped she'd not be made to wear the rouge his mother had.

His uncle turned and looked at him. He said, "I have no idea what I'll do. Where it might make sense to ponder settling. Right now, I cannot begin to turn my attention to the mundanities of it, Luther, so I honestly have no notion. The only thing clear is that the idea of continuing on like we have without her is a repugnation to me. To say that it would give me no joy is to barely poke at it. As much pleasure as I've taken in selling to the yokels, my true pleasure was in making Junie laugh. I know how I always tell you to watch their faces for that smile that shows you've got them. But what mattered to me was, was she having a good time? Was I making *her* smile? A whole other kind of smile."

Ray White paused and tried to wipe away his sweat. He moved the red bandanna, wet through itself, over his face and neck. He made no effort to loosen his collar or undo his vest.

Then he said, "This may be just the liquor talking, but I have the honest sense that I'm going to be a fairly different person from now on." His stubby fingers felt the furrows in his forehead. "You might decide to stay, but I should tell you that I have a hunch I'm not going to be nearly so easy a man to be around for the rest of my days." He was looking in the direction of the bedroom as he spoke. He was quiet for a moment. "No," he said, "it is *not* just the liquor talking. I feel certain I can say that it is not the liquor talking."

He turned in his chair and lifted the bottle from the end table. "As long," he said, "as we are talking of liquor talking." He made an effort to smile, then poured whiskey into his glass.

He looked up at Luther for the first time in a while and his face loosened slightly as though with an idea. "Go get yourself a glass," he said. "It seems to me you deserve a bit of this." Since he'd first sat down with him, Luther had watched his uncle close an eye against a tear or a bead of sweat. But now it appeared that he'd winked at him. "Yes," Ray White added. "It seems to me that it is time . . . it seems only right, now that you're a man, that you share a whiskey with your poor old Uncle Ray. We'll make of it a one-time ceremony, like the testing of the compound." He nodded again toward the shelf by the outside door. "Go on," he said. In a whisper he repeated: "Go."

Luther had no confidence that he'd be able to stand. Within his great confusion, he realized he'd not been told when his uncle had begun to see him as a man. And he wanted now to explain to Ray White his mistake. For Luther knew, in the way the heart knows things, that he was not a man at all. And most of all he wanted to describe for his uncle their sympathetic future, the one he'd foreseen just a moment before, now that each of them could detail for the other his hour of life's most sensuous meanness.

Abruptly, Luther stood and walked out of the sitting room. On a shelf by the door to the outside stairs he found a glass. There was a small window that looked out over the alley, but it had been kept closed and the accumulated heat in the space was astonishing. Luther stood, letting the heat work on him.

When he turned away from the window and walked back toward his uncle, Luther saw him holding up the bottle of whiskey, ready to pour. His hatred for Ray White at this instant was entire. He reached his uncle's side and held out the glass. Ray White filled it half way.

"Now," Ray White said, "just as we drank each spring to the start of a new season, and the hope that we would encounter a vast population of free-spending yokels, we should, handsome Luther . . ."

Luther heard his uncle's voice becoming liquid just before it broke. He looked down at him but couldn't see his face. He watched Ray White's shoulders tremor and he focused, standing over him, on the long white scar toward the front of his bald head.

Then the front door opened and Ray Junior came in. He was breathing with effort after climbing the stairs. He was also smiling broadly, for one of the few times Luther could remember. Together, in silence, he and his uncle watched Ray Junior look around the room. They saw him glance toward the bedroom door.

"Come in here, son," Ray White said. But Ray Junior ignored him. He continued on toward the empty bedroom. He walked through its door and for the moment out of sight. Ray White and Luther waited. The silence Luther heard now was old and too familiar. Memory was in it, and a child's horror of an hour's infinity: of waiting for the sky to clear and the sun to rise.

Ray Junior emerged from the bedroom. His face was pale and his expression was more complicated than it had been in his life.

"Come here," Ray White repeated. In a whisper, he remarked to himself, "Not a trace of his mother in his face." Then he raised his eyes and frankly studied Luther. He said, "That's why I can't fathom your staying. There's so much of her in you." His voice, such as it was, had a soft slushing sound.

Although Ray White had spoken, Luther heard even more the silence that his mother, and now his aunt, had summoned. And he sensed that unless he broke it immediately, the loneliness it was trying to make would be larger than the world. He raised his glass to look at the whiskey, then turned and threw it against a wall. As he did he gave a scream that flew out the open windows into the desultory air. Hearing it, two women on the street just below stopped their conversation and clutched at their chests. An old man dozing soundly on a bench sat up and blurted, "Libby Sue!" speaking for the first time in more than half a century the name of the girl who'd broken his heart when he was eighteen years old.

Chapter

4

*I*n those rare moments over the next years when Luther stopped to
reflect on his life, a resentment took hold as he thought about the
ways in which people had betrayed him. He considered their habits
of dying and desertion; their earnest stupidities and their unimagina-
tive hearts. But again, these reflections were few. At most other
times another anger moved in him, like the coursing of blood, as if
bile were blood. It was fed by what he saw as the treasonous nature
of life in summary. It had less to do, for instance, with the death of
his Aunt June than with the combination of his mother's death, then
his aunt's, and, just as much, with the span of time between them
that had made him a false promise.

Having run from the apartment and begged a wagon ride out of
Pampa, he gave over to an abiding restlessness. He let rail lines and
riverboats set his schedule and direction. The peculiar conditions
under which he'd been raised gave him exactly the gifts he needed
at this time: resourcefulness; courage; a long familiarity with the
social hermitage of the itinerant.

He worked as a short-order cook in Baton Rouge. He worked as a
stable hand. Weeks became months. He worked as a roustabout on
Mississippi River timber rafts. He passed his eighteenth birthday
driving a coal wagon in Marion, Ohio. He found himself, that day,
with the idea of visiting his father, whom he'd not seen in all this
time. While he made his deliveries in the mule-drawn wagon, he
considered a trip to the huge cattle ranch near the Oklahoma border.
The notion of going to see his father was new, though sometimes
he'd stopped and wondered, as he'd gone about some task, what his
father might be doing at exactly the same moment. In fact, Luther
had been more curious about him than he was able to admit. But the
anger he felt toward the people in his past included Aubrey promi-

nently, and anger has its way of denying curiosity.

In Frankfort, Kentucky, he worked for a veterinarian whose principal patients were high-strung thoroughbreds. Here Luther recalled his love of horses and reclaimed his skills at tending them. The veterinarian observed these skills and they impressed him. He eventually let Luther assist in every procedure he performed, including the most vital surgeries. When the veterinarian offered to help him get started on the road to a partnership, Luther declined. The veterinarian was understandably perplexed when Luther left Frankfort the next day.

The year became two and two became three.

The afternoon sunlight was a golden band as it shone through the window of the prostitute's room. It was November in Memphis and the sun was low in the sky through the day. The room was long and as narrow as a hallway, ideal in its dimensions for the shaft-shape of sun. In consequence, Helen, the prostitute, and her mattress and her chair and every other naked surface in the room—including Luther waiting on the edge of her bed—were bathed in the hue of amber tribute.

Luther watched while Helen adjusted her arthritic hips. Her breath whistled as it passed through her lips, which were pursed hard around the stem of her pipe. Luther's smile as he waited was adoring. He'd been meeting Helen, and several other prostitutes who lived and worked on Beale Street, for some months. His regard for these occasions had not fallen from the ethereal. Greeting them, entering their rooms, entering *them,* he felt he'd discovered an exotic domesticity. For Luther, their world had the quality of reverberance and legend and his instincts were to find a context for it. The suitable universe he knew of was the Bible's, which, as we know, had been for him an anthology of mythic tales in a tone of voice he loved. And so, with prostitutes, Luther sometimes fantasized that his movements had acquired the eloquence of Scriptural parable while he felt, at the same time, a boy's lighthearted frolic.

He watched Helen grimace as she listened to the music coming from the park on the other side of Beale Street, where groups of Negroes played stomps and primitive blues all day and night.

Helen took the pipe from her mouth. "Let's go, son," she said flatly. She wiped sweat from her face with the heel of her hand.

Luther thought, *And so it came to pass that the harlot, Rahab, spake unto him, saying, "Now, therefore, arise and come unto me and know me."* He slid forward on the mattress.

Helen said, "Now do like I said and stay a mite more calm. I told y'all before, I ain't no damn farm animal, I'm an aging specimen of human womankind."

Luther's eyes looked about the room. Each detail provided an erotic glimpse for him. The warped floorboards. The water stains on the walls. The expression on the lips of Helen's vagina, which seemed to have gathered into a permanent rictus of weariness and skepticism.

She repeated, "See that y'all remember."

He thought, *And he spake unto her, saying, "I will not fail thee, nor forsake thee."* Every part of him was happy and his steely sunlit penis was happiest of all.

Afterward, he lay listening to a rendition of the "Joe Turner Blues" coming in through the window. The music seemed to have the sunlight in it. It sounded a bit too pleased at being played to convey its complaint. Still, it *was* the rich trochaic blues, and Luther's long feet, hanging over the end of the bed, began to twitch. *And the room overfloweth with music, and his heart did melt, neither did there remain any sadness in him.*

"Oh," Helen sighed, "there goes that damn awful music." She reached for her pipe. "This used to be the sweetest town there ever was. A person used to could open her window and what she would hear when she did would be the birdies singin' in the trees. But then those niggers started playin' that sorrowful excuse for music day and night."

Luther said nothing but, unlike Helen, he loved the Negroes' music. Throughout his time in Memphis, he took an unexamined pleasure in the entwined sensations of humidity and melody. He stood in the park where they often played and listened to them eagerly. His head would move back and forth, demonstrating again what he'd show all his life—a love of music in a man who sang off-key and only fleetingly caught the beat.

"Why'd they have to pick out Memphis? Who they think give them the right to play outdoors like that? Why should I have to listen to it? Ain't I got the right to listen to what I want, including the birdies or even nothin' at all? Why can't they play *real* music, anyway? Why can't they play somethin' by John Philip Sousa?"

Luther stayed in Memphis for more than a year. He worked as a bartender on Beale Street. It was a job, as it happened, that he was very good at. He'd been hired for his size and his youthful stamina. His saloon, not unusually, attracted many brawlers and it was his responsibility to set the rules and keep the calm. The rules were few in most saloons of the time. One of them was to break as little as possible. Another, often, was to vomit outside. Luther had no trouble enforcing either one. His strength was his principal aide. But so was his unfolding sense of mischief, which was easily capable of charming customers whose thirsts and ignorance made them guileless as a group. Some nights, when his temper was pugnacious, he might suddenly impose an arbitrary order on the room. He'd look around and select a victim and order him to leave. Why? the man would ask, I'm sober as a babe. How then, Luther would inquire, spreading his arms to draw the rest of the room in, how then if y'all are sober as a babe can y'all stand there and not be bothered by the smell of that manure on your boots? His voice at this point in his life was an unmodulated near-shout. There ain't no manure on my boots, the man would say, while glancing down to check. Seeing this, the other customers would chortle. Sometimes Luther's victims would argue briefly until Luther put down his cloth and started to come around from behind the bar. Sometimes there were fights, which Luther won easily.

The incident that forced him to leave Memphis was spontaneous. It was late in July and a bizarre summer chill had come in off the river. The temperature dropped to fifty-five degrees and people hurried through the streets with a Midwest-winter haste. The huge summer shad flies that swarmed around the street lamps fell from the air and lay wreathing their bases. Such weather was ruinous to the prostitutes' business since no one, especially the prostitutes, wished to linger outside. The chill sent the Negro musicians out of the parks and behind closed doors. The sounds of their instruments were weak and diffuse and coy as rumors.

But the cold was a boon to the city's saloons and on the night he left Memphis, Luther had been working with little chance to sleep for three days and nights. He had a growing headache and no patience left at all. Another bartender worked with him. The din in his saloon was that of a happy riot. The air was cigar smoke and stank as well of human malodor and pools of spilled beer.

A tremendous fog had followed after the chill, stopping the river's traffic and keeping crews from the steamboats and roustabouts from the downriver rafts docked in Memphis. The group of roustabouts who'd taken a table in Luther's saloon had come in with the fog on their first night in Memphis. If one of them rose to leave for a few hours of sleep, it was only after another had arrived to take his chair. Midway through the second day none of them bothered any longer to leave but simply passed out for a while where he sat. Their coats and sweaters piled up on the floor. Next to them, their long wooden peaveys with sharp metal hooks lay in loose stacks.

Luther's anger toward the roustabouts had been instantaneous. Watching them enter, he'd told himself that the last thing he needed was another group of smart alecks. But there was a deeper reason for his hostility. He had, we recall, briefly been a roustabout himself and it was work he'd hated. More to the point, it was work that had frightened him, the one time in his life he'd been physically afraid. The roustabout designed by God was a terribly strong man who was shaped like a pear and possessed the balance of a tree squirrel. Luther, on the other hand, had inherited his Aunt June's tendency to clumsiness and his tall, broad-chested body was exactly wrong for the low-centered agility he'd needed on the logs. He worked two months on a raft, helping to steer acres of logs down the Mississippi, and whenever it was necessary for him to walk out on them he felt that with his next step he would fall through the undulant floor of a vast, sky-walled and sky-ceilinged room and be crushed to death as its huge mass shifted.

He'd also heard the snickering of the other roustabouts as they sensed his fear and watched him scramble for his balance. He was subjected, as he saw it, to the paradox of hairy brutes ridiculing someone because he lacked a fawnlike grace. All of this had flushed up in his mind when he'd watched the roustabouts sauntering through the door.

They kept fierce and profane arguments going for a while, but by the third day their energy had faded and they marshalled what was left in the exchange of body noises. They'd also begun to violate the first and, yes, eventually, the second rule of saloon etiquette.

Luther did not see the culprit. But as he passed their table, carrying his bar cloth, he smelled the evidence through their commingling odors.

He stopped and looked down. "Who did that?" he asked.

"Did what?" replied a roustabout.

Luther scanned the table. Five of the seven were more or less awake. Their faces were bloated and shiny with sweat. They had rolled up their sleeves, showing forearms big as roasts.

Luther said, "I'll ask again, who did it?" He pointed to the vomit. He looked around the table. His head pulsed.

"That?" answered a second roustabout finally. He was looking down. "That's been there since we come in." His eyes closed and opened again. "Disgustin', ain't it."

"Wipe it up," Luther said. He tossed his bar cloth at the first roustabout. It struck him in the chest, where it lay like a bib. He looked at it for several seconds, sighting with effort down the length of his nose. Three others leaned forward and stared at it too.

The roustabout peeled the bar cloth from his chest and dropped it on the floor. He grinned. "Wipin' floors is girlie work." He grinned again. "And when you're done, bring us some whiskey." Then he suddenly broke into song. "Oh, the wind she stops, then the wind she blows, and a woman comes, then a woman goes. But I know which way the river flows, and that's why I'm married to the ri-ver!"

In the early years of the century, farmers sang to celebrate the harvest; miners sang as they walked in the predawn; and roustabouts, as we know from the matchless genius, Twain, sang river songs around their fires. So, unlikely as it seems, the other roustabouts came awake and joined in, while Luther stared down at the bar cloth on the floor.

"Oh, we're married to the river, yes we are, by damn! 'Cause she don't suffer buggers, and she knows what am!''

Luther knelt down and reached for the cloth.

"We're married to the river, yes we are! Up yer arse! E'en though she shows her temper now and then, of carse.''

His head felt ready to burst, but it was the song, too remindful, too ridiculous, that proved the catalyst. Luther picked up the bar cloth. Then he saw the loose stack of long peaveys with their hinged metal hooks lying nearby. He stood up again, holding one of the peaveys at his side.

The roustabout who'd insulted him stopped singing. He blinked and smiled. He offered both hands, palms up, to Luther, a sort of pulpit gesture. Then he set his forearms on the table. "Now, girlie,'' he said, "where's our drinks?'' He saw that Luther was holding a peavey. "What're you doin' with that?'' he asked.

Luther answered him by raising the peavey and bringing its hook down deep into his forearm, opening a river in his flesh. Blood started, flowing wide and easy. Luther dropped the peavey and walked through the crowd to the door. People stepped aside to let him pass, too startled and too drunk to react. So was the roustabout. By the time he howled, Luther had his hand on the doorknob.

Outside, on Beale Street, he was instantly inside the fog. The cold astonished and refreshed him. He knew the fog would help him hide. Also, he was familiar with the streets and the roustabouts were not. Also, he was sober. He ran two blocks and ducked into an alley he knew was there. In normal weather, Helen and many other prostitutes walked it.

He leaned against a brick wall. Expecting no reply, he whispered Helen's name. For a long moment he listened to his own heavy breathing. Other than the softened rowdiness filtering out from the other saloons, the sound of his breath was the only one he heard. There were no voices on Beale Street. There were no drunken shouts of disorganized pursuit.

He understood he must leave Memphis immediately and he sensed that, with the fog aiding him, he'd have time to reach his room and get some clothes and money. He hurried through the alleys, alert for any noise that was not his boots against the ground. He continued along for fifty yards when suddenly he heard the sound of the blues coming faintly from somewhere above his head. He looked up, then straight ahead, then behind him down the alley. All was fog, and the music's strength seemed to lie equally in every direction.

He emerged from the alley onto Beale Street again and the music sounded closer. He glanced up in the direction of Helen's window. He believed he saw her light. Through the fog, it was the weakest pale blur, the way the moon makes a cream-gray smudge through clouds.

He reached his room and gathered what he needed and when he returned to the street he heard the blues continuing. Hurrying away, he was sure he heard it still.

Which tells us something of the tumbledown quality—sound streaming out and cold pouring in—of the Beale Street rooming houses. Or does it tell us more about the power of the early blues? For as Luther was making his way out of Memphis, a young song-writer named Hilliard Highstreet worked at the piano in his unheated room. (It was his lighted window, not Helen's, that Luther had seen.) Highstreet had sat down to write a song that the chilly fog had been singing in his ear, a chord here, a phrase there, for the past three days. He wore a long wool topcoat and a pair of wool gloves from which he'd cut the fingers. On his head, he wore a beaver-fur top hat, which he'd recently won in a poker game.

He would work through the night and when he'd finished the next morning he would entitle his song "The Foggy Night Blues." It was an especially haunting tune, one of litanic and lachrymose beauty. But it would never be widely known and, like Highstreet himself, would fall into obscurity. Whenever people heard "The Foggy Night Blues" they'd tend to stand and move away without making the conscious decision to do so. One day, watching a small audience in the park do exactly that, Hilliard Highstreet would approach the musicians when they'd finished playing his tune and ask them why they thought this always happened. The trumpet player would respond immediately, as though the reason were obvious. "A person," he'd explain, "hear the truth too clear, he feel more sad than he can stand to be, so he just got to get up and walk away."

Several blocks from Beale Street, heading north along the river-bank to the edge of the city, Luther continued to imagine he was hearing Highstreet's blues.

Chapter

5

On the last day of October, in 1922, Luther sat behind a desk in a two-room storefront office in Laredo, Texas, holding a large plaster model of a penis in his hand. He turned the penis this way and that in order to show its brightly painted lesions of venereal suffering to the fidgeting young man seated opposite him.

Luther wore a beige three-piece suit. Its vest buttons strained against the breadth of his chest. On his desk sat a nameplate identifying him as Dr. Edward Merritt, one of the aliases he used.

He said to the young man, "You're concerned about the cost?"

The young man nodded. "The sign out front didn't say the cost. Twenty-five dollars is my whole week's wages." He was short and thin, with unruly light brown hair. A cowlick rose like a punctuation mark from the crown of his head.

"I understand," said Luther. "I surely understand." He appeared to fall suddenly into thought. His eyes took in their close surroundings. A worn green velvet curtain divided the room in half. He could hear, behind it, the rustling of men waiting their turn.

"Ain't there a lesser price somehow?" the man asked. "Ain't there, say, a smaller-size dose?"

In response, Luther glanced at the full-sized diagram of the male anatomy hanging from a wall. Then he studied the four papier-mâché statues that stood in a row to the left of his desk, showing sequential stages of syphilis in flower. They made the curtained space a kind of fiendish sculpture gallery. He cocked his head in the way that someone might when preparing to launch a philosophical speculation. He absently angled the palm of his hand so that the plaster penis seemed to cock its head, too. He and the penis often worked in accidental concert, as a deft ventriloquist and his dummy. "Let's suppose," he said, "for the sake of our conversation here, that there ain't a thing to worry about. It *is* possible. The Lord willing, anything is possible. There's always the possibility she was a virgin. Every whore in the *zona* was a virgin up until the last hundredth of a second of the very first time, isn't that so? It's possible y'all found one who'd quit the convent the night before and was just opening up for her first day of business." With the mention of Nuevo Laredo's *zona roja,* Luther had swept his free arm in a general southwesterly direction toward the Rio Grande at the edge of town.

He said again, "It's possible." He shook his head in a gesture of rueful skepticism. He looked at the penis. The young man did the same. Luther's lips puckered gravely. The young man cleared his throat. His Adam's apple rose and fell. The penis's silence seemed somehow voluntary. Luther turned its profile to the young man to show a suppurating canker.

"I want the treatment," the young man blurted.

Luther waited a beat, a sense of rhythm that eluded him in music. "There might not be a thing to worry about."

"It don't seem worth the risk."

"Twenty-five dollars?" Luther said. He shook his head and made a clicking sound of regret with his tongue against his teeth. "There's always the chance—"

"I want the treatment," the young man repeated.

Luther sighed and laid the penis on the desk. "Y'all will not be sorry. If nothing else, it will buy you peace of mind."

The young man emptied his wallet and searched all his pockets. He said, "All I got with me is four dollars."

Luther's smile was sympathy. "I'll keep it as a deposit while y'all go fetch the rest." He held out his hand and the young man gave him the money. When Luther stood up, he also rose.

Luther walked the young man past the four statues—arranged as they were they seemed a row of diseased ushers—through a doorway that led into the office's back room. In its center was a high, long table draped with a sheet. A desk, like Luther's, was positioned near the table and behind it sat a man in a white lab coat. Framed diplomas hung here and there.

"Hello, Doctor Barkley," Luther called as he and the young man approached.

The man in the lab coat looked up from a thick textbook. He wore dark-framed glasses whose lenses were circular. He stroked a sandy-brown goatee. He nodded to Luther. "Hello, Doctor Merritt," he said. He set the text aside and stood, moving directly to the sheeted table.

Luther said, "No, we're not quite ready just yet, Doctor Barkley." He turned and winked his reassurance at the young man. "But we wanted to say 'hy-dee' on our way out, just so we'll be familiar with everything when we return with the balance of our fee."

"Ah," said Dr. Barkley. He came forward and, unsmiling, shook the man's hand. He said, "There's nothing to it. Just a quick injection. Cleans you right out. Takes ten seconds at the most and—"

"And yet," Luther interrupted, "though it takes so little time, the cure is complete."

Dr. Barkley nodded curtly. "Of course. Cured completely."

"It is distressing," said Luther, "that the vaccine is so expensive." He looked down at the young man once more. "But maybe it's only fair in the end that we pay according to the benefits we receive. Especially when those benefits come just in the nick of time."

The young man's eyes were looking for the exit. "I'll be back directly," he said.

Luther smiled and pointed to a door that opened to the alley. He watched the young man hurry out. Then his smile fell. He turned to Dr. Barkley, whose name was Robert Burke. He said, "Well, that was awfully damn helpful. The way y'all talk, it's so easy we should be givin' it away."

Burke snorted. His face puckered as he peered through his glasses. He was fifteen years Luther's elder but his bearing and his manner made him seem a man of seventy. He walked back to his desk.

Luther started toward the front. He paused in the doorway and turned back to Burke. "There's a bunch of them waitin' out there," he said. "Just like there's been every day this week. Every week we been here." He waited for some acknowledgment from Burke. "All five weeks," Luther said.

Burke's reply was the turning of a page.

Luther left the room and walked back to his desk. On the other side of the green velvet curtain, someone sighed. Someone else sneezed. Luther moved to the curtain and threw it aside with a flourish he'd perfected.

He took a step into the waiting area, where four men sat. They were as various in size and shape and age as four white men in southern Texas could be. Only the shyness on their faces was the same.

"I'm Doctor Merritt," Luther announced. "Who's next?"

"I am," a teenaged boy said quickly. He stood up. He was parodically bowlegged. He launched himself forward, shuffling like a cripple.

Luther had met Burke on the North Side of Chicago, having come to his office early one morning. The previous night, an itching in his groin and scrotum had wakened him from sleep. In an effort to calm it, he'd gotten out of bed and spent the rest of the night in his boardinghouse tub. Madly lathering his crotch, he found what looked at first like fleas creeping through his pubic hair.

Bizarrely, his discovery served to free his mind. Stretched out in the cooling scummy water, his legs hanging over the edge of the tub, he fell into a state of active reminiscence. As other travelers might recall a series of chateaus as the way to trace past tours through the French countryside, Luther used his most piquant hours with prostitutes to reconstruct his journey from the night he'd fled Memphis.

He'd crossed the Mississippi and headed inland after Memphis. He'd traveled through Kansas, Nebraska, South and North Dakota. Shortly after, he'd enlisted in the Great War, where, by happy circumstance, he spent most of his time in the company of horses. He supervised the cavalry herd at Fort Bliss, Texas, on the border near El Paso. His army days were unremarkable. Once or twice a week, his regiment received its debarkation orders. Each time the orders came, the men prepared all night to ride off to war at dawn. Then, in the morning, the orders were canceled. After the first weeks of this routine, the men began to chuckle and sing with robust insincerity "It's a Long, Long Way to Tipperary" while they packed their gear for the trip they knew they would not have to make. Over time, they developed a glee club's daring harmonies. The horses, of course, had had the wisdom from the first to ignore these calls to action. They stood in rows of insusceptible dignity in their long dark stables at the edge of the base. Luther moved contentedly among them.

After the war, his waywardness resumed and led him in time to

Chicago's North Side. Through all this time, in all these places, Luther ardently sought prostitutes. There were prostitutes in Juarez as well as in El Paso. There were prostitutes in Kansas and in southern Colorado. In Lincoln, Nebraska, there was a frankly beautiful prostitute who managed at all times to keep her straw boater on her head. It was a hat she'd been given during a working vacation in New York City by a celebrating stockbroker on Armistice Day. A Nebraska whore and her Wall Street summer straw! What better paradigm of the commingling of the classes?

It would have been impossible to have escaped an episode of meanness here and there and in the bathtub in Chicago he recalled those times as well. He remembered the prostitute in Denver who kept a gleaming hunting knife in plain view on her bedstand. He remembered the paranoid prostitute in Ft. Smith, Arkansas, who accused him of distracting her to steal her money and fired a bullet from a Derringer which made a neat groove in his thigh.

When he'd climbed out of the tub and gotten dressed, he walked north on Lincoln Avenue to the second-story room of the prostitute he'd last visited. She opened her door, adjusting her blond wig. Her undergarments hung from her body in great disarray. From inside her room came a man's coughing. Seeing Luther, she said, "It don't rain but what it pours."

"No," Luther said, "I just need some advice."

"Doctor Burke," the prostitute said. "Two blocks north." She said, "He's an ornery little shit but he'll see to it you're all right. Be sure to tell him it's me gave you his name. He pays me a commission every time I send him someone."

Just past the intersection of Lincoln and West Webster, Luther spotted a sign in a sidewalk office window that said, "Dr. Robert B. Burke, Male Specialist Physician."

When he stepped inside, he was confronted immediately with the life-sized diagram of the male anatomy hanging from the facing wall. He moved past the ghoulish statuary standing in random arrangement near the door. The room was dark and had about it the sick-sweet rural odor of a creamery shed. In the center sat a desk and empty chair. He waited a few moments before calling "Hello?" He heard a muffled response from the back room and the squeak of bed springs.

Then Burke appeared in the doorway, squinting. "Yeah?" he said. Luther said, "Bernadette, down the street, directed me here." "Shit," Burke said. "Another damn commission."

Burke had given Luther a shot in his hip of the arsenical compound neo-Salvarsan, a discovery of the great German bacteriologist Paul Ehrlich. It had superseded Ehrlich's earlier formula, Salvarsan, and one or the other was successfully used against venereal suffering at this time. Today, we might be at least as interested to know that Ehrlich was the founder of chemotherapy or that he also, among the many contributions in his brilliant career, helped to cure certain tropical diseases, malaria for one, with injections of special cell-killing dyes.

Luther was grateful, of course, to receive the injection and perhaps it was his relief that made his mood unusually garrulous. He found Burke's sourness amusing and he began to ask him questions.

Burke reluctantly responded. He told Luther that male specialists were more common in the South. He said that he'd worked in Tennessee, North and South Carolina before moving north fourteen months ago. He'd been hopeful that a practice such as his would prosper in Chicago. He said, "Anything goes here. The town's loose as a goose. It's got more whores than the Carolinas got people. You'd figure it'd be the perfect place for a practice like this."

Luther asked how he was doing.

Burke snorted and opened his arms wide to emphasize the room's emptiness.

Luther asked, "What's missing, do you think?"

"Patients," Burke snapped. "The trouble is, Chicago's too sophisticated for something like this. You gotta be in a town that's small enough to be unsophisticated but big enough to have a lot of whores. I haven't found it yet. I thought Chicago would be the answer but I didn't allow for the sophistication." He paused for a moment. "Sophisticated people don't like specialists like myself. They ask, why's he do just *one* thing, if he's a doctor? Don't he know how to do anything else?"

Luther looked in the direction of the diploma on the wall. "Are you?" he asked.

"Am I what?" Burke asked.

"A doctor," Luther said.

Burke's face flushed and he pointed to the diploma. "I'm a medical graduate of the National University of Arts and Sciences in St. Louis, Missouri. That piece of parchment cost me four hundred dollars and a slew of correspondence tests." His squint became a scowl. He looked at Luther and said, "I've got some things to do. It's been nice talking to you."

With reluctance, Luther stood. When he'd reached the door, he turned again and said to Burke, "You're *sure* that's been the trouble? Sophisticated people?"

Burke shrugged. "What other could it be? Everything else is identical here to what it was, say, in South Carolina. What it was in Tennessee. I found this office. I set out the statuary. I hung my sign and put my advertisements in the paper. That's everything I done before. I even cut back on expenses, not taking on a partner, so there's nobody else I have to split the profits with, except the whores like Bernadette I pay for their referrals."

Luther asked, "Y'all said you had a partner?"

Burke patted the top of the desk he was perched on. "I had someone sit out front here. He'd say hello and try to make the patients feel at ease. And I always had somebody else to do that, because I used to have the crazy idea that I didn't have a winning personality."

Luther was smiling. "Doctor Burke, I've got a thought."

From the first it was clear that Luther's presence was an asset. He brought elements of counsel and instruction and comradely joking to his role. He was able to draw on his past for each of them. He'd agreed with Burke, that day in his office, that his failure in Chicago was no doubt the result of the city's damnable sophistication, but he'd added that there just might be an argument for the role of the assistant who welcomed the patients. After half an hour, Burke finally agreed to let Luther work for a small commission while they determined if he could help the practice. After two months, they renegotiated and Luther's share rose to twenty-five percent.

But the ideal site, with lots of syphilis and no sophistication, remained elusive. For Burke, this was a reversion to what he'd hoped Chicago would end and he subsided into a crisp and even more humorless competence. But Luther hardly noticed. He was caught up in the challenge of learning new work that echoed in its broadest notes much that was familiar. The similarity to the rhythm of the medicine show's itinerary was beguiling on most days and haunting on others. He was twenty-five years old. He'd lived solely by his wits, his war year notwithstanding, for nearly a decade and he was unconsciously pleased to be giving the major decisions in his life to someone else. He embraced this freedom as the invitation to train at his own pace for some vaguely apprehended assault on life.

One day Burke said, "Think up an alias to call yourself here."

Luther put down his pencil. He was preparing their advertisement for the *Terre Haute Gazette.* He looked at Burke and frowned. "Why?" he asked. "What for?"

"I'm calling myself Doctor Tennyson," Burke said. "As in Lord Alfred B. Tennyson. The only poem I ever read in my whole life that did for me what they claim a poem's supposed to do insofar as stirring up your emotions was 'The Charge of the Light Brigade,' by Lord Alfred B. Tennyson."

"Why is it we need aliases?" Luther asked.

"It's really more like a story than a poem," Burke said. Then he looked at Luther. "Why? Because it makes it harder to trace us back to where we just came from." They had come to Terre Haute after a month in Carbondale, Illinois. Lifting his eyebrows, he added, "I figured a way to cut our expenses, but our landlord in Carbondale is most likely upset."

"In other words," Luther said, "y'all skipped out on the rent."

"Like I said," instructed Burke, pointing to the piece of paper on which Luther had been composing the advertisement, "call me Doctor Tennyson." There was a friskiness in Burke's spirit that was almost raffish. It seemed possible to Luther that Burke might wink at him at any moment. He raised his index finger and said, "Charge!" And then he did: he winked.

But even named Tennyson, Burke recovered his normal personality soon enough. Neither did their pattern of frequent movement change significantly, though their departures weren't always the result of Burke's new way of cutting their expenses. Sooner or later, they still ran out of men to treat. But throughout this time, for a span of some months, Luther enjoyed more than ever that mixture of the familiar and the challenging, held together in some sense of recipro-cal balance. Having accepted the logic of Burke's bookkeeping, he'd quickly justified it. He reasoned that the lengths of time (one week's rent; only rarely, two) and the amounts of money (ten or fifteen dollars; twenty on occasion) were brief and small in the lives of those they cheated. But they were very large indeed to Burke and himself as they accumulated in town after town.

Inevitably, he decided he wanted the same certificate as Burke and when he'd saved enough money from his percentage of their profits he asked him for the address of his alma mater, The National University of Arts and Sciences in St. Louis. Burke said that none of his previous partners had been doctors and he saw no reason why they both needed to be. An argument ensued, the first of many, all of which would have about them the wounding sarcasm of the low domestic quarrel. Luther accused Burke of wishing to keep him dependent. Burke complained of the unnecessary expense. Luther pointed out that he would be using his own money, sacrificially saved. Burke predicted that Luther would next be demanding an increased share of the profits. Luther dismissed this charge as a deliberate change of subject. Then he offered that, since Burke had brought it up, it was hard to make ends meet on the percentage he was given.

Luther received his exams, general delivery, in Louisville and, three weeks later, celebrated the notice of his graduation with the most expensive prostitute in Little Rock, after which he gave himself a preemptive injection of neo-Salvarsan. The next day he proposed that, since he was now a doctor too, his percentage of the profits be raised to forty. He acknowledged that Burke's administrative duties still entitled him to the greater share. Burke asked what had hap-pened to the time when younger men were content to see themselves as students?

Pleased as Luther was to sense his life taking shape, he felt it most poignantly as he and Burke crossed into Texas in a Model T Ford. There were of course many painful memories that might have been stirred by his return. But since he believed he'd found the way to imminent success, he was happy to measure his life against the idea of how far he'd come. So he suppressed a surge of complicated feeling when he realized they were within a long day's drive of the huge cattle ranch near the Oklahoma border. He suppressed another when they passed within miles of the little town of Blossom, where he had secretly watched from behind a pile of rocks while his Aunt June and Uncle Ray made squirming, grunting love underneath a stand of cottonwoods.

Especially, he reclaimed the great Texas sky. It seemed to Luther, though he knew it was foolish, that the magnificence and the threat of the overhanging sky deepened as they crossed the state line from Arkansas. Why was this? Certainly he'd seen other skies that were as huge and influential. He'd seen the Colorado skies and the skies of North Dakota. He'd seen New Mexico's skies, endless and effortless in their painterly brutality. It was not as though he'd ignored these skies. Indeed, he'd been inclined to do more than merely look at skies since the day he'd ridden his horse into Cliffside beneath a particularly evident Panhandle sky to send the news of his mother's death to his father.

But the Texas sky held the episodes of his early history. Its colors and weather were the media of record and whenever they shifted it was like the majestic turning of a diary's pages. The first sounds of death and the first words of betrayal were in the composition of the Texas skies for Luther.

They routinely left towns now after only two weeks. It was not uncommon to stay a few days. In Killeen, Luther's alias was Dr. Ethan Morton. In New Braunfels he was, with a nod to his father, Dr. Aubrey Edwards. He was Dr. David Barber and Dr. James Robinson. Dr. Wendell Matson. Dr. Albert Penny. From his desk, Luther watched and listened to a town outside the window. He was learning to measure the spirit of a place and to sense when the number of sufferers had peaked.

"For the last month, at least," he complained to Burke, "you been leaving a town with half the row unpicked."

Burke said, "Now you want to take over *that* part, too?" He pulled on his goatee.

And so, exhausted, distracted, barely speaking to each other, they arrived in Laredo and suddenly saw that they'd reached an edge of America. It was as though, each of them brooding and preoccupied, they'd neglected their course and had to their surprise simply run out of Texas. They looked around and decided that Laredo was large enough to support a few weeks of business.

Through his window in Laredo, Luther watched its steady, languid life. Fruit stands run by Mexicans were set up along the street. In front of the office was a cart that sold bananas. Luther adored bananas. There was an exoticism, an indulgent sweetness, in the taste of a banana that seemed to him as far removed as possible from the idea of a food crop as defined by his hardscrabble childhood in the Panhandle. Several times a day he left his desk to buy one.

Regularly, then, he stood beneath an awning in Laredo's sultry shade, savoring a banana, and he began to think that here was the location they'd been looking for. He felt a unique ease in Laredo, a mood of sunlit borderlessness in its cultural play. He listened to the Mexicans converse with their customers and call back and forth from their stands to one another. He understood little Spanish and would never know more than a few phrases. But he heard music in the elisions and inflections of the language and he had the thought that he would give his own way of speaking a more pleasing lilt. That he would think such a thing seemed suddenly odd to him. He assumed a remnant of his uncle's advice had given him the idea.

After more than a month of steady business in Laredo, Burke said one night they should leave the next day.

Luther shook his head. "Just this time, pay the rent."

Burke's expression was its common squint. He said it had nothing to do with unpaid rent. He said his experience simply told him that the well in Laredo was practically dry.

Luther said, "Think about it. Laredo's got all those whores and their daughters just across the border in Nuevo. And what it doesn't have is sophistication. We had a patient today told me he was so grateful we'd set up here since he didn't have to dip his pecker any more in lard and bleach and cow shit after he'd finished his whorin', like his daddy had showed him. That's the kind of sophistication they've got here, Burke."

"Another week," Burke said, then turned and left the room.

*   *   *

Luther directed the parodically bowlegged young man to the hard wooden chair. He closed the curtain, then came around and sat down behind his desk. In these opening moments, Luther adopted the deportment of a parson. Along the way, he'd tried everything from bonhomie to censure. He gave the boy a nod and said, "What say we start off with your symptoms?"

The boy's eyes flitted about.

Luther said, "Y'all might be interested to know that before I got to be Doctor Edward Merritt, I was a skinny kid named Eddie Merritt who found himself on one occasion in my life sitting right there where y'all are, in maybe the same predicament or worse."

He reached into the drawer and withdrew the plaster penis. Turning and tilting it, he described his terror and his conviction he would die. He said, "I was sick at heart, and sick in spirit. You see, my mama, she is the sweetest mama in all of Texas and the idea of her finding out what I'd done was something I could not abide." He looked at the boy. "I expect y'all might feel that way about your mama."

"My mama's with the Lord," the boy said.

"Well," Luther said, "God have mercy on her soul. Anyway, I expect y'all still think about your mama the same as I do mine."

"She did what the Lord give her to do," the boy said.

"I expect she did," Luther nodded. "I expect she did." He said, "Anyway, one night after Mama was asleep, I just saddled my horse and rode off underneath the moonlight. I eventually ended up in Dallas and I was walking the sidewalks, hungry and convinced of my doom, when I came on Doctor Barkley's sign in his office window."

"Where's this Doctor Barkley?" the boy said.

"In our surgical area," Luther said. He extended his arm. "Right through that door."

The boy cleared his throat. "Let's go then."

Luther smiled. "It's good y'all understand so readily about the need. But there's the matter of the fee."

The boy frowned. "I wanna meet Barkley," he said. His hands were trembling. His stubbornness was clear.

"Well," Luther said, "it's usual for us first to get clear about the fee."

The boy answered by standing and Luther quickly rose, but the boy was already at the door to the back room, his shuffle still more effortful in his haste. Luther followed him through.

Burke looked up and squinted. Luther caught up with the boy but before he could speak the boy asked Burke, "Y'all are Doctor Barkley?"

"I'm Doctor Barkley, yes," said Burke. He looked at Luther for an explanation.

The boy raised his hand as though to take an oath. Staring at Burke, he said, "Wide is the gate, and broad is the way, that leadeth to destruction, and many there be which go in thereat."

Burke pulled on his goatee. "You here to get the treatment or not?"

"I ain't here to get, but to *give*," said the boy.

"What the hell you talking about, son?" asked Burke. He rose warily from his chair. He looked at Luther. "What's he said to you?"

"He wanted to meet you first," said Luther.

"He hasn't paid?" asked Burke.

"I have paid," said the boy, "according to God's plan."

Luther took a step toward the boy. "We should maybe head back out front and make sure everything's real clear before we proceed." As he extended his hand, the boy reached inside his coat and withdrew a Colt revolver.

"Whoah!" said Luther.

"What the hell!" said Burke.

The boy pointed the revolver at Burke. He said, "Three weeks ago, y'all treated my pa. Y'all promised him he'd be rescued from his afflictions." He turned the revolver on Luther. "Those sores and boils y'all showed me out front."

"Listen, son," said Burke. He was alternately pulling his goatee with either hand. "Sometimes it takes a little longer for the medicine to start to do its work. You'll just have to be patient, you and your daddy."

The boy shook his head. "The Lord had saw fit to set a plague upon my pa for layin' down with whores. The angel of the Lord poured out a vial upon the earth, which was full up to the brim with the wrath of God. 'And there fell noisome and grievous sores upon the men which had the mark of the beast.'" He was directing the revolver back and forth from Burke to Luther. He explained, "It wan't right for y'all to go against the will of the Lord."

Luther cleared his throat and spoke as softly as possible to the boy. "But on the other hand," he said, "y'all might ponder this: Once your pa's healed, he'll have better luck finding favor with the Lord again. Remember what the Lord said to Moses."

"The Lord said a bunch of things to Moses," said the boy.

Luther said, "I'm thinking of the Lord telling Moses how He had no time for anybody with a blemish? How's it go? Whosoever hath a blemish shall not approach the altar—"

"Whether that man be lame or crookbacked or a dwarf or be scurvy or scabbed—"

"That's it exactly," Luther nodded. "So once your pa gets rid of his scabs, thanks to Doctor Barkley here, then he'll stand a lot better chance of getting permission to approach the altar of the Lord again."

"Whether he be a blind man, or lame, or he that hath a flat nose."

"That's right," said Luther.

"Broken footed or brokenhanded or hath his stones broken. Or lame."

Luther said, "Y'all see my point."

The boy seemed to be thinking about this. Then he took a few deliberate steps toward Burke, his body rocking left and right. He said, "It's folks like y'all that destroyed our Babylon. Long before I was born, this was a purty place. Then the whores and all the rest of it sprung up across the border and Laredo was destroyed."

Burke had stopped wringing his goatee and his squint had regained its meanness. "I only been here a month, son, and I didn't have a thing to do with ruining your town, which I am confident I can say was never no damn Babylon."

"That ain't so!" the boy shouted. He raised his revolver again. This new burst of anger appeared to surprise all three of them. "Y'all are just like Jehoram leading his people to a life of whoring."

"Oh, hell yes," Burke snapped disgustedly. "I am just like Gorham."

"Jehoram!" said the boy. "What y'all do in here encourages the people to lay down with whores! They come in here and then they're safe from the Lord's punishment. Elijah said to Jehoram: 'Because thou made the inhabitants of Jerusalem go whoring, y'all shall have great sickness until y'alls bowels fall out.' " He gave a shrug of helplessness. "I can't wait for y'alls bowels to fall out, so I'll have to kill you both."

Burke's color was rising. "You ever seen a man die of syphilis, son? It is not a wholesome sight. Never mind the running sores. The pus and the stench. In the end, that's the least of it. And you'd be the one caring for him, sounds to me. You'd be the one listenin' to his howls."

"If it was the will of the Lord," said the boy.

Burke turned in his frustration and pointed at Luther. "This is your fault, damn it! If we'd done what I wanted, we'd've left a week ago." His face was florid. His eyes were plump slits. "But you had to stay another week and now this lame half-wit's going to kill us because we saved his old man's pecker from falling off!"

"Praise the Lord!" shouted the boy.

"It would be good," Luther said to Burke, "if you would just shut up."

Burke turned to the boy and pointed at him. "Boy, you are a fool and an ingrate. Whoever heard of a son who wants his father to die of syphilis? You should be ashamed."

"He laid down with whores!"

"What else is there to do in this goddamn town?"

"Babylon is fallen!" sang the boy. "It is become the habitation of devils!"

Lunging, Luther nearly touched the gun, but the boy stepped back with surprising quickness. He fired and Luther dropped heavily to the floor. The room shook. "Oh," Luther said.

"Hey!" shouted Burke.

"Babylon is fallen!" shouted the boy again. From the front came sounds of the office emptying, the door opening and slamming and opening again. "The kings of the earth have fornicated with her!" He held the revolver in both hands now as he tried to aim at Burke. Its barrel was drawing figure eights in the air.

Luther sat up. He ripped wide the hole in his pants' leg where the bullet had entered.

Burke shouted to the boy, "It's not how you think! I didn't cure your daddy!"

Luther shook his head and smiled at what he saw. The new wound in his thigh was not an inch from his old one, the crease he'd received from the Derringer bullet of the paranoid whore in Ft. Smith, Arkansas.

"I did not cure your daddy!" Burke was saying to the boy. He had raised his hands in surrender. "Your daddy is gonna die, just like you want."

"Lies won't do y'all no good," said the boy.

Burke shook his head. "You're gonna get your wish. Your daddy's gonna die." He moved toward the cabinet where the supply of neo-Salvarsan was stored. He kept his hands raised.

Luther watched from the floor. His thigh was bleeding badly but just beginning to throb.

Burke reached into the cabinet and removed a bottle labeled neo-Salvarsan. "It's just water," he said to the boy. "All we gave your daddy was a dose of well water."

"Y'all think I'm stupid?" the boy said. "If it ain't but water, y'all take a drink yourself."

Burke turned from the boy and looked down at Luther. He sighed heavily. He looked back at the boy.

"Go on," said the boy.

Burke raised the bottle to his lips and swallowed. The sight of him doing so, and all it meant, made Luther dizzy. He inhaled as fully as possible but had barely enough air to say to Burke, "You son of a bitch."

"Let me see that," said the boy. He took the bottle from Burke. He dipped his finger inside, then put it to his lips. With the revolver, he pointed to the other bottles in the cabinet. "How do I savvy all of them is water, too?"

Knowing now, Luther said, "Oh, they are, son. They are." He was looking at Burke, whose eyes were studying the floor. "When?" he asked Burke. "When did you start with water?"

Burke mumbled, "It's your own fault, wanting a bigger damn percentage every other week." He continued to stare at the floor.

"*When?*" Luther said again. It seemed to him suddenly the single thing he had to know.

Burke sighed. "Just since we been here," he finally mumbled.

The boy said, "So y'all told my pa he was saved when it wan't nothin' but water that you give him?'' He blinked and shook his head hard, as though his effort at thought were a physical act. "Then that means y'all are a false prophet." He said, "The false prophet deceived them that had the mark of the beast. And he was therefore cast into a lake of fire."

"Hold it," Burke said. He'd lowered his arms. "First you quote us how we're damned because we *saved* your daddy. Now you're saying we're doomed because we *didn't*?" He managed a bit of indignation. "Which is it, son? You can't have it both ways."

Luther heard the front door open. He heard boots on the wooden floor.

"It don't make no never mind," the boy said. "The Lord's word is in all words." He smiled and raised his eyebrows. He looked greatly relieved. "If a man's been called to rid the world of sin, it's for sure the Lord has said something on the matter at hand. That's why they call it the wisdom of the Scriptures." Then he aimed the revolver and shot Burke in the chest.

"Shit," said Burke before he fell.

A man hurried into the room and another followed him. Luther saw a sheriff's star on the first man's shirt. Both men were sweating and smelled of whiskey. After them, the Mexican banana vendor tiptoed in.

"Señor Merritt?" the vendor said to Luther.

The boy turned to the sheriff and nodded. He said, "Hy-dee, Uncle Malcolm."

The sheriff looked around at everyone who was standing, then down at Luther and over at Burke, who lay with his legs splayed wide in missionary compliance. "Wilbur, Wilbur," the sheriff said to the boy. "What is it the Lord has told y'all to do this time?"

*C*limbing the steps of his Uncle Ray's front porch, Luther imagined the entire town of Dimmitt pausing to stare at him. A month had passed since he'd been wounded in Laredo and his leg at this point was stiff as a pole. His style of ascent was to swing the leg up after him (he'd retain a hint of this motion in his walk all his life) and his self-consciousness in doing so was extreme. When he reached the porch he paused to take a breath, just as Ray White came hurrying out his door.

"Good God," his uncle said. He stopped. His face fell and its color went away.

"Hy-dee, Uncle Ray," Luther said, "it's been a while."

Ray White moved almost on tiptoes to Luther. He touched his nephew's arm. He seemed to be testing the tactility of an apparition. Finally, he said, "Hy-dee, did you say?" The pinkness was quickly returning to his face. "Son, you talk like a rube from Texas."

Luther said, "For all I know, I might be." He turned and cast his eye meaningfully up and down the dirt street.

"All right," his uncle chuckled, "I take your point. It *has* been a while." He took Luther's arm to usher him into his house.

Luther took a step toward the door and Ray White gasped, surprised, at the sight of his limp. "I'll explain it," Luther said, "in the course of catching up."

It had been, in fact, ten years.

Inside, Ray White offered Luther a maroon armchair in the middle of the parlor, then began to move about in a clearly flustered state. He proclaimed himself flabbergasted. Luther sat, his leg extended rigidly, watching his uncle circle him. He turned the word *flabbergasted* in his mind. It was one, he realized, he associated with his uncle. He wondered why. Had Ray White used it in the punch line of a pitch? Had the word been integral to some forgotten family joke? A strain of sentiment threatened Luther's feelings and to keep it out he concentrated on the pleasure Ray White's nervousness was giving him.

Luther had not expected to find Ray White in Dimmitt. He knew that Dimmitt was where his uncle had been born and raised and he'd recalled Ray White's theory that the town had got its name from some crestfallen German immigrant doing his best to swear in English upon seeing the place. Luther had come to Dimmitt to see if anyone there could tell him Ray White's whereabouts and was told, to his surprise, that since it was Saturday afternoon and the dry goods shop was closed, he would likely find Ray White at home, in a narrow frame house with a shallow front porch, one block west of the single street of commerce.

He watched his uncle settle finally into a chair. He seemed not so much to sit as alight. He wore wool trousers—it was a brisk late-autumn afternoon in West Texas. He wore black high-topped shoes. He wore navy-blue suspenders which drew parallel bands against a lighter blue shirt. His corpulence and his pink complexion gave him still the freshness of a cherub. As for Luther himself, his current temper was a crankiness considered the right of the aged; he felt, with his wound, old and stiff at twenty-seven. Studying his uncle, Luther remembered the one time in his life when Ray White had appeared old, that last afternoon in Pampa when he'd sat, drunk and drained, in his Prince Albert frock coat.

"I'm awfully glad you made the effort to come," Ray White said. He shook his head. "Ah, life. Life, I used to say, is but a series of ironifications. I used to begin one of my pitches that way. Remember? Well, a man could make a case for my ending up back here in Dimmitt, Texas, as the ironification that beats them all. If somebody had said to me ten years ago, 'Raymond White, you will return to Dimmitt, where your rearing was marked by the single idea of escape. You will return to the ancestral homestead to live out your days.' If somebody had said that to me I'd've accused him of deep insult." He chuckled and crossed his short, thick legs. Then he reversed and crossed them the other way. "You remember," he asked Luther, "all the fun we made of Dimmitt?"

Luther nodded.

Ray White smiled. "Remember our German who moaned, 'Ach *dim*mit, ver iss dis place?' "

"Gott Dimmitt, Texas," Luther said.

"Dimmitt straight to Hell," said Ray.

"Dim, Dimmer, Dimmitt?" offered Luther.

Ray White laughed and abruptly sang, "I'm a dimwit from Dimmitt, I'm a dim shit, sad but true."

Luther said, "I remember." He watched his uncle's smile slowly fade.

Ray White said, "I decided to come back here for a short while, just to get my bearings. I knew the house had stood empty since Daddy died. Plus, my sisters are all nearby, married to local ranchers, and the prospect of a little sisterly attention seemed appealing." He sighed. "And I had the notion that it would do Ray Junior good to finish high school in one place."

"Where is he?" Luther asked.

"He's a sergeant in the army," Ray White said. "He's made it his career. I'm very proud of him. He braved the grotesque trenches of the war and was wounded at Verdun. But he fully recovered and was grandly decorated."

Luther heard sincerity in his uncle's voice and he found that this pleased him on his cousin's behalf. He was also amused to catch his uncle's mistake, since only the Germans and the French had fought at Verdun. Or, he wondered, *was* it a mistake?

Ray asked, pointing at Luther's leg, "Is that where you got that? The war?"

Luther hesitated, tempted. He felt suddenly mischievous. But he replied, "No, it's recent. I'll tell you all about it. Go on."

"Well," Ray continued, "my sisters, bless them, *were* a source of comfort. But what I hadn't counted on were all the folks hereabound, all the dimwits from Dimmitt. They were a source of comfort, too. The same people I'd remembered being ignorant as fieldposts but not quite as talkative, they truly saw to us. Their concern when I needed it was of a high order, Luther, and in sum I feel obliged."

"Obliged," Luther said. He smiled. "That's what you said you made the yokels feel—obliged—when you were with the Garland brothers."

Ray White blinked. "It is, isn't it? Yes. That *is* what I said." He smiled. "Are you accusing me of being a yokel? A dimwit from Dimmitt?"

Luther shook his head. "Just noting the coincidence."

For the first time, a silence filled the little house, one to which the musty air and the furnishings themselves—the sagging chairs and the yellowed lace draperies and the antimacassars—seemed to contribute. Luther watched the nervous alertness leave his uncle's eyes.

"Uncle Ray," Luther said, "I need some advice."

After a moment, Ray White said, "Advice?"

"I've had some—what I reckon should be called some professional disappointments."

Ray White smiled. "Never say *reckon,* Luther. I told you that throughout your youth: Impressive speech can be your most effective ally. Never say *ain't* and never say *reckon.*"

Luther nodded. "I suppose that's a start."

The raw bleatings of a brass band could all at once be heard, clearly heard though wafting from a distance. "Oh," Ray White said, "it's starting! I forgot." He jumped to his feet. "Your arrival distracted me. You can tell me, we can talk while we're watching the game." He headed for the door with his old mincing haste.

"The game?" Luther asked. He struggled from the chair.

"The football game," Ray White said. "I was on my way when you arrived. If Dimmitt defeats Nazareth, we'll be champions of the conference."

Outside again, they hurried toward the field and Luther learned of the place that high school football had assumed in Ray White's life. If we know something of the importance that Texans have long attached to the game; if we know that for them it is a mode of worship, its catechism one of vindictiveness and pain, then we might assume that Ray White's interest in the Dimmitt Blue Demons was a good-faith effort to go along with local custom. But as Luther labored to keep up with his uncle, he discovered that Ray White's passion was genuine, born of Ray Junior's desire to play, first expressed in Pampa on the day that June had died.

Apparently, Ray Junior's sense that he possessed a center's skills had been inspired. He'd played the game, his father said, with loveless savagery. As he'd lumbered up and down the field, his cries had been frankly murderous. His desire had clearly sprung from some dark well of violence whose revelation had at first taken Ray White's breath away. He'd had no clue that such brutality had lain dormant in his son. One play especially, in the last game of his brief career— when he'd picked up a teammate who was about to be tackled and thrown him over the goal line for a score as time expired—had attained the realm of myth.

Walking briskly along, Ray White said to Luther, "To confess the truth, I was perplexed by Ray Junior through much of his youth. Of course you never sensed it. No one did. Certainly not his mother. Certainly not Ray Junior himself. But I couldn't understand why he had no interest in the things I loved. I kept waiting for him to pick up the banjo or work up a little skit, to show some spark, some wit! And it wasn't until he found football that I realized you can't expect your children to care about the things you care about. When I saw how talented he was as a football center—when I saw that *his* gift, his genius was for running headlong into people and knocking them down—I understood my parental task.

"So I learned everything there is to know about the sport and I've come to love it." Ray White had slowed for Luther to catch up. He continued, "I only wish his mother could have seen him come to flower, though, of course, she always adored him for what he was, which was her way." He looked up at Luther and said, "I can tell you all this now. We're two grown men after all, and besides, the story has such a happy ending." Then he fixed his look at Luther more closely. He said, "The field's up ahead." He pointed to the open expanse of prairie grass past Dimmitt's last line of buildings. The sky was un-blemished and, of course, fell uninterrupted to the line of the horizon and appeared as flat and fraudulent as the backdrop of a stage.

For the final blocks, before the pasture began, Ray White directed Luther's eye to some details of the town, whose bleakness was the ordinary bleakness of West Texas. He identified more than a few vacant houses. He said this was the result of the influenza epidemic of 1919 that had ravaged Dimmitt and reduced it by a tenth. Luther was paying little attention. He was considering Ray White's enthusi-asm for football and his pride in Ray Junior, the warrior of Verdun. This was not the Uncle Ray he'd anticipated finding.

Over the past ten years, he'd grown comfortable with the rage he felt for his uncle. At first, as we've seen, it was loose and unserviceable. But with time he'd gradually ordered his memories and his anger had become a distillate of their history. Yet his decision to see him had been in no way sentimental. As he'd lain recuperating from his wound, his mind and spirits had fought with each other to the detriment of both, the way flies buzz about in tight, tormenting orbits as though simply to frustrate each other's paths of flight. It seemed to him that before his days with Burke had turned frantic and mean, he'd been close to something he'd wanted. Furthermore, he felt he wanted it still. But when he'd tried to clarify it, he'd been stopped every time by the recognition that he'd let Burke deceive him. Whether due to laziness or greed or some blinding vanity, he had, in the end, let himself trust Burke—he could think of nothing else to call it—and in doing so he'd very nearly got his leg blown off. How, he'd asked himself, had he let this happen? And the harder he'd pressed to separate his mistakes from his ambitions, the more unbearably he'd been reminded of his lapse.

Finally, he'd decided to find his Uncle Ray, who, in spite of everything, still stood as the figure in his life who'd spoken of the mysteries of human behavior. He'd reached this decision with great reluctance. He'd come, again, to rely in a sense on the uncomplicated resentment he could summon toward his uncle. But in the end he could think of no one else or, more to the point, no one better to consult. In thinking about the past, he'd recalled Ray White's rules and observations as inclusive. He'd remembered them delivered with oracular certainty.

But the man beside him now, hurrying toward the field, seemed some addled little stranger whose curiosity ended at the Dimmitt town line.

A set of bleachers rose from the parched and naked plain. They appeared completely filled and as the two of them approached there was a sudden burst of shouting that made Ray White hurry forward with even greater speed. "I'll see you there," he called to Luther over his shoulder. Luther saw him burrow his way into the sideline's standing crowd.

When Luther reached him, his uncle waved him forward to a place by his side.

"Nazareth scored," Ray White explained. "They've just kicked off to us." His face was grim.

Luther looked out onto the field. The teams lined up and a boy from Dimmitt began to call out the signals. When the center hiked the ball, it came back, a wobbling bladder, and fell at the boy's feet. Everyone dove for it and the air sounded with leather slapping leather, a sound more brutal, because more naked, than the rifle-cracks of colliding plastic we hear at football games today.

The referee signaled that Dimmitt had recovered.

Ray White said to Luther, "Let's find a seat, why don't we?"

They reached the bleachers and Ray White started up. Someone in the crowd grabbed his hand and shook it. Someone else did, too. Luther's leg swung from his hip like a hinged implement, requiring people to stand and move out of its way. Ray White headed across toward a spot that had been made for them.

Luther collapsed beside his uncle. Ray White patted his knee. "I'm sorry you had to make that climb but I thought you'd be more comfortable if you could sit down." He paused to watch the Dimmitt player punt the ball, then turned back to Luther. "It's obvious Nazareth's the better team. But Dimmitt's had a great share of glory. It's a shame you didn't visit years ago when your cousin was playing." He winked. "Now tell me how you got that leg."

This Luther tried, without success, to do. The game itself was the least distraction, as the score quickly reached 26 to 0. More critically, Luther was steadily interrupted by Ray White's neighbors stopping by to say hello. A space was cleared on the bleacher in front of them. Ray White leaned close and people spoke into his ear. They were earnest as supplicants. Some touched his arm and patted his cheek, the fawning caresses we've come to associate with movie mafiosi. It was clear to Luther that his uncle was used to receiving the people of Dimmitt in this way. He welcomed them all with a grace note of pomp. He kept a degree of attention on the game. He gave a sound of exasperation now and then.

"This is my nephew," he said to a man, whose face beneath his sweat-stained hat was a history of weather. "This is June's brother's boy."

The man nodded and then said to Ray White, "I's just remem-berin' that time against Pliny, when Ray Junior rammed his knee in that ol' boy's face and broke ever tooth in his goddamn head? Y'all 'member that?"

"I do." Ray White smiled. "I do."

The man looked at Luther brightly. "I suppose y'all know your cousin won hisself the Medal of Honor for bein' wounded at Verdun?"

"I didn't realize it was the Medal of Honor," Luther said.

As the afternoon continued, Luther learned many things about Ray Junior. He learned that he'd played most of his last game with a broken arm. He learned that it was Ray Junior, and not Sergeant York, who'd killed more than twenty Germans and forced 130 more to surrender on the eighth of October, 1918. And as he listened, Luther began to feel more hopeful. For he believed, watching Ray White among the locals, that he was glimpsing the fruits of his uncle's old craft. In fact, it seemed to Luther that Ray Junior's being made a Dimmitt legend was the most artful fable his uncle had ever invented and Luther saw it as evidence that he'd been right to seek his counsel. The only thing missing from the past was Ray White's laughter. Luther found himself wanting his uncle to turn and give him a conspiratorial nod, show him some bright vestige of the prankster. But then he remembered that the two of them had been alone when Ray White said his son had been wounded at Verdun.

When the game ended, fights broke out on the field. Players grabbed one another and kicked at each other's shins. They spun around, holding on, moving up and down the field like pairs of violent waltzers. Several men from Dimmitt spit streams of tobacco juice and threw their hats on the ground and ran toward the opposing sideline to club someone from Nazareth. These fights among the adults were even more pathetic.

From the bleachers, Luther watched them all disappear into the dust they were raising. Beside him, Ray White shook his head and said, "Oh, dear." Luther imagined that his uncle might actually stand and command them all to stop. But instead, he rose and said, "Let's head home."

When they reached the house, Ray White helped Luther up the steps as best he could. On the porch, he said, "Wait a moment. The sun's about to set. Every night, I come out and sit in that chair and watch it." He pointed to an enormous rocking chair that had been his parents'. Its size was inexplicable, for Ray White's mother and father had also been short, fat people. "I cherish the spectacle as a reminder of our years together, when we stopped every day at dusk to watch the falling sun."

Luther wasn't sure how inclusively his uncle had used the pronoun *we* and he felt, to his surprise, a wish to know. His interest was a wave sweeping over him, its strength and suddenness as though hormonal. Yet he found himself unable to ask. Standing at his uncle's side, he waited for him to say, "Do you remember that, Luther?" But Ray White said instead, "Mother Nature is a democrat, small d. Rich or poor, we all own the sky."

The sun was orange and soft enough to look at. Just before it disappeared, it cast the fields of Dimmitt in a wide smoky light. Then the opening shades of darkness came and Ray White nodded smartly. "Now come on and I'll fix us some supper and you can tell me everything." He started in.

Behind him, Luther shook his head as though to clear it.

He sat in a chair at the kitchen table while his uncle fried steaks. Smoke rose from the stove and formed a nimbus around Ray White's bald head. Fat popped in the cast-iron skillet.

He brought plates of steak and fried tomatoes and pickled okra to the table. Then he hurried down to his cellar and brought up dark-brown bottles of beer. As he poured it into glasses, he said, "This is my own recipe. People here are always saying to me, 'Where's your garden, Ray? Y'all should have a garden, enjoy the sunshine.' I tell them I *am* a gardener: I raise beer in the sunshine of my cellar. They look at me like I'm crazy."

He said, "Let's drink to your . . . being here." They raised their glasses and drank. "It just occurred to me," he said, "that brewing my home recipe is what I do instead of mixing up a batch of the compound every spring." The fragility in his voice and on his face was sudden. "I wonder why I never had that thought before?" He shook his head. "Your being here, I suspect."

"I suspect." Luther took another swallow and watched his uncle's face. He knew he needed him to be alert, but at the moment Ray White seemed lost in rumination. So Luther cleared his throat and said, "This is why I came to see you, Uncle Ray."

He started his story with his meeting Burke. It seemed to him the years before weren't directly relevant, and except for his months in Memphis, they were indistinguishable in his mind. He said, "At first, it was working beautifully, Uncle Ray. I'm speaking of Burke and myself. And it ended up with Burke shot dead and me with a bullet in my leg.''

"What?" Ray White asked. "You fought a duel?"

"Not exactly," Luther said. He recognized that he had his uncle's attention. Continuing, he adhered as faithfully as possible to chronology while Ray White listened and nodded and said not a word. Luther ignored his food. He led his uncle on a journey through these United States, in the company of Burke and himself and the scabrous statuary. By the time they'd reached Laredo and the young boy named Wilbur had fired his Colt revolver, night was fully settled, and had been for a while. Outside, the dogs of Dimmitt called to one another. The kitchen's thick windowpanes slightly muffled their barking dialogues as they made and accepted lewd offers of sex.

Ray White stood and began to clear the table. He was clearly mulling over all that he'd just heard. He reached toward the counter for two more bottles of his beer and then gestured toward the parlor. "I'll wash these dishes later."

Luther settled again into the maroon armchair. As before, Ray White sat opposite him. He massaged his forehead. Luther watched the tail of his uncle's long scar wriggle.

"The obvious points," Ray White began, "are ones I'm sure you've already seen yourself."

"I wouldn't be certain," Luther said.

Ray White fingered a lace doily on the arm of the chair. "Well, maybe not. Because the thing in all you've told me that I find most astonishing is his giving those fellows injections of *water*." He shook his head. "My Lord!"

It seemed to Luther he was being judged unfairly. His temper flared. He drank from his beer and when he spoke his tone was sarcastic. "Well, Uncle Ray, your compound wasn't exactly what you claimed *it* was, either."

Ray White waited some moments before saying anything. He displayed his nervous habit of crossing and recrossing his legs. "I think," he said softly, "that you're confusing very different ways of medicine. You and Burke, you were working in an area into which I never wished to venture. You attracted people whose maladies were physically based and required treatment with . . . let's say, for the sake of my point here, pharmaceutically valuable medicines."

Again, Ray White waited for some time before continuing. "It always seemed important to me to keep in mind the idea of medicinal equivalences. As I said, I've always seen two basic categories of sickness. There are first of all those ailments born in a person's imagination, and in those cases the effective treatment should also depend on the imagination." He paused to take a swig of beer. He smoothed the doily over the chair arm. He said, "I would place the compound in this category. So, in all the most important ways, I would disagree with you when you say that the compound was not what we claimed it was."

He looked at Luther. "This is something I thought I'd spoken to you about when you were young, but I see you frowning, so I must not have. I'm sorry. I apologize."

Luther snapped, "You talked about a lot of things I've forgot."

Ray White said, "No doubt." Then he added, "I realize I sometimes go on about this and that. But I'm trying now to give you what help I can."

Hearing this, Luther suddenly felt foolish. "I'm sorry. I'm touchy, is all, about messing up with Burke."

"Luther," Ray White said and shook his head, "that's what human beings do: mess up." He smiled. "You're already way ahead if you can admit you did. Do you at least remember me telling you that my greatest ally in selling to the yokels was their refusing to admit that they'd been fooled, that they'd messed up? And that they'd buy some of the compound again the next year, just to prove that they *hadn't* been fooled the year before?" He didn't wait for Luther to answer. "This all fits in with what I was saying about medicinal equivalences. If the sickness is imaginative, then the treatment must be likewise.

"On the other hand, if the ailment is physical and it doesn't rely on the imagination, then the medicine must *not* be imaginative. It must be more, well, the way I always put it to myself is that it must be more prosaic. I always loved that word, *prosaic*. I looked up its meaning the first time I ever heard it and I was amused to discover that it means the opposite of the nature of its sound. 'Pro-*zayy*-ic.' Very lilting, light and rhythmical.

"But, to what I was saying, it never made any sense to me to try my hand in the prosaic area. I could never see how the odds made sense. Failure there is final, and then where are you? I saw the tragedy of prosaic ailments day after day during the influenza epidemic. There were people all around me here in Dimmitt who received the right kind of prosaic medicine, and they *still* died." He shook his head. He said, "I used to say that the one necessary ingredient in any medicine was the mind's belief in it. But the people I saw, their minds' belief was complete, it was *desperate,* and it was not enough." His voice thinned in recollection. A plaint had entered it. "Of course, your Aunt June's death was the first and only confirmation of that unfairness I ever needed."

He spoke this from a place so far away that Luther had to lean forward to hear it.

"Anyway," Ray White said more strongly, "I always felt it was necessary to keep clear where the prosaic meets the imaginative. There's a borderline where the two come together and that's where I tried to operate, just on the imaginative side of that border, with a full view of the prosaic which I attempted to describe for the yokels as splendidly as I could. It doesn't hurt—in fact it's of course a help to your ambitions—if *they* confuse the two. But if you can't keep them separate in your mind, then you're bound for trouble." He shrugged. "Or so I always believed."

He rose slowly from his chair, holding his empty beer bottle, and motioned to Luther to hand him his as well. Then he headed into the kitchen. Outside, the dogs had quieted. Luther's leg needed stretching, so he stood and began to circle the parlor. He looked more closely at the furnishings, which seemed of a piece with the walls and the floors. It was as if the rugs, the mantel's candlesticks, the ancestral portraits with their fierce expressions and mad glinting eyes had themselves been elements of the original construction, as structurally vital as the windows or the ceilings.

Ray White returned with two fresh bottles. "This is a young batch," he said, handing one to Luther. "Tell me what you think."

They drank. They moved their lips, pursing them in the act of their critiques like fish breathing air. And as they did this, a vague sense of the deeply familiar once more surprised and nearly overwhelmed Luther. "It's fine," he said weakly.

Ray White sat down again and said, "If you can stand to hear your uncle yap a little longer, there's a few more things on my mind."

Luther said, "I'm sorry about earlier. I took your words as personal criticism, I suppose."

"Well, of course, they were!" A hint of cheerfulness had returned to him. "And they will be again, so it's up to you."

Luther nodded. "I'm going to pace for a while." He set off again to walk the edges of the room. His heavy limp made a rhythmic slide-*boom!*

Ray White said, "I said there were some obvious points and the most obvious of all is that the two of you, you and this Burke, didn't need to be illegal—that business of not paying your rent and all the rest of it, leading up to his giving them water in Laredo. I know he was in charge of all that. Fine. But for the future, keep in mind the difference between illegal, on the one hand, and lawless, on the other."

Luther came back to the chair and sat.

Ray White wiggled forward to the edge of the cushion. He raised his index finger. "Listen to the words themselves. They tell you everything. *Il-legal*—not legal. *Law-less*—without laws. My question is, why would anyone choose to violate a law when there's so much opportunity to discover places where there are *no* laws?"

Now it was Ray White who stood and began to pace. He held his bottle of beer by its neck. "Of course, the laws *will* follow eventually. But the law is *not* an explorer. It waits to arrive until things get nearly civilized, so the great advantage you have over the law is in that stretch of time—ten years? five years?—however long it lasts, you've always got a lawless stretch of time when you can make your own rules within the unruliness."

He stopped to drink deeply from his beer, then began to circle Luther's chair while keeping his eyes on the recurring woven roses in his rug. "Obviously," he said, "this means staying on the move and looking over your shoulder for signs of the law approaching. But that's the trail-blazing spirit of the pioneer, Luther. It's how this country continues to get made. Without it, we'd all still be stacked up on top of one another, smack up against the Atlantic Ocean, breeding and freezing and dying in hordes."

He stopped his orbiting in front of Luther and smiled. "I envy you, Nephew. I'm a happy old man, secure in my daddy's house. I'm actually content, which I find a miracle. But seeing you again, and being reminded of the possibilities, I'm maybe a little less happy and a little less content than I was yesterday." He finished his beer in a swallow and belched. "But that's all right," he said. "That's all right."

He went into the kitchen and returned with more beers. He sat down again. "Where will you go?" he asked. "What are your plans?"

"I haven't decided," Luther said. He assumed he'd made that clear over the course of the day. He took a drink. A silence fell between them. Including those they'd had with supper, this was the fifth round of beers Ray White had opened and his recipe was strong. But Luther remained sober and his deepening sadness was a clear-headed one. He was forced to recognize that at least one of its sources was the world that being here had brought to mind and so he asked, more logically than it might have sounded to Ray White, "Pa's the same? I haven't heard from him. I haven't been in touch."

Ray White said, "Nobody has."

"He's not at the cattle ranch?" Luther asked.

Ray White said, "I got a letter from his foreman when I sent your daddy word of Junie's leaving us. I thought I should offer to wait on her service 'til he came, if he wanted. But according to the foreman, he'd got hurt in an accident more than a year before. Some cow fell on him or something and after that he couldn't do the work any-more. Apparently, he just rode off one day without explaining his plans to anyone."

Luther said, "Well, that's what he did best."

"They figured he'd gone home to Cliffside," Ray White said. "But he didn't do that. He's never set foot on the place again so far as anyone knows."

In fact, Aubrey Mathias had fallen from his horse while trying to direct a hundred head of cattle through a narrow gate. For some reason the cattle suddenly panicked. They sent up high moans, ignoble sounds, and collisions ensued. Aubrey was knocked from his saddle and trampled by a bull. His right shoulder was shattered at its socket, leaving his arm with barely any motion.

His intention, the day he rode away, *was* to return to the farm near Cliffside. But soon into the journey, the idea of living there alone began to settle in and it became less appealing with each accomplished mile. He pictured the house, hardly bigger than his cabin on the huge cattle ranch. He heard its quiet unbroken by any voice but his own.

It occurred to Aubrey then that had he not relinquished his son's raising, Luther would be waiting for him at the farm. He asked himself how *that* might have been: him and his son? Would that have been enough, *that* other voice, *that* other presence? He held this speculation for the length of a few miles and concluded that giving up his son had been a horrible mistake. A brief keen pain came into his heart. The father and his son! Working side by side!

He pictured his wife's neatly dug grave, now overgrown with wild grasses, and from that it wasn't difficult for him to begin to think of the whole farm as a grave. Without consciously deciding to do so, he abruptly turned and headed north. He crossed into Oklahoma. He stopped in Panhandle towns for food and liquor. He camped each night beneath the skies, a routine as natural to him as the breath of sleep.

More and more, he came to love the nights. He thought about things this way: He lived at night as he often had, but his days of aimless riding were new and they were hell. His mind worked to its lamentable limits to think of some work he could turn to now, but physically damaged as he was, he could not imagine a life he might fill.

He began to have to drink himself to sleep because, as he lay looking up at the skies, he would think to himself that too soon it would be day. And then, too soon, it would be.

He'd been heading generally northwest, more west than north. But the ordeal of spending each day trying to will the sun to move more quickly down the sky became one day more than he could stand. So he turned again and aimed himself directly east.

Eventually, of course, he came to the Mississippi River, which he'd never seen. He was in Missouri. He rode into the river town, as it happened, Clemens's Hannibal, and spent the afternoon in a saloon on the docks. All around him he heard talk of the river and its work and as the day continued he began to picture himself in the midst of such a life. From what he could gather, it seemed as though working on a raft would be something like living on a ranch that floated on water. It sounded to Aubrey as though the work of persuading cantankerous logs to move one way and not another was no different from directing huge herds of stupid cattle. He was very drunk.

Suddenly he announced at the top of his lungs that from this instant he wished to be a river man! Knowing his son's history, we can see this moment as one of some coincidence. He proclaimed his wish to walk on logs and see that they behaved! Everybody in the saloon whooped and cheered. In a gesture of welcome and initiation, a roustabout standing nearby tossed Aubrey his long-handled peavey pole and Aubrey instinctively reached to catch it with his arm that wouldn't move. The pole bounced off his chest and clattered to the floor. Had its blade been pointed toward him he would have been harpooned. The saloon rocked with laughter but its spirit was good-natured. People assumed he was merely too drunk to catch the pole.

The instant the peavey bounced off Aubrey's chest, he began to sober. He stood at the bar with a merciless clarity returning to his thoughts. He remembered the moment just before he'd walked into the bar. Then he remembered his waking up that morning.

He bent down and with his good arm picked up the peavey. He handed it back to the man who'd thrown it to him. Then he paid his bill and said good-bye. With a deeply chastened air that quieted the saloon and confused everyone, he walked to the door and out into the night. And that's the last we know of Luther's father, Aubrey.

Luther sat with Ray White's news of his father. It seemed to him in keeping with how the night had generally gone and he felt suddenly too weary to learn anything more. He felt it was much too arduous and too painful to learn things. He'd learned today of his uncle's self-serious embrace of life in Dimmitt. He'd learned that his cousin, the dolt, had become the stuff of myth. And for the past hour or more he'd learned how stupid he himself had been. Yes, this he'd suspected; yes, he'd come to Dimmitt for his uncle's advice. But how lovely, he found himself thinking at this moment, it would have been to learn that none of what had gone wrong had truly been his fault.

He said, "It's like having him dead and yet he isn't. Pa, I mean. If he was dead, at least there'd be that I'd know." He cocked his head and said, "Maybe he *is* dead."

"Maybe so," Ray White said. "But if he isn't, and I suspect he isn't, then he's got his reasons for disappearing." He added, "Of course, that's looking at things from *his* standpoint." He finished his beer in three short swallows. "But what you say is true. I grieve Junie's death each and every day and yet I'd rather have those final moments I was witness to than some mystery of her whereabouts. Imagining such a thing for even a moment chills me utterly."

Luther watched his uncle's face go through a sequence of distress. "Then don't," Luther said.

"Don't what?"

"Don't imagine it: Aunt June not dead, but only disappeared."

"Oh, no," Ray White said. "That wasn't what I was thinking. To be honest, I was thinking, with us talking of her last days, how much I wish we hadn't parted the way we did."

"You just said you're glad you were with her."

Ray White shook his head. "I meant the way *we* parted, Nephew. You and me."

Luther felt his heart clench and he had to look away. After a moment, he said, "Well, I won't lie to you, Uncle Ray, I wish the same." Now he realized he wanted to say deeply wounding things, to say them quickly and loudly to head off all response. He found completed thoughts poised in his mind. He recognized that they'd been ready for years.

Ray White nodded solemnly. "I appreciate that," he said. "And I accept your apology."

Luther flinched. "Apology?"

"Your regret," Ray White explained. "That you left the way you did." He did not seem detached from his words. He seemed at peace with them. It should be added that, like Luther, he was sober.

Luther did not know what to say. None of his punishing phrases fit with this. He heard Ray White speaking calmly. "I understood how upset you were. I know how much you loved your aunt. But just disappearing that way. Not even waiting for Junie's burial. And then no letters, not a word in all these years." Ray White crossed his legs and took a deep breath. "You were just saying how not knowing your daddy's whereabouts made you feel strange. Imagine how I've felt, wondering about you?"

There was in Ray White's voice a palpable sincerity of weariness and ruin. In response, Luther was having difficulty breathing. Suddenly he sensed that he'd glimpsed another sort of clarity, intimate and final, from the one he thought he'd come for. But the moment was not, for all its pain, instructive. For Luther did not understand that when one has, as Ray White had, lived all his life in principalities of illusion, it's no more possible to see the truth of the past than it is to draw a line down the middle of the air.

Ray White said, "That afternoon, after Junie died, it was so unbearably hot in our rooms. I must have lost ten pounds in sweat while I sat there waiting for you boys to come home."

Luther said, "You're saying it was *me* who told *you* I wouldn't stay?"

Ray White said, "When you let out that scream . . ." He shook his head. A rueful smile appeared. "People in Pampa wondered about that scream for the rest of the day. Ray Junior and I were walking up and down the streets, looking for you after you ran out, and everybody was talking about that scream." The sad smile held. "They had it coming from at least four different windows."

Luther sensed his old rage returning, that first loose fury he'd loved feeling for so long. He believed at this instant that he could love it again and he felt if he stayed in this house a minute longer he would kill his Uncle Ray. He waited until he was certain he'd stopped trembling, then slowly rose from the maroon chair. He swung his leg back and forth like a scythe to stir its blood. Without a word, he headed toward the door.

Ray White watched, then frowned. "Where are you going?" he asked. He quickly stood.

At the door, Luther turned and said, "Thank you for the advice, Uncle Ray."

Ray White said, "I thought you'd be staying the night, at least."

Luther said, "It'll be a help. All of it will. Especially what you said just now. That's especially helpful."

Ray White started to say something, but Luther raised his hand to stop him. "Thanks for the supper, and the beer. Your beer tastes a whole lot better than the compound ever did." He opened the door and looked back at his uncle, whose face was pinched. "Now listen, Uncle Ray. Don't you be thinking about me like you do Aunt June.

Dead, I mean, instead of disappeared. I wouldn't want you sleeping any easier, thinking I was dead."

Ray White said, "Luther—"

He pulled the door shut on whatever Ray White was saying and hurried as best he could down the steps. His presence on the street caused a nearby dog to bark and another one to answer. He moved away from the house into the Texas night. There were no stars in the limitless sky, which appeared to be using all the darkness in the world.

BOOK TWO

◆　◆　◆

1927

Chapter

7

Luther sat sipping whiskey in the dining room of Some Other Hotel in Del Rio, Texas. His second-story office was directly across the street. He habitually stopped in at the end of the evening after eating his supper and finishing his night's reading. The hotel's name was actually the St. Charles and it was at the time the only hotel in Del Rio. It had come to be known locally as Some Other Hotel three years ago, after a Customs Service agent, assigned a length of Texas border, had stopped in Del Rio to investigate a rumor. He'd heard, he told the sheriff, that liquor was being secretly served in many rooms throughout Del Rio, especially in the dining room of the St. Charles Hotel. "That would be against the law," the sheriff said. "It would be, yes," said the agent. "It must be some other hotel," said the sheriff. The Customs Service agent instantly agreed. He said he was pleased to know that Del Rio was honoring the Volstead Act. He offered the sheriff a thick stack of forms and asked him for his signature. It would verify, for a supervisor at the Prohibition Bureau in San Antonio, the agent's thorough search for liquor in Del Rio. "Happy to," replied the sheriff. He scribbled the name of his wife's second cousin across the bottom of the page. Then he walked the agent to the door. He pumped his hand and squeezed his shoulder and said, "Y'all come back."

With Luther at his table were Robuck Winter and Peter O'Malley. Winter was a hapless drifter from Bovina, Texas, forty miles straight west of Ray White's Dimmitt. His ignorance took the form of an irrepressible energy.

O'Malley sat across from Luther. He was a man of placid temperament whom everyone called Irish, though his handsome features suggested no ethnicity. They were so regular and symmetrical as to appear designed by an uninspired God who'd fallen back on drafting instruments. Considering his pleasantness and his immemorable beauty we might assume that O'Malley had been born and raised in California. In fact he came from Iowa and had *dreamed* of California. He'd been headed there, having left Des Moines in 1925, and had gotten to Texas when his money ran out and his zeal went with it. He'd just come from his work as the organist at the Princess Theater, two blocks up South Main. He'd played appropriate underchords of gravity and frolic for the current week's feature, "Wild, If You Are Too," while Douglas Fairbanks, Jr., frowned and smiled and swooned and scowled and looked out from the screen with his gaze of edged hauteur.

Luther was describing the shooting on South Main Street he had witnessed from his windows that afternoon. He said, "The one that fired the shots was standing there completely barefoot, yelling at the other one, 'Y'all stole my boots!' " Luther's voice was cast to the corners of the room. A dozen men or so sat around in easeful postures. Their expressions as they listened were childlike. They looked tickled. They looked sly, as though they'd all played parts in the high-noon incident. "And the other fellow, his tragic mistake was to try to be the voice of reason. He yelled, 'What about your *socks*? If I stole your boots, ain't y'all gonna say I stole your socks, too?' "

Robuck Winter leaned forward and said, "Stole your socks, too!" As usual, he was drunk. His smile looked forced and sickly. His teeth were widely set.

Luther said, "So the first one looked down and appeared to realize all of a sudden that he'd, by God, got somehow barefoot! His toes started wiggling, like they were waving up at him. He kept staring down and they kept waving up. This went on for I would say a full minute. Finally, he looked up and said, 'I was only gonna wound y'all for stealing my boots. But peelin' off my socks, that's some sort of perversion.' Then he took out a gun and put two shots in the other one's chest."

"Killed him?" Peter O'Malley asked, smiling.

Luther nodded. "All the way to death. He drew that gun like there was as much thought to it as deciding it was time to scratch an old itch."

O'Malley whistled softly. "Who were they?" he asked. "Local fellas?"

"No, cowboys," Luther said. "They worked for Payne Daugherty over toward Uvalde."

"Payne Daugherty raises mohair," Robuck Winter said. "Y'all surely remember that I worked for Payne myself when I first come to Val Verde County. He had him cattle *then,* but now it's mostly mohair."

Luther ignored Winter. He turned in his chair to face the bartender. "Didn't it start in here, Vernon? Weren't they drinking in here?"

"They were, Doc," the bartender said. "But they's already seriously drunk when they arrived." The bartender smiled. "And the one done the killin', he'd lost his boots before he got here."

"But what about the socks?" Luther asked with mock alarm. "It's that perversion with the socks we want to know about." His own laughter seemed to push the room's along. Several men shook their heads and slapped their knees.

Luther winked at O'Malley. He said, "The killer, at that point, he could hardly *stand.* He was pitched to the left and I mean pitched *severely.* His aim when he's sober must be ten feet to the right."

O'Malley asked what had become of the two of them. Luther said that the killer was in jail and that Payne Daugherty had come to claim the dead man.

Robuck Winter said, "When I quit ol' Payne, he was so poor he saved his spit in a jar so he could use it again. Then he followed my advice and took to ranchin' goats and now he owns half the county."

A small teenaged boy appeared in the doorway of the dining room. Luther's back was turned to him. Peter O'Malley waved and said, "Hey, Langston. What is it?" The boy worked as the usher at the Princess and O'Malley assumed he was looking for him. The boy hurried over to the table and put his hand on Luther's shoulder.

"Doctor Mathias," he said, "can y'all come with me?"

"What's the trouble, Langston?" Luther asked, looking up.

"I ain't exactly sure," said the boy. "There's a woman walked into the Princess a short while ago. And we all think she's Alyce Rae."

The Alyce Rae?" O'Malley asked.

"Who's Alyce Rae?" asked Luther. "The name's familiar, but who is she?"

"Alyce Rae," declared Robuck Winter, "she's that little gal who swum across the English Channel."

O'Malley shook his head. "Alyce Rae is Billy Boswell's wife."

Langston the usher said, "They met on the set of *Lasting Impressions.* She played the younger sister to Billy Boswell's fiancée and we all think this woman who come into the lobby is her. But the thing is, she says she ain't sure *who* she is and she don't have no purse, no identification that a person could look at."

He described the woman walking into the Princess as he and the owner, Irene Pugh, were cleaning up. She'd stood quietly for a moment. She was dusty and unkempt. When Langston had asked if he could help her, she'd said in a near-whisper that an urge she didn't really understand had drawn her into the theater. Langston had kept his wits about him. He'd said, from what he'd seen, many women felt that way about Douglas Fairbanks, Jr., but the picture was over and they were closing up. The woman had said nothing in response to that. She'd seemed to be trying to hold something back. She'd said at last, "I don't know who I am." That's when Irene Pugh had blurted, "Why, girl, you're Alyce Rae. I'd know y'all anywhere. Those big doe eyes and blond hair and that pointy chin that shapes your face into the perfect valentine? I see you all the time in *Motion Picture* magazine, posed by your swimming pool with your husband, Billy Boswell."

"I'll be damned," said Peter O'Malley at the table in the St. Charles. Like Langston the usher, O'Malley followed the lives of the stars whose performances he accompanied on the organ each night.

Luther said to Langston, "So she claims to have amnesia."

"No, like I said, she claims she don't know who she is. She's actin' unpredictable, so we took her down to the jail for her own peace of mind."

Luther said, "You put her in jail for her peace of mind, next to a drunk who killed his best friend? That was a fine idea, Langston."

The other men in the bar had been listening closely. On cue, like a chorus, they'd said, "Amnesia?" and "Jail?" Now a higher eager interest came over them all. "Speak up, Langston!" someone shouted.

"What's she look like?"

"Is she passed out?"

"She say why she run off?"

Luther shook his head. He said to Langston, "It'd be easier to get Doctor Cathcart to take a look at her."

Langston shrugged. "Doctor Cathcart goes to bed by now."

Luther sighed. He said, "Let's go." He pushed his chair back and stood up.

Robuck Winter said brightly, "I'll come too. I's always curious why she'd wanna swim that far."

"By God, I'll come too," said a drinker at the bar.

"Let's us all go."

"Now ain't *this* somethin'? A killin' and a movie star all in one day!"

Luther turned and said to everyone, "If she asks for any one of you, I'll have Langston come and fetch you."

It might seem surprising that Langston the usher would summon Luther to treat a woman in jail who was probably Alyce Rae. It's true that the boy had first thought of Dr. Cathcart, Del Rio's licensed M.D. But with Dr. Cathcart gone to bed, he headed quickly for the St. Charles to look for Luther, who was still primarily known as a male specialist physician. And his reasoning reflects the country's changing attitudes as the twenties neared their end.

Moving beyond the suspicions of their ancestors, people had begun to recognize a bold and more merciful world of medicine in America. This is not to say that their fondness for balms and salves had been replaced, and especially in the smaller towns and hamlets, the sources of remedy were seen as equal and circular: If the way science worked was inexplicably magical, so the older work of magic was invisible, like science.

This notion of equality extended to the many kinds of healers. To doctors of medicine. To doctors of osteopathy. To electro-medic doctors offering cures based on the paths of magnetic currents traveling through the body. To sellers of radium water, offered as a measure against impotency. To doctors, like Luther, with eclectic degrees. This view was arguably truest on the Mexican border, where, then as now, there was a certain laissez faire in medical matters.

Luther had been dispensing neo-Salvarsan in Del Rio for four years. After leaving Ray White's house in Dimmitt, he'd traveled slowly west and south. He'd ruminated. He'd recuperated. He'd read what he had and what he found along the way: the weekly tabloids; a discarded copy of *The Magnificent Ambersons;* now and then a chapter of Ruth or Deuteronomy. He let his bitterness toward Ray White grow. But he also considered what his uncle had told him. In spite of everything else, Luther sensed there was utility in Ray White's advice and he felt he'd be a fool to ignore it in a spirit of revenge. He saw revenge, in fact, in *not* ignoring it. So he thought, as he traveled, about Ray White's distinguishing physical illnesses from those a man contracts in his imagination, diseases often spread by the virus of loneliness. He thought about his uncle's reading of the frontier spirit. He thought of his unlikely ease in the town where he'd been raised.

When Luther first saw Del Rio, on the western Rio Grande, it appeared to him a smaller version of Laredo. At once, Laredo's pleasures came keenly back to him. He saw the same wide dirt streets. He saw the flat façades with their awnings and shutters against the strong desert sun. He saw South Main Street lined with the Mexicans' cane-roofed fruit stands.

He walked slowly about the town. He guessed that roughly ten thousand people lived there and he was roughly correct. As he walked, it felt as if the stiffness in his leg were lessening. The dry, hot air seemed to work lubriciously. He smiled to himself: an imaginative cure for his prosaic wound?

He walked along in the shade of live oaks and pecans. He saw a block of grand homes of sand-hued limestone set back from the street. He followed for a while a deep, narrow creek that bent and turned through the town with the whimsy of a root. After half an hour, he returned to South Main, where people moved along beneath covered sidewalks.

He moved out of the heat—the sun was now directly overhead—and continued his walk beneath the sidewalks' roofs. After a block, he stopped in front of the largest fruit stand. He saw oranges and grapes and pluming stalks of bananas. Luther leaned against a post and listened to the vendor speak to his customers. The plainsong of Spanish reached his ears, its braided chords of loss and romance.

Listening in the shade, Luther felt extremely happy. He stepped forward and smiled.

"Buenos días, señor," said the owner.

"Buenos días," Luther said. He pointed to a stalk of bananas. The owner reached for one and Luther stopped him. "I want the whole stalk," he said. He moved his arms in large circles. The owner laughed and lifted the biggest stalk free. He handed it to Luther, then said, "Wait, *señor."* He took something from his pocket and handed it to Luther. It was a photograph, worn soft as felt from frequent handling. Its surface was chipped and fissured. Luther could barely make out the image of a chubby Mexican girl in a white dress. He looked up at the vendor, whose face was bright and urgent. "My daughter, Angela," the vendor happily explained in English. "She is beautiful, yes? You come tonight and I make you special price to fall in love with Angelina! A favor to you because you buy so many bananas!"

Luther looked at the photograph and then again into the vendor's beaming face. "She is the best in Acuña," the vendor said. "Guaranteed, señor. My Angelina is the best in whole state of Coahuila!"

This had never happened in Laredo.

When they reached the jail, Luther told Langston the usher to go on home. The boy couldn't hide his disappointment. "But it's almost for sure that she *is* Alyce Rae, Doctor Mathias. What if she starts talkin' about her life with Billy Boswell?"

Luther said, "I'll remember everything and I'll tell you all about it."

Inside, he nodded to the night watchman behind his desk and looked across the room to the two dark cells. One was empty and in the other slept the cowboy who'd killed his friend that afternoon. His snoring was extraordinary. Luther noticed that he now wore socks, though there was still no sign of boots. Then he looked to the far corner of the room and saw her, sleeping also, beneath a light blanket on a long Mission bench.

The night watchman whispered, "It didn't make no sense to put her in a cell. But the poor little thing's been extremely agitated. Not so's to give me any trouble. Just fretful is what I mean." He added,

"Me and Irene Pugh helped her wash up a bit. We was real gentle. She's got her a serious sunburn." The night watchman was a sour-tempered old man named Ulrick Clyde, who at the moment had light and grand excitement in his eyes.

The two of them watched her sleeping. The killer cowboy's snoring filled the room. It moved in perfect synchrony with her breathing, thereby creating an unfortunate impression.

Ulrick Clyde whispered, "Have y'all ever seen anything so purty?" His head was cocked to one side. "I believe I could die now without a great deal of regret, knowin' I've lived to see something so purty as she is right there."

Luther moved across the room on tiptoes, but his size made the wood floor creak with each step. He lowered himself into a chair beside the bench.

She was extremely fair and her face and arms were pink from the sun. Her eyelids were delicately veined. They seemed almost tinted with a blue-shaded opacity and yet also too translucent to shut out light. She stirred and mumbled something and a small bubble of saliva formed at the corner of her mouth. Her short blond hair had lost much of its wave and when she moved it fell lankly across her face. Luther reached over and brushed it back. He waited for her eyes to open, but they didn't. She moved her hand in sleep to wipe away the bubble of saliva, then she rubbed the end of her nose. Luther saw these gestures as a napping child's. On occasion, in Memphis, he'd watched the infant daughter of a frequently visited prostitute. The child sometimes slept soundly in her crib while her mother went about her work beside her. Now, as Luther studied this woman, images of the child and her mother came to mind and passed like specters back and forth through one another.

From his cell, the killer cowboy released an outlandish noise and she smiled as though responding to a sound in her dreams. She opened her eyes. They were uncommonly large and round and, in Luther's view, uncommonly beautiful. He was trying to name their color but it seemed to change as they darted about and the light caught them differently. They appeared mostly green but a green that alluded to blues and browns and grays. She blinked and said warmly, "Was that you, darling?"

She sat up, drawing the blanket more tightly around her.

"Are you cold?" Luther asked.

"A little," she said. She looked at Luther and frowned. "Where's Douglas?" she asked. Her voice was surprisingly low and husky.

"Douglas?" asked Luther.

"My Dougie," she said.

"Well," Luther said, "I don't know about that." He paused. "Are you wide awake?" he asked. "Take your time waking up."

She blinked and nodded. "Yes, I'm awake," she said. She cleared her throat and said more formally, "Where is my husband, Douglas Fairbanks?"

Luther looked around before he answered. "Let me ask you this," he said. "Are y'all entirely certain Douglas Fairbanks is your husband?"

She started to reply with seeming confidence. Then she stopped. She shook her head. "I guess I'm actually not sure. It was what was in my mind when I woke up just now. I was remembering how I've been looking for him for some days. And then I saw his name on a big sign in front of a hotel. They were apparently advertising the fact that he was staying there. And I remember thinking to myself, 'The poor dear can't find a night's privacy, even in a little hick town like this.' " She shook her head. "That seems very real to me. But also, it doesn't. It feels more like a dream. It *sounds* more like a dream, too, doesn't it?"

Luther said, "It might be you're a little bit confused." He hadn't sensed himself bending quite so close to her while she was speaking. He sat back abruptly and his head bumped against Ulrick Clyde, who'd tiptoed over to stand behind him.

She said, "I must have been dreaming. And I clearly am confused, because I need to ask both of you who you are. And where I am."

Ulrick Clyde said, "My name's Ulrick Clyde, ma'am. I helped y'all wash up a while ago and since then I been sittin' over there makin' sure y'all got some sleep."

She said, looking around the jail, "Have I done something wrong?"

Luther said, "I sincerely doubt it."

She studied the room for a moment. "The details are sweet. It reminds me of the one they've just built on the MGM lot." She glanced at Luther, then looked away. "Why did I say that?"

From his cell, the killer cowboy said, "Excuse me, ma'am." Luther and Ulrick Clyde spun around to look at him. "Excuse me," he repeated. He stood, leaning into the bars. They pressed against his huge stomach, dividing it into loaves. It was clear that he was not yet sober. "Nobody here'll tell me where my boots are, ma'am, and I was just wonderin' if y'all might've seen them?"

"Did you leave them in the cabana?" she said without a pause.

"Say, I'll bet I did," the killer said.

Luther asked, "Does Alyce Rae. . . is that a name you know?"

She thought for a moment. "Perhaps," she said. "Yes, I think it is. Why?"

"Thank ya', ma'am," the killer said. "I'll look out in the cabana."

"And what about Billy Boswell?" Luther asked.

"Of course," she said. "Who doesn't know Billy Boswell?"

"We think *your* name might be Alyce Rae," said Luther. "We think that might be who you are. And if it is, then your husband would be Billy Boswell." He softly offered this to her, with several pauses.

She thought, frowning hard. "And not Douglas Fairbanks?"

"Not if it's the case that you're Alyce Rae."

The killer asked, "Just where is it now again?"

She turned to him. "Where's what?" she asked.

"That cabana," he said. "And also, *what* is it, while I'm askin'?"

She looked back to Luther and, behind him, Ulrick Clyde. She thought a bit longer before letting out a sigh. "I'm very confused," she said.

"Don't worry, darlin'," said Ulrick Clyde. "Y'all don't *have* to be. Y'all's photograph is everywhere in the movie magazines."

Luther said, "Go slow with all that, Ulrick."

But the old man was too thrilled to hold his information in. "Irene Pugh showed me two magazines that she owns just herself. It's clear from their photographs that y'all *are* Alyce Rae."

"Really?" she asked vaguely. "Do you have one I might see? Do you have one that shows me standing next to Billy Boswell?"

Chapter

8

*T*he police had called just a few hours before to tell him she'd been found and now Billy Boswell stood, surrounded by the floor-to-ceiling mirrors that lined his vast dressing room, preparing to leave for Texas and his Alyce. She'd been missing from their mansion for the past eleven days.

Billy was a lithe and fine-boned man. He was thirty-two years old. His physical beauty had a kind of ultimate finish. His features worked so harmoniously it was impossible to imagine how any one of them could, on its own, begin to age. His hair was black. His face was long and his magnificent chin was invariably termed "chiseled" in the motion-picture magazines. His complexion was swarthy, which of course was not apparent beneath layers of makeup on black-and-white screens.

Eleven days before, Billy had returned home from a late-night meeting with the insomnious studio owner Abe Zietman and found that his wife was not in their bed. His response was a primeval scream that woke the servants. Half an hour later, when the police arrived, Billy was hysterical and already drunk. The detectives suspected that he was not really drunk, but was for some reason playing a drunk much too broadly. They silently critiqued his hiccups as too demonstrative by half. Perhaps, in these years of Prohibition, they'd gotten used to watching people underplay inebriation.

Billy was an emotionally fragile man in the calmest of times. He was not a little paranoid. He was prone to spasms of weeping that broke without warning through a grand sunniness. He was currently trying to wean himself from the visits of an astrologer he'd long retained. He'd decided that the unsettling accuracy of her forecasts and her snarl of contempt as she offered their details had been the sources of his nightmares for the past several years. But he remained in the thrall of Émile Coué, the savvy little Frenchman who had recently spread a strain of fatuous psychology throughout the country. The popularity of Coué's doctrine had weakened long ago among Billy's Hollywood friends, but several times a day Billy still stood in his dressing room, his eyes roaming among the mirrors' images of himself, and recited Coué's litanic pap: "Day by day, in every way, I am getting better and better."

Now he knotted his tie and ran his hands along his neck. He was emerging from a hangover with a fresh and manic giddiness at the news that Alyce was safe. Whatever his swings of mood and self-esteem, Billy held his love for Alyce Rae at the steady pitch of zealotry. She was a former beauty queen from Detroit and a Paramount starlet who'd shown no hint of talent before retiring from the screen when the two of them were married.

Through the open windows of his adjoining bedroom, Billy could just hear the idling motor of his limousine. His chauffeur was waiting to drive him to the train station. Listening vaguely to the limousine, Billy was startled by the ring of his dressing room phone. When he picked up the receiver, he heard only heavy breathing.

"What is it, Leland?" Billy asked. He'd instantly recognized the severe asthmatic wheeze of his press agent, Leland Wheelock.

After several moments Wheelock said, "Billy, what time should I tell the photographers to be at the station?"

"What photographers?" said Billy. "What are you talking about?"

"I'm talking about you boarding the train to set out on the journey to retrieve your beautiful Alyce." Wheelock paused to breathe. "I'm talking about the photographers who'll capture your departure. It was a masterful idea, Billy. And just when your career could use this little nudge."

Billy said, "You think all this was a publicity stunt? My God, Leland, I thought she was dead! Or that she'd left me, even worse!"

Wheelock stammered an apology, though he was privately saddened to hear that Alyce's disappearance had not been staged. He'd thoroughly admired it as an elegant piece of craft.

"Billy," Wheelock said. "Billy. Let me think for just a second."

"What?" Billy leaned toward a mirror to inspect the bruises of sleeplessness crescented beneath his eyes.

Wheelock said, "We can still use it, even though it's true. So let me ask again, when do you leave? When do you swing yourself up onto that step, the cowboy to the stirrup heading off for Texas, and give the sweeping wave while the nigger shouts 'Aboard!'?"

"No press!" Billy shouted. "I've been insane with worry. I've been in mourning, Leland."

Wheelock thought he heard the too-familiar sound of a hitch in Billy's throat, signaling the onset of a serious weeping fit. "Billy," he said more softly. "Billy. You really should have let me know all this was merely true."

"Good-bye, Leland," Billy said.

"What I'm saying to you, Billy, is that I've told the press already."

"What?"

"They don't know just when you're leaving. That's why I was calling."

"You told the press!"

"Some are waiting down at Central Station. Dozens more are by their telephones, expecting my call."

"You idiot!" In his mirrors, Billy watched the back of his hand fly up to his forehead, the hotly controversial I'm-feeling-faint gesture he'd first used in *Darkest Before Dawn*.

Wheelock said, "Billy, any first-rank professional would've done what I did. If you don't give them these stories, they'll pretend you don't exist when they know you really need them. They'll say, 'Billy Boswell? Wasn't he that tailback at Southern Cal who got the clap and died?' "

"Leland, I'm hanging up the phone."

"All right. I won't call anyone else. But you'll have to have *some*-thing for the boys who are already there. I know Wally Jacobson is, from the *Times*. Don't forget he adores you. Don't forget the review he gave you for *Two Dirty Sweethearts*. And Billy?"

"What?"

"Tell me you made up the amnesia, at least. The amnesia was brilliant."

Billy flung the phone across the room. He stood still for a few moments. He was imagining what he would face at the station. In his mind, he heard the photographers shouting, "Look this way, Mr. Boswell!" He felt an urge, strong as lust, to call his old astrologer.

Then, through his panic, a saving thought occurred and it caused him to hurry through the door toward his bedroom. He stood before his wardrobe and began to open doors and drawers. His hands moved over garments in quick and fluttering motions. As he rummaged, he realized that he could not actually wear a costume as such, anything that would draw the least attention to himself. He would need to appear somehow fully ordinary and outside any notice.

At the bottom of a drawer, he spotted an elegant silver wig and a costume Vandyke beard, trig as a gigolo's. He remembered the Halloween party at Abe Zietman's, when he'd worn them. He pictured himself in the wig and the beard once more. He envisioned an old man moving slowly through the station. He could not imagine a more effective deception. Who could be more unlike him than a dignified old gaffer shuffling poignantly toward his train?

He hurried down to the first floor. In his butler's closet he found what he was looking for: a pair of baggy pants and a plain, dark jacket. He took them from their hangers and rushed back up the stairs. In his dressing room again, he got out of his suit and put them on. With a makeup pencil of Alyce's he drew age lines fanning out from his eyes. He slipped on the wig and the beard and then he thought of something more.

He left the room. In the back of a closet in the hallway, he found a cane. It was a memento from Chaplin, one from the Little Tramp's numberless collection; he'd presented it as an elegant gag on Billy's thirtieth birthday. Billy saw a straw hat on a hook and took it down as well.

Using Chaplin's cane, he shuffled back into his dressing room and stood amidst his mirrors. He looked at himself critically and, as best he could tell, there was not a sign of Billy Boswell in the many angled images his eye had learned to catch peripherally.

Two hours later, he was sitting in a burgundy plush seat of the Southern Pacific's Sunset Limited, heading east into the desert. A portly man with a portly leather salesman's case sat across from him. He'd told Billy that he was going to Texas also. He'd been ready to talk but Billy had cut him off with a curmudgeonly nod and turned his head toward the window. For he still wore his disguise and he was worried that the salesman would see, from this close range, that the hair was a wig and the beard was false.

Billy watched the desert outside his window deepen toward sunset. A trail of engine steam cirrused past his view. The Pullman was only slightly cooler than it had been when he'd boarded. Inside his wool coat he was sweating heavily and the thick silver wig was a hat that held his heat in.

In his hastily made plan, Billy had assumed that he would remove the wig and beard and scrub his face clean as soon as the train had left the station. He hadn't been much concerned about dealing with his celebrity once he was on board; it had been the idea of publicity cheapening his departure that had sickened him.

But two things had happened that kept him still disguised. No sooner had he settled into his seat than he'd glanced up to see Wally Jacobson, the reporter from the *Los Angeles Times,* moving through the car. Panic had bloomed in Billy. He'd looked immediately away and fixed his eyes on the view. Taking deep calming breaths, he'd asked himself how he could possibly avoid Wally Jacobson for the next thirty hours and it had been clear that he had no choice but to remain in his disguise. "Goddamn it," he'd muttered aloud.

Across from him, the portly salesman had leaned forward and said, "With all respect for your age, sir, I revere our Lord, Christ Jesus, above all things."

Billy had mumbled an apology. To give his voice the sound of age, he'd adapted Leland Wheelock's asthmatic wheeze.

And then Billy began to realize that in a way he was enjoying himself. He had never in his life played a more demanding part. For the first time in years he felt he was acting. As a stunning silent star, he was typically directed to project only his Apollonian beauty on the screen. The last thing audiences desired when they paid to see Billy Boswell was to find his presence diffused inside a role.

To avoid conversation with the portly Christian salesman, he placed the straw hat over his face and pretended to take an old man's epic nap. After that, he went early to the dining car. He sat alone and, to prevent anyone from joining him, repeated over and over in his mind the phrase, "I despise you, each and all," hoping through a kind of perversion of Coué to send waves of misanthropy out into the room. As he began to eat his dinner, he had a moment of inspiration and began to make his hand tremble as it held a fork of food. He congratulated himself for thinking of this touch.

And then, without warning, his heart suddenly filled with a passion for Alyce and he had to put his fork down, for his trembling had become real. He looked away, out the window, to try to hide his weeping. In his mind he smelled her perfumed hair. He sucked her sweet pink toes.

Luther stared inattentively at the opened pages of Dr. August Steinach's book, *Sex and Life*. Earlier, at his desk, he'd tried with no more success Dr. Serge Voronoff's *The Conquest of Life*. He already knew the contents of both books thoroughly, but that had nothing to do with his inability to concentrate. Indeed, he'd been rereading the books continually for the past few months, thinking himself the fortunate monitor of a dialogue between brilliant adversaries.

He closed *Sex and Life* and got up from his reading chair. His rooms were hot at eleven o'clock at night, their windows opened to the sounds of South Main. He walked through his kitchen and into his office and raised those windows as well. In the darkness, he looked across the street to the third floor of the St. Charles, where he saw, behind closed draperies, that the lights were still on in Alyce Rae's suite. He was surprised, for she'd seemed exhausted when he'd left her at eight. Perhaps the nurse was reading after getting Alyce settled.

He stepped away from his windows and wandered around his office before sitting down in the chair behind his desk. He leaned back and lifted his long legs up onto its surface. He heard the rattling of an automobile passing below. Moments later he caught a whiff of its exhaust fumes.

Tell me again? Alyce Rae had asked him at the door of her suite. *Tell me again when my husband will be arriving.* She'd frowned. Her eyes had been gray-green at the moment of her question and enormous with the predicament of memory.

"The morning after tomorrow," he'd told her, repeating again the information he'd received in Billy Boswell's telegram. "He's due in on the ten forty-five. We'll make sure you're there plenty early."

"You'll come with me to the train?"

"If that's what you want."

"Yes. It is." She'd taken hold of his wrist a moment before and continued to hold it lightly.

"But that's another day still. For tonight, Mrs. Hurd has everything you need." He'd nodded to the nurse moving officially about the room. "Y'all should sleep long and late in the morning."

"I *am* very tired."

"Good night then," he'd said. Her grip lingered on his wrist.

"I'll see you tomorrow?"

He'd nodded. "I'll stop in around noon."

In his office, he turned on the lamp. On his desk lay Voronoff's *The Conquest of Life.* He opened it, removed his bookmark, and read, "Decrepit old men are, in reality, eunuchs. They have been emasculated not by the criminal hand of man but by the cruel hand of nature. When they cease to function, when they lose their affective ardor, there occurs in their physical, moral, and intellectual condition a characteristic modification that makes them, for all practical purposes, akin to eunuchs."

Luther had prospered modestly in Del Rio as a male specialist. Ranch hands from throughout the territory came regularly to see him. Steady numbers of men stopped by his office after visits to Villa Acuña's *zona roja,* just across the border. But in his desire for something else, for something more, he'd recently begun to offer a second specialty, one based on the experiments of Steinach and Voronoff.

Steinach was Viennese, Voronoff a Russian with a clinic outside Paris, and they'd separately described, in interviews that had found their way into American tabloids and caught Luther's eye, the emerging field of rejuvenation. The two agreed on that term and on the physiological explanation for their great successes. But they disagreed hotly on the question of the most responsible methodology.

According to the interviews, many men of middle age or older, long subsided into sloth and indifference, were receiving from Steinach injections of what he called the hormonal essence of monkey gonads. Others were choosing instead Voronoff's surgical implantations of the gonads themselves. In either instance, patients claimed to have been transformed into figures of rediscovered sexual vigor.

Luther had noted in his reading that a good many of these patients were French and he'd taken that into account. But even so he'd been intrigued and had sent for Voronoff's and Steinach's books. He'd read them, fascinated. Both were written, at least in their translations, in the euphemistic prose suggested by Voronoff's phrase "affective ardor." Both were comprised of detailed case studies and were replete with photographs that employed contrasting light and angle and facial expressions (listless sulks before; bonny smiles after) to show revitalized subjects in the miraculous aftermath. There were photographs of rodents and frogs, dogs and goats. There were hapless rams in the first realm of senescence. And there were photographs of human males, chronologically aged or prematurely so. Each of these subjects, according to the authors, had been given a new testicle eager to release its hale and boisterous hormone.

What most held Luther's interest was not what the two agreed on, but rather the irresolvable argument between them. Steinach's answer to the anticipated crisis of supply to meet demand was the one of poetic spareness: the masceration in his laboratory of monkey glands to make a solution for easy and limitless injection. While Voronoff, acknowledging that monkey glands were indeed the appropriate substitute, insisted that injections would prove only temporarily effective. He'd opted instead for grand expansion and had financed baboon-breeding farms in Africa, ensuring plentiful inventories of the gland itself.

Luther shifted his long legs on his desk. He read from Voronoff, "If Goethe, that universal genius, produced admirable works until the end of his days, it was because he preserved the reproductive faculty down to the last years of his long life. This great genius was a great lover, like Victor Hugo—like all geniuses in fact—but only the poets have the courage to tell of their loves."

Oh, look, Alyce Rae had said that afternoon. *There I am. There we are.* She was pointing to a picture of herself and Billy Boswell in one of Irene Pugh's motion picture magazines.

"That's your living room, then?" Luther had asked.

"It must be." She'd frowned. She studied the photograph for several seconds. "Yes, of course it is. With the dining room through those French doors you can just see behind us." It seemed to Luther she was trying to convey a sense of certainty, not only for herself but to put him at ease.

He'd said, "There's no need to hurry yourself about any of this."
Her eyes, as he'd watched them, had become a shade of aqua.

He closed Voronoff's book and set it aside. Again he turned off his
desk lamp, got up from his chair, and walked to the windows. Below,
the air of South Main was as quiet as a poised moment.

Her lights were still on.

In the hours he'd spent with Alyce, Luther had learned a great deal
about her. He'd seen many photographs of Alyce with Billy Boswell.
He'd seen one of them kissing while dressed in wedding clothes.
Alyce's gossamer veil was God's own cloud surrounding her. Billy's
beauty, in his morning coat, was stark and epicene. "Do you recognize your glamorous friends, Alyce Rae and Billy Boswell?" the
magazine's caption asked. "They've kissed lots of people on the
screen, but this is one kiss where they're certainly not acting!
They're going to be married and we're sure you'll agree they're not
just pretending to be in love!" In earlier magazines Irene Pugh had
saved, he'd seen photographs of Alyce when she'd first arrived in
Hollywood, a teenaged starlet posed in bathing suits. Her loveliness
in these earliest pictures had shone from a face of unguarded enthusiasm, and looking at them, Luther had felt something like concern
for her safety.

At the end of the day, when the temperature had cooled a bit and
people were in their homes preparing to eat supper, he'd escorted
her up the street to the facade of the Princess and shown her the
marquee advertising Douglas Fairbanks, Jr., in *Wild, If You Are Too.*

"I suspect," he'd said as he pointed up, "that's the hotel sign that
was in your mind. That it's what gave y'all the idea Douglas Fairbanks, Jr., was your husband."

She'd shaken her head and laughed uncomfortably. "How incredibly strange," she said. "I feel, I don't know, *ashamed.*"

"There's no reason to, none whatsoever."

"Embarrassed, then."

"Not that either."

"I feel . . ." She searched. "Just so silly and stupid."

"No, n—"

"And frightened."

"Ah," he'd said. "Well, of course that's understandable."

She said she remembered nothing of the eleven days she'd been lost: where she'd been; how she'd traveled; whom she'd met. This bothered Luther more than anything else. He pictured her wandering, confused and defenseless, about the countryside. Imagining someone coming upon her and recognizing her vulnerability, he became enraged.

He'd watched her grow steadily more alert every hour and more fully reacquainted with her life before she'd disappeared. As far as he could tell, she seemed for the most part to feel, not just say, she was Alyce Rae. Still, there'd been momentary lapses. When they'd returned to the hotel from seeing the Princess marquee, she'd said to him at her door, "I'm so grateful to you, Douglas." Seeming not to have heard herself, she'd taken his hand and squeezed it with a strength that had surprised him.

Standing now at his windows, looking up and down South Main, something caught his eye. He was sure he'd glimpsed the draperies parting at her bedroom window. But when he looked more closely, they were closed, as they had been, and while he was looking her suite went dark. He felt a sense of being caught.

He stepped away from the windows and back into his room. He moved about his office, again turning on his lamps. It was past midnight and Luther's mind was racing. This was not unusual. He never assumed sleep and never fought sleeplessness. Over the years, from the time he'd been taken in by his aunt and uncle, any number of things had kept him awake: his energy; his anger; the elements; the sound of animals; loneliness; exhaustion itself.

A long work table stood in a corner of his office and a carpenter's vise was attached to one end. He walked to the table. He selected a small, ripe lemon from several in a bowl and placed it in the vise, closing the jaws to hold it firmly without squeezing it. Next he went to his desk and found in the top drawer several surgical scalpels. He chose one and, back at the table, placed his free hand in his back pocket so it could be of no help. Leaning over the vise, he began to shave the lemon's skin.

In his heart, Luther had found himself allied with the boldness and ambition of Voronoff's enterprise. It seemed, as he weighed the two treatments side by side, that there was in surgery a more appropriate operatic grandness. He also recognized, not insignificantly, that surgery was beginning to flourish in America. There were regional medical centers springing up across the land. There was a place in Minnesota, hard beside the Arctic Circle, called the Mayo Brothers Clinic, where procedures were performed with the speed and efficiency of Henry Ford's assembly lines. Luther perceived this as a new sort of surgery with refinement and dash, not the squared-off amputations, the blunt drawnwork of old. Peoples' internal workings were being inventively rerouted. Crude protrusions were being removed, not only curatively but, Luther sensed, in a newfound spirit of cosmetic aspiration: goiters that swelled a neck like a bullfrog's ready to belch; tumors ballooning from shoulders and sides that caused their bearers to list and fall down.

But practically, Luther had no source of supply, as did the great Voronoff, and he'd not performed an act of surgery since leaving his job as the veterinarian's assistant in Frankfort, Kentucky. So he'd decided for the present to offer a bogus Steinachian injection. He'd placed an advertisement in last week's *Del Rio Times-Herald* that read, "Dr. Luther Mathias, Eclectic Physician. Educated at the National University of Arts and Sciences in St. Louis, Missouri. Now offering the specialty of Rejuvenation!" At the bottom, the advertisement asked, "Are you a Manly man, Full of Vigor?"

Still, he vowed he'd find a way to offer Voronoff's surgery. He'd been devoting much thought to the problems of supply and economics. And he'd devised this exercise of shaving lemons clamped in a carpenter's vise in order to reclaim the surgical deftness he'd once demonstrated on priceless thoroughbreds.

He loosened the vise, turned the lemon, and retightened it. When he'd first begun to practice, several weeks ago, he'd used grapefruits. Within a week or two, they'd become too easy. He'd now progressed to the point where he could strip a lemon bald. He could shave its skin away, making profiles in the process, peels falling to the floor. Working over the vise several nights a week, he etched silhouettes of dogs' heads. He rendered men with beards.

In description, this activity certainly sounds bizarre. But what often distinguishes the successful from the hapless eccentric is how it all turns out. Had Demosthenes continued to stammer all his life, he'd have been locally dismissed as the fool who went down to the sea every day and stood there chewing rocks while the waves smacked his face.

Luther finished a cameo he tried to make look like Aunt June. Displeased with her nose, he threw the lemon away and put another in the vise.

We can only speculate whether Steinach, in Vienna, or Voronoff, outside Paris, actually believed anything they claimed. But regardless, there would be, by the end of the decade, many thousands who believed in *them*. It would be a roster studded with the prominent— industry chieftains; European heads of state; also, to confess, more than a few writers. Yeats would make his pilgrimage to Steinach in Vienna. Acquaintances would claim to know of Maeterlinck's visit to Voronoff.

Luther hadn't been the least interested in whether Steinach and Voronoff believed themselves. He'd given no consideration to the soundness of the biology. Instead, as he'd read, he'd found his mind's eye slowly adding to a vision of a vast pasture filled with people. It was unfenced and its borders were somewhere outside his frame of vision. But the people in the pasture were crammed shoulder to shoulder. They were crowded so tightly that should one of them have fainted he'd have had no room to fall. There were thousands and thousands of people in the pasture and on the face of each was the smile of sorrow and wonder.

I'm so grateful to you, Douglas. She'd smiled, turning to him at her door, and when she'd said it he'd been at the same time wounded and stirred by the nature of the confusion. Her eyes, in the hallway, were a smoky-shaded green.

Cutting idly on the lemon, he began to think about the strangeness of amnesia. He asked himself how it could happen and he wondered if he might ever have had it himself. If you forgot what happened while it had you in its hold, wouldn't it follow that you'd forget having had it? He'd been entirely alone for long periods in his life, so he might have been amnesic for months and never known it. He pledged to sit down soon and account for every month of every year from the day he'd left Ray White in Pampa.

He asked himself what inspired amnesia in the first place, assuming no blow to the head, no accident. He'd found no sign of a cut or a bump when he'd delicately examined Alyce's skull.

What, then, could her amnesia be, if not a form of escape, if not the mind's clandestine flight? What else could it be but someone running from a life she could not yet leave?

He looked down at his lemon and saw that the profile he'd been making was that of a man with a striking Gallic nose and an elegantly chiseled chin. He leaned close and studied the profile for a few seconds more. Then he raised his scalpel and stabbed the lemon through. Its juice geysered up and hit him in the eye.

On the second afternoon of his train trip to Del Rio, Billy Boswell sat, holding a newspaper directly in front of his face, as the Sunset Limited cut across New Mexico. He was not really attending to the paper, so it was nothing Billy read that made him suddenly hear again Leland Wheelock's voice praising his scheme: *And just when your career could use this little nudge.* All at once, Billy felt his stomach tighten and his newspaper slid through his hands to his lap. When Wheelock had first spoken these words, Billy had been much too upset to take them in. But they'd returned unbidden and were sounding in his ears and Billy thought to himself: Use a little nudge? What on earth was Wheelock saying?

Yes, all right, it was true that his last two pictures hadn't done quite as well as expected. But Abe Zietman, the studio chief, had been reassuring at their meeting the night Alyce disappeared. It's just a little pause, Billy, Zietman had said. He'd patted Billy's cheeks. He'd given them love-pinches. Look at the newspapers, Zietman said. Hell, the whole country is catching its breath. Even General Electric and A.T.&T. are taking a rest. If General Electric can stop to catch its breath, surely it's allowed, yes, for Billy Boswell, too?

On the train, Billy got up and began to pace the aisle. He was six steps into it before he remembered he was old. He glanced around to see if any of the passengers had noticed. He looked directly into their faces. Suddenly he was seized with a craving for their recognition. He longed to feel that soft, sweet breeze of adoration caressing his face. He'd had enough of his immersion in a role.

The conductor passed through, announcing, "Lordsburg!" People briefly turned to look out the open windows and glimpse the dribble of adobes.

Billy plopped down into a seat in the open lounge. As the train started forward again, a passenger who'd just boarded walked into the car. He wore a light-colored suit that was filthy with red dust. He declared to the lounge in a booming voice that he had just proven himself the mental equal of a fly that spends its days sniffing horses' bungholes, for he'd been waiting for the train since eight o'clock that morning, standing outdoors by the tracks in this cream-colored suit. He did a slow pirouette so that everyone could see. Huge stains of sweat beneath his arms and down his spine were an almost rusty red. He sat down and belched and began to run a comb through his thick mustache.

It was predictable that when his confidence faltered any incident at all might undo Billy, and the overbearing presence of this dust-covered rube caused him to lose what was left of his perspective. His Alyce came to mind again and Billy thought, Amnesia? Did she mean him to believe that she had simply walked out the door, away from their mansion, in a daze of amnesia? Where had the servants been? Wouldn't they have seen her? Where was the chauffeur? Wouldn't he have asked to drive her? Oh, Alyce! It had all been planned and the servants were complicit. Billy felt tears forming. His hands fluttered up like birds to cup his eyes.

"Damn stuff grinds the shine right off your eyeballs, don't it."

Billy lowered his hands to see that the man in the red-stained suit now sat across from him.

"What?" Billy asked.

"The dust," the man said. "I seen you teary-eyed. All these windows open, it's like they dumped the entire damn desert in here." He shook his head in sympathy, then looked into Billy's face and held his stare.

Billy jumped to his feet, suddenly a codger as nimble as a hare. He raced for the bathroom and opened the door with such force that he surprised the dozing attendant.

"Yessir!" the attendant shouted.

"Leave me alone!" Billy said. "I'm feeling vomitous."

The attendant hurried out and Billy locked the door. He stripped the wig from his head and the beard from his jaws. He bent to the sink and began to scrub his face. He rinsed the soap and scrubbed his face again. When he'd finished a third time, his complexion was bright pink.

He looked into the mirror and saw himself for the first time in two days. He breathed a sigh of relief. Yes, he was Billy. Yes, he was handsome.

He sat down on the toilet and, remembering the words as best he could, repeated the detective's description of how Alyce had been found. After a few minutes he was able once more to see that everything suggested that she *had* been amnesic. His instant sense of shame was typically outsized.

Sitting there, he began to try to picture their reunion in Del Rio. He saw their kiss in close-up, his profile to the camera. But any wider shot of them was distinguished by hitching posts and water troughs and dirt streets pocked with horse dung.

There was a knock on the door and the attendant called cautiously, " 'Scuse me, sir. You 'bout finished up bein' vomitous?"

"Nearly," Billy answered. He looked down at the floor where the wig and beard lay. They looked to be the pelts of tiny silver animals.

It was becoming obvious to Billy that his rescue of Alyce deserved a richer setting than Del Rio could provide. But since that was impossible, there should at least be an atmosphere teeming with occasion. When he thought of himself stepping quietly from the train, it now seemed frankly penurious as a pageant of romance. He was beginning to see that his arrival should be equal in its moment to the pain all this had caused him. And what of Alyce's pain? Who knew what she'd been through? Yes, their reunion should be a well-attended moment in their marital history. Reporters and photographers could make for the two of them a kind of album of the day.

He stood up and left the bathroom, the wig and beard stuffed into the jacket's pockets, and strode boldly through the aisles. He was searching for Wally Jacobson. Again he caught peoples' eyes and now, at last, he heard their murmurs in his wake. As he passed his own seat he saw the portly Christian taking inventory of his case. Billy glimpsed several sizes of medical syringes, snug in their pockets like rows of gleaming weaponry.

When the Christian looked up, Billy flashed a smile. "Hello," he said. He smiled still more brilliantly. He sat down. "You know," he said, "I must apologize. Let me introduce myself. I'm Billy Boswell."

The salesman shook Billy's hand and squinted and said, "Well, so you are. Praise the Lord if this isn't rich." He smiled. "I have to tell you I was curious whether you was gonna keep your act up all the way to Texas."

Billy's smile fell but then he offered that it had obviously been foolish to hope that his disguise could pass so close a scrutiny.

"Oh, the disguise was good enough," the Christian said. "It was the way you been trying to *seem* old that give it away. That business with the cane, for instance, wouldn't've fooled a half-wit."

Billy abruptly stood and excused himself. He hurried off and spent the next few minutes moving among the passengers. He shook hands and signed autographs and made leisurely chitchat. Because they'd only seen him on the silent screen, some of the passengers, though they naturally knew better, were surprised by the fact that when Billy moved his lips an actual voice, and a melodiously rounded tenor voice at that, passed from them.

It was then that Wally Jacobson hustled up to Billy. He glanced at Billy's baggy pants and wrinkled shirt, then asked him if he might consent to an exclusive interview. Billy smiled and shrugged resignedly. He said, "I guess you've got me." He followed Wally Jacobson back to the lounge and they settled into a corner, facing each other. Wally Jacobson scooted forward in his seat, his notebook ready.

Billy was ready, too. For more than an hour, he spoke without pause of the horror of the past two weeks. Of his fearing Alyce's death. Of his vision of meaninglessness without his wife, his Alyce. He watched Jacobson's pencil flying across the page and it felt to Billy as though this ancient act of note-taking, the sacred calling of the Scribes, was giving his suffering the respect and authenticity it hadn't had until now. Billy offered to Jacobson that he'd eaten nothing, not a morsel, for the first four days and that he'd blacked out frequently. He said that without the strength he'd found in the teachings of Coué, he could not have gotten through it.

He searched his brain for more that he might say. The two men moved even closer together. Their postures grew intimate. Their lips were nearly touching. Outside, the dusk flew past their windows in several streaks of brownish gold. Billy described for Jacobson his wrapping, like a boa, one of Alyce's loveliest negligees around his neck in order to feel that he was with her wherever she was. He began to whisper. The softness of his voice was an expiatory sibilance. As he spoke, his understanding grew that every revelation he was giving Wally Jacobson was an act of paying honor to what he and Alyce had been through. He knew he spoke for Alyce. His only frustration was the nagging sense that there were moments of deeply private behavior he was forgetting to reveal.

In El Paso, at nightfall, Jacobson hurried off the train to wire a dispatch to his paper. He asked that a regiment of photographers be waiting in Del Rio.

Meanwhile, Billy fell back, exhausted. His spirit was light. He lay down across the seat.

When Jacobson returned, he found Billy sleeping, his legs tucked fetally. He reminded himself to ask Billy, when he woke, where the hell he'd been hiding on this train the past two days.

It was 10:57 when the train approached Del Rio. Billy had slept the whole night through curled up on the seat, while the Sunset Limited traced a soft southeast meander that mimed the Rio Grande's. Wally Jacobson had given up on Billy's waking before morning and had left him there, breathing soundlessly. He'd been roused by a porter not an hour from Del Rio, as they'd passed through Langtry, Texas, near the Pecos River crossing.

In Del Rio, the heat of the day was prematurely full as perhaps fifty people milled about beneath the depot's beige brick arches. Not surprisingly, Peter O'Malley was among them. He'd played accompaniment to dozens of Billy Boswell's pictures and his eagerness to catch a glimpse of Billy was ardent, though not enough to make him obvious in the crowd; he blended in as usual with his handsome indistinction.

There were several photographers readying their equipment. There was also a cluster of teenaged girls, whispering and giggling behind their hands. But aside from them, and even though this crowd had come to see a moving-picture star, most of those gathered were middle-aged men in suits and wide-brimmed hats. At this time in our country, women were not made to feel that they could drop what they were doing in the middle of the day and stroll up to the depot to pass an hour of idleness. Instead, they stayed home, firing their stoves and stoking their grudges for the sexual uprising two generations hence.

Luther waited, with Alyce Rae and the nurse, Mrs. Hurd, in a new blue Buick he'd borrowed from one of Del Rio's wealthy ranchers. He'd driven the two women the short distance from the hotel to the depot and had parked the Buick alongside the tracks. He sat behind the wheel, sweating freely.

He turned in his seat to speak to Alyce in the back. "It should be here any minute now," he said.

Mrs. Hurd, beside Alyce, was beating the air with a hand-held fan. Her face was dour with her assignment.

Alyce smiled tightly and nodded at Luther. He sensed the great nervousness she was trying to conceal. She was masking more successfully her discomfort from the heat. She was wearing a loose yellow sundress and a white broad-brimmed summer hat, which Mrs. Hurd had bought for her at a shop on South Main. If not exactly stylish by Hollywood standards, the dress and hat emphasized the youthful aspect of her beauty.

Suddenly they heard the approach of the train and, after a few moments, saw it easing in. It came to a stop and gave off groans and vicious hisses.

On the platform, everyone came to attention. The teenaged girls were as interested in seeing Alyce as Billy, and their looks jumped back and forth from the train to the Buick. They saw Luther emerge from the driver's side and open the rear door. When Alyce stepped out, a high-pitched sigh issued from the platform. As she stood in the sunlight, the hem of her loose yellow dress just touched her knees. She lowered the veil of her broad-brimmed hat.

Mrs. Hurd got out and took Alyce's arm. Luther fell in behind them and they started toward the platform. Now everyone's eyes shot quickly from Alyce to the train's closed doors. Climbing the steps, Alyce and Mrs. Hurd kept their gazes straight ahead. As they passed the crowd, Luther heard one of the teenaged girls whisper, "It's like we're at their wedding."

He felt a fist of sickness in his stomach. He fought to calm his tremendous wish to protect Alyce Rae. Waves of jealousy and sadness were moving in his heart. As he stood behind her and traced the flow of her hair to the shaved nape of her neck, Luther experienced that ache of disappointment that we feel upon waking from a dream we'd believed, in sleep, to be our glorious life.

The train's car door slid open, the crowd leaned toward it, and the portly Christian salesman stepped out into sunlight and a dismissive groan of letdown.

Then, a moment later, Billy Boswell appeared, with the reporter, Wally Jacobson, hovering just behind him. There was a gasp of excitement. There were three or four squeals.

Luther watched Billy step from the train. He was smaller and more slender than Luther had expected. Against the glare of the sun, Billy held his hand over his eyes. He searched the small crowd. He appeared dazed by the heat and the brightness of Del Rio.

"Over here, Billy!" the photographers called.

Then Alyce and Mrs. Hurd came forward to greet him, and from just behind them, Luther watched Billy's face break into a beatific smile. He reached for Alyce Rae and lifted her veil, then spoke a kind of moan which could be clearly heard. It had, to Luther's ear, the sound of real distress and he could only assume it was Billy's reaction to the sight of his wife's recuperating wanness. The sound also startled many of those gathered, who, like the passengers on the train, had only seen Billy on the silent screen, where his wildly working mouth uttered soundless sentences.

Billy took Alyce Rae's heart-shaped face in his hands and in doing so turned the two of them so that their profiles were to the cameras. Luther saw Alyce's face break into an awkward smile.

Billy leaned forward to kiss her but was stopped by her voice.

"Hello, Douglas," she said quite formally.

"What?" Billy stammered.

"It's been a very long separation," Alyce said. "You feel almost a stranger to me."

Behind them, Wally Jacobson began to scribble in his notebook.

Mrs. Hurd took a step toward them and placed her hand on Billy's arm. She said, "Oh, I'm sorry, Mr. Boswell. I was worried this might happen. Miss Rae's been so excited to see y'all, but she's still a tiny bit prone to her little lapses. And whenever she has one, she thinks she's married to Douglas Fairbanks, Jr.''

"Hello, Pulitzer!" cried Wally Jacobson, writing furiously.

Luther watched Billy's color leave him, watched his eyes' rapturous light darken toward despair. He knew it was his place to step forward, and he would, once he had control of the smile on his face.

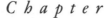
*L*ate at night, on the day Billy Boswell arrived, Luther drove his
Model T out of Del Rio on the wide dirt road toward Villa Acuña. It
was the same Model T he'd owned with Burke and by now its springs
had begun to give out. It sagged badly to one side. It looked like a
high top hat suavely tipped.

Luther was devoted to a young whore named Lydia Mendoza, who
lived in Acuña's *zona roja.* Lydia was short and approaching obesity. The outline of her body was a series of soft parentheses. At the
age of nineteen, she'd begun to lose her teeth. But her black hair was
lovely, falling almost to the backs of her knees, and it shone with a
night sky's integral iridescence. She was also talented in the strict
terms of her work and could seem to bring a spirit of interest to each
occasion. But what held Luther's loyalty was her uncommon cleverness.

Her brush-roofed mud hut was immaculate. She obsessively
poured lye into the outdoor trench where she and her twelve-year-
old sister shat and urinated. With a hand broom, she drew intricate
Aztec patterns around the edges of her hut's dirt floor, creating the
illusion of a richly woven rug. She rewove it where necessary after
each customer.

Unique among the whores of *la zona,* Lydia Mendoza kept a
schedule of appointments. It was expansive and accommodating but
she honored it strictly. No easeful attitude of *mañana* marked her
manner. The first thing she'd bought with her earnings was a watch!
She was a phenomenon: a full-blooded Chicana for whom the minutes moved linearly, whose instinctive sense of time was an Anglo
actuary's.

She'd been a prostitute since the age of fifteen. Her father was a
vaquero of randy temperament, who'd not been seen by her mother

for ten years. Lydia had gone to work one month to the day after a period of mourning her mother's death from typhoid. She'd quickly seen that, having set for herself the life of a *mala mujer,* she might as well use her disgrace to advantage and openly pursue her curiosity and ambition. She understood that, being a woman in her culture, the admission of ambition alone would have cast her as a *mala mujer.*

As he eased the Model T over the wooden ribs of the Rio Grande bridge, Luther had a moment's thought, as he often did when he crossed the river, of how narrow and unimpressive it was. It seemed to him that, given its role, it should be a magisterial body, like the Mississippi. But the Rio Bravo? The Rio Grande? It had all the grandeur of a local creek. Naked Mexican children played unsupervised in its weak current. Its banks were scruffy and unkempt. *Coriza* reeds and ugly thistle grew inhospitably along them.

On the Mexican side, he nodded to the border guard, who recognized him and knew where he was going. The guard nodded back and smiled.

He entered Mexico. The dirt road from the bridge curved slowly to the right and led into Villa Acuña, but just before the squat rows of the central village began, he turned left and followed a rutted path that climbed the hillside.

He was thinking about the mole behind Lydia Mendoza's left knee. He thought it beautiful. He liked very much what she'd done to him last week, which had allowed him to watch it close up for some minutes. He mused about the variety of positions people assume when they dance the dance of love. But beneath his thoughts, he'd not rid himself of an uneasiness he'd been carrying through the day.

The Model T dipped and sputtered up the hill. Mange-spattered dogs ambled out into the path. They snarled without conviction. Here and there, a confused rooster crowed, while the huge black buzzards sleeping everywhere slept on.

His uneasiness had started the moment he and Mrs. Hurd had closed the door of Alyce and Billy Boswell's suite. Billy had insisted a nurse was no longer needed, so Luther had escorted Mrs. Hurd back to her house on Garfield Street. Walking along in high sun, they'd encountered perhaps a half-dozen stragglers from the crowd at the depot. Luther had declined their invitation to say any more about the events on the platform: Alyce's confusion; Billy's answering despair.

Neither did Luther or Mrs. Hurd speak of it to each other. But Luther was so absorbed in his thoughts that he didn't recognize, until he'd heard himself thanking Mrs. Hurd and bidding her good day, that neither of them had said a word while they'd walked.

Walking back to his office, what he'd seen in his mind were Alyce's eyes. On the platform at the depot; in the back seat of the Buick as she'd sat beside her shaken husband; in the suite at the St. Charles after both she and Billy had seemed to calm down and assured each other that everything was clear and everything was fine: Through it all, Luther believed, her eyes had sought his. They'd moved through every shade of green, a chroma of need, all the while asking Luther not to leave her; not to leave. Wasn't that what they had said? Wasn't that what he had seen?

He pulled the Model T to a stop in front of Lydia Mendoza's hut. It sat low on the hillside, the first one of the *zona*. Fifteen or twenty more, some even humbler, fanned out above hers to the top of the hill. The Model T coughed and sighed. Luther set the brake, stepped out, and stood in the still air. Even at this hour, cooking fires smoldered, their rising after-smoke like listless streamers. The *zona* was relatively quiet. Beneath the dogs' barking and the occasional answering chicken, the sound of human voices was a sourceless murmuring. He saw slits of candlelight defining doorways here and there. The absence of a breeze allowed the many smells to mix. Tonight Luther found them not so putrescent as usual. There was as always the stench of the open sewers. But he also caught the aroma of garlic. He smelled flowers, a plural and fecund scent impossible to specify. And as he stepped through Lydia Mendoza's doorway, he recognized the fragrance of her perfume, a subtle scent that in fact she mixed herself.

"*Buenos noches,* Dr. Luther," Lydia said. She sat on her mattress in a circle of candlelight, writing in a tablet. She smiled and set the tablet aside.

Luther stepped carefully toward her, trying not to smudge the Aztec border in the dust. He had to angle his head to keep from scraping it against the brush ceiling. He inhaled, acknowledging the scent of her perfume.

"Rosa's sleeping?" Luther asked quietly. He nodded toward the sheet that hung from a length of hemp and divided the hut into halves.

"*Si,*" Lydia said. "Please do not wake her."

In the mornings, the two sisters sold Lydia's perfume from a stand in the marketplace. Lydia had composed a song that they sang for *turistos* browsing among the stalls. In three verses of erotic juvenalia it described nights of ecstasy if one wore the perfume. Few of the *turistos* understood the words. They tapped their feet and smiled and, charmed, bought many bottles.

Luther sat down next to Lydia. "Is that why Rosa's afraid of me?" he asked. "Because I come late at night and wake her up?"

It was true that Lydia's younger sister was terrified of Luther. She had always been. She had screamed, *"El blanco grande!"* and burst into tears the first time he'd entered the hut. Now, if she was awake when Luther came, she ran outside and hid all night.

Lydia shook her head. "She say to me last week that she is afraid of you because you are her fault."

"I'm her fault?" Luther asked.

"She thinks she is the one who first make you, in a bad dream she have once."

Luther smiled. The idea pleased and displeased him.

"She thinks she make you in a bad dream and now you are a huge *Yanqui* monster who escape from the dream world and she is not able to put you back. She is very worried for making you and letting you escape."

Luther lay back on Lydia's mattress and stretched his arms and legs. He felt comfortable and free in this hut. His head rested just below the swatch of colorful cloth that Lydia hung from the wall behind the mattress. He took a deep whiff of the perfume, which she had squeezed into its fabric. Its scent was nearly enough to cover the smell of the garbage and the open sewers. On those fortunate nights when the breezes blew out toward the desert, it *was* enough.

Luther said, "A *Yanqui* monster."

Lydia said, "But her eyes get so big and her face look so afraid when she tell me this. My *pobrecita.*" She laughed.

Luther looked up at Lydia. Her soft body tremored with her laughter. Her breasts moved beneath her brightly patterned dress. He abruptly sat up and reached toward her mouth. Lydia stopped laughing, a trusting expectancy on her face. He placed his thumbs between her lips and rolled them back—not harshly, but with a veterinarian's pragmatism—to inspect her teeth. "Did some more fall out?" He released her lips.

She shrugged. "And so?" Her attitude was sullen. *"La luna* rises. A woman's teeth falls out."

"Let me buy you new ones," Luther said.

"I have say to you, I do not want them." Lydia's feelings on this matter were defiant. She regarded her missing teeth as motivating features. She believed that ideally she should be offering men a body free of ugliness and that, given her weight, a mouth of new teeth would only minimally improve her appearance. So she used the way her mouth looked to her advantage. To inspire herself to work harder, she often smiled into a mirror.

Lydia said, "If it is your need to help me, then buy me a big mirror. If it is your need to buy someone new teeth, buy new teeth for Rosa."

"Hers aren't falling out."

Lydia shrugged. "She is so far only twelve. But every night *la luna* rises." She nodded her head. From the other side of the sheet, Rosa mumbled in her sleep.

Luther touched Lydia's cheek and turned her face toward his. He said, "Laugh again for me."

Instead, Lydia smiled aggressively. Then she said, "A *turisto* in the marketplace say to me today, 'Your perfume is the way the breeze will smell in Heaven.' "

Luther said, "A poet, that *turisto*. A man who knows his breezes."

Lydia said, "My secret in my perfume is that I use the oil of love."

He leaned forward and felt her nipples through the sheerness of her dress. "I know," he said. "You've told me."

She watched his fingertips trace her breasts in slow circles. She said, "You would want to know what is the oil of love, but I would never tell you."

"No." Luther smiled. "I don't want to know. Everyone should have a secret."

She sat up straight to better offer him her chest. She whispered,

"It is something very common that you already know what it is. But I call it something grand, the oil of love, and that way I make it into some other thing that is my secret."

"That's the best way I know to make a secret," Luther said.

When he approached the bridge to recross into Texas, the bottom of the sky was beginning to lighten. Looking down to the riverbank, he could see in the milky grayness of the dawn two men fishing with long cane poles.

He was unusually tired and he was also ill at ease. He'd been distracted during his hours in Villa Acuña. As always, Lydia had nimbly led the dance of love but he had stepped on his own feet in trying to follow. He'd had ample chance to see the mole behind her left knee but he'd been aware of Rosa sleeping on the other side of the sheet. He'd heard her whenever she'd stirred and he'd imagined that he was haunting her dreams. Each time she'd made a sound, he'd felt falsely accused.

Another border guard stepped forward from under the sign swinging loosely from its pole. The sign demanded ALTO. The guard was uninterested in the pretense of the sentry. He waved Luther past. His grin was simple and slovenly. The Model T swayed and shook as it made its way across, and as he reentered Texas, he moved the accelerator lever to increase speed. He drove past the *coriza* marsh bordering the road.

Now a vision of Alyce Rae came sharply into his mind. He imagined her awakening in a corner of the same room where he lay and walking toward him, opening her silk pale-green robe to show him that she wore nothing else. When she reached his bedside, she sat down on a wooden chair. Then he imagined her lifting her legs and placing her small white feet on its rungs. As she did this, she smiled and the two expressions, her pose and her smile, were versions of each other. She lifted her shoulders to let her robe fall away.

In Lydia's hut, he'd finally risen from the mattress and peered over the dividing sheet at the sleeping Rosa. "You didn't make me," he'd whispered. "You didn't make me."

He imagined Alyce's fingers closing over her cunt and saw them move against each other like babies in a litter snuggling to the teat.

He saw her lift her hand to her lips, and in this way her two mouths kissed. She looked at him and offered him her fingertips as a gesture of inclusion.

The Model T had drifted across the road and now it plunged into a shallow ditch and came to a sudden stop in the marsh. The force of the impact caused it to sway forward and then settle back, an exaggerated tip, like an emphatic *adieu.*

Hidden in the *coriza,* three hoboes looked up at the sound of the Model T. A few years from now this same marsh would be thickly settled with Depression refugees, but for the moment these three were trail-blazing pioneers. One of them, particularly delirious on mescal and benzene, saw the glow of Luther's headlights filtering through the reeds as the divine signal he'd been waiting for and with the wit he had left he plunged his knife into his heart.

We have the idea that traveling by train was once sublime. But in fact, our dependence on trains was an imperfect and often unrewarding one. Trains were noisy. In summer they were hot, making open windows necessary. The air inside the cars became a mix of dirt and coal dust, as we have already seen. Even more to the point, trains were often late, not the models of reliability their mythologists would have us believe. They broke down regularly and, when they did, waited many days for replacement or repair. The population of the time was well aware of this. There were even tall tales told of trains disappearing, laboring away from their point of departure and simply not arriving at the next town down the line. Especially in the American Southwest, such tales persisted. Trains of the Southern Pacific line leaving Marfa, Texas, and never reaching Alpine. Search parties following the tracks out from both towns, trudging across the desert through the mesquite and the sage. Meeting midway and forced to shrug their shoulders.

On the morning following Billy Boswell's arrival in Del Rio, the train to Los Angeles did not appear. Billy had expected to spend the balance of one day and then a night in Del Rio before he and Alyce boarded the 9:15 A.M. At most, he'd imagined the two of them taking a quick stroll through town at dusk while they glimpsed the amusing rusticity of border life. He'd allowed that he would graciously sign some autographs, if the locals were not made too shy as he walked among them. Then he'd pictured Alyce and him hurrying back to the hotel as the ardor that had kept them in their suite all afternoon once more overtook them.

His only concern had been that their room have a veneer of comfort befitting their reunion. He'd assured himself he was being realistic. He certainly had no expectation of luxury. He knew well enough that these border towns drew barbarous populations whose idea of opulence was a room with two spittoons.

He'd envisioned all this as he'd entered Del Rio after waking from his deep dreamless sleep on the train. But then he'd stepped from the car and heard his wife mistake him for Douglas Fairbanks, Jr.

From their hotel window, Billy peeked through a slit in the brocaded drapes and looked down at South Main Street. It was jammed with the curious in front of the St. Charles. All of Del Rio was aware that the Boswells hadn't left. Everyone knew the Southern Pacific schedule and had reasoned correctly that they'd planned to depart on the 9:15 A.M. In no organized way, the idea had grown that the town should see the couple off in festive fashion. Many felt that the small crowd Billy Boswell had discovered when he'd stepped off the train had been, in the end, a failure of Texas hospitality. Many more felt this way once they'd heard the details of the confusion on the platform. So hundreds of people, even wives and single women, had headed early for the depot to say good-bye. They'd stood there in the morning heat until nearly ten o'clock, when the Del Rio agent had walked over to the car where the Boswells waited and leaned in to tell Billy he'd just received a telegraph message that the train had broken down as it was pulling out of the San Antonio station.

Billy let go of the drapes and moved away from the window. He sat down on the couch and took a cigarette from a slim silver case. He lit the cigarette and inhaled deeply. He picked a bit of tobacco from the end of his tongue.

Alyce came into the room from the bedroom beyond. He looked up and offered her his most brilliant smile. He said, "You look dazzling, my darling." He was both sincere and accurate. Her shining yellow hair softly framed her face. She was wearing a white silk negligee he'd thought to pack for her. His first choice had been the black one he'd wrapped around himself like a boa while he mourned her disappearance, but he'd noticed it was tear-stained.

"Is there any word about the train?" she asked.

"Not yet," he said. "I'll let you know immediately." He did not relax his smile. "You should get back into bed and get some more rest."

Alyce said, "You should get some rest, too."

Each time Alyce spoke, Billy held his breath until she'd finished, braced for the horror of her calling him Douglas or still some other name. He smiled again and shook his head. "No, no. I'm perfectly fine."

Alyce said, "All right. But darling, you really mustn't worry."

Billy cocked his head at a pirate's jaunty angle. "Of course I'm not worried!"

He watched her turn and walk back into the bedroom. He was able to keep his lips closed as he moaned, muting it to a quick inhuman squeak.

When she'd closed the bedroom door, he got up and walked again to the window. He moved the drapes aside and peeked out once more. He looked at his watch, which read 10:30. He could see that still more people were gathering. The size of the crowd was what he'd expected when he'd stepped off the train. Looking down to the street, Billy said to himself that he must be, at this moment, his best and highest self. He imagined that he was standing on a rung of Life's Ladder reaching all the way to Heaven. He told himself that he must now take a step up onto the next rung. He said, All right, here I go, and he determined it would be his best self taking it. It would be his most excellent and powerful self.

As he imagined raising his foot to step up to the next rung, he continued to peer down at the crowd and he said to himself, Here comes that big hick phony doctor. He saw Luther walking up the street, looking rumpled and exhausted.

Luther couldn't imagine why the crowd had gathered. But his mood was ugly and he was so tired, after trying in vain to free his Model T from the ditch, that he hadn't the energy to care. He saw that everyone was craning his neck and looking skyward, as though some rare and quirky drama of the heavens were beginning. He reached the wrought-iron stairs to his second-story office.

"Good morning, Doctor Mathias!"

Luther looked up to see the portly Christian salesman from the train on the top step. He raised his portly salesman's case in greeting.

"Oh, hell," Luther said, seeing him. He'd told the salesman yesterday he was too busy to give him any time.

"Praise the Lord!" said the salesman, to counter Luther's profanity and erase it from the air.

Luther began to climb his stairs, favoring his leg as he did when he was tired.

"Ain't this the grand occasion?" said the portly Christian, smiling. He pointed to the crowd and when Luther asked him what was going on, the salesman began to explain it in detail.

In Luther's office, the portly Christian laughed and began the story of Billy's behavior on the train. He demonstrated Billy's unconvincing stiffness and his cane-assisted gait. In spite of his ill humor, Luther found himself listening with pleasure. The portly Christian's description added to Luther's growing impression of Billy as a fool. He'd all but forgotten the intimidating image he'd held of the handsome and unimaginably wealthy Billy he'd seen with Alyce in the photographs.

The portly Christian opened his case and removed his samples of scalpels and syringes. Luther sat forward in his desk chair, and while he made his selections the portly Christian idly scanned the office. As usual, he saw the life-sized drawing of the male anatomy hanging from a wall. He saw the bookcase of bound volumes. But he didn't see, as he always had, the papier-mâché statues.

He asked, "Are you in need of new statuary, Dr. Mathias? I have connections with a company that's making a much improved line."

Luther said, "I'm expecting to phase myself out of that area of my practice."

"You're dropping the men's specialist procedures?"

Luther got up and walked to the window. He raised it, admitting the morning dust and several fat summer flies. The crowd below seemed to have peaked. Here and there within it, clusters had formed. Several card games had begun. A group of women had made a sewing circle. He said, "I've ordered a new sign and I've placed new advertisements in the paper." He walked back to his desk and opened a drawer. He found a copy of last week's *Times-Herald* and turned its front page.

The portly Christian took the paper and saw the advertisement. It was graphically bold and filled a quarter of the page.

"Rejuvenation?" he asked. He sensed something heretical in the air. The word itself was too close in its sound and its allusion to the miracle of Christ's rebirth to sit comfortably with him. He suspected a kind of poaching on one of God's specialties. On the other hand, for all he knew, a rejuvenation doctor might require vast quantities of syringes.

Luther asked, "Have you heard of Dr. Eugene Steinach of Vienna, Austria?"

"No," said the portly Christian, "I don't believe I have."

"Of Dr. Serge Voronoff, living now in Paris, France?"

"I'd have to say no, again."

"They are men of great genius," Luther said. He got up from his chair and came around and sat down beside the portly Christian. He leaned over and looked the Christian in the eyes. He said, "They've discovered things. . . ." He raised his hands and held them wide apart, as though to show the record-breaking length of the things they had discovered.

The office door opened and a patient came inside. He was big and sloppy and dressed in farmer's overalls. He took off his hat. He walked on his tiptoes and stood in a corner. Luther sighed. Suddenly the full weight of exhaustion descended. He suspected he was about to hear some sordid narrative of what tempted a man, alone for weeks with a flock of sheep, when the desert nights grew cold. Seeing the farmer, Luther was reminded that he must give himself a shot of neo-Salvarsan.

When the portly Christian had left, Luther waved the farmer over. He listened inattentively, though his face did not betray him. He caught only bits of the farmer's story: a day-long drunk that had undermined his judgment; the lice-infested hair of a whore in Acuña. Before the farmer had even finished his confession, Luther reached into a drawer and withdrew the plaster penis, for now a needed vestige of the work he wished to leave. The farmer stopped talking, though Luther didn't notice. His mind was across the street in the St. Charles. He was trying to imagine what Alyce and Billy might be saying to each other.

The farmer stared at the penis. Luther absentmindedly turned it, showing its lesions. It seemed to be carrying the presentation by itself.

Luther first saw the two of them in a kind of silent-screen close-up. Then they appeared to him at a wider distance. Billy looked ridiculous. He was scampering around the suite with the speeded-up jerkiness of his movements in a film. But Alyce glided elegantly, as she had in the fantasy that had driven Luther off the road. She wore the same pastel green robe. Her small white feet were bare, as they had been. Her languor seemed to show that her mood was sure and easeful.

In the chair, facing Luther, the farmer was pale.

"Thank you for coming so directly," Billy Boswell said. He smiled and stood aside for Luther to enter the suite.

Luther brushed past him and reached the center of the room in three long strides. He looked around for Alyce Rae. "Is she all right?" he asked. He saw that the bedroom door was closed. "Your note seemed fairly urgent."

"Really?" Billy laughed. "I apologize then. There was no urgency intended." He said more quietly, "Alyce is doing splendidly." He nodded toward the bedroom. "She's catching up on some much-needed sleep."

Luther was confused. Billy's sealed note, which the St. Charles bellboy had delivered to him, had asked him to come to the suite as soon as possible. Luther had been struck by the childlike fashion of the penmanship and assumed the messy scrawl had been a sign of Billy's haste.

Billy said, "May I fix you a drink or is it too early for you?"

Luther looked around once more. His mind was having a hard time letting go of what he'd expected to find. Everything was quiet. Everything seemed calm. Finally, he sat down in a frayed and wobbly armchair.

Billy repeated, "Will you join me, Doctor Mathias?" He opened a suitcase and lifted a flask of whiskey from one of its pockets.

Luther said at last, "I'd drink some whiskey, surely." He looked at Billy and saw him really for the first time since he'd entered the suite. He wore a magnificent white linen suit that gave his complexion an even more impressive swarthiness. He stood before Luther in three-quarter profile. He held the glasses in his hand and poured their drinks with a casual grace. Watching him, Luther was thinking that this was not the same man who'd stepped from the train the day before and been instantly reduced to a simpering child. This was not the inept mimic, as described by the portly Christian, nor the helter-skelter fool of his own fantasy. Altogether, Billy stood flawless in manner and appearance and Luther received this flawlessness as unexpected news.

Billy handed him his drink and sat down on the couch. He proposed a toast. "To Del Rio," Billy said. "A queenly little city of manifold charms."

"Queenly," Luther said. "I must say I've never thought of Del Rio as queenly." The whiskey's bite was deep and refined. "That's a generous sentiment, Mr. Boswell, with all the inconvenience we've caused you. I'm sorry about the train."

Billy waved his hand dismissively. "These things happen. I'm grateful for it, actually, since it's given me the chance to see you again in a . . . in a calmer atmosphere." He said, "I wanted to thank you for the care you've given Alyce. She's spoken of you in the most glowing terms."

Luther sensed his heart move to a new place in his chest. He took a drink of whiskey and said, "She's been a perfect patient."

Billy smiled brightly and took a sip himself. He crossed his legs in a single fluid motion while reaching in his jacket for his cigarette case. "I must admit," Billy said, lighting his cigarette, "that when I first heard something of the nature of your . . . practice, and then saw your advertisement in the local newspaper, I was—"

They both turned toward the sound of the bedroom door. Seeing Alyce framed in the doorway, Luther was taken aback, in part by a sense of himself as a conjurer. For she appeared to him nearly as she had in his erotic hallucination. Her robe was silk, though it was white and not the pastel green in which he'd dressed her, and as she walked toward them he could see that she wore a white silk negligee beneath it. She wore elegant cream-colored slippers with a slightly raised heel.

She took his hand and smiled. She said, "I thought I heard a familiar voice out here." She went to Billy and kissed him tenderly, in the perfect hollow of his sculpted cheek. She said to Billy, "What a splendid idea, darling—inviting Doctor Mathias up."

Billy lit a cigarette for her and she took it from his fingers. Luther had not seen her smoke. He found it fascinating that she did.

She sat down on the couch while Billy walked over to the dressing table to get another glass. She said to Luther, "You know about our train not coming?"

"I was saying how sorry I was."

"Surely," Alyce laughed, "there must be something you can do about it."

Luther's reaction was to think, Yes, there *must.* A few seconds passed while he considered what it was. Billy returned and handed Alyce her whiskey.

Billy and Alyce began to speak of trips they'd taken. Solicitous of Luther, Billy refilled his glass the moment it was empty. Billy's was the chipper inanity of a stranded good sport. He recalled a time when their ocean liner was late in leaving Spain. He told of being on the French Riviera when Alyce had kept their chartered yacht, with nine others aboard, waiting at the dock because the shop in which she'd seen a dress hadn't opened yet. Alyce laughed demurely and scolded Billy for telling tales.

As he listened, Luther sensed Alyce moving far away. Her manner became, more each moment, the same as Billy's. He watched her sip her drink and smoke another cigarette. Though she frequently turned and, with her eyes, included him, she continued to speak only to Billy. She contributed her perspective to Billy's anecdotes. She offered one of her own, wherein the two of them on holiday absolutely drank buckets of ghastly tasting rum and, heathenishly drunk, behaved themselves quite scandalously. Using even more adverbs, she furthered the details. She laughed. She placed her hand on Billy's shoulder and softly kneaded it. Once, she stroked his cheek. There was a comely assuredness in her gestures. She looked, as ever, fresh and youthful.

Finally, she leaned to the ashtray to rub out her cigarette and a lock of her hair fell forward, toward Luther. It felt to him in spite of everything like a private exchange between them and he received it exactly in his cock.

She said, "Now I'm going to leave you two to the brandy and

cigars." She looked at Billy. "I'm feeling as though I could nap a bit more, darling. Can you believe it?"

"Of course I can!" Billy said.

She said to Luther, "I've done nothing but sleep these past two days." Abruptly, she stood and came to him and shook his hand. For just a moment, because she looked directly at him, she seemed to Luther again as she had been. Then she turned and, passing Billy, stopped and kissed his cheek again. She said to him, smiling shyly, "Darling, I didn't mean that to sound like a complaint."

The two men watched in silence as she closed the bedroom door. They looked at each other and nodded. Neither had a sense of what the other's nod meant. The tone of Alyce's departing words to her husband had been affectionate, but Billy appeared to have received them like a slap. He stood, holding his drink, inscrutable inside his gracile beauty. Finally, Luther coughed, just to give the room some noise.

Billy reached for Luther's empty glass and took it over to the table where the silver flask sat. Luther watched him closely, though the back of his white linen suit was what he saw. Billy took a long time pouring the whiskey, and when he turned around again, some of his swarthiness appeared to have returned.

He handed Luther his fresh drink and walked over to the drapes. He drew one to the side. Looking down at the crowd, he gave a sweeping wave. Luther could hear his fellow citizens reply with their applause. From the window, Billy said, "I'm a fortunate man, Dr. Mathias, to have such numbers of patient, loyal fans. And to truly appreciate that good fortune is to be made *better* by it."

"I suppose that's true, Mr. Boswell," Luther said.

"Of course it's true!" Billy said, still looking down. "I appreciate my good fortune more today than I did yesterday and *measurably* more than the day before that. And tomorrow, I'll appreciate it more than I do today!" He turned away from the window and lifted his glass. "Let's drink to being made *better* for truly appreciating one's good fortune."

Luther raised his glass. "Happy to," he said. "I often drink to far humbler sentiments."

"Well, yes, of course," Billy said. He came over and sat down on the couch once again. Luther listened for a sound from the bedroom.

He imagined her lying on the bed. He imagined her turning onto her side, the curve of her hip a lovely white-silk mound.

"We were talking before," Billy said. "And I never finished thanking you."

Luther imagined her, a mischievous child, standing with her ear pressed to the door.

"But I'd started to say that when I first got an inkling of the nature of your practice, I was alarmed, to be frank." He awarded Luther an incandescent smile. He said, "It's clear that my concern was misplaced."

"I'm sorry y'all were alarmed."

Billy took a drink, then said that, with some hours to pass today, he'd read a copy of the Del Rio *Times-Herald* and had come across Luther's advertisement. He said, "Perhaps, Doctor Mathias, you could tell me something more about just what it is you do."

Luther waited a moment to order his thoughts. He said, "Your question comes at a time when I'm giving less attention to my former specialty, which is suggested by the sign y'all may have noticed hanging just below my office window." He moved forward in his chair. "From now on, I'm hoping to devote the bulk of my attention to a new area of restorative medicine. So, in regard to your question, just what it is I do, my sign suggests what it was I've been doing up to now, while the advertisement in the newspaper announces my new specialty, that is to say, what it is I hope to develop from now on." Listening critically to himself, he heard the absurd redundancy of his sentences. He shook his head, disgusted. He sounded to himself like a member of the state legislature. He said, "Let me speak plainly."

"Yes," Billy said.

"A few months ago, I read some interviews—y'all maybe saw them yourself—with two international geniuses of medical research. And this led me to read their books, which describe incredible experiments on the endocrine glands." Luther was assessing as he spoke the effectiveness of his opening. Should he have begun with the science? Should he have started with an exemplary anecdote, then shifted quickly to the data? He said, "I think it's a physician's responsibility to monitor new developments in science. And this is the newest, Mr. Boswell. It is new and it is remark—"

"Doctor Mathias," Billy interrupted, "I love my wife very much. I have friends in Hollywood, actors, other people in the community, who think about love in ways that would shock and offend a good, simple man from the Plains like yourself. And they find my fidelity to Alyce puzzling, given my, well, my status, you could say. They say to me, 'But Billy. You could have any woman in the world.' And I say to them, 'I have *every* woman in the world. I have Alyce Rae.' "

Billy was speaking her name freely, with no particular hush, and this took Luther's thoughts again into the bedroom. He wondered to himself just how loudly *he* should speak. "She's surely very beautiful," Luther said. Raising his voice, he said, "Your wife is a *very* beautiful woman."

Billy turned to look at Luther and Luther saw the fullness of his sudden sadness. "When she disappeared, I was frantic. The idea of life without her was not just tragic. It was unacceptable. So you can imagine my joy when I heard she was safe."

Luther said, "I can imagine that your joy must have been . . ." He searched for the superlative but Billy couldn't wait.

"I'm *still* joyous," Billy insisted. "I'm more joyous today than I was yesterday and I'll be even more joyous tomorrow!" He nearly jumped to his feet and walked again to the windows. He took hold of the drapes and peered through the crack, then turned away and came back to the couch. He said, "Alyce seems to have found nearly all her memory and she says she loves me more than ever. In fact, she says she loves me in whole new ways."

Luther nodded and managed to smile. "Then everything's fine." He heard *whole new ways* echoing in his ears.

Billy said, "You see, this has all been so traumatic. First she was gone from my bed, *our* bed. Then I heard she was alive but had amnesia." The quiet sobbing started, taking Luther by surprise. He averted his eyes from Billy's face and settled on watching Billy's left shoulder lift and fall. "Then," Billy whispered, "I arrived here to greet her and she mistook me . . ." He made a prolonged sound, like the sky-honk of a mallard, which Luther thought Alyce had to have heard.

"And now she loves me more than ever."

"*Yes.*" Luther tried to give his voice a lift of encouragement.

"And she wants to show me that she does."

"I see."

"In whole new ways."

"Uh-*huh*."

"But the train hasn't come to take us home. And we've been stuck in this room." He turned away. Luther glimpsed the glistening in his eyes and on his cheeks. "With her wanting to love me."

"Yes."

"In . . ."

" . . . whole new ways." Luther motioned for Billy to sit back and relax. Billy collapsed into the pillows. Luther had become the host in the room. He saw that Billy was once more the pitiable figure he'd assisted from the train. He'd understood some moments before why he'd been summoned.

With effort, Billy stopped his sobs. "I've just been so . . . thrown off," he said.

Luther watched the torment on Billy's lovely face. When it was clear that Billy had nothing more to say for now, Luther began.

He said that the difficulty Billy was experiencing had become increasingly common and was no cause for shame. He said that he found it a particularly cruel trick of Dame Fortuna. He saw Billy wince, so he softened his voice even more. He'd set his glass on the floor. His hands were on his thighs and his chest was thrust forward. His arms were cocked like a frog's front legs. He said, "I have to believe that it's a symptom of the pace of the times. This is a new world, Mr. Boswell. The goddamn energy and muscle and opportunity out there"—he waved his arm in the direction of the windows—"it's brand new, Mr. Boswell. It is new and it is ours."

Billy said that a motion picture studio owner had recently said much the same thing to him.

"But these same aspects also take their toll."

Billy said the owner had said something like that, too.

"In my office," Luther said, "I have a store of the rejuvenating emulsion Sexalin." He had just last week decided what he'd call his blue-dyed water, his innocuous cure for an imaginative malady. "Sexalin is easily injected in the hip. It's a distillate of male sex glands. Of monkey gonads, to be plain. The gonads of monkeys have proven in experiments to be particularly successful. No doubt because they're so nearly human. They're our next-door neighbors, after all, along the great chain of being. I import my supply from the most modern laboratory in Europe, outside Paris, France. It's true, I'm afraid, that the Europeans began to study this matter some time ago. It's true, they got there first. But if the past belongs to Europe, I say, who, in the end, gives a goat turd for the *past*?"

Luther's concentration had grown narrow and he'd forgotten about Alyce Rae in the bedroom. Pausing for a moment, he thought of her again. He strained for any sound—the creak of bedsprings, her modest cough. He heard nothing. Was she listening? Was she bored? Was she again in deep, sweet sleep, beyond the reach of either of them?

He got up from his chair and sat down next to Billy on the couch. He said, "Mr. Boswell, an injection of Sexalin will solve your temporary dilemma completely." He spoke as warmly as he could, then told himself he should probably not speak too warmly. It was his first experimental pitch and he'd begun to feel the reckless confidence to take the tone of it this way and that. He said, "I could tell y'all much more about the things that have already been accomplished. I could tell of old men made young. I could certainly say, because it's true, that an injection of Sexalin would revitalize your interest. But I realize your *interest* is not the issue here."

Suddenly a look of agitation came into Billy's face. He stood and walked over to pour himself another drink. Luther sat back on the couch. He cursed himself. He wondered what he'd said that had caused him to lose the hold he thought he had.

When Billy came back, he sat in the frayed and wobbly chair. "Doctor Mathias," he asked, "have you ever heard of Émile Coué?"

Luther said that he hadn't and Billy began, somewhat haltingly at first, to explain the idea of picturing the very best version of oneself and then working to raise oneself to that ideal. He quickly warmed to the words. He admitted the metaphor of the ladder climbing heavenward. Finally, he described the witless credo of positive belief and of shoring up that belief with the frequent repetition of the little shyster's jingle.

Then he stopped and when he spoke again his voice was one of rue. He said, "For these past two days I have tried to apply Coué's teachings to all the setbacks you now know about." He shrugged his shoulders. "They haven't worked at all."

Luther felt greatly relieved. "Mr. Boswell," he said, "I mean no insult." He leaned forward, so intent on engaging Billy's look that he seemed to be trying to sight up his nostrils. "But everything you've just been describing to me is—I'm obliged to say it—it is so much hocus pocus." Was that her clearing her throat? Laughing softly in her sleep? "I am speaking, on the other hand, of the latest medical science."

Chapter

10

*I*t struck Luther, as he rode in the back of Billy Boswell's cream-colored limousine, that his life had become a distinctly local one. The lush foliage of the hills above Los Angeles brought this sense sharply to mind. He watched thick hedges, tall as fortress walls and intricate with rose vines, flow past the windows of the limousine. As it rounded the curves, taking Luther higher into the hills, he caught quick glimpses of the orange-tiled roofs it was the hedges' work to hide. He was impressed as he rode by this evidence of double duty—of both verdure and sentinel service—that the owners of these hills had insisted of nature. His fascination with the landscape spoke to him of how long it had been since he'd seen anything other than Del Rio's surrounding desert.

In fact, it had been four years. This was not, in 1927, an especially long time for people to stay put. But compared to his Bedouin days before he'd settled in Del Rio, his present life, in the midst of this new scenery, seemed an aberrant and suspect existence.

He felt the limousine slow and heard Billy Boswell's chauffeur mutter something. Looking over the chauffeur's shoulder, Luther saw through the windshield an animal standing in the road. It looked, as nearly as he could compare it to anything he knew, like a small, sleek camel.

He heard the chauffeur say, "Goddamn it." The limousine slowed to a stop.

"What is it?" Luther asked.

"It's Pola Negri's goddamn llama." The chauffeur was a gaunt young man who'd stood ankle-deep in fetid water in the trenches of France. Having been raised in Seattle, he'd been weary of wetness even before he'd gone to war and he'd emerged from the experience with a deep need for aridity. He'd also acquired the habit of lacing his conversation with the curse *goddamn*. He'd found limitless applications for the phrase, as armed forces linguists of later generations have discovered for the word *fuck*.

"A llama?" Luther asked. He leaned forward to get a better look.

"Pola goddamn Negri's." Billy's chauffeur pointed out the window to his right. Luther looked in that direction. He saw an especially verdant hedge, which hid, he presumed, the estate of Pola Negri.

"She lets it run loose half the time," the chauffeur said. He honked the horn and started forward. As the limousine squeezed past the llama, it spit prodigiously on the windshield.

"Goddamn it!" shouted the chauffeur. He adjusted the visor of his cap. "Sorry," he said into the rearview mirror, "but that's the third time this week he's spit on this goddamn automobile."

Luther began to think about his past, when new landscapes had been a matter of routine. He recalled those days, when the hills of Ohio and the riverbanks of Illinois and the dozen shades of ochre of an Oklahoma mesa replaced each other as his momentary setting with the ease, so it seemed, of one of Ray White's canvas backdrops falling into place.

His yearning nearly reached the pitch of melodrama. But in fairness, it sprang from a uniquely vulnerable state of mind. For six weeks now he'd been working to promote rejuvenation in Del Rio and the results so far had been extremely disappointing. Because men throughout the region had from the first sought him out in steady numbers to cure their fears of social disease, he'd been puzzled by their indifference to the promise of rejuvenation. He'd continued to advertise heavily in the Del Rio *Times-Herald*. He'd hung his new sign and regarded it with pride from the street below. Still the patients hadn't come and he'd begun to wonder if something peculiar to the town was part of the problem. The idea of settling fresh was not necessarily pleasant, for he'd been satisfied with life and its prospects in Del Rio.

The limousine made another sweeping turn and continued its ascent. Luther reached into the breast pocket of his suit coat and withdrew Billy Boswell's telegram. He'd read and fingered it so often over the past two weeks that its paper was worn soft and its edges were feathered. He read again: "Please come at once. Stop. Have

vital questions. Stop. Will arrange travel and assume all costs. Stop.
B. Boswell.''

When he'd received the telegram, Luther naturally thought of the
note Billy had had delivered to him in Del Rio. He'd been reliving that
day, in any case. He'd been remembering Billy's welcoming splendor
as he'd ushered Luther into the suite. He'd remembered how he,
Luther Mathias, had sat on the couch while the country's largest
screen idol broke into sobs, and how he'd felt the control of the
moment shift to him. He'd remembered Billy's willingness, his open
eagerness. He'd remembered his postinjection words of desperate
hope.

And woven like a specter through all of it was Alyce.

He folded the telegram again and absently rubbed its halves
against each other in the manner of an Arab fondling worry beads.

The limousine made a hard turn and Luther's thoughts were broken by a sudden dense shade that fell around him. He saw through
the windshield a corridor of palm trees flanking either side of a
white-graveled drive and meeting overhead to form a leafy roof.

At last the chauffeur pulled the limousine to a stop in front of a
Tudor-style mansion. Luther stepped out. He was tired from the
train trip and his bad leg ached. His height grew as he stretched and
looked about. The limpid California sunlight seemed to bathe the
mansion's every surface, undercutting the impression of wetness
and cold to which Tudor architecture perversely aspires. The chauffeur withdrew a rag from his back pocket and began to rub the dried
llama spit from the windshield.

The grounds rose gently before falling again toward the mansion,
and Billy Boswell suddenly appeared at their crest. He was dressed
for golf, wearing pale-blue knickers and knee-length argyle socks.
His shoes were white. He carried a putter.

He waved at Luther and started down the lawn's long slope. His
step was bounding. As he watched, Luther kept expecting Alyce to
appear any moment on the horizon, following after Billy. He'd repeatedly played a scene of greeting in his mind and he could not
quite see the fact that she was as yet absent.

Billy reached him and offered his hand. "It's marvelous to see you
again," he said. He tapped Luther's shoulder with the head of his

putter, as though knighting him. He said, "I thought we'd head over to my club and play a round of golf."

Luther was taken aback. "I don't have any golf clubs." He glanced down at Billy's knickers. "Or clothes." Most of his attention was still awaiting Alyce.

"I've got plenty of both," Billy said.

"I don't know how to play golf," he said.

"Nonsense," said Billy. "Of course you do." He told the chauffeur to bring Luther's suitcase to the guest cottage. He turned to Luther and his arm swept inclusively in the direction of the mansion, saying, "You should find everything you need." He took Luther's arm and placed it through his, like an usher at a wedding. The linking of arms struck Luther as bizarre. They headed up toward the guest cottage.

"How is your wife?" Luther asked.

"Alyce is my angel," Billy said.

Luther could stand having his arm in Billy's no longer. He slipped it free and slid his hand into his pocket.

"How was your trip?" Billy asked.

"Long," Luther said. "But no delays to speak of. Pola Negri's llama spit on your windshield."

The most self-exalted among us may just believe that, not only their concerns and desires, but also their size and proportions are everyone's ideal. Yes, this begs the boundaries of egomania, but how else can we explain Billy's assumption that Luther Mathias, five inches taller and with a much larger frame, would find a way to squeeze into his golfing clothes?

Billy said, "It was short-sighted of me." They were standing, Luther still dressed in his suit, at the edge of the fairway of the first hole at Billy's country club. Billy was apologizing for the third time for the fact that Luther had been unable to wear anything he'd brought along for him. He seemed to have been genuinely surprised. "I wanted to speak to you in complete privacy and out here on the course seemed the perfect place."

A teenaged caddy, wearing a gray cloth cap that spilled on one side to his ear, stood thirty yards away, as Billy had ordered him to do. He was smoking a cigarette and looking sullen for his banishment.

Luther said, "Again, it really doesn't matter." He was telling the truth. He'd never swung a club and had no interest in the game. He'd watched O'Malley and others flail away and curse and sweat while they trudged over the course that the town of Del Rio had tried to render out of desert.

In the locker room, Billy had introduced Luther as his cousin to all the rich and famous members who stopped to say hello. He'd said, "Cousin Luther owns a little property in Texas on the Mexican border." Each time he'd said this, he winked broadly, and everyone concluded that Cousin Luther was a cattle baron whose property was one of those legendary ranches larger than an eastern seaboard state. This also allowed the rich and famous members to accept Luther's unseasonable dark wool suit as an amusing example of frontier parsimony.

Some of those Luther met were motion picture stars of Billy's magnitude. He was introduced to Taunton Malloch, then riding the great success of *Hooligan House.* He met the notorious lecher Crosley Duke, who, two weeks later to the day, would die from his week-long participation in the Hubba Hubba Club affair, that event of epic debauchery by which Hollywood licentiousness has been measured ever since. Luther also met members who were wealthy in ways having nothing directly to do with motion pictures. Among them was Haskell Albright, whom Luther liked instinctively. Albright, the owner of, among other things, the *Los Angeles Times,* won from Billy the promise to meet later on the veranda.

On the course, Billy stood over his ball and commenced a series of tics and flexes that he performed before each shot. At last he swung and the ball flew toward a rough. The caddy reached them and handed Billy his wooden-shafted niblick, then gave them both a baleful glance and headed off.

Billy looked at Luther. His expression had turned serious and lively, the look of one who's bursting to share a piece of gossip. "I've been reading the books," Billy said.

"The books?" Luther asked.

"The ones you told me about in Del Rio." They were walking at a stroll, postponing their arrival at the rough, where the caddy stood. "Voronoff's *The Conquest of Life.*"

"Ah, yes," said Luther.

"And Steinach's," Billy said.

"Sex and Life?" Luther asked.

"Yes," Billy said. "Also some of the books by various associates. Paul Kammerer's book? And Harry Benjamin's?"

"Kammerer and Benjamin. Good for you, Mr. Boswell." Luther felt Billy waiting for his thoughts on Kammerer and Benjamin. He'd not read either book. As they walked along, he emitted a series of noncommital hums, varying his inflection to make it seem he was reviewing the authors in his mind before responding.

When they'd reached the rough, Billy glanced down at his ball and almost immediately swung. He barely paused to watch the results, but dropped his club for the caddy and hurried over to stand close to Luther. He whispered, "Voronoff's point, that all human progress is the triumph of man over nature, bothered me so much at first I couldn't sleep! But he persuaded me in the end when his *own* humanity became clear." He smiled and motioned for Luther to come along.

In this way, they proceeded from hole to hole. The execution of each shot was an instant's distraction for Billy before he resumed his discourse on the literature. Stripped of the anguish and the ceremony he normally brought to his game, he was shooting the best round of golf in his life, but this was taking place entirely outside his notice.

His words issued rapidly. He spoke of the thrill it gave him to imagine Steinach peering into his microscope and observing the seminal fluid's two-cell composition: the cells of external secretion, where those busy guppies, the spermatozoa, swam; and, embedded within, the interstitial cells, which secreted their hormones directly into the blood. He began to quote passages nearly verbatim, raising his index finger and moving it in the air to mark their meter. Again, his enthusiasm. His dear vapidity. (Which was, when all was said, the quality in Billy that lit up the silver screen. Forget the jutting chin. Forget the chiseled profile. It was his exquisite ignorance that enthralled the movie camera, which couldn't get enough of a face so void of cynicism.)

Luther's mood fell to a self-pitying pout. He'd taken off his coat and given it to the caddy. He'd loosened his tie and rolled up his sleeves. But he was still very hot, his throat was parched, and he was following Billy Boswell around a damn golf course when he'd imagined sipping gin with Alyce Rae by the pool. He thought about Billy's telegram and its promise of vital questions. He now suspected that Billy *had* no vital questions and had only asked him to Los Angeles to serve as his audience.

They reached Billy's ball and again he swung immediately, but at last his inattention served him badly. The ball rose and veered, making almost a boomerang's turn toward the practice greens spread out around the clubhouse.

Billy stepped urgently to Luther. "For me, it was Steinach's man, Kammerer, who put all the moral questions to rest best of all." He looked hopefully up into Luther's face and waited.

"Yes," Luther finally said. "When all's said and done, it just might be Kammerer."

Billy's smile was that of a boy receiving praise. He said, "Of course, Voronoff's answer is the more philosophically profound, but when I read Kammerer saying, if rejuvenation is unnatural, as the clerics charge, then we should stop all efforts to prevent the body's decline, we should all stop using toothpaste to prevent tooth decay—I thought, *Voila!* "

"The homely image says it best," Luther said.

"Absolutely!" Billy said.

We know that Luther had read Steinach and Voronoff with great attentiveness. But for him, their thrum and metaphor was grandly economic. Within their laboratory drama was the beguiling innuendo of supply and demand, shipping and storage. He read the statistical results and studied the photographs and his mind was captured by the slippery metaphysics of maximum profit: the planned obsolescence of Steinach's injections versus the implied permanence of Voronoff's surgery. Small but frequent fees against a large lump sum.

They moved along in the direction of the clubhouse, where Billy's ball had finally come to rest on the fringe of the largest practice green. Billy was reciting some experimental statistics from Voronoff. "After they injected that French bull, Jacky, he screwed the cow

Grisette four times on the nineteenth of January and three more times on February ninth!" Luther was ignoring him as best he could by concentrating on the splendor of the course itself. He found its man-crafted beauty aesthetically impressive. Pruned palm trees hemmed the fairways and made great perfect circles of fringed shade. The grass was a brilliant and unvarying emerald. The greens were as flawless, in a uniform pastel.

As they approached the clubhouse veranda, the call of Billy's name began to fill the air.

"Hey, Billy! Looking good, kid. Looking sharp."

"Where you headed, Billy B.?"

Members sat beneath umbrellas at white wicker tables. Their attire ran from the resplendent to the garish. Many were with their somehow less flamboyant-looking wives or girlfriends.

"Billy!" a man shouted from the veranda.

"Billy!" shouted the man's wife. "Billy, we saw you in *Big, Bold Broadway!* last night. You were spectacular, sweetie!"

Luther was distracted by the redound of Billy's name. It might have been heard as a trilling exchange, the cries, perhaps, of articulate macaws.

"Billy!" another man shouted. "Hey, Billy! Come on over!" This voice particularly boomed through the air, causing Billy to look up and see Haskell Albright, the owner of the *Los Angeles Times,* who was standing up and waving his arms in wide crossing arcs.

"Oh, lord," Billy said to Luther. "We might as well get it over with or he'll follow us all over the course. It's shameless the way Albright sniffs up to movie people."

Nothing we know about Haskell Albright suggests that this is true. He was arguably the most influential man in Los Angeles. He owned hundreds and hundreds of blocks of the city and vast reaches of the encompassing desert and in at least one entry in the journals that survive him he refers to actors as "dickless little shits." But Billy was ready to believe that anyone who was prominent in town, while having no connection with the motion picture industry, spent all his time scheming ways to insinuate himself into the lives of the stars.

Albright's greeting was a gust of high spirits. He slapped both Billy and Luther on the back and gave Billy's buttocks the crude squeeze of the locker room. He ordered iced teas for the three of them. He was a handsome man with silver hair whose outline made impressive wings at his temples. He was nearly as tall and broad-chested as Luther, leaving Billy, seated between them, looking delicate as a doe.

As soon as their drinks arrived, Albright sat back in his wicker chair and stared out at the eighteenth green and it was clear that his spirits had all at once altered. He was palpably preoccupied and seemed to believe he was alone. He openly farted and appeared not to notice that he had.

Billy looked at Luther and rolled his eyes.

Luther took a long, grateful drink, nearly emptying his glass.

Albright mumbled his disgust at something he was watching, either on the course or in the privacy of his brain.

Moments passed. Billy raised his glass and took a showy swallow. Then he said, "Haskell, we'll do this again. I want to finish my round and then we have to run."

Albright turned to Billy, looking confused. He blinked. "Oh, hell, forgive me. My mind strayed for a second and I'm being goddamn rude." He said to Luther, "This isn't the Texas etiquette you're used to, is it, Cowboy?" He reached over and punched Luther's shoulder.

Luther smiled. His response to Albright in the locker room had been warm and now he found that he was liking him even more. His crassness was refreshing. Luther drained his glass and said, "The hospitality I needed was a glass of this iced tea."

Albright called loudly for another glass and once again apologized.

Billy said, "Not at all, Haskell, but I really do want to finish at least nine."

"How's Alyce feeling, Billy?"

"Splendidly!" Billy nearly shouted.

"Give her my love. I'm sorry she isn't here." He turned to Luther and winked. "Don't take offense, Cousin Cowboy. It's just that Alyce is about a thousand times prettier than you."

"No offense taken," Luther said, smiling. "Hell, Mr. Albright, I think she might even be prettier than you."

"Hah!" Albright said. "That was pretty good! I liked that."

"She's in Detroit," Billy said.

"She's *where*?" Luther asked, his head snapping toward Billy.

"That was pretty funny, Cowboy. You're all right."

"What's she doing in *Detroit*?" Luther asked.

"Visiting her parents," Billy smiled. "They're having a sort of early Thanksgiving."

"Maybe I should send *my* wife to Detroit," Albright said.

"When will she be back?" Luther asked. He was trying to make his interest sound casual.

"Or Pittsburgh," Albright said. "Some place where the air's filthy and turns your skin black as a nigger's."

Billy's telling him that Alyce was away felt to Luther like a withdrawn promise.

"Or Alaska," Albright said. "Let her suck the dick of some reeking Eskimo."

"She'll be back in a week," Billy said. "I miss her terribly."

Albright said, "I stopped by my house today, on my way out here, and found my wife doing the old wham bam with my nephew on the hallway stairs. He's been living in our pool house and going to UCLA."

"Haskell!" Billy cried. "No wonder you're distracted."

"Right there on the stairs. Going at it like dogs."

"Oh, my God!" Billy covered his face with his hands.

"I've never seen such action," Albright said. In the tone of his voice was an airy amazement. "They were pumping each other like a couple of wind-up toys."

"Haskell, stop!" Billy said. "I can't believe what I'm hearing."

Luther thought, What the hell is going on? Still he felt he was obliged to say something condolent. "I'm sorry, Mr. Albright. That must be quite a shock, coming on a sight like that."

Albright said, "That's why I mention it. That's what I find incredible. Because the truth of it is, I do not give a shit. I've been sitting here playing it over and over in my mind, trying to get myself pissed off. Obviously, I *should* be. But here I am, relaxing in the sun on the veranda of my club, and I'm forced to admit that I do not give a shit."

"You're just in a state of shock," Billy offered weakly, "like Doctor Math—like Cousin Luther just said. Coué teaches that we literally flee our bodies when—"

"Figuratively," Albright said.

"What?" Billy asked.

"You said literally when you meant figuratively. Say what you mean, Billy. Say what you mean. What does the future hold for America if people go around saying literally when they goddamn mean figuratively?"

Billy was fidgeting in his chair. "Coué says that we flee our bodies, if you will, when we're in distress because that's where our pain resides. And this mental flight leaves our bodies unprotected . . . as though there's no one left at home to tell the pain that it simply has to go now. Coué—"

"Jesus, Billy, shut up," Albright growled. "You told me last week you were finally through with that Coué crap, the way every other gullible asshole in America was about three years ago. My body is right here and I am sitting entirely the hell inside of it." He turned to Luther and said to him, "He's a sweet man, your cousin Billy. He has three outstanding attributes: He is sweet and he is handsome and he is handsome some more."

Albright winked at Luther and punched him in the shoulder again. He shifted in his wicker chair and looked out at the fairway. "No," he said, "I wish it was that simple. I wish I *was* in shock. Normally, I would be pleased to charge people admission while they watched me roast the gonads of anybody I caught even whispering about this. I hate the way goddamn gossip spreads in this town. I goddamn hate it, as you know, Billy. But here I am, casually telling you both about it and what I'm seeing is, the reason I don't give a shit if my wife is doing the humpty-dumpty with my nephew on the stairs is because all I care about are my money and my businesses. And, especially right now, whether the goddamn federal government is going to leave me alone and keep its hands off my radio station." He turned to Luther. "I own a radio station," he explained. "The first one in Los Angeles." His voice was more calm, but edging toward the stentorian.

He shook his head. "This seems to me a sad commentary on the turn life has taken in America. Here I sit, actually concentrating, actually *trying* to remember what it looked like, my nephew's white behind bobbing up and down—"

Billy made one of his high, peeping sounds.

"—his cheeks sucked in like his ass just ate a lemon, and I can't even hold the picture in my mind for more than a few seconds, because as soon as I feel myself starting to get pissed off, I start remembering what it is I'm *really* pissed off about, which is the letter I got a week ago informing me that those brainless bastards on the Federal Radio Commission are going to decide next year how powerful a station can be, and where it can broadcast its signal. Once they start doing this, you can bet—this is coming, Billy, count on it—the next thing they'll tell me is what kind of advertisements I can play on the air." He struck the table with his fist. Several people nearby turned to look. "It's the same thing as the Will Hays Office telling you how much of Clara Bow's tits you can see in a movie, Billy, as if anybody wanted to see Clara Bow's tits except Clara Bow."

As he listened, Luther couldn't help but assess the quality of Albright's monologue. He was thinking, He's damn good. He builds the volume real well and his timing is first rate.

"Believe me," Albright said, "I wish it was different. There's nothing that would give me more pleasure than the thought that I might wake up tomorrow morning a frothing maniac, counting the seconds until I could strangle my wife and cut my nephew's nuts off. Isn't that what should happen? Isn't that the way it used to be? I mean, it's disgusting what I saw. Hell, it's almost *incest!*

"But frankly, I know it's not going to happen." His voice seemed to Luther that of someone offering up a parable.

Albright suddenly stood up and looked down at Luther. He said, "Come here with me a minute."

Luther glanced at Billy. Billy's eyes were disks offering no parables whatsoever, nothing more subtle than a glaze of mindless panic. Albright had left the veranda and was walking along the edge of the fairway. He stopped and looked back and motioned for Luther to join him. Luther hesitantly rose and left the table.

When he reached him, Albright put his arm around Luther's shoulder. He said, "You're awfully young to be so damn rich, Cowboy. Invite me down to see your ranch sometime." Then he pointed at the sky. "See that?" he asked.

"See what?" Luther asked.

"That tower," Albright said, "above the tree line. Over there."

"Yes, I see," Luther said, and so he did. It was a magnificent tower of crosshatched-patterned steel. It rose above the palms and stood alone in the eastern sky.

"That's mine," Albright said. "That's my station, KHJ. As I said, it's the first radio station in Los Angeles and I'm a legitimate god-damn pioneer just as much as Daniel Boone could ever claim to be. Now I ask you, did the government pay to build that tower and think to broadcast beautiful symphonic music? And did it occur to the government that the silence between songs is exactly the same thing as empty space on a newspaper page? And that businesses would pay to fill up that silence with advertisements for their products, just like they pay for advertising space in a newspaper?"

Albright removed his arm from Luther's shoulder. His broad chest appeared to have swelled beneath his golfing sweater. He turned to look at Luther. "Do you see why I'm so upset, Cowboy?"

"I do," Luther said, "and I don't blame you. Now that I under-stand, I surely do." The pleasure he was taking in Albright's outrage was considerable.

Albright returned his gaze to the sky above the palm trees. He said, "At Christmas, I decorate that tower. I have huge colored lights winding around it all the way to the top. It's a beautiful sight and the people just love it. You can see it for hundreds of miles. It looks like God's own Christmas tree."

Someone shouted, "Fore!" and Albright turned to look. A ball was flying toward him on a low line just above the ground. He waited till the last instant, then casually hopped over the ball as it screamed past, the perfectly timed reflex of a schoolgirl skipping rope with her expert lackadaisy.

Luther heard Billy's soft knock on the guest cottage door. He was sitting in a chair looking out some casement windows at huge protozoically shaped beds of roses. He felt refreshed after a long bath and a change of clothes to slacks and an open-collared shirt. He stood and walked to the door.

"Were you able to nap?" Billy asked. He'd also changed and now wore a silk shirt and trousers in not quite identical shades of cream.

"I didn't try," Luther said. He stepped outside and closed the door behind him.

They set off across the lawns. Luther noted that the buoyancy had returned to Billy's stride. During the drive home from the country club, Billy had maintained a silence as thorough as a climate and the fear on his face had been unguarded. When they'd reached his estate he'd been able to suggest that they meet again in two hours, after Luther had had a chance to nap. He said he'd have the kitchen send out some sandwiches.

Luther had devoured the sandwiches. Then he'd drawn his bath and lain back in the cottage's short tub as best he could and considered all that had happened so far. His mind was full, to say the least. He'd thought of Pola Negri's llama. He'd thought of Billy on the golf course with his frantic rush of talk. He'd thought with admiration of the glum cuckold, Haskell Albright, and heard again his lordly baritone of complaint. He'd wondered why Billy had taken them to his club in search of privacy when they could have spoken right here in the guest cottage. Was he afraid that the gardener or the chauffeur or the butler might eavesdrop? If so, eavesdrop on what? It would be convenient to describe Luther lying in his bath and receiving an epiphany in which these events ordered themselves to reveal the terms of his future. But such tidy discoveries occur only to the heroes of simplistic fables. In life, our understanding presents itself in increments.

So his response to the day, as he soaked in the tub, had been not so much reflection as pure sensation, an encompassing hum, and strong within it was the absence of Alyce. He'd tried to picture her in Detroit and he could not. She existed, in his mind, in three locations. Here, where she led the life he'd seen in magazines; in Del Rio, where he'd tended to her; and in the erotic chambers of his imagination, where she was ever suppliant and perpetually nude. She did not exist in Detroit.

When he'd finished his bath, he put on a terry-cloth robe that came to the middle of his thighs. He'd walked across the bedroom and fetched Billy's telegram from his suit jacket and read it yet again.

Now Luther walked with Billy beneath an overhead door into the darkness of a vast garage that had originally been the estate's stables. He followed him through another door and back outside to a cozy flagstone terrace. He saw wings of the garage extending on two sides, framing the terrace in the shape of a block U and directing your eye to the back of Billy's mansion.

Luther's gaze, therefore, followed this suggestion and it was then that he saw the large gray baboon. It was crouched in its cage, which sat on a flat-bed near the open end of the terrace.

"It arrived last week," Billy said, "from Ethiopia." He walked to the cage. Luther followed. The two of them stood, looking up at the baboon. Then, Billy leading, they began to circle the cage. He said, "The Ethiopians once considered them sacred and you can certainly see why. Isn't he magnificent? With that elegant cape of hair? He looks like he's dressed for an evening at the theater."

He was referring to the hair on the baboon's head and shoulders, which did fall down his back like a long gray cloak. But otherwise, it would require Billy's inimitable sensibility to see in this baboon the cut of the *bon vivant* settling into his orchestra seat. As Luther circled it, he noticed, for instance, its puffed-out cheeks, which were filled with chunks of canteloupe. He was reminded of Del Rioans he saw every day whose cheeks were swollen with chewing tobacco. Luther noticed, as well, the baboon's long muzzle, which suggested to him a Collie's needle snout. And then there was the matter of the way the baboon smelled.

Luther said, "He's quite a specimen. He's a baboon, all right." That part of him that had always warmed to animals was genuinely admiring. The baboon seemed somehow both familiar and exotic. He added, "I pictured a baboon bigger."

"He weighs eighty-five pounds," Billy said. "That's about as large as a male gets. You're probably thinking of a gorilla."

"I probably am," Luther said.

Billy said, "Selenka concluded—but then you've read Selenka."

"Not for a while," Luther said.

"Well, you remember he concluded that the higher apes and man have a common origin and come from beings that are now extinct." Billy stopped and looked up at the baboon. As on the golf course, he raised his index finger as though for the direction of the wind.

Seeing this, Luther thought, Oh, shit, he's going to quote me some Selenka.

"Quoting Voronoff on Selenka," Billy said, "it makes sense that an ancestor of the anthropoid ape procreated an offspring of genius which became a human being, while its inadequately endowed brethren remained monkeys."

They had finished their circling of the cage and were standing again at its front. The baboon began to pace back and forth in a galumphing fashion so typical as to smack of rank self-parody. It chattered in a high staccato.

Billy said, "This is the same species, a *hamadryas* baboon, that Voronoff used for his first implant in a human being. He chose them in particular because they're polygamous and prolific and they live in droves. The natives are terrified of them. They march in hundreds, destroying everything in their path. What a sight that must be! Can you imagine hundreds just like him, bearing down on you?"

Billy's fervor was high and his plot was thickening and Luther found himself inevitably intrigued. It was one thing to read and speak of Voronoff's apes; it was another to speak of one in its presence. "Well, it's quite a thing to own," Luther said. "I can see why you're excited." Then he said, glancing up toward the back of the mansion, "What's Miss Rae think of it?"

Billy was quiet for a long moment. So was the baboon. Finally, Billy said, "She hasn't seen it. It arrived after she'd left."

He sighed again and looked up into the sky. He said, "After Alyce's amnesia ended in Del Rio, she and I were so eager to enjoy our reunion. That's why I turned to you that day. That's why I was so frustrated."

Luther felt the return of a painful uneasiness. He cursed himself for bringing up Alyce's name. He said, "Like I told y'all at the time, any man would've been. It was an entirely natural reaction, like I said."

Billy lowered his eyes and looked at Luther. "I guess you could say that both of us, first her, then me, we were both in the grip of an amnesia, in a way."

"You certainly could say that. I would call that the perfect way to put it."

"So, with all that eagerness we'd stored up, those first nights on the train coming home were just incredible."

Conflicting sensations were in Luther's mind and heart. His sense of jealousy wanted nothing of this, but an eagerness, a voyeurism, wanted it all. He said, "I take it, then, that my Sexalin was helpful."

"Oh," Billy said, "oh, yes! I assumed I'd made that clear. Oh, indeed it was. Once, just afterwards, when we lay side by side, we were perspiring fiercely, I think it was the second night, somewhere in Arizona, and Alyce whispered to me, 'If God made love, that was how He'd do it.' "

Luther looked above the roof of the cage at a second-story window of the gloomy Tudor mansion. He declared it in his mind to be the master bedroom window. He imagined Alyce Rae standing at it now, looking down on them from behind a parted curtain.

Billy sighed. "And I said in response, 'But God would not be sweating.' And then Alyce said, 'He would be if He were making love to me.' "

The baboon released a piercing whinny through its nose.

Billy turned to Luther. His smile was seraphic. "I'm sorry," he said. "That was indiscreet of me."

Luther said nothing. He continued to look up at the window.

Billy said, "When we got home, Alyce lived each day at an almost ecstatic pitch. It was as though she was rediscovering certain things but also experiencing them for the first time. She virtually swooned at all the seeming newness around her, even while it was perfectly familiar. Certain views. Certain people, friends. And especially . . . us." He shot a glance at Luther.

Luther heard Billy's choice of the historical tense. He was thinking, too, of Billy that day in the suite of the St. Charles. Now, as then, he seemed particularly alive with his intimate confession. But unlike then, and though the scenes he was recalling were of ecstasy and eros, his voice was sliding into one of hard resolve.

"It was such bliss," Billy said grimly. "So naturally I sent for the books. I wanted to learn everything about their work. I wanted us to stay exactly that way, a couple of just-recovered amnesiacs forever!"

Luther imagined seeing some shadowed movement pass behind the window.

"It's returned," Billy said.

"She has? Where?" Luther looked to Billy for direction. He looked left and right and back toward the house.

"*It's* returned," Billy said. "My *amnesia,* as we decided a moment ago we might call it? It returned from out of nowhere. We were just finishing dinner one evening, perhaps three weeks ago. The candles were casting Alyce's face in a miraculously beautiful light. Soft and amber. Like the light on a Renaissance madonna, but allowing her at the same time to appear brimming with a spirit of the most *modern* playfulness. I was swept away, as I often am, as I have always been. I went to her and took her in my arms. . . ." He sighed and shook his head.

"I realized, in the house an hour ago, that seeing Haskell today was meant to happen. I can confess to you now that he upset me terribly, though I'm glad I was able to hide it at the time. But now I see that his story, it was providence. It was a gift."

The baboon had been chattering distractedly all the while but now he made a higher, more complicated noise, like overlapping talk among a group of melon eaters.

Billy waited on it. Then he said, "As much as I know how deeply Alyce loves me, there was a lesson in Haskell's story which convinced me even more that I can't rely on her love to see us through times like this. It's not fair. To *her,* I mean. I'm a young man, and this has already visited me twice. What might happen when I'm forty? Fifty?" Billy shivered perceptibly but his mouth remained sternly set.

He said, "Steinach's injection? Its result was lovely, I don't mean it wasn't." He turned to face Luther squarely. "But I'm not interested in those intense peaks and sudden valleys. I want the permanent summit."

"The surgery," Luther said. He sensed that if there was ever a moment to maintain a professional solemnity, he was living one. Still, as he spoke the word *surgery* he could not keep himself from turning to the baboon and trying to catch a glimpse. But the baboon was sitting in profile, his hairy hands folded demurely to affect a kind of codpiece.

"I have no choice," said Billy. "I'm obviously vulnerable to this malady. Thinking about it these past several days, I've journeyed to the heart of my truest self to ask, Why? And I've come to understand that it's the price I pay for the highly strung temperament my art requires."

He moved a few steps closer to the cage and gave the baboon a long inspection. Then he walked back and turned once more to Luther. His chin was high. His voice was, too. He asked, "Can you do it?"

"Do it?" Luther asked.

"The surgery. Have you performed the implantations? If you have, I want you to do mine. I don't want to go to France. That's why I brought the baboon over *here*. I've realized, thinking about how you and I came to meet, that it's as though Alyce led me to you, as though she found you for me. I've realized that there's a powerful force of predetermination at work between us. I'd be an utter fool if I ignored it."

Luther lifted his eyes to avoid Billy's look. It seemed to him that the curtains at the window had moved. Hadn't they been parted? Hadn't they just closed? He was certain they'd changed, but as it happened he was wrong.

*L*uther regularly attended, as did most of Del Rio, the films at the Princess Theater on South Main. Seeing the actors on the screen, their grand gesticulations and their histrionic faces, reminded him of his own performances in Ray White's medicine show. His clutching of his young chest as a bullet pierced his heart. His rolling of the eyes in wild rotations of pain or mourning or unutterable joy. He usually arrived early to hear one of Peter O'Malley's thunderous medleys. Indeed, O'Malley's playing possessed a spirit that was entirely lacking in his personality and listening to him, Luther had come to love organ music.

There were many in Del Rio who went to the Princess more than once during a picture's run. These were unprecedentedly popular years for motion pictures in America and such was not uncommon habit in the country at the time, though it had always seemed nonsensical to Luther. Yet without hesitation, he went three nights running to watch Crosley Duke in *The Furies of Love*.

Crosley Duke was a second-rate actor of the silent era, his presence on the screen that of an overweening ass, regardless of the part. But people throughout the country were standing eagerly in line to see him star in *The Furies of Love*. In Del Rio, Irene Pugh had never sold so many tickets for a picture at the Princess and she never would again. Not for one of Charlie Chaplin's, not for Billy Boswell's. Certainly not, until last week, for Crosley Duke's. But until last week, Crosley Duke had been alive.

News of his death in the Hubba Hubba Club affair had spread across the land. Alive, he'd been merely well known, but as a dead orgiast his infamy was grand. Wherever people gathered there was heated speculation. Just what had gone on? And on? For a week? How had Crosley Duke actually died? Which overdose had killed him? Liquor? Sex? Was a week of sex potentially lethal? Was it possible?

The Furies of Love had finished its run in the country's major cities when the news of Duke's death broke and the studio had immediately rushed it back into the theaters. But in the smaller towns, the timing of the picture's distribution was ideal. The Princess, for example, got its print the day Duke died.

Luther had returned from Los Angeles exactly three weeks before and he was reminded of the date as he sat in the darkness at the back of the Princess. On the screen, Crosley Duke, playing a debonair dilettante of independent means, sat in an opera box with his future brother-in-law on the eve of his wedding. Both men wore tuxedos. Their black hair was slick with brilliantine. They were listening to the debonaire dilettante's fiancée, his companion's sister, singing from the stage. She was beginning an aria from an opera called *The Furies of Love*. It had been written by the debonaire dilettante played by Crosley Duke. It was the dilettante's first opera and it was improbably brilliant. But, as the audience in the Princess had earlier learned, the dilettante had not written the opera at all. In an effort to win the heart of the beautiful diva, whom he honestly adored but who'd regarded him as a vacuous playboy, he had purchased the score from its impoverished composer. The composer vowed silence in exchange for lots of money. And the scheme had worked! When the dilettante presented her with the score, the diva began to scan it with indifference. Then, hearing in her head the music she was reading, she became overwhelmed by its beauty and by the previously inapparent genius of the debonair dilettante.

As he watched, Luther felt the disorienting pleasure of seeing on the screen someone he'd met just three weeks ago in life, a sensation further complicated by that person's spectacularly dissolute death. He watched Duke's eyebrows lift and fall to suggest the dilettante's rapture—the substance of Duke's talent was contained in his expressive eyebrows—and he recalled for some reason the softness of Duke's handshake. Luther remembered that he'd noticed, in contrast with Duke's grip, the unusual hairiness of the backs of his hands. This was true, too, of his thick wrists and forearms, something not visible at the moment on the screen.

From the rear of the Princess, Luther scanned the audience. He thought to himself that everyone here was rapt with interest in the glamour of the dead man, while he had seen him alive in all his commonness and knew, for example, that the backs of his hands and his wrists and his forearms were hairy as an ape's.

The future brother-in-law turned to Duke's dilettante. Their heads were matching cameos. The brother-in-law's lips moved. On the screen, the titles said, "How very very *beautiful!*" Duke's lips moved in response. The titles said, "Oh, yes! She *is!* And I'm the luckiest man alive!" (The irony of this utterance was not lost on the people in the Princess, who gasped and murmured when they read it on the screen.) The brother-in-law smiled sweetly. "No," the titles said, "I mean that your *opera* is beautiful!"

Luther had performed his surgery on Billy Boswell at seven o'clock in the morning, the day after their inspection of the *hamadryas* baboon. The operation took place in Billy's vast dressing room. Though its mirrors were distracting, its many banks of lights could be directed to give it the brilliant shadelessness requisite for surgery. Luther had spent the previous evening in seclusion. Before retiring to his cottage, he'd asked Billy to send out a dozen lemons and the kitchen's sharpest paring knife. He'd offered no explanation of his request, leaving Billy to assume anything he wished. He'd fashioned a vise for the lemons from bookends and heavy rocks from the garden. He'd peeled them expertly.

Then he'd studied those passages in Voronoff that alluded to technique. He'd always had the impression that these descriptions were precise, but rereading them he realized they were frustratingly vague. There was reference to agitating the existing veins and arteries at the site, of scratching at their endings so they would grow and penetrate the new testicles. Voronoff spoke of this as tilling the soil before planting the seed. He spoke of humility in the face of Nature.

But mostly, he recounted an unfailing series of successes. Postoperative rams, "aggressive and bellicose," seeking the females once more. A goat, ten years after surgery, manifesting "an amorous ardor to which the female shows a ready complaisance, without the slightest suspicion that the masculine attributes of its gallant swain have been borrowed from a comrade.''

Luther's mind wandered back as he read to the days he'd served as the veterinarian's assistant in Frankfort, Kentucky. He remembered an operation that required him to clean the ventricle of a prize thoroughbred. The horse had won two legs of the Triple Crown the year before and had then been sold for an extraordinary sum to pass his days on a stud farm, a life that inspired moronic jokes of envy among men who read about it in the nation's sports pages. But as things had turned out, the horse's flesh was willing while his heart had proven weak.

In the darkness of the Princess, Luther listened to the fibrillating accompaniment of Peter O'Malley's organ. He watched Crosley Duke and his mind summoned what statistics he'd culled from news accounts of the Hubba Hubba Club affair. A full week, night and day. As many as a hundred participants at one point. Alcohol sufficient to supply a small city for the same length of time. Three deaths so far. Two young women still in comas. Survivors mumbling incoherently as they stumbled into daylight, vowing lives of chastity in exchange for being spared.

On the screen, the debonair dilettante suddenly sat forward as something caught his attention. His brows shot up. His eyeballs bulged. O'Malley's organ intoned crisis. The future brother-in-law could not help but notice and his own eyes caromed in their sockets with confusion and concern. His lips moved. The titles said, "Is something wrong?" The dilettante's fear appeared to grow wilder. Then the screen showed what he had spotted—the anonymous but no longer impoverished composer, splendid in newly purchased evening clothes, seated in a box across the way! His eyes were closed. His head lolled in a subtly rhythmic way to the gorgeous sounds that he in fact had written. The camera cut back to the bug-eyed dilettante, whose lips finally moved. "No," the titles said. "Nothing is wrong . . . *nothing*!!

*   *   *

Having assumed that Luther would agree to perform the operation, Billy had hired a woman to assist it. Her skills were such that she had also been the one to anesthetize the baboon at dawn and remove the vital gland. She was a former surgical nurse who now ran the large monkey house at a zoo in Montreal. In his planning, Billy had been characteristically fanatic. He'd reasoned, like the mastermind of a complicated heist, that the fewer involved the better. He'd given the entire household staff the rest of the week off. And instead of hiring both a surgical nurse and a monkey expert, he'd found, who knows how, a single person with the exact blend of skills and had paid her handsomely to keep her mouth shut.

Luther had been amazed when he'd walked into Billy's transformed dressing room. The mirrors gave him angles of himself he'd never contemplated. Everything he might need was there. The operating table. The full range of instruments. The Canadian zookeeper to serve as his assistant. He imagined briefly what it must feel like for an actor walking onto a meticulously made set.

Then Billy came in. He was elegantly dressed in a blue silk robe and soft leather slippers. He was working futilely to project an easy confidence. He looked around and asked Luther if he'd slept well. Luther said that he had. This was a lie. Billy's face was ashen. To Luther, it looked as white as his mother's when he'd left her in the house to ride into Cliffside.

Billy disrobed, struggling with the knot in his sash. Though obviously nervous, he showed no self-consciousness in being naked. Indeed, he paused for an instant to regard his body in his mirrors. He straightened his left arm and turned it clockwise to assess his summoned triceps. Then he lay down on the table and took a very deep breath.

As Luther had lain awake in the guest cottage, a soft breeze had carried the fragrance of the roses from the garden through the open windows. Over and over, he'd recalled that afternoon's moment of decision on the terrace, when he'd lowered his eyes from the second-story window where he'd imagined Alyce standing and said calmly to Billy, "Yes, of course I can do it." Each time he'd replayed it, he'd been freshly pleased with the confidence of mind that had come over him. It had been clear to Luther, at the instant Billy asked him, that he was being made an offer he'd be a coward to decline. His preference all along, as we know, had been for the grandeur of the surgery and he'd felt as though Billy were asking him into a bright and luxurious room that was the very future he hadn't yet been able to find on his own. *Yes,* he'd said calmly, *of course I can do it.*

Then Billy had asked if three hundred dollars, on top of his expenses, seemed an adequate fee. And Luther had felt at that point so confident that he was able to put a pause between the question and his answer. "Well," he'd finally said, "since it's you, I guess that's fine." He'd given his voice a tone of reluctant compromise.

"Forgive me," Billy said. "Is five hundred more appropriate? I apologize if I've insulted you."

Luther's night had continued with the fragrance of the rose garden filling the room, while he'd drifted in and out of sleep beneath French linen sheets, feeling certain when awake that he'd reached the precinct of success at last. For the rest of his life, when he caught the scent of roses, he'd remember how it had felt to pass that night in the thrilling wait for greatness.

The Canadian zookeeper came forward to administer the anesthesia. Billy looked up at Luther and with his thumb and index finger gave him a jaunty A-OK sign.

On the screen, Crosley Duke was rendering a panic-stricken stare. As the dilettante, he rose slowly from his chair in the opera box. The future brother-in-law's eyes lifted in concert with the dilettante's rising form. Then the screen showed the no-longer-impoverished composer in his box. A movement across the way now caught *his* eye. Suddenly his expression altered as well, not so much to fear as to steely defiance. Next the audience in the Princess saw the beautiful diva delivering the aria. Her hands were clasped to her bosom, her eyes raised ceilingward. She turned her gaze toward her fiancé's box in order to sing to him. But seeing what she saw, her face fell.

And now a wide shot filled the Princess screen. The dilettante standing in his box, upper right. The no-longer-impoverished composer standing in his, upper left. And below them, in the middle of the stage, the bewildered diva, looking first to her fiancé, then to the composer. Literally a triangle, should your eye connect the points.

It was not until Billy had left consciousness that Luther felt his confidence wavering. Lying before him, fully anesthetized, Billy seemed utterly vulnerable to Luther. He felt his forehead bead with sweat. He had simply not considered the absoluteness of responsibility that Billy would hand him by slipping bravely into sleep. Suddenly Billy's view of life seemed to Luther, if not substantial, at least formed in a world beyond his comprehension. Was Billy's trust a mark of some hidden complexity or was it instead a confirmation of his fatuousness? The prize-winning thoroughbred, from all indications, had been no more nor less trusting as it waited submissively for its anesthetic to take hold. Luther himself had offered no one a particle of his trust from that day in Laredo when Burke's betrayal had been exposed by Wilbur, the Scripture-certain assassin.

Luther glimpsed the many angles of himself in the mirrors. He looked at the Canadian zookeeper. Like his, her face was masked. She handed him a scalpel. He looked down at Billy's slender member and his ruddy, waiting scrotum. There they were! Among the most famous genitalia in the United States of America! Luther consciously reminded himself of his prowess with the lemons.

The zookeeper loudly cleared her throat. Luther looked up at her again. She arched her brows. Her eyes grew wide. With her face covered, it was impossible to read what her eyes alone were telling him. Luther considered that they were showing him fear. (Their attitude appeared not unlike the debonair dilletante's.) In fact, they were asking Luther if he would mind getting on with it. No matter that he misread it, her look brought Luther's mind back to the task at hand. He bent forward with the scalpel and made a longitudinal slice in Billy's scrotum above the left testicle.

Struggling to continue, the diva looked up to where her brother was trying to wrestle her fiancé back into his seat. Then she looked across to the opera's true composer, who now stood with his back arched and his chest swollen like a captain in the masthead braced against the heavy squalls. The titles showed his thoughts: "No amount of money is worth the cost of keeping silent! This opera is *mine* and all the world shall know it!"

The diva's eyes shot from box to box. The audience at the opera stirred. The audience in the Princess stirred. Some in each audience pointed toward the boxes.

On the screen, a look of deeper alarm crossed the diva's face and following after it the inflicted wound of clarity. It was obvious that she suddenly understood. The music she was singing seemed to be explaining everything. In the beauty of the music were the pure notes of truth. She was edging unconsciously toward the composer's box. She began to send her voice expressly up to him.

The dilettante watched the dream he thought he'd captured vanishing before him. The titles said, "She knows! Somehow, she knows! But *how*?" (As a dilettante, he had no hope of understanding that art's message can never stay suppressed.)

The act of making the incision restored Luther's calm. The zookeeper was proving an unflappable assistant, which should not have been surprising. She had after all performed a surgery of her own to get the gonad, which waited nearby in a high mound of ice. With forceps, the zookeeper parted the scrotal skin. Billy's blood trickled in thread-thin tributaries. Luther eased a flat, thin probe into the incision. He moved it behind the fatty tufts of epididymus to the vas deferens, tough and muscular. He was allowing himself a quick tour of the territory. Nothing he discovered puzzled or surprised him. He glanced at the baboon's gonad. He pictured it nestled in Billy's scrotum, following Voronoff, each implanted organ in its natural place. An improvement on Nature, but not a violation of her. "I started from the principle," Voronoff wrote, "that we must conform to Nature when we dare substitute ourselves for her." Luther felt no second loss of confidence. Physically, his hand and heart held steady. So none of these factors had anything to do with the sense that swept over him and served to give him pause.

He looked up at the huddle of himself in the mirrors. He looked at the zookeeper. Their eyes met.

*   *   *

The dilettante leaned over and gripped the edge of his opera box. The titles said, "Without her, I am nothing! Without me, she is everything she has been . . . and, alas, even more." (This last with a glance toward the opera's true composer.) He turned to the future brother-in-law and shook his hand. The future brother-in-law was exhausted and in a state of resignation allowed his hand to be shaken.

"I must try with one last gesture to show her that my *love,* if not my art, was true!"

Though he knew what was coming, Luther, in the audience, felt his heart beating faster and his throat tightening.

The dilettante climbed up on the edge of his box. He jumped and hit the stage with a horrible force. O'Malley's organ resounded. The dilettante lay at the diva's feet. She knelt and took him in her arms. He looked up into her eyes. His gaze was weak. He had no strength to speak but his titles were verbose. They said, "Think of this, my darling, as the final note in the opera of love that I *did* write for you. Don't you see, I simply had to show you that though my—"

"Don't try to talk," the stricken diva said, or sang, for it appeared she was incorporating the dilettante's leap to his death into the opera itself. She looked down at him. He closed his eyes. Her titles said, "You were not a great man. But your love for me made you truly want to be!"

Sounds of sobbing began in the Princess.

The true composer sat slumped in grief, doomed to live with the result of his need to claim his authorship.

The diva's titles said, "Most of all, you've shown me that you knew how greatness sounded!"

Then the dilettante's body performed a little seizure of final relaxation. Crosley Duke, dead on the screen as he was dead in fact!

The screen filled with "THE END."

There was long applause. The lights came up. Women were dabbing at their eyes and blowing their noses.

*   *   *

So it was neither confusion nor a further flight of confidence that interrupted Luther as he was bent over Billy. Holding the probe completely still, he tried to visualize the procedure. In a tender exploration, he gently altered the probe's angle. Hello in there! it seemed to be saying. But after several seconds, he was forced to conclude that a transplant was impossible. The networks of veins and arteries were so microscopically small that they could not conceivably be isolated and agitated, that tilling of the soil that Voronoff had described.

For the first time, Luther sensed what he saw as Steinach's and Voronoff's dedication to their schemes, the elaborateness with which they'd worked things through. Truth be told, he felt for a moment deeply inspired and an additional admiration for the two of them filled him. But then, returning to the moment, he faced the unavoidable conclusion that any attempt to replace Billy's gonad with one of the baboon's might do serious harm. It might likely make Billy sterile. It might send deadly infections coursing through him.

He withdrew the probe and looked at the zookeeper. She continued to hold the forceps steady. He imagined himself explaining his train of thought to her. In his head, he heard his words beginning. They seemed, at worst, to be admitting his ignorance. At best, they were those of a fool lacking foresight. He watched filaments of blood meander weakly down Billy's scrotum.

Luther bluntly studied the zookeeper. She was holding her pose, as she had been, the forceps in her hand. He had no idea what she'd brought to all this but when her eyes met his again he began to shake his head. Not a word, nothing audible, was offered.

After a moment, the zookeeper responded in kind. The two of them stood, shaking their heads at each other. They looked like synchronized figurines on the deck of a cuckoo clock. Between them, the incised Billy lay asleep. His mirrors caught it all from at least a dozen angles.

Several people greeted Luther as they filed out of the Princess. They commented on the film. They asked him if he knew that the actor they'd just seen, the one named Crosley Duke, was in actual life a dead man. They wondered if he agreed that watching a dead man die in a motion picture was a mightily strange event to contemplate. Luther smiled and nodded and said yes, it surely was.

Out on the street, as he had the past two nights, as he had to some degree since his return from Hollywood, he felt he was leaving one dream and moving directly into another. South Main Street seemed a high suspenseful dream. Walking along toward the St. Charles dining room, he imagined O'Malley's Princess organ embellishing his steps. His state of mind was similar to that romantic self-regard with which he'd watched himself in the rank rooms of whores and had set his movements to the music of Old Testament narrative.

As a child, with his aunt and his uncle in the wagon, he had sometimes sensed, as he was close to sensing now, that the moment he was living had a literal shimmering surface. Yes, there were times, in the years with June and Ray, when the world had seemed so magical he'd imagined he could extend his hand and run his fingers over the bright face of his day. But at the same time, he had known it was something one could do only if the moment were a day in a dream.

Still without exchanging words, Luther had signaled the zookeeper to pass him the tray that held the needle and the thread. Then he'd closed Billy's incision with a tiny ladder-row of perfect stitches. He worked as alertly as when he'd closed the horse's heart.

It was not until noon, after they'd gotten Billy comfortably set up in his bedroom, that Luther and the zookeeper, whose name was Charlotte, spoke alone. Eating a lunch of cold chicken and fruit in Luther's cottage, he saw her for the first time without her surgical mask and discovered that she was an extremely strange-looking young woman. Her face was jowly and her nose was long and rubbery. In this regard she was fortunate to have lived when she did, for had she been born half a century later, her features surely would have been described as Nixonesque.

Charlotte asked, "When are you leaving?"

"Tomorrow," Luther said. "And how about y'all?"

"When he asked me, I agreed to stay on a few days afterwards."

Luther nodded. He took a bite of chicken. He said, "I've got no inkling what y'all make of this." He paused. "But it seems to me, and I say this with Mr. Boswell's interest uppermost in mind, it seems to me that what he doesn't know won't do him *any* harm."

Charlotte gave him a slow smile. Improbably, it was lovely. She said, "I look at it this way. If Mr. Boswell knew, he might ask us for his money back."

Luther smiled as well. "Well, yes, I guess there's that."

"But he'll surely . . . wonder," Charlotte said. "I mean, how things . . . how *he* might have . . . changed."

Luther thought as he chewed. "Just tell him not to go inspecting himself for a month or else he'll risk disconnecting things."

Charlotte shook her head. "Is he that gullible?"

Luther answered with a sweep of his arm that included the two of them and the fact that they were there. He said, "I had an uncle who used to say that the most important ingredient in a medicine was the mind's belief in it." He didn't add, he'd conveniently forgotten, that his uncle had since amended his opinion. Then he asked, condescendingly, "Do y'all see my point?"

Charlotte said, "I see it fine. Try telling it to the baboon."

*T*he talk was of *Cristeros* as Luther entered the dining room of Some Other Hotel.

"I wouldn't be surprised if they rode right down South Main," Vernon the bartender said. "If it's true they're heading for Villa Acuña, what's to keep them from just coming on into Del Rio when they get through killin' Mexicans?"

Luther looked around and sat down at his usual table.

"Because," offered a big, beefy man at the bar named Rheinhold Bayless. "Because they remember Texas whupped them once and they know we'd do it again. A Mexican can't remember where he left his butt hole but he remembers every minute of when somebody whupped him."

The *Cristeros* had been busy bringing violence to the state of Coahuila. Theirs was a movement that had risen on the fervor of the ancient contest between the church and the state for the peoples' obeisance. In the government's latest try at writing a constitution, it had set the number and restricted the nationality of priests. Across town on his throne, imperceptibly alive inside his chrysalis of silks, Archbishop Diaz's reply was to suspend all religious exercises. The *Cristeros*—some of whom were fanatics made desperate as addicts by the church's refusal to let them worship, some of whom, it was said, were bored *Villistas* happy for the chance to reenact the good old days—had been expressing their displeasure by riding into a town and killing all its teachers.

Luther signaled to Vernon for a bottle and a glass. He listened uninterestedly. Over the past few days, he'd felt a sense of great frustration and his brooding tonight had an adolescent's depth of purpose. For it seemed to him that in Los Angeles he had visited his

future, but he hadn't yet grasped how or when he'd join it. It was as
though his days with Billy were a scene from a motion picture that
had been edited with no sense of narrative: the happy culmination
too close to the beginning. Where was the middle, the way of struggle and discovery? Tonight he was feeling especially irritated and
had decided to get drunk.

Luther heard Robuck Winter, at the hotel bar, turning the talk
away from the *Cristeros* to detail the ease and rewards of creativity.
"First, I just remember somethin' I did in my cowboy days, then all
I do is put some rhymes in it." He explained that he'd recently
decided to become a western singer after seeing a picture at the
Princess starring Steve "Saddle" Horne. In its campfire scene, Horne
picked up a guitar and began to strum it while the other cowboys
closed their eyes and nodded their heads. Robuck said that though
the film was silent, he'd heard the music in his mind, and sent away
the next day for a guitar and an instruction book. Inevitably, he'd be
asked to make recordings.

Vernon brought the bottle of whiskey to Luther's table. "What do
y'all think, Doc?" he asked. "Would the *Cristeros* come across the
border?"

"If they do," Luther said, "we'll set Robuck loose on them and
he'll sing them to death."

An hour passed, through which Luther drank, and he was no
longer sober when Peter O'Malley came into the room. "Irish!"
Luther called and waved O'Malley over. Robuck Winter looked up
and, seeing O'Malley, eased away from the bar and headed over to
join their table.

Luther had been tempted to tell O'Malley of his trip, in part
because he knew how fascinated O'Malley would be to hear about
the stars he'd met. But Luther also knew that telling only *some* of
what he'd seen would be impossible and he'd signed a document for
Billy that swore him to say nothing. More critically, Luther sensed
that the authority he'd felt since returning from Los Angeles had its
source in the fact that he held enormous secrets.

Still, at the moment he felt the urge to tell them. To stop it, he
threw back two successive shots of whiskey.

"Y'all been to see the tire?" Robuck Winter asked O'Malley.

O'Malley said, "This morning." A gigantic tire, billed as the World's Largest, was on display for four days at the Val Verde County Fair Grounds.

Robuck Winter said, "I went out to ask the fella in charge if he'd be interested in some entertainment to go along with the display. But he said he didn't think my western songs would match up with their theme."

"Western songs?" O'Malley said.

"Robuck's going to be a famous western singer," Luther said. "He's going to get rich singing rhymes about how he fell off his horse and lassoed his own foot." Luther's sarcasm sounded oddly absent-minded, for his thoughts had stayed fixed on Billy Boswell's need for secrecy, and now a statistic from Voronoff's book drifted up to him: that ninety-eight percent of those who'd had the surgery wished to keep it private. Luther drank another shot. He looked around at all the drinkers in the room. He felt a sudden sense of beneficence. He believed he'd begun to understand why these local men were not coming to him as they had when his practice had been to calm their fears of venereal disease. Then, their urgency had overcome any shame. But rejuvenation was new and it was strange and even in Europe, even in France, where people were interested in little else but artful wantonness, there was an aura of skittishness about it.

"Irish," he blurted, "I want you to come and work for me."

O'Malley said, "What do you mean, Doc?" His smile was uneasy. He'd seen Luther turn suddenly mean when he was drunk and the sloppy force of his voice suggested he was ready to do that now. "What would I do?"

"Play the organ," Luther said. "What the hell, isn't that what you do?"

"But you don't have an organ."

"Jesus," Luther said, "I don't mean right now. I mean the organ in the house I'm going to build."

"I didn't know you were going to build a house."

"Now you do," Luther said.

"And I'd play the organ just for you?" O'Malley asked.

"In the evenings," Luther said. "At the end of my day." He was stopped for a moment by a burst of hiccups. "It's a gift I've decided

I'm going to give myself. You'd probably take on some other chores, too."

Robuck Winter sat up straight and said, "I could be your private balladeer."

Luther said to O'Malley, "Y'all know how I enjoy your playing."

"Thanks, Doc," O'Malley said.

"But I'd want you to expand your style a bit. Can you play the blues?"

O'Malley shrugged his shoulders. "Sure. Why not?" He was trying to avoid any humoring tone.

"I love the organ," Luther said, "and I love the Memphis blues."

Robuck Winter said, "I tell you, Doc—"

"And I hate, I goddamn *hate,* someone twangin' on about the cowboy's life underneath the open skies." He turned back to O'Malley and offered him his hand. "Then it's a deal, Irish. We'll have a good time, I promise."

O'Malley hesitated just a moment, then reached across and shook it.

Luther whispered, "Trust me, Irish. I know we will." His bleary eyes tried to hold O'Malley's. His grin was crooked. He said, "I've already seen how good it's gonna be."

He began to describe the home he planned to build. He would have a long driveway lined with palm trees. There'd be stables for horses. Perhaps a fountain in front. There'd be magnificent rose gardens.

O'Malley pretended to be listening with interest. His eyes blinked. He pinched himself in his thigh to stay alert. Luther's descriptions became even more earnest and dwelled longest of all on his future rose gardens. It seemed to O'Malley that, more than imagining them, Luther had already seen them.

This we know to be true, which alone could explain Luther's tedious narrative. But in fact they were inspired by Alyce Rae, who'd surprised him in the cottage as he had finished packing.

I thought you were in Detroit! Answering the quick knock on his door, he'd expected to see Charlotte, come to say good-bye or to say she'd reconsidered and was telling Billy everything.

"Billy thinks I am," Alyce had said. She hurried past him and walked to the chair that looked out the window. She was dressed in riding clothes. They were crisp and unwrinkled. She appeared freshly bathed. She smelled sublimely of powders and cologne. She turned back to Luther and said, "I'm leaving tonight, I've been staying with a friend, but I couldn't go until I'd found out how he was." She said, "Of course Billy musn't know I've come, he'd be furious with me, he insisted I not be bothered with it all, but he's all right, isn't he, he's going to be all right?"

Luther saw that she was terribly nervous. Her voice was high and breathless and she was apparently unable to speak a short sentence. He walked over and sat across from her. She seemed to him as she had when she'd first appeared in Del Rio. Agitated, frightened, colt-ish in her spirit.

"He's fine. He's asleep. Charlotte—did you meet Charlotte?—she's the nurse he hired, she's with him." He intended to speak vaguely, hoping Alyce would reveal how much she knew.

"He was trying to keep it all from me at first, urging me to visit my parents for an early Thanksgiving. That's when I knew something was going on. I *detest* Detroit and Billy knows I do."

She lit a cigarette and took two drags. She looked up at Luther and her smile was as quick as a muscular tic. Her green eyes, as he saw them, were taking some of their color from the sky's dusky light.

In the bar, Luther finished his detailing of his future house and grounds. Robuck Winter had fallen asleep. His head was cradled in his arms atop the table. Luther looked at O'Malley. He said, "You look tired, Irish. Go home and get some sleep."

"I probably should," O'Malley said.

Luther shook Robuck Winter's shoulder. "Wake up, Robuck."

Robuck grunted.

Outside, Luther said good night to O'Malley and started across the street. When he reached his steps, he paused. He looked up at the sky. Its stars were clustered, dense as salt where they'd collected. Despite the whiskey he'd consumed, he now felt wakeful and restless after talking to O'Malley. The images he'd depicted lingered in his mind. His agitation had returned full blown and he had no wish to climb his stairs and go to bed. He decided he would drive to Villa Acuña to see the mole behind Lydia Mendoza's left knee. He turned from the wrought-iron steps and walked toward his Model T. He climbed up, set the spark and throttle, got out and turned the crank.

Alyce Rae had said, "Billy and I have been fighting for weeks, just one long, terrible argument. I'd accused him of hiding something from me, of wanting me gone so he could carry on behind my back. It was horrible, and it seemed it wouldn't end. He kept saying that everything was lovely, but we both knew it wasn't, that things had *not* been lovely." Her face showed a sudden new alarm. Then she shook her head and laughed nervously. "I was thinking just now how flagrant I'm being, but I suppose I'm not telling you anything you don't already know." She stabbed her cigarette into an ashtray and lit another one.

She had never seemed as young, as *new*, to Luther, and yet had never looked as womanly. It was as if her beauty had completed its last details the moment before she'd knocked on his door.

He said, "You can tell me anything."

She studied his face. She seemed to be working to calm herself. "Yes," she said finally. "I guess that's so. I mean, because of what you helped me through, it's as though you already know my most unguarded self. I've been thinking quite a lot about that, actually." She looked down, avoiding Luther's eyes, and picked at imaginary lint on a leg of her riding breeches. "Quite a lot."

Luther watched her fingers pincering the cloth of her breeches. "Have y'all been riding?" he asked.

She looked blank before appearing to understand his question. "Oh," she said, glancing up, "heavens no."

The road out of Del Rio toward the border was empty and Luther took full advantage of its width. The Model T wove from side to side at a leisurely speed. All the while, it tipped debonairly to the left.

Luther had no appointment and he smiled at the thought of waking Lydia. She would blink her eyes, rising stupidly from sleep. She would curse him for surprising her. Lydia hated surprises as much as she loved sleep, an act to which she brought an appetitive aggression.

A smoky cloud hung in the distance, over Mexico.

The night air blowing through the Model T had a sobering effect. Though there was scant chance of meeting anyone, Luther began to steer a straighter course. He'd not visited Lydia since returning from Los Angeles. He thought of Lydia's little sister, Rosa. He'd remained in part insulted that she thought of him as monstrous. Why, given the conditions of her life, had she found *him* terrifying? He decided as he drove, as the chill night air blew across his face, that he would win Rosa over. He felt buoyed by this idea. He felt magnanimous. He would buy Rosa clothes. He would, as Lydia had suggested, fill her teeth with gold when they'd begun to rot. He felt suddenly impatient for their decay to begin so that he could.

The road was a ghostly white strip. He followed its last slow bend toward the bridge. In the sky, the low smoky cloud hung even more dramatically over Villa Acuña. Its color was the road's.

Alyce Rae had said, "He never would tell me exactly what he was planning."

Luther waited. He wasn't sure if this was her way of asking him to do so.

She said, "Then he finally admitted his deception was only his plan to send for you, and when he said that, I was even more confused. In part, I was relieved, but then I felt guilty for having accused him." She paused and breathed. "I've been so frightened for him. Whatever the reason he sent for you, it all seems so, such . . . desperation." She looked directly at Luther and asked, "Is it?"

"Is it?"

"Desperate?"

Again, Luther waited before replying. He said, "Billy—well, the *two* of you—you can either one answer that better than I can."

Alyce stabbed her second cigarette into the ashtray and lit a third. She said, "I just realized I don't *want* to know what you've done. I thought I did, but, no, I don't. But if you've helped him . . ." A kind of primness suddenly showed. "I thank you, for both of us." She looked out the cottage window to the rose gardens. From this angle, her darting eyes took on more of the dusk, which made their green more gray. She said, "Hearing that, it sounds incredibly selfish to include myself in thanking you."

Luther offered her his open palms, the gesture of a magician showing his audience he hid nothing. "With your husband's devotion and all, it's natural to think of yourself as included."

She exhaled and watched the smoke. Luther watched it, too. She shook her head. More slowly, she said, "These have been extremely strange times."

"I'm sure that's so," Luther said.

"Extremely," she repeated, seemingly to herself. She put out her cigarette. "Last week," she said, "one morning last week, I thought I remembered all of a sudden what had caused my amnesia." She was gazing out the window. Her features were momentarily softened behind the rising cigarette smoke and appeared the deft imprecisions of an Impressionist's brush. "It was nearly noon, I guess, now that I think about it." Her voice was nearly contemplative. "But I was sitting at the table finishing a late breakfast. I suppose that's why I first said it was morning." She said, "I was eating shirred eggs."

Then she put her hands on the arms of the chair and quickly got up. "All right. I must go," she announced. Her full impatience had returned. "I shouldn't have come, I shouldn't have let you know I was still here, but I had to find out how Billy was."

Luther sat frozen in his chair. He'd been eager for what she'd seemed about to divulge. Now he felt slow as a dullard. He rose uncertainly. He stood and looked down at her high brown boots. "Are you going riding *now*?"

She looked down at them, too. She shook her head. "I've never ridden a horse in my life." Her voice sounded oddly and sincerely perplexed.

"Then why is it you're leaving?" he asked.

"I'm supposed to be in Detroit, remember?"

"Y'all hate Detroit." He moved to stand next to her at the window. "Remember?"

"But I still have to go, it's all been arranged. Mother and Father are expecting me."

He reached for her face and lifted her chin. He was sure she'd played with him a moment ago and he felt, in response, free and inconsiderate. A thread through his desire was now retaliation. He ran his fingers down her neck and along her collarbone. She let him. His fingertips traced the V of the neck of her white silk blouse. Alyce made a quick inbreathing sound. He said, "Why is it you're wearing these riding clothes then?"

She hesitantly reached up and ran her fingertips along his cheek. She said, "I don't know. Maybe because Billy likes the way I look in them."

"I don't," he said. He put his hand over her mouth to stop her from speaking. Then he took it away and kissed her. His fingers moved to unbutton her blouse. He parted it and got down on his knees to kiss her breasts. She lifted her shoulders to help the blouse fall away. He could feel her trembling, and yet her movement was a shrug of subtle languor, almost suggesting torpor. It was a gesture of extraordinary sexual elegance which she'd performed once before in his imagination.

Through the Model T's windshield, Luther saw that the Rio Grande bridge appeared inexplicably crowded. He drew his long body up to get a better look. He slowed the Model T. He'd met no one on the road and there appeared as many as a dozen automobiles gathered at the bridge. They'd made a tight row blocking its entrance. Their radiators faced Texas. The flat tops of their roofs, one next to another, formed a long, neat shelf against the backdrop of black sky.

Luther drove to within a few yards of the blockade. He stopped and set the brake. Now he could see in his headlights that in front of each of the automobiles stood a man with a rifle. All the men wore tan Western hats with the shining stars of the Texas Rangers pinned to their fronts. The silver stars made a magically even-rowed constellation in the night.

Afterward, Alyce and Luther had lain atop the French linen sheets. She'd begun to speak softly of loving to be used. She said she felt that's what sex was for a woman, that sense of being filled up, of being absolutely used. She'd touched the bullet scar on Luther's thigh, then traced its outline with the tip of her finger. "It's very beautiful," she'd said.

Luther got out of the Model T and walked up to the nearest Texas Ranger.

"How do," the Ranger said. He put his hand to the brim of his hat.

"What's the trouble?" Luther asked. He could barely detect a face beneath the hat. He smelled smoke.

The Ranger said, "Mexico's all closed up tonight."

The smell was strong and only then did Luther realize that the smoky cloud above Acuña was instead a cloud of smoke. It was rising particularly from the hill above the village. Beneath it, through it, he saw the glow and lick of fire.

"It's them damn *Cristeros,*" the Texas Ranger said. "They rode into Villa Acuña after sundown and once they finished killin' a few schoolteachers, they headed straight up the hill."

"To the *zona,*" Luther said. He felt himself growing cold.

The Texas Ranger laughed. "They set fire to ever damn whore hut in the *zona,* then they waited outside and picked 'em off as they run out." He laughed more openly. "The brush roofs of them whore hovels made superior kindling. There ain't a whore left in Acuña. We all of us said here, all of us was sayin' "—he nodded left and right to the row of handsome hats—"that it's about time them *Cristeros* got their logic straight and started killin' whores instead of runty little schoolteachers."

Luther looked toward the hill. He tried without success to specify the concentration of the smoke. He knew exactly where Lydia's hut sat at the low point on the hillside.

"No," the Texas Ranger said, "if they was—I'm talkin' now about the *Cristeros*—if they was to go at it right, what is the sense in killin' schoolteachers when ever dust heap in Mexico with three Chicos and a rabid dog sharin' a shit hole has got its *zona*? How I see the world, it's the *zonas* where there's the evidence of Godlessness."

Luther gathered himself and suddenly charged toward a gap he thought he saw in the line of Texas Rangers.

"Hey!" two Rangers shouted. He surprised them so, he nearly made it through.

Luther screamed Lydia's name while the Rangers held him. Then he shouted it again, and as he grappled with the Rangers he shouted Rosa's also. His voice was wounded and bestial, but though it left his mouth strongly, it quickly thinned and died in the air.

The border remained closed for a week after the fire as rumors of *Cristero* violence grew shrill. The cavalry was summoned from Fort Clark in Brackettville. Hour upon hour, the mounted soldiers patrolled, keeping their horses to a narrow route amidst the spongy *coriza* marsh along the river. Through the nights the horses' neighs were of boredom and complaint. The Texas Rangers, for their part, guarded the crossings into Coahuila and had the most to do with the rumors' growing scale. Turning travelers back, they more often than not provided vague descriptions of the butchery beyond. They seemed reluctant to mention the bloody firing squads. They apologized for having to add that, by the way, women and children were being slaughtered. They wished everyone to understand that in sealing off the violence and making sure it stayed in Mexico they were merely following orders and should not be seen as heroes.

Luther ventured early every morning to the Del Rio bridge, hoping each day he'd at last be allowed to cross. On the seventh morning, he steered his Model T toward the phalanx of Rangers and two of them stepped back and gravely waved him through. Luther was startled and stalled the automobile. Strong as his daily disappointment had been, he'd begun in a way to expect and ritualize it.

"What's your business in Acuña that can't wait?" the Ranger asked.

Luther said, "I need to see a friend."

"Y'all be careful," the Ranger warned from beneath his wide tan Stetson. "Far as we can tell, everthing's back to normal, but I wouldn't stay any longer than I had to if I's you."

"*Buenas dias, El Doctor,*" the Mexican border guard said. He smiled and touched the tip of his rifle to the brim of his hat. Belts of bullets X'ed across his chest. He was swelled with self-importance by the rifle and his clichéd display of ammunition. "I am very surprised to see *you* this morning. You are most often at this time of the day going the other way across the bridge." He laughed.

There was an eerie normalcy at the bottom of the village but as Luther started up the hill, a sudden barrenness was profound. The hillside was denuded. There were skeletons of trees. Here and there an obviously human bone lay amidst the ashes like so much banal refuse. Vultures wheeled in the sky.

Luther saw that the *federales* assigned to clear the devastation had leveled whatever had remained of the mud huts. They'd raked everything into huge piles and had subsequently set a second round of bonfires. Smoke breathed from the ashes and hung vagrantly in the air. He noted that the open trenches had been filled to some degree in the general cleaning up but they were starkly visible as never before. From the Model T, he watched a vulture, as though in frustration, drop from the sky and settle on an ash pile and peck viciously at a twisted picture frame, the closest thing to carrion left anywhere on the hill.

As he approached the spot where Lydia's hut had stood, Luther heard the crack of flames, syncopated and processional. He imagined their heat. He heard the terror of the prostitutes as they were being shot, their cries perversely musical, flutish with surprise.

He slowed the Model T and came to a stop. He stared at the ash-gray spot, raked smooth and flat. He imagined Rosa waking from her light sleep and seeing a *Cristero* standing in the doorway. What had she thought? Had she thought, *El blanco grande?* He heard Lydia's scream weaving through it all like the principal thread that held the madness neat and tight.

Then he steered the Model T through a wide returning arc. And as he headed slowly back down the hill toward the border, he thought of Ray White's gratitude in having got to watch June die, in knowing she was dead and not just disappeared. He heard his mother's death cackle. He sensed his father's arms surrounding him as they'd ridden back from Cliffside. He felt his father's breath feathering his ear as he'd told him he'd be living with his Aunt June and Uncle Ray. He thought about people dying and people disappearing and all the possibilities of response from those they left.

*   *   *

It was the following day when Luther received the two letters, though he would always remember them arriving the same morning he'd returned from Villa Acuña.

He walked into the post office on East Broadway Avenue and removed the letters from his box. He had a moment's trouble understanding what he held. He noticed first of all that both the envelopes were a luxurious parchment in a tasteful cream shade. Next he saw that in fact they were identical and that they'd been mailed the same day from Los Angeles. On the flap of one of them, the return address was embossed in rich gold leaf. On the flap of the other the address had been crossed out. He walked outside and climbed up behind the wheel of his Model T. He loosened his collar and opened the first envelope.

Dear Dr. Mathias, Billy Boswell wrote on a plain piece of paper in his remarkably childlike scrawl. I am, alas, surrendering, against my better judgment, to the wish to communicate with you once more. You and I are, of course, both keenly aware of the document you signed before my witness which holds you to a lifelong secrecy in the matter of our recent collaboration (shall we say?). You'll forgive the stern tone of the foregoing sentence. I invoke it only to underscore the seriousness and delicacy of this pact. It is not, I assure you, a reflection of my mood, which is one of enormous relief and joy, and the cause that compels me to write this note to you. For I simply had to tell you that my life is once again full, in that most vital and treasured way, indeed it is *optimally* full, more so than one (than I, in any case) might have possibly imagined.

It is clearly all your doing, the result of your research, which you've artfully translated into surgical (now I've employed the word, how incautious of me!) acumen. I can only express my immeasurable gratitude for shepherding me into that world of genius and plain good sense pioneered by Messrs. Steinach and, especially!, Voronoff.

I now resume my days at a pinnacle of energy and commitment, once again fully able to give my art to my public and my all to my

dear wife, my life, my Alyce. (Please, I trust that you not read that
as some tasteless *entrendre*. I am being quite sincere.) I am certain
you'll respect this confidence between us and understand full well
the impossible complications that would ensue—with a huge and
irrationally adoring audience to please, and a hungry tribe of news-
men forever ready to invade my cherished privacy—should a hint of
our venture ever surface.

And so it is in that spirit of trust and admiration that I once again
and finally emphasize my heart and my soul's debt to you. I remain,

Forever thankful and,

Yours sincerely,

B. Boswell

Luther shook his head and stroked his chin. His heart had begun
to beat more quickly, the way the heart works harder in the midst
of some inclemency. He looked up at the pedestrians on East
Broadway Avenue. From the Model T, he acknowledged them with
a nod and a minimal wave of his hand. Still feeling the effect of
Billy's prose, Luther opened the second envelope while he
watched Del Rio pass.

Dear Luther, Alyce Rae wrote. I hope this finds you well and prosper-
ously attending to the concerns of your little town. I find myself
wondering, in these days of late autumn, how the seasons show
themselves in your part of the world, as we live here, as Billy likes
to say, through four seasons of summer. Not that I mean for a
moment to complain (my recent visit with my parents in Detroit
reminded me just how horrid a thing weather can be).

Both Billy and I are extremely well. Billy is deeply immersed in
shooting *Let Me Show You How,* his new picture for the Zietman
studio, and I've never seen him so eager for each day's work to begin.
His only complaint is that he's being forced to work with that insufferable Harold Lloyd, who somehow persuaded Mr. Zietman to let
him try a serious role. Billy says that he's absolutely ghastly and has

no business in a dramatic picture. Nevertheless, it's thrilling to feel Billy's renewed enthusiasm.

I suppose that's why I've chosen to write to you, even as I ask that you regard this letter as a matter of utmost secrecy. Whatever aid you gave Billy, I continue to wish to be ignorant of, partly, I must confess, because I find I don't want to tempt the skeptic in me. But I did want you to know just how grateful Billy is to you, though it's impossible for him to communicate his thanks directly. (What a time the press would have! as I know you understand, particularly in the aftermath of my embarrassing episode, which kept them hovering about for weeks after our return.) Still, it seemed quite unfair not to let you know that Billy speaks of you privately with great admiration. Indeed, he's said he believes that you have very special gifts.

I will close having said that, and adding my own appreciation for your help and concern—and *most importantly,* in *all* things relevant to Billy and his peace of mind—for your *absolute* and *total* discretion.

> Yours very sincerely,
> Alyce

Luther pictured the two of them locking the doors of their baronial dressing rooms and settling in to compose their secret letters. He conjured them bent over their desks and imagined the distinctions in their poses and their attitudes: Billy's gushing impetuosity; Alyce's agonizing search for tone and strategy.

He read Alyce's letter a second time more slowly, recognizing line by line her hedges and her compromises. In the cool morning, in the seat of the Model T, as people on East Broadway waved and tipped their hats to him, Luther fell into a reverie. He supposed she hadn't spoken of their hours and her concern because she hadn't felt sure enough that only he would read it. Was that it? Was that why she'd decided to write to him obliquely? But if she had so mistrusted him, she'd never have sent the letter.

Yet she had, she'd needed to despite her misgivings, and it was quite enough for Luther that she had. For he sensed in what she'd written a certain heat and scale, a balance of admission and imposture that felt sufficient, felt appropriate. He had her letter, and he had the memory of the air's thrilling tension in the cottage and of the whiteness of her skin in the sunlight through the windows. He agreed with her wish that this be the past. There, it posed no risk of becoming less than it had been. It might only become better, which was, as Luther increasingly would use it, the past's particular grace.

BOOK THREE

◆ ◆ ◆

1933

*E*very night, two hours before his broadcast, Luther Mathias left his medical clinic and headed for the quiet of his old second-story office. He needed this time to ready his mind for what he would say on the air that evening. Pausing at the door of the clinic, which filled a former boarding house on the corner of Garfield and Griner, he issued an order to his receptionist as a way of saying good night. "I'm off to prepare," he was likely to say. "I am not to be disturbed unless there's an emergency." His accent had become buttery and ineffable, a subtle amalgam of drawls and twangs, and who, after all, can finally define a drawl as distinct from a twang? Over the years, he'd weaned from his habits any lingering tendency to say *y'all* and had smoothed to indistinction all other mannerisms that might, he believed, unprofitably define him to the national audience listening to him on the radio. In his nightly broadcasts, he often referred to himself in the third person. He was one of the first public figures in America to adopt this bizarre and, today, quite common mannerism. Such descriptive attention to Luther's way of speaking would be rightly judged excessive were his voice not now heard by thousands every night.

Today, as usual, he hurried out the door and headed east down Garfield in the lavender twilight. He felt the sun's vestigial warmth on the back of his neck. His white lab coat filled like a sail as he moved down the street. He fixed his look on the second-story roof lines of South Main Street. Crows roosted there, barely discernible. He met no one's eye. Someone called to him from across the street. He replied, "Good evening, my friend," but his words were pitched to the line of roosting crows.

Passing the bank, he crossed South Main, climbed the wrought-iron stairs, and entered his old office. He was still living in its back rooms while his grand new home at the edge of town was being finished. The office's tall narrow windows were now visored with stiff green awnings, like bookkeepers' eye shades. He removed his lab coat and suit jacket. He loosened his tie. A janitor at the clinic had come an hour before to raise the windows and let some air into the room.

He sat down behind the desk. The room was otherwise empty. There were no full-size anatomical diagrams on the walls. There were no medical books on the shelves. All the props and paraphernalia had been moved two years before to his office at the clinic. A large bulletin board hung behind his desk, but it was covered with notes and schedules pertaining to his radio station.

Alone in his old office at this hour, Luther was able to fashion a sense of privacy. He sometimes found himself imagining a scenario in which he'd mysteriously disappeared from the face of the earth, to the frantic concern of his patients and his staff and his thousands of listeners. He could spend pleasurable minutes inside this fantasy. He imagined the tabloids' hysteria. The thousands of people wandering through their days in a state of perplexity and grief. He imagined years of ensuing speculation and evolving theory, holding the country in a fever of obsession comparable to its interest in the Lindbergh kidnapping.

In the early spring of 1928, some five months after his adventures in Los Angeles, Luther had written to Haskell Albright, the exasperated cuckold and publishing tycoon, to set in motion his wish to build a radio station. At the time he'd chosen to write to Albright, Luther was certain that aspects of his scheme were badly flawed or worse. But he was also convinced he'd thought of everything he could. The moment had come for a more experienced assessment and he'd hoped from the instant he'd begun to think things through that Haskell Albright would be the one to provide it. Indeed, Luther saw the prospect of Albright's involvement as among his plan's most attractive possibilities. Albright's behavior, that day at the club, had seemed to Luther admirably indifferent to what others thought of him. It expressed a power that needed to please no one else, the federal government notwithstanding, and this was just the sort of power Luther wished for himself.

Also, to Luther's ear, Albright's tirade on the veranda had been laced with insight and prophecy. Back in Del Rio, he'd continued to think about it until he'd hit on the idea of a radio station as a way of announcing the joys of rejuvenation. Consequently, he determined that he wanted Albright's advice; also, he wanted the help of Albright's money.

His letter was brief and aimed to tantalize. It did not mention the idea of the station itself. Luther wrote that he'd been thinking, since his return to Texas, of Albright's understandable frustration with the Federal Radio Commission's interference and he'd come up with a way he might be able to help out. Luther assured Albright, should he suspect this seeming charity, that there was something in it for him, as well. Luther kept in mind Albright's understanding that he was Billy Boswell's cousin and an unmannered Texan of vast property. This allowed his tone to suggest that he and Albright were equals and that his proposal might, whatever else, be amusing to discuss: one rich sumbitch trading notions with another. He knew that if he met with Albright again he'd eventually need to tell him the truth. But that would be the closing skit. First there was the pitch.

In no time at all he received Albright's response. "Get your ass out here yesterday," his telegram said. "I'll hear any idea to screw the F.R.C."

Haskell Albright's cavernous office at the *Los Angeles Times* was one floor above the bustling newsroom. The noises of reporters and editors below rose up through Albright's carpets and became a hum on the soles of Albright's shoes. In fact, he often took them off and worked in his stockings so that he could sense the burr of news being made on the bottoms of his feet. It gave him the feeling that he was recharging his energies and his powers of thought. It was a superstition he allowed himself.

The office was filled with Louis Quatorze antiques. There were chairs and couches and tables grouped everywhere on Oriental rugs, which made it feel less cavernous but more manorial. There were so many of these Louis Quatorze islands floating on the carpet-sea of Haskell Albright's office that visitors, when they entered, sometimes had a moment of trouble finding him among them.

Luther did not. He spotted Albright right away, sitting on a couch in a far corner. This was easier than it might otherwise have been because the couch was made up with sparkling white bed sheets. Two fat white pillows lay against one arm.

"Cowboy!" Albright shouted. He stood up and came toward Luther.

"Haskell," Luther answered.

When they were seated, Luther asked if Albright had been feeling poorly.

"Never better. Why?" Albright said. Then he followed Luther's eye to the sheets and pillows. "Oh, those," he said, then explained that he'd been living in his office for some time now and would be for the foreseeable future. He said everything he needed was there—a bathroom, a closet big enough to hold some clothes—and, best of all, the thing he didn't need was *not.* "Now my skinny slut of a wife is free to do the old snake and shake with anybody she can find, morning, noon, and night, for all I care." He said that he'd moved out the week after he'd caught her screwing his nephew on the hallway stairs. He'd been camped on the couch in his office ever since.

Luther said, "I'm awful sorry, Haskell. I remember that day when you told us about it, y'all were distressed to find that you didn't give a shit. I take it," he said, nodding toward the couch, "this means you found yourself a way to."

Albright threw back his head and erupted in laughter. When he was done he said, "Forgive me, Luther. Your sentiment was heart-felt, I realize, and I didn't mean to be rude. It just tickled me, because nothing could be further from the truth." He said, "As it happens, my wife is the second meanest person in Los Angeles and it's just her misfortune that I am the first. She insists she used to be sweet and good when we got married and I drove her to become the bitch she is today. She might be right, I frankly can't remember, but what I'm saying is, I did not move out because she broke my heart. I moved out because every living human being in Los Angeles knew the story within a week after it happened. Hell, I shouldn't have been surprised. You know your cousin. Tell Billy Boswell something like that and you might as well have broadcast it over the radio. It drives me goddamn insane to think of everybody talking about me that way and I was an idiot for mentioning it in front of Billy." He said, "It was an aberrant slip on my part to talk about it in public, but the point of it is, I've got an image to protect. How would it look if I *hadn't* moved out? What the hell would this country be coming to if a man with my reputation just let a thing like that go by?" He laughed. "Hell, in your part of the country they still shoot fornicators in front of a crowd of picnickers, don't they, Luther?" He leaned back and smiled and winked. "But enough of that," he said. "Tell me how you think we can screw the F.R.C."

Luther began with the unvarnished truth. He told Albright how much he'd enjoyed their meeting. He said that a great deal of what Albright said that day had stayed with him. Most of all, Luther said, he'd been impressed by Albright's cleverness in equating the format of a radio program with the blocks and columns of a newspaper's pages. He said that the memory of the radio tower rising above the palm fronds of the scalloped horizon had stayed vividly in his mind. He said, "The image of it nagged me like a clue I had to solve." And, "On top of it all," Luther said, "I kept remembering y'all saying that someday the commission was going to be telling you how strong your signal could be and even what you could broadcast."

Albright nodded sharply. "Count on it, Cowboy," he said.

"I have no doubt but that you're right," Luther said. "I have *no* doubt."

"The goddamn federal government," Albright said. His eyes were bright.

"Del Rio," Luther continued, "as y'all can guess by its name, is right *on* the border, so folks go back and forth across the river and think nothing of it. In fact, it never fails to impress me what a puny little river it is to be an international border. Hell, there's a local creek that runs through Del Rio that's almost as wide as the Rio Grande is."

Luther next described the moment he felt he'd begun to solve the clue. He said he'd been leaving Villa Acuña one afternoon when he was struck by Mexico's accessibility—it was in some sense simply the next town over—and at the same time its, well, to put it simplistically, its absolute foreignness. Luther said, "I know this is hardly an original perception, but I think it might be a useful one in the context of your concerns."

His idea was plain enough, Luther said, and here is what it was: Build a station in Villa Acuña, just across the border, but beyond the reach of our government's laws, insusceptible to its irritating whims. Aim the signal back into America and make it as powerful as you can, as you wish. "I am no engineer, Haskell," Luther said, "and so I don't know the details of how a person would do this. But I'm sure he could. The Calles government is just like old Diaz's. It'll do anything for American businessmen. All it wants is the usual *mordida.*"

"The *mordida*?" Albright asked.

" 'The bite.' The bribe," Luther said.

"Ah, of course." Albright smiled. He sat quietly for a long moment. His face was working hard through a run of squints and frowns. Then he got up and walked toward his wall of windows, weaving among his Louis Quatorze islands. When he reached his desk, he leaned on it and worked his feet free of his shoes. He flexed his stockinged toes so that they kneaded the carpet. He said nothing.

At last, still standing by his desk, he said, "Two questions. First, I don't know that you could get a radio signal to travel that far and sharpen it that narrowly, all the way back to my listeners in Los Angeles. So why shouldn't I build it directly south of *here*? And second, what's in it for you, Cowboy, if I put up a station somewhere in Mexico?"

Luther nodded and smiled. "The answer's the same to both questions," he said. "I'm not talking about your station in Villa Acuña. I'm talking about your investing in *my* station in Villa Acuña."

Sitting at the desk in his old office, Luther picked up the day's stack of twenty letters, which Peter O'Malley had selected with the help of four stenographers from the hundreds that arrived in Del Rio every day. As the stenographers removed and filed the dollar that Luther insisted must accompany each correspondence, they quickly scanned its contents. They knew generally what to look for and if a letter seemed like one Luther might want to read on the air they passed it on to O'Malley.

Luther glanced at the letter on the top of the pile. It was written by a man named Oscar Nesseck, who farmed wheat and barley near Dillard, South Dakota. "Dr. Mathias," it began, "Mrs. Oscar Nesseck and I want to tell you how much joy it brings us to hear your voice over the radio. We get your signal most nights, though there's always the frequent fadeouts, of course. You are a blessing from God so far as we're concerned, as we go several weeks at a time without seeing so much as another human face. Especially with the wind and dust like they is presently, there are many days when we cannot see out to the barn which is a distance of thirty yards."

Oscar Nesseck asked Luther if he'd heard about the dust storms, if word that the Dakotas were blowing away had reached as far as Del Rio. In a long paragraph he detailed what had become his family's daily life. He described them waiting in their house for a sense that the sky was lightening from black to deepest gray—the shade that had come to define daylight and the signal for him and his son to wrap bandannas over their faces and hurry outside. He wrote of how they groped toward the barn where the mules and milk cows stood stunned to immobility by the ever-blowing dust. He said that when they reached the animals they inevitably found that foot-deep dunes of dirt had shoaled in around their legs. Meanwhile, Oscar Nesseck wrote, his wife spent her waking hours inside their house sweeping dirt into piles. She sealed its walls with gummed paper strips normally used for wrapping postal packages, then sat at her table and watched the walls darken from dirt that blew in through pores too small to see.

Oscar Nesseck observed that God always seemed to offer something good—which is why he believed Luther's voice was Heaven-sent—to balance His punishments, and that the dust storms were the hardest punishments he had so far known. He said it was obvious to him that the world had done something unforgivable to get God this angry, though he couldn't for the life of him think what it might be. The coming repeal of Prohibition was the best he'd been able to conjure, he said.

In the margin of the letter Luther scribbled "story of Job."

At last, Oscar Nesseck described his symptoms. "I am dizzy several times in the course of a day. I fall down. I myself am of the opinion that the black I cough up from my lungs is the culprit. Many nights, I vomit dirt."

Luther turned the letter over and here was where he read, "Also, Dr. Mathias, I am now having trouble with that part of me which inspires my private needs, or used to. It is a concern which I am shy to spell out here, though I trust you will be able to guess what I mean, as I have heard you address these matters regularly on your radio program with a way of saying things that makes it clear you understand."

Luther circled this paragraph. Its tone of blushing vagueness was the one he always looked for.

In closing, Oscar Nesseck wrote that he and his wife were sure they knew what Luther looked like, just from the sound of his voice. They had decided he was tall and broad-boned. They pictured an open, friendly face. He was fair-complexioned and had brown hair that made a high wave in front. "Would we be close, Dr. Mathias?" Oscar Nesseck asked. "I bet we are."

Luther put the letter aside and worked through the rest of the pile, choosing four more of the twenty to read on the air. He made appropriate notes in their margins. He wrote "microscopical exam" and "contiguous and in juxto-position with prostate gland." He wrote "dementia praecox." In these moments he was a poet of a thrillingly severe language of pseudo-medicine. His pencil hovered momentarily over the page while his mind sought persuasive phrases. Their rhythm and their tone were all that mattered to him.

Haskell Albright, naturally enough, had been surprised to hear that Luther wanted a radio station for himself and he responded with a series of fundamental questions. Luther's answers provoked still further questions, but he'd thoughtfully anticipated his meeting with Albright and he was not caught unprepared. It was, all in all, a delicate exercise in altering misconceptions and Luther was exactly as honest as he needed to be. When Albright asked, "Why don't you just build the thing with your own money?" Luther said that Albright was speaking of money he didn't have. "I thought you were Billy's cousin," Albright said. "I thought you were rich. I thought you owned about ten thousand cows." Luther nodded. For all the reasons that he wished to preserve Billy Boswell's good will he saw no need to say that he wasn't his cousin. So he replied, "I never said I was rich. Just because *Billy's* rich, that doesn't mean I am." Then he smiled and added, "Just look at it, Haskell—your assuming I was rich—as an instance in your life when you saw into the future."

When Albright asked him, simply, *why* he wished to build a station, Luther nodded and paused. Then he matter-of-factly began to explain his rejuvenation specialty and his need to reach a wide population. He told Albright he had learned that his was not a call that local men, burdened by the sense they'd be found out, responded to. Luther had thought hard about how he should present the concept and the credo to Albright. At first, he'd decided he should make it immediately clear that there was a distance between rejuvenation's rationale and his belief in it. He was eager not to seem a fool in Albright's eyes. But finally Luther felt there was always the chance, however infinitesimal, that Albright would himself hear a note of something attractive in it all. Or that he might take offense at a salesman's open cynicism. So Luther had concluded that he should play it safe and count on being able to shift his tone as necessary.

"Rejuvenation," said Albright.

"That's right, Haskell," Luther said. He regarded Albright's face. It was absent all expression.

Albright nodded. "I've heard about it," he said. "They were talking about it at that dinner for Wallace Reed a while back. God, what a hideous affair *that* was. I can't imagine what I had in mind when I decided to give it. Because I feel sorry for Wally, I guess, the pathetic fop. Anyway, I heard people talking about it. Somebody there said that Larry Lancaster, I think it was Larry, had been to Paris to see your man, Vodka."

"Voronoff," Luther said.

"That was a joke, Luther," Albright said. "Your man's a Russian, isn't he? Vodka's Russian, isn't it? 'V'? 'V'? I was making a joke. You're awfully goddamn earnest, all of a sudden." He looked at Luther. "So," he said, "you think this rejuvenation is the thing mankind's been waiting for."

Luther held his reply in the hope that Albright's face might now give him something. When it didn't, he decided to risk his sense of Albright's attitude. "I think," he said, "that it's what *I've* been waiting for."

"Meaning?" Albright asked.

"Meaning, that with your help at the start, I'll make a fortune."

Albright nodded slowly several times. "You know," he said at last, "while you were talking just now, I thought I was going to have to go into my closet over there and put my trout waders on." At last, he smiled. "That's how high the bull crap was rising in this room, Cowboy."

"Oh, Haskell," Luther said, smiling, too. "I can stack it like that all day long and far into the night." Together, he and Albright laughed for half a minute. Then they got down to work and over the next several hours they decided the financing, Albright's graduating percentage, and his willingness to refer engineers and technicians. They even speculated on the general nature of the station's music and its features, anything that might fill the hours not devoted to Luther's voice. Albright urged Luther to think of other things to sell to listeners. "I have no idea what they might be. It's your part of the world, they're your people, Cowboy."

Luther was elated. At one point, he stopped and mentally sniffed the air, pretending to himself that it held the scent of roses. At the end of the day, on a gust of enthusiasm, he said, "Hell, Haskell, y'all can sell your station here. Let somebody else worry about the F.R.C.!"

Luther thought he glimpsed a patronizing thinness in Albright's smile. "As I imagine it," Albright said, "the programming on your station's going to be awfully goddamn primitive. I mean by that that I suspect it *should* be, the kind of listeners you'll attract, with the exception of the occasional cultured fool like Larry Lancaster who couldn't make his pecker stiff if he kept it in a splint. But you see, Luther, I've got my name to protect." And therefore, Albright said, he'd continue to own in a highly public way his Los Angeles station with its symphony broadcasts and, as a matter of fact, he would insist that his interest in Luther's stay a secret.

Luther fought off a sense of insult. He said, "Fine. If we make the kind of money I think we will, it won't matter a wart on a rat's hind end what the F.R.C. tells your station it can't do."

Albright looked at Luther. "I'm serious, Cowboy," he said, "about keeping it a secret." There was suddenly a meanness in his eyes unlike anything Luther had ever seen. It was as though he'd called it up from some bottomless reserve he hoarded in his soul.

Albright said, "What you plan to do is tawdry and unsavory. So I'm following a hunch here that keeping my involvement a secret is something you can do. It's a hunch based mostly, I suppose, on the simple fact that you don't live in this town. The idea of a secret in this town is when you don't tell your dog. People here think I'm successful because I'm brilliant and ruthless, but in fact it's because I'm the only living human being in Los Angeles who can keep a secret. You can't begin to measure the advantage that gives me when I'm trying to sell somebody something for a lot more than it's worth and I know more about him than he knows about me."

"I can keep a secret," Luther said. "It's one of the things I do best."

Albright's claim, that alone in Los Angeles he valued secrecy, had brought Billy Boswell and Alyce Rae even more to Luther's mind. The lengths to which Billy had gone to keep his surgery a secret. The document, swearing secrecy, he'd insisted Luther sign. Alyce's clandestine visit to the guest house. Their subsequent letters, written in secrecy, urging secrecy.

Once Luther had known he'd be returning to Los Angeles, thoughts of Billy and of Alyce had begun to occupy him. He'd thought about what to tell Billy. He'd even briefly imagined offering Billy the chance to help finance the spreading of the message, to help thousands of others just as he'd been helped. But he'd decided, given Billy's personality, that he'd be inviting trouble. Instead, he'd simply tell Billy that his letter had inspired him to spread the healing word to many, many, many men.

Over the months, Alyce Rae had filled Luther's mind—where he could think of her with a sense of cool achievement, where the past remained the past and the future would repeat it—but he'd been surprised, as he prepared for his trip, by the degree to which she also stirred his heart. He'd reminded himself of the conclusion he'd come to after receiving her letter. But then he would feel again the air's thrilling tension in the guest cottage bedroom, he would watch the shade of her eyes move among its many greens, and he'd say to himself that he simply had to see her. On the day he departed, he hadn't reached a decision.

Though we've been skeptical of the myth of idyllic train travel in America at this time, its most basic feature, its enviable pace, remains unarguable. People traveling by train were placed in pockets of time, away from their ordinary lives, in which to contemplate, to speculate, to change their minds and moods. We know how this experience worked on Billy Boswell as he rode from Los Angeles to Del Rio to claim his Alyce. But for Luther, traveling preoccupied in the opposite direction over the Sunset Route of the Southern Pacific, it gave a chance for his mind to overcome his heart. So by the time his train pulled into Central Station he'd decided what to do. He would see Billy alone. He'd describe his grand plan, thanking Billy for inspiring him. He'd mention Albright's help and money, an impressive thing indeed, implying Albright's confidence. And he'd rely on Billy to convey all this to Alyce.

But when Luther received Haskell Albright's look of meanness, he saw the risk in letting Billy know he was even in Los Angeles. And so, as it happened, neither Billy nor Alyce learned of his visit.

The telephone rang in his old Del Rio office. Luther lifted its earpiece and said into the receiver, "This is Doctor Mathias," though he already knew it was Peter O'Malley.

He heard O'Malley say, "It's nearly seven-thirty, Doctor M."

Luther glanced at the schedule that was tacked to his wall. He read,

7:15–7:30—Fiddler Bob (sponsored by Man-O-Ree laxative).
7:30–7:45—Fenoglio the Master Accordionist
(by Hamlin's Wizard Oil).
7:45–8:00—Brother James and Sisters, gospel singers
(by Kolorbak hair dye).
8:00–8:30—Dr. Luther Mathias and The Medical Question Box.
8:30–9:00—Cowboy Buck Winter
(by Peruna and the Buck Winter Songbook).

"Is Bob finishing?" he asked O'Malley, who monitored the programming from his apartment in the St. Charles.

"Yeah," O'Malley said.

At the radio station in Villa Acuña, Fiddler Bob, the Champion Fiddler of Arkansas, was filling the studio with a sweet assault of mountain music. He was a tall, skinny man with oily black hair, whose playing style was clean and impetuous. He paused briefly when he finished a song to lean into the microphone and announce the next one in a high Ozark twang. Then he straightened up, pushed his hair back off his forehead, and began again, letting the music elaborate itself.

Outside, as Fiddler Bob played, hectic veins of lightning burst from the tops of the three broadcasting towers. Around this sudden jagged brilliance green coronas of light shone strongly, then dimly, then radiantly again, all in all a lustrous excess caused by the station's extraordinary power. Luther's chief engineer, a man named Travis Fenbow, had built a massive transmitter of jerry-rigged genius: cables and amplifiers and cooling ponds of water, through all of which ran, with an intestinal intricacy, a network of treated glass tubes that glowed from the heat of the water it directed. Luther himself had no idea how any of it worked. When he'd first discussed the building of the transmitter with Fenbow, he'd contributed only one specification, as Haskell Albright had insisted: that it be powerful enough to send its signal to Los Angeles. Albright had told Luther that he believed in investments he could actually see and touch. The hell with stocks and bonds. He liked to own things that he could, on a whim, direct his chauffeur to drive past. This is why he owned newspapers and put up buildings and bought vast tracts of land. Albright figured, then, that if he couldn't drive past Luther's station on his way about town, he wanted to be able to *hear* the goddamn thing.

As it happened, the best and cheapest land Luther found for the station was the barren hillside of the burned-out *zona roja*. No one in Villa Acuña had been interested in resettling it. The people of the village sensed the spirits saying no. And they feared that the *Cristeros* might return to take revenge on anyone who built upon the ashes of that night. When Luther first pictured his station at its summit, he'd asked himself how he'd feel about driving up the hillside every night and he'd decided it would be the ideal way to honor Lydia.

And so the lively scratching of Fiddler Bob flowed from the microphone, through the enormous transmitter in the adjoining room, and out to the station's three three-hundred-foot towers atop the hill, an amplified transmission of five hundred thousand watts that fanned northward from Acuña through the evening ether (the term of the times) and broadly into the American night.

"I'll be ready to go in two minutes," Luther told O'Malley.

"I'll be waiting on South Main in the Packard," said O'Malley.

It was not until Luther's return trip from Los Angeles, while the train took on passengers at the Langtry, Texas, station, that his reviewing of his arrangement with Albright yielded the term *partner*. He had taken on another partner. He thought the actual word. Then he said it to himself as he looked out at the desert and watched a massive tumbleweed, God's untidy try at baling, scurry by.

C h a p t e r

14

*F*iddler Bob also served as the station's principal announcer. When in this role, he called himself Brother Bill Loomis and he spoke at the register of his natural Texas bass. Now he was bending to his microphone to finish reading an advertisement for Kolorbak hair dye. "Send just one dollar to Kolorbak, Del Rio eight, Texas. That's Kolorbak, K,o,l,o,r,b,a,k. Del Rio. D,e,l,R,i,o, Texas. And remember that Kolorbak is fully guaranteed for as long as you live. The makers of Kolorbak don't see any use in guaranteeing it after you have died. We're sure you all agree!"

He nodded his head deliberately three times, then continued, "And now it's time for Doctor Luther Mathias, helper of mankind, who addresses you at this hour each weekday evening from the study of his beautiful home in Del Rio, Texas."

Luther sat behind a desk in the station's second studio. "My dear friends," he began, "this is Doctor Mathias saying good evening to you all as I do at this time every evening." He spoke closely into the microphone. His eyes were shut and the picture of a crowd gathering around him was forming in his mind. He saw their slightly uplifted faces. He heard their unanimous hush, that most eloquent of sounds.

"As I speak with you all tonight, I look out the windows of my study and across my rose gardens bursting with blooms and I am struck once again by the splendor of this special place of sun and plenitude, this desert Eden, Del Rio, Texas." He said, "I am watching at this very moment the blanket of night lowering itself over the mesquite and draping the stately salt cedars. How fortunate Doctor Mathias is to have found this paradise of palm trees and sweet Old Sol in which to do his healing work." Luther opened his eyes. The picture of the crowd was firm in his mind. He imagined himself standing above it on the seat of the medicine show wagon. He saw his words drifting down and softly touching all the faces. He saw their expressions easing toward the necessary smile.

Luther said, "I take up now some of the correspondence that has come to the Medical Question Box. It is Doctor Mathias's wish that he could answer each of your letters at length, but to do so would consume every waking moment of every day, and would leave no time to minister to the many patients at the Mathias Clinic."

He said, "Here's a letter from L. R. in Hoyt, Nebraska, a plea for help written from the slough of suffering and frustration." He read from the letter's detailing of gastric ulcers. The seizing nausea. The in-sucking cramps. He edited nimbly as he read. (No euphemism came to him for L. R.'s blood-streaked shit.) "Now, listen carefully, L. R. I want you to send immediately for my formula Number 16. Be sure you're writing this down. That's Doctor Mathias's Number 16, in care of the Mathias Clinic, Del Rio, Texas, and I will send you, collect, a three-month supply. The cost to you will be fifteen dollars, and I will pay the postage." He paused, then spoke more softly. "I know you're listening, my friend, and if you'll do as I say you will soon be restored to a life of health and vigor."

As it happened, L. R. was not listening. Only minutes before the broadcast had begun he'd been called from his chair in front of his radio. He'd risen with painful effort to answer a knock on his door, and had been asked by a neighbor if he would come with him to look at the man's stalled Chevrolet. L. R.'s gift with engines was legend around Hoyt. But though he missed his diagnosis, though he got no help from Dr. Mathias, his letter was heard by Arthur Deedle, in What Cheer, Iowa, who listened every night to the Medical Question Box. Deedle came to full attention when he heard L. R.'s letter, for the nature of his troubles seemed to match L. R.'s exactly. They also fit Whitcomb Blunt's, in Paris, Colorado. And the details of L. R.'s suffering were precisely those that Chester Halsey had borne for months in Small, Missouri. When he heard Dr. Mathias speaking of them, Chester Halsey felt as though the Doctor's hands were moving over his body. He felt as though the Doctor's touch were visiting his pain. And so, like Arthur Deedle, and Whitcomb Blunt, and dozens more across the country who were listening to their troubles in the lines of L. R.'s letter, Chester Halsey took a dull pencil and addressed a note, asking for the formula. Two mornings after Arthur Deedle had mailed his order to Del Rio, he stepped outside, looked left and right, and seeing no one watching, sprinted twenty yards in a kind of palsied trot. It was a foolish burst of effort that left him alarmingly weak for the next ten days. But the lesson for Arthur Deedle, what he thought about as he lay in his bed, was that he'd run twenty yards for the first time in years. Indeed, nearly everyone who ordered Dr. Mathias's Number 16 this evening would begin to feel new hope spreading through them as they waited for three ink-blue bottles of generic aspirin, worth perhaps a dollar fifty, which a crew of local women in a large room at the clinic filled from a supply kept in huge brown jars.

Luther looked at the clock. He shuffled the letters in his hands. He quickly proceeded to identify gallstones. He diagnosed a crippling prostate. He prescribed massive doses of his Number 20, the same generic aspirin in an impressive jade-green bottle.

Next he picked up Oscar Nesseck's letter. He saw his notes in its margins and the circle he had drawn around its paragraph of confession. He reached for a Bible he kept on the desk.

"Doctor Mathias is speaking now to that good man in Dillard, South Dakota, who wrote recently, and he's also addressing his loyal wife, the loving mother of their brave son. Let me say to you first, my friend, that my prayers are with you and your family as you struggle through the days of dust and desperation you describe so movingly in your letter." He paged his Bible as he spoke. "And I want you to know that Mother Nature is demonstrating her merciless temper hereabouts as well, so that the hardship she is currently causing you up there in South Dakota has begun to be felt by the good people of Texas, too. Not in Del Rio, which God has for His own reasons which we dare not question seen fit to bless with sun and flora and an abundance of clear water, all in perfect proportion. No, not here. But very close by, in the Quemado Valley and most certainly all across our Panhandle, a drought grows worse and worse by the day, reminding us of the words of Job, whose despondency reached such depths that he came to curse the very day of his birth." Luther found the passage in his Bible and read. " 'Let that day be darkness,' Job said of his birth day. 'Let not God regard it from above' and 'neither let the light shine upon it.' "

He turned the Bible's slick, thin pages. He said, "I am sure that you must feel that way about your days of darkness in Dillard. I'm sure there are times you must believe that you'll never see again the light of the sun through all that black dust. I'm sure you suspect that God has chosen not to regard you from above. But I urge you, friend, to keep the story of Job's suffering in mind and remember that his faith was so tested that he would say at his lowest point, 'Mine eye shall no more see good.' "

Again, Luther quickly turned the Bible's pages. "But as a devout man of God, you know very well that Job did see good again, once he'd accepted the Lord's will. And the Bible tells us that 'the Lord blessed the latter end of Job more than his beginning.' " He closed the Bible and pushed it away.

In Dillard, South Dakota, Oscar Nesseck had gone rigid in his chair beside the radio the moment he'd realized Luther was referring to him. He'd felt his heart pause and contract in his chest. His neck instantly reddened. Peripherally, he saw his wife, Mary Ellen, also assume an alert posture in the room's other chair. He felt her eyes on him and he refused to turn and meet them.

Oscar Nesseck was a wide-framed, awkward man. He had a long face and very small ears, which were shaped like snail shells. His cheeks were permanently chapped. Were he to appear as a character in a historical romance of the Great Plains, he'd inevitably be described as raw-boned. He was raw-boned.

"Friend in Dillard," Luther said, "I can't quiet the wind. I can't take the dust out of the sky, and I know that you're not asking me to. I know from the sincere tone of your letter that you understand such things are God's province. But I *can* help the problems you are having with your health, for that is within my province, the province of modern medical science."

He turned the letter over to the circled paragraph. "Now friend, this is naturally a matter of deepest anxiety to you, which, if it's any consolation, you know from listening to me every night afflicts hundreds, even thousands, of good men like yourself. It troubles them just as severely and unfairly as it is troubling you and I want to say to you that you should feel no shame whatsoever, although your letter hints to me that you do. You are concerned, of course, and that is proper. But there is simply no reason for you to feel embarrassed or defeated, if you will only remember that the restoring of your sexual interest and activity—yours and anyone's who likewise suffers—this is the very mission of the Mathias Clinic. It is the sum and substance of the healing that goes on daily in Del Rio and which gives all of us here our sense of reward.''

In truth, Oscar and Mary Ellen Nesseck had never enjoyed an especially sexual marriage. This had as much to do with his deep confusion—his waves of lust against a broad idea of sin—as with Mary Ellen's reticence. Still, over the twelve years of their marriage, they had infrequently joined in apologetic sex and on these occasions Oscar Nesseck had met at least the definition of performance. But as he'd become more obsessed with his troubles—the relentless wind, their impending ruin—Oscar Nesseck had mostly forgotten about sex. If he thought about it at all, it seemed, like so much else, a feature of his life before the plague.

Then, some months ago, he'd begun to hear Luther Mathias's nightly broadcasts, which his radio received with acceptable quality. If the dust storms were a curse to South Dakotans, they were a blessing for Luther's radio station, for in many parts of the Plains his signal was the only one with power enough to penetrate the thickened skies. Weaker local stations, what few there were in 1933, sent their sounds into the air and all a listener heard was a wild and angry static, as though the voice of the blowing dust itself were being broadcast.

Both Oscar Nesseck and his wife had welcomed Dr. Mathias into their home as a guest against their loneliness. His voice was warm and it was wise. It spoke regularly and lovingly and fearfully of God, as the Nessecks did themselves. But as Oscar Nesseck listened every evening, he began to be reminded not so much of his sexual past as of his new indifference. And the more he thought about it, the less able he was to end it.

In the studio in Villa Acuña, Luther's words took on a lively delicacy. "Now I want you to listen carefully, my friend, for if you are serious about being restored to sexual health, you must make plans immediately for your journey to Del Rio."

He said, "You have heard me explain—in the plainest language I know—how and *why* my operation works so completely and predictably. You have heard me speak of my years of research. I know you have heard me describe the way all the various glands—the pituitary, the pineal, the thyroid, and et cetera—how they form a linked chain of command inside each and every one of us.

"You have listened faithfully to Doctor Mathias explain the order of power, that is to say, the hierarchy of these glands inside us all, and have heard his conclusion, which is also shared by the other international experts in this field: that it is the sex glands which are the prime, the predominant, the all-powerful of glands."

Oscar Nesseck had already tried certain remedies. One afternoon, alone in the barn, he lay down in the hay and took out his penis and thought of the flesh-dimpled stripper, lines of dirty sweat penciling her rolls of fat, who had thrilled him at the carnival in Dillard when he was twelve years old. With her image in his mind, he stroked himself for several minutes but his penis continued to lie in his hand, limp as his hope.

One recent morning he'd walked to his wife as she'd sat at the table and without a word began to unbutton her dress. She'd looked up at him as he worked down the row that ran between her breasts. His look was concentration; the tip of his tongue was in the corner of his mouth. Confusion, then interest, then confusion crossed her round face. He peeled away her undergarments until she sat before him, naked to the waist. He sat down and looked at her breasts. He could not remember the last time he'd seen them in daylight, although daylight in Dillard was now no more than dusk. Neither Oscar Nesseck nor his wife moved. Neither spoke. Oscar Nesseck's eyes did not stray. Perhaps a minute passed, an extremely long time to behave in this way. Oscar Nesseck concentrated his look on his wife's long nipples, which curled like commas from their areolae. And all that Oscar Nesseck was aware of, as he watched Mary Ellen's chest gently rise and fall, was the sound of the wind and the grit of dust on the surface of the table. He got up and walked to her and helped her rearrange her clothes. That night, he wrote his letter to Dr. Mathias.

"I know, my friend in Dillard, that you yearn for those yesterdays of sweet and Heaven-sanctioned ardor, and consequently you would wish Doctor Mathias to speak candidly. Therefore, I'm certain you will hear me in the healing spirit that's intended when I say that the only thing wrong with you is that your master engines, your sex glands, your gonads, are experiencing what you might think of as a blocked fuel line. So that even though you're as healthy as in your younger days, when you were that strong and frisky stallion among the mares in the corral, your gonads are not able right now to release their fuel. And the result is that you are sitting around like a feeble old geezer in a rocking chair, and that flame, that flame which used to burn so strongly, is now but a snuffed-out wick of memory.''

Moving back and forth between two adjoining rooms on his clinic's second floor, Luther had this afternoon performed five operations. They were identical in every nuance of procedure and technique. The quickest had lasted nineteen minutes; the longest twenty-three. In each room, two nurses assisted him. The women were gowned in white. Bands of white cloth were carefully wound around their heads and faces in the antiseptic fashion of the day. They looked like stylish summer Muslims, were there such a thing, wearing seasonal white purdah. They looked like mummies whose bindings had excluded their eyes.

"You have heard me read over the air how many dozens of letters from my former patients? Letters which describe the painlessness of the Mathias Operation. You have heard their expressions of relief and rejoicing—I can think of no more fitting word—at their return to the realm of the sexually vigorous.''

To begin each surgery, one of Luther's nurses took the patient's scrotum in her hands and very gently stretched its skin between his testicles until it formed a puckered axis. Then the other nurse injected a needle of local anesthetic along this axis. No longer was a suction mask of general anesthetic used, as it had been in Los Angeles in 1927, when Billy Boswell had drifted innocent in sleep.

Luther's nurses maintained a rigorously professional decorum. They gave the atmosphere of the operating room not the slightest opportunity for a word or a wink even modestly risque. If anything, they erred on the side of earnestness. Many nurses at this time, in this culture, were not especially trained or necessarily schooled. Many, if not most, did work of simple maintenance, their jobs some hybrid of handmaid and charwoman. In fact, nursing was regarded by some in this part of the country as less than respectable work for women. Nurses saw men naked. They touched their flesh; they bathed them. Not surprisingly then, the women who nursed at Luther's clinic were open to more than the usual suspicions, given what they did, the parts of men they touched. Imagine the rumors. Imagine the jokes.

Luther met this attitude as he had come to meet any problem: with the money required. He paid his nurses very well.

"So, dear friend in Dillard, I put it to you. Will you come to us here in Del Rio right away? Will you make your decision, tonight, that some find hard to make, even though they are suffering, as you are, from this deep and needless shame? Even though they are living through years of what could be the most gratifying pleasure, but are exhibiting instead the gelding's sad and pitiful resignation?"

When Luther entered the operating room, his eyes looked only at the patient. He shut them and nodded in a reassuring gesture. He said something soft and friendly, which, muffled through his surgical mask, the patient could not understand. Then he turned to his work. In his hands, surgical tools had become responsive as digits. He held an instrument he wasn't using in a V of his fingers, then moved it into place as dexterously as a magician walks a coin across his hand.

"Will you take that first step back to virile manhood? I am here to help you take it, but you're the one who must decide."

After making certain that the patient was anesthetized, Luther held out his hand to receive a scalpel and with it sliced the scrotum in exactly the way he'd opened Billy Boswell's. Using forceps, a nurse parted the skin, just as the Canadian zookeeper had parted Billy's. Then Luther eased the probe into the incision and moved it toward the vas deferens. With the flat blade of the probe, he lifted the vas and it emerged through the incision, a hatching inch worm. In the glare of the overhead lamp, it appeared new as birth and intricately coiled. Luther's blade held the vas free of the scrotum. A nurse was ready with a vial of mercurochrome, which she, like all his nurses, had been told was the testicular extract, ground from young and fertile monkey glands, that would rinse the cord to patency as it worked its resurrection. It was, of course, now red, where it had formerly been bright blue.

Luther made a second incision, an eyelash slit, along the length of the vas and directed two drops of mercurochrome into the cut. Then he eased the vas back through, stitched the scrotum up, made a slice above the other testicle, and did it all again.

Such was the surgery that Luther had devised: a prosaic cure for an imaginative ailment. Ray White, of course, held that the two should not be mixed, but he had worked in a time of primeval science and could not have imagined the persuasive power of blood and gleaming instruments and fastidious procedure that Luther had combined to create a solemn rhetoric.

"Everyone here at the Mathias Clinic, my staff of assistants and kind, caring nurses—truly angels of mercy, each and every one—they stand ready to serve you from the moment you arrive. All my medical knowledge and my gifts as a surgeon—which I can take no credit for, but which God in his doling out of human talents among His children determined to assign me—are available to you when you come."

As Oscar Nesseck sat listening to Dr. Mathias speak personally to him, he was held in the grasp of two conflicting feelings. It seemed, first of all, as though there were now another presence in the room and after all the months of ever-growing isolation it inspired an unsettling sensation in him. In the time since the dust storms had begun, his house had grown steadily smaller in Oscar Nesseck's mind and was no longer nearly large enough to accommodate the three of them—his wife, himself, and now the living radio—and Oscar Nesseck felt an impulse to bolt from his chair.

But just as powerfully, Dr. Mathias's exclusive attention to his troubles seemed to Oscar Nesseck an intimate miracle. It is not hyperbole to say that he felt something close to a sense of being chosen. So he sat where he was, the urge to flee and the wish to stay resulting in a posture of astonished equipoise.

"It is obvious to me, from the words of your letter, that it is what you truly want to do. It is clear you understand that your coming to the clinic will be an action taken not just for yourself, but for your blessed wife and for your future of sexually contented married life, which is, after all, her due as well as yours, according to God's plan." Luther was leaning pronouncedly into the microphone. Sweat now glazed his forehead and ringed his neck beneath his opened collar. "Will you take the necessary action and book passage for what you should think of as a well-deserved vacation, considering all that you've been through, on the sun-kissed banks of the silvery Rio Grande?"

Mary Ellen Nesseck spoke at last. "It's you, ain't it, Oscar?" she said to her husband. "Ain't it?" she repeated when he failed to answer her.

"No, it ain't," Oscar Nesseck said. He continued to keep his eyes on the face of the radio.

"Why would you put that in a letter? I can see why you might want to write to Doctor Mathias about the dizzy spells, but why would you ask him about the other?"

"It ain't me he's talkin' to," Oscar Nesseck said. He was nearly faint with confusion. His eyes narrowed on the radio, which suddenly seemed less ally than betrayer. It had never occurred to him that Dr. Mathias would read his letter on the air.

"Who else could it be, Oscar?" Mary Ellen Nesseck said. "In Dillard? With a manly complaint?"

"Could be any of a dozen," Oscar Nesseck snapped defensively. "You heard what Doctor Mathias said. There's thousands of sufferers, and no shame in it either."

Sweat had started down Luther's cheeks and had spread beneath his arms. In the time since he'd begun his broadcast, a steady transformation had as usual taken place. He'd entered the studio with his acquired public air of cool reserve but he had about him now the intimate coarseness of a bayou politician. He said, "Now, when you come, be sure it's with your money order for five hundred dollars. I know that might seem like a lot of money to you. But I can assure you it is an amount that barely covers the staggering costs here at the Mathias Clinic." It was also the amount he'd received from Billy Boswell and Luther had kept it as his price, a sort of talisman.

"It is the simple proposition of your spending just four or five days, an investment that will yield a return of a lifetime of rediscovered desire. To a patriotic and highly intelligent American such as you are, there's surely no doubt what your decision will be."

In his room at the Mathias Clinic, a man named Taggart Boyle, from Paint Rock, Texas, was sitting up and maneuvering his bed pan beneath him, readying himself for his first postsurgical piss. He'd held it in as long as he could, but now the moment had arrived. He saw two purple circles, evenly described, spreading from his incisions. He felt a muted soreness around his balls, but that was all. Taggart Boyle had been assured that there would be negligible discomfort following the surgery but he had not been able to persuade himself of that. On the contrary, he'd told himself to be ready to hurt. He'd remembered what he'd felt when he was kicked one morning by his best milk cow. How, he'd asked himself, could the aftermath of this be any less than that blinding pain? His sack had been cut open, twice! His balls, his balls! had been somehow sliced.

He sat perched above the pan. He contracted the muscles of his inner thighs, wishing release while also fighting it. A drop came and then a flow. It made a sound as it struck the metal pan, the musical *pah-zing!* of an udder's milk against the side of a bucket. Again he was relieved at the absence of true pain. He looked down into the pan. He saw that his urine was red. He panicked for an instant, thinking it blood. Then he remembered he'd been told he would know of the surgery's success by the strong and lovely red that would color his first urine. Now he watched and saw that it was a red more exotic than blood's. He relaxed as he pissed this quite impressive red and felt doubly reassured by the pan-filling evidence that something surgically profound had indeed been done to him.

"I'll be waiting to see you in Del Rio. Write to me immediately, tonight, to reserve your room, as the demand for the Mathias Operation grows more urgent every day and the space at the clinic is naturally limited."

Luther glanced up at his clock again. It was twenty-nine minutes after eight. He saw Travis Fenbow placing on a turntable a transcription disk, which he assumed was Cowboy Buck's; Cowboy Buck, the former Robuck Winter, who'd become in these five years radio's most popular western singer.

Luther believed that the performers on XALM should resort to transcriptions sparingly. He'd decided, when the station began five years ago, that live performances made discernibly better-sounding music than did transcriptions and he told everyone who auditioned for him as much. In truth, the overlays of static and the thin, tinny quality of radio reception at this time blurred meaningful distinction between true and transcribed sounds. But Luther held to his belief absolutely.

"My friend, I can break through those clouds which the winds of ill fortune have blown into your life to darken your blue skies of youthful zest. But only if you come to the clinic in Del Rio will the sun of bright amours shine for you again." He paused a perfect beat.

"And if you do, it will." He swallowed and whispered. His voice was barely audible. "This is Doctor Mathias saying good night. Until tomorrow night, God bless you all." He closed his eyes and slumped back in his chair.

Travis Fenbow nodded and when Luther opened his eyes Fenbow gave him the OK sign. Still slumped in his chair, he watched Brother Bill Loomis bend to his microphone again.

Mary Ellen Nesseck listened to Brother Bill say, "You've just heard Doctor Luther Mathias's Medical Question Box." She moved her foot absently back and forth in front of her. She was brushing a small pile of new dust this way and that. "Oscar," she said, to her husband's profile, "did you ask Doctor Mathias if it's right how I imagine his looks?"

After several seconds, Oscar Nesseck shook his head. "I guess he don't say anything about that if he reads your letter over the radio."

In the studio, Luther remained motionless in his chair. His thumb and index finger stroked the bridge of his nose. He seemed held by an echo and an energy of some musical piece he'd just finished playing. He'd been known to stay this way for four or five minutes after a broadcast.

When he stood up at last and came around from behind his desk, Peter O'Malley walked over to him.

"Irish," he said quietly.

"Ready to go home, Doctor M?" O'Malley asked. He gave Luther his broad and uncomplicated smile.

"Not quite," Luther said. His voice was vague, from somewhere else. He was watching the turning-table needle moving over the transcription of Cowboy Buck Winter's inimitable whine and primitive guitar. He watched coral-colored wax curling out from the needle as it cut through the coated surface of the disk.

Luther asked, "Irish, is Robuck drunk at the City Club again?" Luther thought of the thousands of Buck Winter Song Books leaving the post office in the course of a year. He thought of the dollar paid for each one. He thought of the quarter that was his from each of those dollars and the nickel from his quarter that belonged to Haskell Albright.

"I don't know," O'Malley said. He was telling the truth.

Luther said, "That's the fourth time in two weeks he's used a transcription."

"I'll find out," O'Malley said. Like everyone else in Del Rio, O'Malley had altered his behavior toward Luther as he'd grown prosperous and famous. This was especially subtle in O'Malley's case, since he was now Luther's closest aide. A working logic had evolved between the two of them that fit comfortably with O'Malley's personality. At other hours of the day, he gave Luther information and volunteered opinions. He felt free to describe his own day's banalities. He was often voluble. But he'd learned to keep his distance in the minutes after a broadcast while Luther projected, as he was doing now, a paradoxical sense of distant intensity, a force of personality that drew you in and gave you nothing.

Luther listened for a moment to one of Cowboy Buck's lyrics of love and loss and equine loyalty. He winced and shook his head. "Let's get out of here," he said.

Outside, Luther and O'Malley headed toward the Packard. Its shade of blue was coincidentally that of the glass aspirin bottles used for Number 16. They passed a small gathering of Acuñans sitting on the ground. Luther seemed not to see them. They were clustered for warmth in the cool desert night, their bodies layered with serapes. There were perhaps two dozen of them, a customary number who came every evening to sit outside the studio and watch green veins of lightning burst from the tops of the broadcasting towers as the air spilled its waste of light and language into the skies. That, at any rate, would be Travis Fenbow's, would be a Yanqui engineer's explanation of the night sky's flashing magic.

They watched Luther pass and whispered, *"El Doctor."* They roused their dozing children and pointed Luther out to them.

Chapter

15

*L*uther sat behind his desk in the walnut-paneled study of his enormous new home studying a delicate-featured man who was barely five feet tall. He wore an old wool suit that fit him much too loosely and made him appear to be a figurine. On his feet, he wore dainty patent-leather shoes tied with wide ribbon laces. He labored to keep a grip on a thin sheet of wood, three feet square, which he held in his tiny arms. There were nests of scratches and dark gray gouges on its surface.

Peter O'Malley stood beside the man, whose name was Ronnie Truehart. "I think," O'Malley said to Luther, "that Mr. Truehart might prove popular with listeners." He placed his hand on Ronnie Truehart's shoulder. "I watched him perform this afternoon. He's very good."

Luther shook his head. He said, "I don't think so, Irish. A tap dancer? Don't people need to *see* a tap dancer? Somebody singing or playing or talking, that's another thing entirely. But tap dancing, don't people have to watch the dancer dance his dance? That's essential to the appeal, isn't it?" He turned to Ronnie Truehart. "Am I right about this or not, Mr. Truehart?"

Ronnie Truehart hesitated.

Luther said, "Now don't take this personally. I'm just thinking out loud, you understand."

"Of course," said Ronnie Truehart. He smiled weakly and looked up at O'Malley. He shifted the sheet of wood in his arms.

Luther leaned back in his high leather chair and stared up at the great dark beams that crossed his new ceiling. He heard, from the ballroom adjoining his study, the sound of voices rising in competitive social chatter. As he listened he thought, A hundred and twenty-five people do make a considerable noise.

O'Malley said, "You know how much we need another program in the early evening hours." He looked down and smiled at Ronnie Truehart. "I don't mean we need to hire just anybody, Mr. Truehart. I think you're very good. As I said, I think you'd prove popular with listeners." He looked again at Luther, whose gaze remained on his ceiling beams. O'Malley said, "I think Mr. Truehart would be ideal for a sponsor like Luvolife tablets. People would listen to him tapping away to beat the band and they'd imagine his legs moving loose and easy, and when he was finished the Luvolife announcer would remind them of their aching joints and their rheumatoid stiffness.

"Or Sunway vitamins," O'Malley continued. "You know they've told us they'd prefer to sponsor something besides Mrs. Ogburn's operatic solos."

"Mrs. Ogburn. Oh, Mrs. Ogburn," Luther said to his ceiling. "Just when was it, what moment of what day, when your voice became indistinguishable from that of a forlorn duck?"

O'Malley winked at Ronnie Truehart. Ronnie Truehart gave his weak smile and rotated his neck inside his collar.

Luther listened to the voices of his employees coming from his ballroom. He was pleased that he'd decided to give the party, though he'd considered postponing it until the massive organ he'd designed was finished and installed. The organ's pipes were to be embedded in a living room wall, starting from an air reservoir located in his cellar and running the full height of the house. But there'd been numerous delays. The pipes themselves had been mismeasured and had had to be returned. The company in Boston retained to make the pedals had gone out of business, a victim of the Depression.

Listening to the sounds of his guests, Luther felt an eagerness to see his new home alive with people. He wondered if a hundred twenty-five would fill the ballroom. Since he'd moved in, ten days ago, no one but O'Malley and himself had been in it. On his first night, Luther had walked in deepest darkness across its polished floor, which had shone in the moonlight like a smoothly frozen pond. The room had felt to him as vast as a night beneath the Texas sky, inciting something close to a vague memory that had disturbed him a little.

"Where are you from, Mr. Truehart?" Luther asked. He still hadn't taken his eyes off his ceiling.

Ronnie Truehart smiled brightly, as though he'd just heard his cue. "A little town called Red Hook, Kansas, Dr. Mathias. I was born in Red Hook and I've lived there my entire life to date."

Luther lowered his look and sat forward in his chair. "And how did it happen that you found your way down here to the border to audition to tap dance on XALM?"

"Well," Ronnie Truehart said, "I listen to your station as a regular indulgence. We're lucky in that we get the signal clear most of the time. And I enjoy so many of your performers, especially Fenoglio, the accordionist, and Brother James and his Sisters. Their gospel songs are wonderful. And one night I just started dancing to the music in my living room."

"You tap dance to gospel music?"

"Well, no, I meant Fenoglio."

"So," Luther said impatiently, "you started tapping away to Fenoglio's accordion and then one night you came up with the idea that you could be on the radio, too."

O'Malley heard Luther's sarcasm, nearly scorn, and it confused him. There *was*, O'Malley recognized, something about Ronnie Truehart that made one uncomfortable. Maybe it was no more than his size and the impression his little body gave of a porcelain brittleness. But O'Malley believed a program of tap dancing was a fine idea and his motive, as always, was nothing more complicated than loyalty.

"All right," Luther said, "let's see you dance." He made hurry-up rotating motions with his hand. He himself didn't know why Truehart's presence annoyed him. Perhaps it was simply his wish to join the party. Or perhaps his mind remained engaged with all the matters he'd been reviewing with O'Malley the previous hour. The progress on the new warehouse to hold the growing inventory of pills and tablets and bottles and boxes. The plans for larger offices where employees could record and sort and answer listeners' correspondence, collect their money, and fill their orders. The shortage of rooms for those arriving in Del Rio for the Mathias Operation. The status of the government's approval of a new post office to handle the mountainous volume.

There was also Haskell Albright's recent demand that XALM's signal become even stronger or in any case pointed more powerfully toward Los Angeles. Albright had just built a new house himself and he'd not discovered until he'd moved in that he now received the station sporadically at best.

Luther watched Ronnie Truehart place his sheet of wood on the carpet, then straighten up again and stretch the cramps from his arms. He took off his suit coat and handed it to O'Malley.

"I guess you'll just have to imagine Fenoglio's accordion," Luther said.

"That's not a problem," said Ronnie Truehart. He swung his arms forward as if to spark some inner engine and his feet started over the surface of his board with syncopated sweeps of caressing epilepsies.

Luther closed his eyes and turned in his swivel chair until the back of his head was what he offered Ronnie Truehart. He judged all those who auditioned for the station in this way. He didn't want to see them. He wanted to hear the personalities they would send into the air. He wished to know what their sounds would invite him to imagine.

Ronnie Truehart watched Luther turn his back to him and he looked in confusion to O'Malley. O'Malley's smile told him not to worry and Truehart responded with a more assaultive energy. His feet swept the board with the dancer's shrewd economy while explosions of click-stomps shot about the room. Turned away, with his eyes closed, Luther listened. He cocked his head, left then right. Ronnie Truehart watched this motion and decided it was Luther's way of setting the beat, but in trying to follow it he very nearly stumbled.

What Luther was hearing confirmed his suspicion that a program of tap dance was a dreadful idea. Ronnie Truehart danced well enough, but his sounds did not inspire the necessary mystery. They were sprightly little flurries of shallow narrative and they lacked, Luther felt, the deeper oddities that music and speech by their nature contained. But he also realized he was having trouble listening to Ronnie Truehart at all. Mostly he was hearing the sounds of his guests, while his mind kept returning to the pressures of his empire, pressures that he relished as they proved to him his power.

Luther spun his chair around. Truehart immediately came to a stop. He backed his way off his board in two quick clicks.

He was panting and sweating to a degree that surprised Luther. "I still think I'm right on this, Irish, but let's try it for eight weeks and see how folks respond. Get in touch with Luvolife and Sunway tomorrow." He looked at Ronnie Truehart and said, "I'm sure you're uncommonly talented, Mr. Truehart." He started to explain his reservations again, then asked himself why he should bother.

"I'm so very grateful for the chance," Ronnie Truehart said. His little chest swelled, robined out, then he exhaled.

He bent down to pick up his board, but haste and nervousness caused him to let it slip through his hands. He groped a little desperately as he tried to get a grip and his graceless moment gave Luther a thought. Smiling, he blurted, "Mr. Truehart, we're gonna make you blind."

Ronnie Truehart stood instantly and said, "I beg your pardon?" His eyes were a fawn's.

O'Malley asked, "How's that, Doctor M?"

Luther laughed. He turned to Ronnie Truehart and said, "As Irish here has heard me say too many times, Mr. Truehart, there needs to be a little undercurrent of complication in whatever people hear on their radios and the sound of your dancing alone doesn't have it. But if they were to imagine, for instance, that you're blind, then listeners could sit there in their chairs and shake their heads and say, Would you listen to that Ronnie Truehart dance, and he's *blind*! If you give them just one little detail like that, they more than make the most of it. It agitates them. They imagine something strange, or heroic, who knows what, it doesn't matter, the important thing is you've given them a clear little particle that's also open-ended and keeps the story from being finished: He's blind, but is he a little tiny blind man or a big fat blind man? Is he a young blind boy or is he an old man from the swamps, blinded by rickets in his infancy? Did his mama teach him to dance that way? Did he learn while attending some special school for the blind? All the while they're listening, they'll be working to finish the story for themselves."

O'Malley shook his head and returned Luther's smile. "It's a very good idea, Doctor M. It's very good."

Luther said, "I trust that's all right with you, Mr. Truehart?"

"Well," Ronnie Truehart said, "I don't know. I'm not sure I can think of myself—"

"Here's how you can think of yourself," Luther interrupted. "Here's your choices: You can be Blind Ronnie Truehart, radio's most extraordinary tap dancer. Or you can be Ronnie Truehart on his way back to Kansas, carrying his sheet of wood and his silly little slippers in his hands." His voice was calm and conclusive. Sudden bursts of sound from the ballroom nearly covered it.

Ronnie Truehart paused just an instant, then he nodded.

"Fine," Luther said. "Irish will work out your wages and all the other details. Now prop up your sheet of wood someplace and he'll take you out and introduce you to all the nice folks in the other room. Fenoglio's out there. He's a feed store clerk from Waco named Clayton Fenig and he's a little shy at first, but he's a good man and you are certainly right—he can *play* the accordion."

"Fenoglio's *here*?" Ronnie Truehart said. "But this is the hour we hear his program in Red Hook."

"I let everyone use transcriptions tonight so they could come to the party." Luther watched a new blankness transform Ronnie Truehart's face at the mention of the word *transcriptions*. He said, "Irish will tell you all about transcriptions and why you should never use them except in rare emergencies." He paused. "Although, in your case, I'm not sure it would make a great deal of difference." He pointed to Ronnie Truehart's gleaming feet. "Please change back into your other shoes. I hate to think what those might do to my new floors."

Luther watched Ronnie Truehart hurry to a corner where he'd left his bag. He leaned his board against the wall and bent down to undo his ribbon laces. When he'd changed and stood again, he seemed to Luther a child awaiting praise for having learned to tie his shoes. The unctuous dwarf, Luther thought. He decided he would fire him after six weeks, no matter how many Luvolife tablets he sold. He would say Blind Ronnie Truehart somehow fell and broke his neck. Tripped over a hassock in his unfamiliar lodgings.

*   *   *

Fifteen minutes later, Luther stepped through the door from his study to his ballroom and his guests almost instantly stopped their talk and turned. The men began to clap and the women sang glad shrieks. Luther gave the crowd his unspecific smile, strong and diffuse enough to reach the far corners. His employees stood about in scattered clusters. He assessed the degree to which they filled the paneled room and was pleased to see that they looked comfortably distributed beneath the huge chandeliers.

He'd been exclusively guided in planning his house by his lasting impressions of Billy Boswell's Tudor mansion. The walnut paneling throughout had been his own idea and any consideration of scale and harmony had played no part in the planning. He'd thought of each room, in effect, as independent. The result appeared a notion to connect free-standing barns and the finished structure from without looked incohesive and carbuncular. Its white stucco exterior and red tile roof were its only unities. The roof strove to merge its many gables.

Everyone in the ballroom remained quiet. Luther raised his hand and said, "Welcome to my home, Desert Gardens. I hope you're having a fine time and I hope you like the house."

A woman standing next to Luther said, "It's beautiful, Dr. Mathias!" A woman next to her said, "I love how they carved your initials in the wood everywhere!"

"In Old English!" a third woman said.

Luther said to the women, "I was worried when I planned it that I didn't have a woman's touch to consult. I'll consider your approval a compliment, if I might." He smiled. The women competed to insist how much they loved his home. All three of them were young and skinny. They looked remarkably the same. Luther assumed they worked in some way for the clinic, for he thought he knew everyone on the small staff at the station and he had no idea who these women were.

He looked out over the room. Cigarette smoke rose to the chandeliers and had begun to nimbus thickly about the crystal baubles. Luther stood a head taller than all but a few of the people. His chief engineer, Travis Fenbow, for one, nearly matched his height. Fenbow was leaning against a wall to Luther's right. Luther spotted him and mouthed his wish to speak to him. Above the heads of others, theirs nodded in unison.

Then Luther raised his hand again and said, "There's a whole lot to eat here, and a whole lot to drink, and I'll be sorely disappointed if there's anything left at the end of the evening."

The people cheered again and a Mexican woman came up to Luther with a tray of whiskies. He took one and stepped forward, heading for Travis Fenbow. As he made his way, he smiled and waved and touched peoples' shoulders, evenly distributing the heartless intimacy of a candidate. Reaching Fenbow, he smiled and shook his hand.

"I suspect I know what's on your mind, Doc," Fenbow said. He was grinning.

"You heard about Haskell's 'request'?" Luther said.

"Irish told me about it yesterday." Fenbow was a Texan from Corpus Christi, but like Luther had endured an itinerant youth and had ended up in Los Angeles, where he'd helped to build Haskell Albright's radio station. Over the years, Fenbow had developed a wry affection for Albright and the opposite regard for Los Angeles. Whenever he was asked why he'd disliked the city so, he said, "Y'all can be poor there and not even know it." Whatever this meant, he refused to say anything more after adding, "Y'all know, I was raised up Baptist."

So he'd been pleased when Albright had asked him if he'd like to go home and build XALM.

Luther shook his head. "I don't know why he doesn't just build an antenna on his roof."

Fenbow smiled. He made a sucking sound with his tongue in front of his teeth and ran his hands along the hollows of his cheeks. "Y'all know Haskell. I suppose he figures that'd be easy and ugly, and the only time I ever seen him prize those two qualities was when he was lookin' for a woman."

Luther laughed. "What can you do?"

"A few things," Fenbow said. "I'll fiddle with the tuning capacitor and I think I can maybe add some power to the transmitter, maybe even enough to drive a couple more amplifiers."

Luther said, "Whatever it takes. I'm dumb as mud on these

matters." He beckoned another Mexican woman. He took a glass of whiskey from her tray and handed it to Fenbow. "Let me buy you a drink, Travis." Then he said, "I'm sure you know how much I value your work." He was suddenly speaking seriously. He held his eyes on Fenbow until the length of his stare made Fenbow uncomfortable and caused him to glance down at the floor. " 'Preciate it, Doc."

Luther winked at Fenbow. It seemed the gracious gesture of a victor. Then he stepped off into the crowd.

For the next two hours, he mingled democratically. He urged everyone to eat his food and drink his liquor. He pointed to the long tables at the end of the room where turkeys and beef roasts and mutton were being carved and Mexicans in cowboy hats stirred vats of barbeque. There was a conscious finish on his manner as he moved among the people, though it lost in its smoothness nothing of its force. In fact, the pugnacity that had carried him in adolescence drove Luther at this point, and on this night, in his life. Its anger was as ardent. Its distrust was as deep. But he'd learned to dispense it socially with a modulated calm and one especially felt its charge, a kind of high heat under pressure, for its being held in. What he lost on such occasions was his spontaneity. As he moved among his guests, he pictured his tall figure gliding here and there with no hint of a limp.

He spoke to some of his nurses. He spoke to several attendants at the clinic. He spoke to clerks who booked reservations for the Mathias Operation. A stenographer who'd had too much to drink pulled on his coat and stood on her tiptoes and whispered in his ear that she'd loved him for some time now.

Late into the evening, he stood alone at the serving table next to a grand ham. Its rosy slices lay in a laminate fan. He drained his glass and looked around the ballroom through the smoke and the din. He saw tiny Ronnie Truehart, appearing even smaller in this room among the crowd. He was talking to Fenoglio, looking up into his face. Ronnie Truehart's expression was earnest. Fenoglio looked confused and somewhat fearful.

He saw Robuck Winter at the far end of the room, among a circle of XALM personalities. He was dressed in a black shirt and matching

pants. Fringe ran along every seam. His head was raised toward the
ceiling, his chin pointing high in the profile of the coyote's to the
moon. Brother James Washington, the gospel singer, stood next to
Robuck. He was a small old man, gnarled as a tree, his bald head a
shiny tuber. Next to him were Ma and Pa Lester, the station's rural
comedians, who'd come to town last year, toothless and sun-
ignorant, from the mountains of Virginia. Their skin even now remained the shade of udders.

Luther watched Robuck for a time and he felt so pleased with the
evening that a flush of magnaminity came over him. He thought, say
what you will, the son of a bitch did what he said he was going to do.
He got another drink and started off in Robuck's direction.

But as he began to make his way, he found his progress through
the crowd proving slower than before. Most of his guests were em-
boldened now by drink and many of them stopped him to thank him
for the party. Then they told him how plainly they saw their good
fortunes: that in the midst of the Depression they all had work. As
they spoke, they held his sleeve. He felt the men's grips tighten on
his arm. He felt the women's fingernails dig in. Everyone who
stopped him was fawning and sincere. They told stark tales of their
relatives in other parts of Texas. They told of children, their mal-
nourished nieces and nephews, who had died of common colds. They
said they regularly got letters from friends and siblings elsewhere,
reminding them how lucky they were to live in Del Rio and asking,
Did they know it? Did they know their great good luck? Oh, they did,
they said to Luther. Oh, my stars, indeed they did. Several women
wiped tears from their eyes as they spoke.

As Luther proceeded, he experienced ten, a dozen, and still
more of these encounters, and who among us would not have
been moved? He was impressed by their uncanny similarity of
story and sentiment. He wasn't humbled, but rather felt an even
greater sense of his own consequence, and it made him realize he
was obliged to speak to it. When at last he reached the other end
of the room, he had only a rough idea of what to say, but he was
keenly interested to see how well he'd do. This was precisely the
attitude he would refine toward his broadcasts, a passionless and
professional self-evaluation. He would never fully believe in what

he said. But he had come to believe utterly in himself, and in the future would assess and admire his power until the distinction be-came, on most nights, immaterial.

He found a chair and stepped up onto it. He straightened his posture to reach an even greater height. Seeing him, O'Malley began to move through the crowd, tapping people on the shoulder and pointing up at Luther. Across the room, Travis Fenbow did the same.

When it was quiet, Luther said, "I know it's getting late, but before you all head home I just want to say that if you all think you're indebted to me, as some of you have said to me tonight you feel you are, then I'm just as much in your debt. But most important, you all are in each *other's* debt. The reason the Mathias Clinic is growing and working to extend its healing hand, that reason is all of you!"

Shouts carried through the room, a chorus of harsh vowels.

He said, smiling, "I couldn't help noticing, as I walked among you tonight, that you tended to gather and stay, shall we say, among your own." He extended his arm to the left side of the room. "The nurses at the clinic in a group over here." He pointed elsewhere. "The clerical staff over there." He turned to his right and pointed again. "The radio station folks over here."

People blushed and laughed, embarrassed, as Luther made this observation. They felt small, as social citizens, felt themselves un-schooled and rude.

Luther said, "That's only natural. But when I noticed it, it brought to mind a powerful incident in my own life, which I hadn't thought about in years. I think you'll see what made me remember it, since it pertains to all of us forgetting about our individual jobs and think-ing of ourselves as the extended Mathias family."

He raised his eyes and tilted his head slightly, as if to get a better sight line on the memory. "This happened to me early one morning in New York City, New York. But it was an important morning in everyone's life here in this room, no matter where you happened to be at the time. It was the morning of Armistice Day."

Then Luther began to describe an extraordinary crowd that had jammed New York's Times Square in the early morning hours of November 11, 1918. "More people than you could hope to imagine," he said.

The people in the streets, he explained, were there to make sure that the end of the war had finally come. Four days before, word had swept the city that the armistice was signed and the falseness of that rumor had been absolutely shattering. So these people seemed to reason that if they moved the need for peace outdoors it would be impossible for the news to be untrue again. Luther said, "As a soldier in the war, stationed in New Jersey, I was among them. I was twenty-three years old."

He told his employees how he had joined an orderly current flowing down Broadway and into Times Square. There, a mass of celebrants had gathered and was growing. In other parts of the city, crowds were vomitously drunk. Outside Grand Central Terminal, the kaiser's effigies burned in a row of vigilante revenge. But the air of Times Square was benign and sanctuarial.

"I was standing in the crowd when I saw a beautiful girl wearing a long blue coat make her way forward and climb the steps of a platform in front of Liberty Hall." Luther shook his head. His smile was finely pained. "I remember that she was hatless. Her hair in the sunlight was a shining lemon-yellow color. There she stood all alone on that platform, and yet without any effort she began to command the crowd's attention. Which tells you two things. First"—he smiled—"how beautiful she was. And secondly, how . . ." He paused and looked toward his ballroom's windows. "How much the crowd thought, and felt, as one."

We know that Luther spent the war tending Cavalry horses and ventured nowhere north or east of the outskirts of El Paso. But among those in the ballroom, only Peter O'Malley knew it, too. What all the others knew of Luther was scant and, as happens when fame or wealth occurs to someone in our midst, Luther's history as an equal and a common man among them had faded in Del Rio in proportion to his rise. What his employees were left with then, the information they all held, was what they'd been told the day they'd started work for him: that the Mathias Operation was not a miracle (though patients in the aftermath were apt to think it was), for that word suggested the inexplicable. No, the surgery was a restorative astonishment based on years of pioneering science.

The people gathered in the ballroom had come to live with this

idea in a handful of ways. Some took it as truth and thought no more
about it. Some received it skeptically, but decided that if it *were* a
sham their own work was no part of it. A few, more detached, were
amused by what he'd wrought, while many were amazed by the
scope of his ambition. Some had had to fight through their disap-
proving consciences, which still rose up, a nagging virus, now and
then. And more and more of them each day held the simple fact of
Luther's great success as proof that he cured people. But no matter
how they felt about his work and theirs, their more abiding thought,
as they had said to Luther earlier, was that they had a job while the
country was in ruin.

Luther described how the young woman on the platform suddenly
began to sing the Doxology, that melody of wondrous and resurrec-
tive beauty, and she sang, he said, with great assuredness.

"As she sang," he said, "I began to move unconsciously through
the crowd toward her until I realized I'd reached the edge of the
platform and was looking up at her."

Not only did Peter O'Malley know the truth of Luther's military
history, but he'd also heard this story before. Luther had told it to
him long ago as a parable suggesting how he, O'Malley, might think
about an audience. For O'Malley had tried for a time to play the
organ on the radio. He'd had his own program, *The Organ Interlude.*
It had seemed an obvious idea when Luther proposed it and O'Malley
had been delighted with his chance. But he'd found that when he
played in the studio he could not envision any listeners for his music.
He pressed the organ keys and stared into the microphones and he
couldn't shake the sense that only they were listening. He lectured
himself before each program. He knew objectively that there were
listeners by the thousands. He saw their mail. He saw the quantity
of products they ordered. He even tried picturing himself as his
audience, listening to his console in his suite in the St. Charles.
Nothing worked. As soon as Travis Fenbow cued him to begin his
opening theme, the sensation returned that he was playing to a dark
and empty house at the Princess Theater, after the picture had
finished and the crowd had filed out. So he went to Luther to ask for
some help. Luther thought for a while and then told him the story of
the young woman, singing to the crowd on Armistice Day. He'd

suggested that O'Malley might imagine himself on the platform of Liberty Hall, looking out through the morning over thousands of people who waited, poised and attentive, for him to begin.

O'Malley tried the next night to imagine this audience, and he tried again every night for a week. Then he went back to Luther and said it was no use. He simply needed to be able to see his audience. It needn't be large, size was not the issue. But he knew that nothing he might try could make him feel there were people out there bending to their radios.

Listening to Luther in the ballroom, O'Malley smiled a smile of recognition. It brought to mind his excitement when Luther had given him his program. And it brought back, too, the memory of Luther's first relating the story, which, he'd said, he'd heard in the bar of the Brevoort Hotel in Chicago from the man who'd witnessed it, a young soldier in the war.

O'Malley's reaction to Luther now placing himself in the story amounted to nothing more than a pulse-beat of surprise quickly lost in fondness as he recalled how Luther had used the story to try to help him.

Standing on the chair, Luther was shaking his head. A look of self-bemusement crossed his face. He said, "The next thing I knew I was mounting the first high step of the platform myself. I can't explain it, except as the reaction of a young man too inspired by the spirit of that occasion to feel any inhibition. And when I reached the step, I turned to look back into the crowd and I saw, I vividly remember this, I saw that every man and woman had the same look on their faces." Luther said, "Above me, she was singing, 'Praise Him all creatures here below,' and on every face there was a certain singular smile, which I'll never forget. Then I reached up and touched my mouth and realized that I was wearing the smile, too. So I just stood there for a moment, smiling out at that vast crowd and receiving all their smiles in return. Then I stepped down again and joined them and I've never in my life held a more rapturous feeling in my heart."

Luther paused to shape a silence before underscoring his point about the power of unanimity he'd experienced that morning and how they'd begun to create that same spirit in Del Rio. But before he could resume he heard someone at the back of the room begin to sing.

"Praise God from Whom all blessings flow. Praise Him all creatures here below."

He recognized at once the horrid quavering of Mrs. Ogburn, the station's operatic soloist.

"Praise Him above ye Heavenly Host."

He couldn't see Mrs. Ogburn; she was a short and almost perfectly round woman with dyed black hair, but her voice was hers alone, a mournful alto weighted down by her ego and the gravel of age and maddeningly close to being on key.

"Praise Father, Son, and Holy Ghost." Mrs. Ogburn's voice had been acceptable in her youth and middle age and she'd offered it in choirs and recitals countywide. She was rare among the personalities on XALM in that she'd been born and raised in Del Rio. But since she'd begun to sing on the radio, she returned the greetings of people who'd tolerated her for years with a vagueness that said, And do I know you?

Standing somewhere at the back of Luther's ballroom, Mrs. Ogburn said to everyone, "Let's all sing it through together." And she started to sing again, "Praise God from Whom all blessings flow." Nearly everyone joined her, their voices great with feeling, and those few men—too shy, too drunk—who didn't mumble-mouthed the words as they did in church on Sundays.

Luther's employees sang the Doxology through and their final "Ah-men" rose and crested. Then they let go a series of "Yah-hoos!" that broke like a parody of a Texas crowd sound.

Luther climbed down off his chair. His fury at Mrs. Ogburn had passed once he'd seen that her singing had assured the mood he wished. Yet again he moved through the crowd, heading this time for the front door of the house so he could be there to bid them all good night as they filed out.

He hurried through into the adjoining living room, past the sheets hanging down to cover the unfinished organ wall. He reached his front alcove and pulled open the enormous carved-wood door and stepped out for a breath of air. He watched the water cascade from his driveway's lighted fountain, watched it fall in tiers of green, then red, then blue.

At this point in his life, Luther carried a sense of Alyce Rae that was not quite history, not quite imagination, but which amply borrowed from both. His emotional memory of her began with what had actually happened and in his mind he'd deepened its details and lengthened its time. So Alyce's days in Del Rio, before Billy had arrived, had acquired more episodes, more walks through town, more dependence on Luther's care, all marked with expressions of mutual solicitude. And their hours in the guest cottage had become unfinished. From its windows they'd watched a sunset of vermilion striations. And while they watched, Alyce had confided to Luther that she must leave Billy, for his good as well as hers. They'd made love again and again; it was as though continuous, as though all their talk and all of Luther's thoughts were also her smile as she'd opened herself to him, were also her breathing as she'd moved beneath him. But the erotic agitation that first edged his memories of her had calmed over time to something lush and textural, something more familiar and yet somehow more distant.

He also had what he knew about her presently from his regular correspondence with Haskell Albright. Because they were all—Luther, Alyce, Billy, and Albright—for their reasons bound to secrecy, nothing had been said in the intervening years to let Albright know that Luther wasn't Billy's cousin. So it was natural for Albright to mention having seen them. But his reports frustrated Luther, since Billy's untempered vanity was more often than not the point of the story while Alyce, in her grace and growing beauty, had simply been there too in some far corner of the narrative.

His sense of Alyce, then, was frequent if not constant, suspended in a burnished and sustenant melancholy. But it was vivid on occasion and it had been through this evening. For when Luther watched himself moving impressively through a moment, he thought of Alyce watching him as well. She seemed stationed at some low-floating vantage, which caused Luther to imagine glancing up to catch her eye. *What do you think? See how it could be?* He'd imagined their exchanges several times tonight. He was imagining it right now as he watched his fountain fall.

Behind him, he heard the first of his departing guests approaching. He inhaled the cool air and turned back toward the house. The white gravel of his drive crunched beneath his step. He moved inside to receive their gratitude. And he savored the thought that this was what he'd glimpsed, this was what he'd sensed when he'd lain in Billy's guest bed, taking in the scent of roses as he'd waited for the morning and his gifted life to dawn.

"And now," said XALM's announcer, Brother Bill Loomis, every weekday evening, "we invite you all to enjoy once again the heart-stopping, foot-tapping, tap-dancing wizardry of Blind Ronnie True-hart, who demonstrates by his brave example that the loss of one God-given sense is generously compensated for by the refinement of another, which in Blind Ronnie's case is his amazing sense of rhythm!"

Not even O'Malley could believe the success of Blind Ronnie's quarter hour. The first months' orders for Sunway vitamins threatened the company's ready inventory and Sunway's president wrote to Luther demanding a contract to sponsor Ronnie for two years. He wrote a second letter to Ronnie himself, which expressed his admiration for the dancer's artistry. The letter deemed Blind Ronnie an example for the country, as it endured these fearful times, of what could still be accomplished with sufficient grit and courage. In its closing, it circled clumsily around a final question. "I cannot help but wonder about the origin of your circumstances, over which you've so magnificently triumphed. But this is perhaps an insensitive curiosity, and if you choose to ignore it I shall of course understand. My deepest hope is that you won't be offended. My deepest regret would be if you were."

Nearly all the letters Ronnie received asked the question more directly. "How is it you're blind?" his listeners wrote. "Please tell us what is the story as we are interested to know." He heard from many people who were blind themselves. They described their unfolding enjoyment of tap, an appreciation they'd only just discovered.

Although Ronnie's popularity had taken Luther by surprise, he assumed it was due to the blindness he'd given him. He'd been pleased, too, to be able to say to Mrs. Ogburn that since she'd attracted no new sponsor she could now sing her solos for her husband in their parlor. He instructed Ronnie's secretaries, when they composed his replies, to say, "I'm sorry, but my blindness is too distressing to discuss. I'm sure you understand and thanks for your concern, which is my daily source of strength." Luther also realized, as Ronnie's fame began to arouse the local curiosity, that the dancer should be blind whenever he ventured out.

Ronnie was a determined, even dogged, young man who'd left Red Hook, Kansas, for XALM on the wings of a pure and unlikely dream: to tap dance on the radio. And that doggedness had already begun its alteration toward ambition. He'd monitored the surge of activity his program had produced. He'd seen the listeners' mail and he knew what it meant. He'd kept the gushing letter from the president of Sunway. He realized, that is, that he was not without leverage. So when Luther instructed him to be blind in Del Rio, his emotions passed through deep irritation at the thought of all the inconvenience in store for him, and settled on a demand he was sure he could win.

He said to Luther, "If I have to act like I'm blind every time I walk outside, then I'll need some assistance. Someone to help me with whatever might come up in the day-to-day life of a blind man." Ronnie said, "I *do* understand why you want me to seem blind. But I can't very well shop for food or drive myself, for instance, can I?"

So Peter O'Malley went to work, calling associates throughout the region, and found a young widow from the hamlet of Big Wells, east of Eagle Pass, to serve as Ronnie Truehart's personal assistant. Her name was Betty Neal and she had a young daughter named Nettie. "Nettie Neal?" Betty liked to say when she addressed her. Her husband had died on the family ranch, killed by lightning in a wild summer storm.

Betty Neal dressed in the style of a Jazz Age flapper. Her sense of fashion had been shaped by a series of photographs in a particularly racy moving picture magazine of the previous decade. Such magazines reached Big Wells only by mistake. She had found it, while taking a walk, in a roadside ditch that ran past her deceased husband's parents' home place. She'd decided to take the walk that day in the hopes of improving her mood. She'd just had a conversation with her father-in-law in which he'd told her she'd inherit the family home. Since her husband had been an only child, Betty had vaguely assumed this would be the case. But as she'd heard her father-in-law speak the words, a sense of dread finality had passed through her. So she'd taken a walk to try to ease her gloom and with her eyes fixed on the roadside she had seen the magazine. Its pages were stuck and curled from rain, but its salient pictures had barely survived. Betty was a young woman of dreamy and superstitious mind and she seized on the finding of the magazine as a cosmic gift. Oh, Betty? she heard the heavens say as she bent down to pick it up. This is for you. This will be of some help.

She'd taken the magazine home and studied the pictures. She sensed in them a spirit of insouciance and élan that showed her how she could distinguish herself in Big Wells no matter what might happen for the rest of her life, or, more to the point, no matter what might not. She cut her hair short and shaved the nape of her neck. She bought dry goods and sewed short-skirted flapper dresses, for which her boyish body was perfectly suited.

Of course, Betty's clothes and lavish makeup made her a social outcast in Big Wells, and her dead husband's parents were deeply shaken. They were good Baptist people with no gift for ease. They watched Betty's transformation take place and they searched their minds and hearts for the words to express their shock. For weeks, they couldn't sleep. They passed the nights in their living room's two stuffed chairs, offering each other shrugs and suffering expressions. Over months, their distress dulled into something heavy and permanent. That Betty Neal sensed their dismay and said nothing to acknowledge her change or explain its motives speaks to the hard, selfish streak that ran through her. She stayed devoted to the style she'd taken from the mud-spattered pictures long after she knew it had passed out of fashion.

So she was thrilled to leave her life in Big Wells and move to Del Rio to take charge of Blind Ronnie's. When they met her, Luther and O'Malley were amused to see that she was almost exactly Ronnie's size and that her face was shaped like Ronnie's, too, long and squirrel-snouted. Since such a frame and such features are more acceptably feminine, they gave Betty Neal a gamin appeal.

She was quick to insist that she could keep a secret, even from her daughter, Nettie Neal. O'Malley assured her that he would learn soon enough if she ever let it slip that Blind Ronnie could see. Betty said he needn't worry because she never would. However, she said, she felt she must confess that she'd never enjoyed Blind Ronnie on the radio. Luther thanked her for her candor and said that didn't matter.

Hiring Betty worked out well. She did all of Ronnie's shopping. She drove him everywhere. She ran his daily errands. Her presence inspired a round of rumors in Del Rio, too numerous and too obvious to detail here. Whenever she and Ronnie appeared together, they looked like the tiny couple atop a wedding cake. Because of the deception they shared, because they forged a kind of domesticity, a peculiar bond did begin to form between them, though to Ronnie's frustration he could never make it sexual. For Betty simply couldn't take him seriously as a valid sexual creature. She thought him cute, in the way of a cuddlesome toy. She liked to tweak his pointed chin. She liked to rub his little head.

All the while, Blind Ronnie's popularity increased and the sales of Sunway vitamins grew and grew, as listeners worn sore and made old by the Depression heard the rat-a-tat flourishes that burst from Ronnie's feet and yearned for a limber, inexhaustible health.

17

In her biography *Shrill Naif: The Life of Billy Boswell,* the neo-postfeminist critic Phoebe Angstrom argues that Billy's film persona was actually a prophetic prototype, that his striking beauty (her phrase for it is "safely strident") combined with his angelic ignorance was the source of a lineage she traces to most of the popular actors of today. If, Angstrom writes, Billy were working now, "the surpassing shallowness radiating from his presence on the screen—whose effect was contradictorily compelling, a beckoning and beautiful emotional Black Hole—would be in great demand." But, alas, Billy's times were not our own. They were the final years of the silent era, when his skills, such as they were, fit his roles ideally, and the early talkies of the thirties, when the studios responded to the first years of the Depression with new grim genres that had no place for Billy.

Many films, in the beginning of sound, told the stories of women who'd been wronged, who'd been scorned. If they'd once led lives of glamorous city wealth, their husbands had deserted them, run off, committed suicide. If they'd once enjoyed lives of pastoral innocence, they'd been cruelly preyed upon, all they'd had taken from them. Now these fallen women lived in tenement rooms. They lived alone or with a small child in a state of what *Variety* called "unofficial motherhood." It was broadly hinted that they did what they had to do to live. Morality was a luxury of the sunny past.

Other pictures showed crude young men trapped in lives of petty crime. They lived in tenement rooms, across the hall from the fallen women, whom, if they met, they treated brutally. They wore grimy undershirts. They curled their upper lips. They lost their tempers and threw violent tantrums. When they did, their hair fell across their eyes.

In neither of these genres were there starring roles for Billy Boswell. His grandly played heroes of gorgeous earnestness had *been* the sunny past. So he found himself, for instance, playing a wealthy concert pianist opposite Kay Coolidge in *The Law Is What You Make It*. But it was very much the supporting role to Coolidge's tragic heroine, the abandoned Clarice Langston, and Billy could not hide for a moment his brooding confusion at being asked to step away from the center of the screen. With his silent-star image presumably in mind, studios offered him more of these debonair savior roles. He played an only son with a huge inheritance who served on charity boards and fell in love with a beautiful young woman he met while distributing food to the hobo camp where she lived with her brother. He played a humanitarian aviator. In *Where Went My Youth?* he played a society lawyer who married Candace Lane's country waif. In all of these pictures he supported the female star and in all of them he was dreadful. It was as though he'd been told to dance with a strange woman, then advised, just before the camera rolled, that he should let her lead. Indeed, in certain scenes in these films he seemed almost literally to stumble.

Then, toward the middle of the decade, the spirit of motion pictures began to lighten. One after another, comedies were made, pairing men and women who traded ceaseless wisecracks and found love against the backdrop of the still-evident Depression. Once again, leading men could be both good and virile. Once again, though they shared it, they occupied the center of the screen. Thank God, Billy Boswell thought, and with his usual ferocity he insisted to himself that the dark days had passed.

It might seem that Billy would have been well suited for these roles. He remained, after all, supernally handsome; he'd not aged a day in a detectable way. And his image, from the silents, was something close to heraldic. Both these qualities were called for in picture after picture. Combined, they offered audiences a mid-Depression figure of American virtue and high sex appeal.

But these romantic comedies were something new in Hollywood. Their focus was more often on their heroines, women of savvy independence who manipulated men of lovable incompetence. So an actor needed an instinctive understanding of this stronger woman. He needed, too, a good-humored unselfishness. He needed to convey a more complicated dimension below a bemused surface and he needed a portion of irony to animate his sense of humor.

Billy, of course, had none of these qualities. His humorlessness was especially betrayed, though he argued with vehemence, often to himself, that he had in fact an exquisite sense of humor. When he insisted to producers that this was so, a funereal grimness came into his face.

Billy loosened a button of his double-breasted suit coat. He was very hot. He felt faint. He shifted his position on the hard kitchen chair and squinted out through the glare of the lights that ringed the set. He heard the low bored chatter of the stagehands as they mingled in the darkness behind the camera and the lights. He could only glimpse their simplest moving shapes. He heard them suddenly break into quiet laughter, which he suspected was somehow at his expense.

Behind Billy, at the sink, Jeanne Craigie stood with the young director, MacKenzie Holmes. Jeanne Craigie was a lovely, slender brunette whom Billy had not met before the filming had begun three weeks before. She was perhaps a year younger than Holmes and though this was her first starring role, she'd played the smart-aleck best friend in a number of films over the past few years and she seemed to know every technician on the set.

"Remember," Holmes said to Jeanne Craigie, "in this scene, you're very nervous. You've invited your boss, who you adore, up to your apartment to show him your idea to save the company, and everything is on the line. Your actions need to show how nervous you are." He stepped behind her and placed one hand on her shoulder and the other at her waist and said, "Like this."

Billy turned to watch the two of them move along the kitchen counter through a halting little tango of fussy inspections.

"Good!" said Holmes. "Perfect."

"You're so full of shit, Mac," Jeanne Craigie said. Her voice was low and gravelly, not unlike Alyce Rae's, though not as full-throated. "You just wanted an excuse to put your hand on my butt." She laughed and so did Holmes. Billy cringed and raised his eyes to the girders and planks overhead. Holmes and Jeanne Craigie volleyed good-humored profanity. Billy was sure he heard the word *cock-sucker* but he couldn't determine which one of them had said it.

Above Billy, a sound man moved back and forth positioning microphones. He wore a wide solid tie, loosened at the collar. Billy's look continued higher until the ceiling gave back its sealed-in darkness. This startled him for a moment. The sets of silent films had usually been open to the air, had had no need to be concerned about rogue off-camera sounds, and despite the evidence of how thoroughly things had changed—the overwhelming heat from kettle-drum-shaped lights, the bulbous microphones dangling just above his head—Billy was unthinkingly surprised not to see the sky. There had always been the sky.

In his mind he saw, as though he'd left it yesterday, the lavish living room set of *Lasting Impressions,* the film where he'd met Alyce Rae. He saw himself, when the shooting stopped for lunch, guiding Alyce to a corner and looking up past the set's crisscrossed supporting carpentry to watch the clouds gauzing thinly in the sky.

He was flooded with memories. They moved quick as newsreel images across his brain. He saw himself on the set of *The City Sheik,* bantering wittily with Clara Bow. He heard her clean chimes of laughter. Was that before or after she'd made *It*? he asked himself.

How could all that seem so vivid and yet so long ago? How was it possible that all the world had changed?

He heard his name being spoken. He lowered his eyes and blinked.

"Billy?"

He saw that MacKenzie Holmes was standing directly in front of him and bending down to meet his eyes.

"Are you with us, Billy?" MacKenzie Holmes asked. "I called to you half a dozen times."

Billy reddened. "I heard you perfectly well," he said.

"Then you're clear about this scene? No questions?"

"It's a simple enough scene," Billy said. "Of course I'm clear."

MacKenzie Holmes straightened up again. "Yes, well," he said, "the timing has to be exactly right or it just won't play."

Billy made no effort to subdue his sigh. He said, "Why don't we just shoot it?"

Holmes looked past Billy and smiled. "Ready, Craigie?"

"I'm with Billy," the actress said. "Let's just shoot it." Billy was certain he heard mimicry in her tone.

He watched the director turn and walk toward his chair. Holmes was a fair-complexioned young man with thick sandy hair. He moved with a squared-off athletic confidence. His build was also an athlete's, and Billy had been told by a cameraman last week that Holmes had played football with Red Grange at Illinois. He was young enough, barely thirty, to make it a possibility, but Billy told the cameraman it was a lie Holmes told all the time.

Billy detested Holmes. He detested the analytic pedantry with which he spoke of comedy and his tireless references to his time as a boyhood assistant at the Hal Roach Studios, where he'd watched and learned from "that genius, Stan Laurel." Good God, Billy had thought, Stan Laurel? A genius? He detested the vulgar camaraderie Holmes shared with Jeanne Craigie, though he'd heard before the filming that she cursed like a sailor and that she and Holmes were very close friends. For these reasons, he also detested Jeanne Craigie. But most of all, he detested everyone's attitude toward him, which had seemed, from the first day, to be condescension.

"It's an honor, Mister Boswell," MacKenzie Holmes had said. Billy had thought to himself that he was only a few years older than Holmes—seven or eight years older at the most—and yet he'd instantly felt like an old man being teased.

"Please," Billy had said, "let's get something straight right away. My name is Billy."

"Fine," Holmes had said. "Then it's an honor, *Billy*."

Holmes dropped into his chair. A woman at his elbow handed him the script. He lowered his head to study it, then looked up again and scanned the set. Billy shifted at the table to catch Jeanne Craigie's eye. Her expression as she watched Holmes was one of sisterly amusement. Billy detested it. He turned back to wait for the scene to begin. He took a deep breath and rebuttoned his jacket. He ran his hand along the length of his lapel. Holmes's head continued to bob up and down, his eyes moving from the script to the set to the script. He asked Jeanne Craigie to move a foot to the left. Billy felt that he might begin to scream at any moment.

You Can't Beat Love was Billy's third romantic comedy. He'd made *Once Upon a Dime* in 1933 and, a few months later, starred with Vivian Bryan in *Every Which Way*. Both had failed badly.

In *You Can't Beat Love*, Billy's Arthur Demarest and his older brother, Lawrence, own the Demarest Corporation, founded by their late father, Milton, and long the principal employer in the nameless small city where the story takes place. The company makes kitchen appliances, most notably eggbeaters, and through the first decades of the century it enjoyed great prosperity with the Demarest Deluxe.

But with their father's death and the onset of hard times, Arthur and Lawrence face a financial crisis that defines them as characters and sets the story's conflict. Though Lawrence (played by Langwell O'Banion) claims otherwise, he cares nothing for the company's family heritage or its civic responsibility. He cares only for keeping as much of his wealth as possible. With the Demarest Corporation losing money every day, he's persuaded the board to vote to close it down, putting hundreds of workers onto the streets.

Arthur, on the other hand, is good and innocent, but has no heart for business. Though he legally holds as much power as Lawrence, he's ignored by his brother and the rest of the board. He's a terribly earnest bumbler who, two years before, was called back from Paris—where he was trying with no success to be a painter—by his dying father, himself a patron of the arts, who loved Arthur especially and wished him to take an interest in the company.

Arthur is deeply troubled by the thought of employees losing their jobs, but he sees no way to do anything about it. (He also dreams of returning to Paris, even as he imagines the specter of his father looking down on these developments with great disappointment.) Arthur has confided the news of the company's closing to his secretary, the beautiful and resourceful Elaine McGraine, played by Jeanne Craigie, who admires Arthur's seriousness and lovingly tolerates his absentmindedness, even if it sometimes makes her job that much harder. Elaine is the local girl from the other side of the tracks, whose own father worked for the Demarest Corporation until he retired. She has his cleverness and common sense, with a tough, crackling wit and an intelligence quite her own. After sharing the news with her father, the two of them determine that something must be done. Together, in his shop, they design a Demarest Deluxe with substitutable attachments that allow it to whip and stir and

grind and dice, anything a housewife might think to do to food. And
so, with high hopes and her secret love for Arthur, Elaine asks him
up to her modest apartment overlooking Main Street without explaining what she has in mind.

From his low canvas chair, MacKenzie Holmes said, "The camera
is rolling, and . . . *action.*"

Billy, as Arthur, looked around the kitchen. He said, "This is a
lovely place, Elaine. Very nice. Very nice."

"Oh, Mr. Demarest," said Jeanne Craigie's Elaine, standing behind him and gathering the ingredients for her demonstration. "This
is a dump and I know it. But, there's no place like home, and there's
sure no home like this place!" She was taking down several bowls
from her cupboards and hurriedly filling them one by one, a puddle
of cream in the first, quartered apples in another, slices of leftover
roast beef in a third, and on down a row that ran the length of the
counter. She moved with the choreographed clumsiness MacKenzie
Holmes had shown her.

"No, I'm deadly serious," protested Arthur.

"Are you ever," Elaine murmured, smiling warmly. In her nervousness she was making an increasingly loud racket with the bowls
and pans. Clangs and crashes occurred, and then an unidentifiable
soft thumping sound. "Oops!" Elaine said. She turned and smiled
weakly and mumbled to herself. "Never seen egg yolks bounce like
that before."

But Arthur was oblivious to the building noise. He only continued
to inspect the room, looking out at the camera and up at the sharply
angled ceiling. "It reminds me of Paris," he said.

"Paris," Elaine said, again looking over her shoulder. She rolled
her eyes, at the same time continuing her frenzied assembling. "Of
course! Paris! I've been trying to think what it reminded me of." The
cacophony increased. There were harsh metallic rings and cymbal-
shards of sound.

"My *atelier* on the Left Bank," Arthur said, "had these same
slanted ceilings and little dormered windows." He'd begun to speak
very loudly to be heard, while giving no indication that he was aware
of anything unusual going on behind him. "The *light* was better in
my *atelier*!" he screamed. "But it had the same coziness I feel here!
And when you looked out over the slate rooftops in the morning,

it—" Suddenly Billy shot to his feet. "This is ridiculous!" he shouted.

"Cut!" said MacKenzie Holmes. He stood and hurried to Billy. When he reached him he placed his hand on his shoulder. "What's the matter, Billy?"

Billy jammed his hands into the pockets of his double-breasted jacket. "This *scene* is what's the matter. It's utterly absurd, as I've already protested. I'm screaming like an idiot at the top of my lungs about the charms of Paris while the entire kitchen is crashing behind me. I feel like a complete fool."

MacKenzie Holmes looked away and exhaled softly. Jeanne Craigie had joined them. She stood with her arms crossed, staring down at the floor. Without lifting her head, she raised her eyes to peek at Holmes.

"Well, Billy," Holmes said very gently, "as I've said, your character, Arthur, he's sweet, he's kind, and that's why Elaine loves him— besides the fact that he's so handsome, of course—but he's got an artist's temperament, even if he's not talented enough to succeed as one, and so he moves through life in a daze most of the time, which does make him look a little bit like a . . . fool." Holmes pronounced the word as delicately as possible.

Jeanne Craigie continued to study the floor. She quietly cleared her throat.

"But *no* one," Billy said, "would be unaware of the sounds of a train wreck going on behind him."

MacKenzie Holmes nodded. "Yes, it *is* a highly stylized scene. It's raised to a farcical register, I know. But, trust me, if it's played correctly, it will be funny. Your shouting has the possibility of being very funny."

Billy said, "The noise makes it impossible to deliver my lines. I'm about to get a migraine, I'm sure I feel one coming on."

Again Holmes nodded. "If you start to feel ill, we'll stop for the day, of course. But remember what we talked about? How the scene is written so that you speak your lines about Paris, getting gradually louder, in a *pattern* with the sounds Elaine is making? How you don't so much try to shout over them as around them? It's a kind of call and response, if you can get a feel for the rhythm of it. It's a dialogue between you and the pots and pans. 'My *atelier* was so divine.' 'Crash!' 'I looked out over the morning mist on the Seine.'

'Bang, slam!' 'And my heart never failed to soar at the beauty of the sight.' 'Kaboom!' And all the time you're raising your voice more and more." Holmes was eagerly nodding his head in an effort to get Billy to admit the scene's potential. "Think of it as a duet, Billy, you and the pots and pans trading riffs, like syncopated jazz." He paused and smiled, but held his look on Billy. "Okay?" he asked. "Does that help?"

Billy took a deep breath. My God, he thought. Syncopated jazz! Once again he raised his head and looked straight overhead. He looked past the sound man standing on the scaffolding and smoking a cigarette. The darkness near the ceiling appeared to have thickened, seemed, as Billy felt it, like the very lid of life.

He mumbled the complaint that all the laughter in the script was at his expense.

"What?" Holmes asked.

Billy lowered his eyes. "I said, 'Let's finish the scene.' "

"That's the spirit, Ace," Jeanne Craigie said. She winked at Billy and tweaked his earlobe. "Just relax your sphincter and we'll have some fun with it."

All through the morning and into the afternoon, they repeated the scene. Just how many takes were shot has been variously remembered by those who were there. In his memoirs, MacKenzie Holmes, who did indeed play football with Red Grange at Illinois, says that he's certain there were more than thirty, an unthinkable number in those days. He writes of having to stop and ask the commissary to send over more eggs and cream and apples. He claims that by midafternoon, he, not Billy, had the migraine headache. He recalls that during a break at some point he walked past Billy, who looked limp with exhaustion, his swarthiness turned jaundiced, and caught him talking to himself. He heard Billy mumbling heatedly that in the days of silent art, an actor wasn't asked to converse with pots and pans. Holmes's tone in writing this is one of some affection.

In any case, MacKenzie Holmes decided to stop work for the day when the scene had reached its midpoint and Billy's Arthur Demarest turned in his chair and, seeing the mounds of food, the spills and the smears, the bowls of ingredients madly arrayed along the counter, said to Elaine, "Oh, how thoughtful. You've made some canapes."

*   *   *

It was nearly five o'clock when Alyce arrived home. She turned her red convertible into the long driveway and entered the nightshade of the cathedrally arching palms. She'd been playing tennis most of the day and had lingered with friends for a drink afterward. She still wore her tennis whites. A soft white sweater draped her shoulders. Her hair was lifted off her neck. Its shape in the breeze was a yellow wing. She glanced at her watch and began to consider what she might do until Billy got home. She'd gotten used to eating as late as ten o'clock whenever Billy was making a picture and staying on the set until well into the evening.

Through their life together, Billy had always been voluble after a day of shooting. He would call to her as he hurried through the door. His reverberant greeting gave her name several syllables. She would bring him a drink and, if any light remained, they'd sit in the sun room and let the deep pink sky turn dark in panorama. He'd ask her what she'd done that day and sit smiling while she told him. Then they'd go in to dinner and while the wine was being poured Billy would begin to tell her of his day on the set. He'd grow more and more animated. His monomania prevented him from shaping his anecdotes, from populating them with anyone who'd contributed in other than a subordinate way.

Alyce had never minded. In the first years of their marriage, she'd come to see their late suppers as gay episodes of her sophisticated life. They'd been one of the ways she contrasted who she was from who she'd been. She'd grown up an only child in Detroit and her punctilious father, a district attorney, had called her to dinner at precisely six o'clock. Alyce's memories of the meals of her childhood were aural. She remembered the scrape of knife and fork against plate. She remembered the ticking of the dining room clock, growing as ominous each night as the sound of a timed explosive. She remembered the salivous slush of even mastications, seemingly in cadence with the ticking of the clock, as her parents, Fletcherites, mirthlessly chewed. She heard in her memory no lilt of voices, no conversation. This silence in their home prevailed most other times, as well. Whenever her parents spoke to each other, they'd seemed to wish to keep their words below any possibility of being overheard or felt.

She steered her convertible to a stop at the top of the circular drive and was startled to see Billy's Cadillac. Hadn't he announced this morning that he'd be working quite late? For some months now, she'd been aware that she was likely to forget what Billy told her he'd be doing through the course of a day. She might pause in the middle of lunch with friends and ask herself where Billy was. Had he mentioned where he'd be? Had he said when he'd be home as he'd left the house after another morbid morning of waiting around for his hangover to clear?

She glanced in the direction of the mansion. It suggested to her, in its stolid Tudor gloom, a preposterously capacious funeral chapel.

She'd been driving along the ocean just above Santa Monica, feeling nothing more specific than a desultory sadness, when she'd consciously realized that her daily sense of Billy had become so vague. Her recognition made her feel suddenly quite cold and she'd pulled off the road and shut off the ignition. She'd reached in the back seat for a sweater and wrapped it around her. She'd lit a cigarette and looked out at the water. The tide was coming in, the sea recurrently spilling itself with its measured profligacy. As she'd watched, hugging herself to get warm in the high blue sunshine, she'd wondered for an instant if there were something mentally wrong with her, if this new way of glimpsing Billy at a soft and edgeless distance meant a youthful senility had come over her. The possibility seemed to Alyce almost hopeful.

As she sat in her car, looking out at the ocean, her eyes filled with tears and her shoulders began to tremor. Her chill deepened. It lay on her bones like a frost, her fear and grief too deep for the sun to be of help. For several minutes she'd cried noiselessly, as though mimicking the sound of her life with Billy now. They'd started, the silences, with the slide of his career. Three years, perhaps. That long ago, she knew. If she'd come, years before, to see Billy's bluster for what it was, she'd also learned to rely on it. But he'd lost his ability to disguise the silences and it was this that terrified her. They were at first brief brave pauses in his clenched ebullience. But over time they lengthened and their despair thickened. And from the start they held an anger so active that they seemed when recollected to have made their own sound. They were vastly different in this way from her parents' bloodless and desiccated hushes.

*   *   *

She stopped in the foyer to set her tennis racquet down and light a cigarette. She looked at herself in the oval gilt-framed mirror. She thought to herself for a moment, wondering how a woman knew for certain that her beauty was unthreatened, what ways of assessment other women brought to bear. She heard someone approaching, but recognized the lumbering steps of Michael, the butler.

Appearing, he said, "Hello, Mrs. Boswell."

"Hello, Michael," Alyce said, turning. "Mr. Boswell's here?"

"In the sun room, I think," Michael said. He was a pallid, flabby man with a churchly demeanor, perhaps twenty years younger than he worked to seem. "I'll bring you your drink in there?"

"No, nothing for me," Alyce said. She had it in mind to change before seeing Billy—her whites were still slightly damp against her skin—but she found herself moving directly down the hall. Her tennis shoes squeaked on the lustrous smoke-blue tiles.

She opened French doors and stepped into the flora and wicker of the sun room. "Hello, darling," she said.

Billy stood near a mullioned glass wall among splayed-leafed aspidistra. He was looking out at the dusk's ordinary brilliance. Alyce said, "I'm surprised you're home so early."

He turned around and stood not quite fully facing her. He said, "I'm surprised you're home at all." He seemed, from the angle of his stance, to be addressing the person standing next to her. Despite his words, his voice was soft and weak and this very contrast gave them a disembodied menace.

"What is that supposed to mean?" Alyce said. "It's five o'clock in the afternoon." She saw the empty glass in his hand. She glanced to the end table to see very little whiskey left in the carafe.

"Just . . ." Billy sighed and shrugged his shoulders. He pursed his lips. "I hoped you'd be home, that's all."

"I thought you'd be late," Alyce said. "You told me when you left this morning you'd be late." She tried to hide her uncertainty that that was what he'd said.

"I did, yes. I know. I'm sorry. I was just disappointed when you weren't here. I'm sorry."

She moved into the room and sat down on a wicker couch. A

pattern of pink and green vines wound through the fabric of its pillows. She put her cigarette out. Billy passed in front of her to the cut-crystal carafe and she saw his face more clearly. It was swollen to a haggard asymmetry that made it plain he'd been crying. She watched him slowly fill his glass.

"What happened today?" Alyce asked, straining to keep even the faintest judgment from the words. She'd been practicing them in her mind all the while he'd taken to pour his drink.

Billy gave her only a glance in reply. For the instant he met her eye she saw an unhappiness so private it startled her to have glimpsed it.

He crossed in front of her again to the opposite end table and picked up his working script of *You Can't Beat Love*. He lowered his eyes and squinted. He took a sip of whiskey, a movement that seemed to threaten his balance. Alyce had no idea of what else to say until he'd spoken.

Billy looked up. His eyes found Alyce on the couch. He said, "I was thinking today of *Lasting Impressions*." He smiled. "Do you ever think of it?"

"Of course I do," she said. "How could I not?"

"Frequently?" Billy asked, having trouble with the word. "Do you think of it," he paused, "frequently?"

"Yes."

Billy smiled. He raised his glassy eyes and looked past her. "You were so wonderful in that picture. You were . . . vibrant and clever, but also so . . . *sweet*." He nodded and smiled and said again, "Sweet."

Alyce laughed uncomfortably. "You're being generous, darling. It was a very small part."

"*No!*" Billy insisted. The force of his voice startled her again. "No, I'm not," he said. "I remember it perfectly, how wonderful you were. I remember everyone saying so." His expression had a witness's beseeching solemnity. "I remember it perfectly," he repeated.

"Thank you," Alyce said, wishing simply to calm him.

She'd played, in *Lasting Impressions*, the younger sister of Billy's character's cold-hearted fiancée. She'd briefly appeared as a beautiful, somewhat ethereal young woman, home from college for the holidays, in whom Billy's character sensed too late all the nobler qualities he should have chosen in a woman. It was the only time the two of them appeared together in a picture. Alyce's was a quick, one-note role and she'd known she was playing it only passably. She had, at that time, recently come to realize that she had neither the talent nor the guile necessary for stardom. She'd had no idea what to do with this knowledge. She'd been living in a state of fear. Each time she'd gotten a new part, she'd felt it would surely be the one to result in some disgrace that would thrill the industry and follow her until she died.

Billy said, "I've been thinking how much I wish you hadn't decided to retire."

"You can't mean that," Alyce said.

"Why can't I?" Billy snapped. "I mean it . . . ut-ter-ly. I've been thinking"—he interrupted himself to sip his whiskey—"how marvelous it would be for the two of us to star together again."

"I had no idea you felt that way. I've never heard you speak of wanting such a thing."

Billy found his petulance. "Well, I do." He still stood beside the end table, holding the script.

"But I've never regretted retiring," Alyce said.

"Oh," Billy said, frowning. "Well, but just imagine it. What fun it would be. How much audiences would enjoy it. Seeing you again. Seeing us together." He raised his whiskey to his lips and got its final drops, then peered into the empty glass. He stared into the air just above Alyce's head. "They need your sweetness," he said. "It's gone. Your," he took a deep breath, "vibrant sweetness. It's all gone from pictures now, and they need it. Don't audiences want to see . . . a sweet and beautiful woman any longer? A vibrant and sweet woman?" He answered himself, "Of course they do."

She said softly, "Dinner will be a while. Why don't you lie down and take a nap?"

She watched him set his empty glass on the table and lift the script to his eyes. He held it tightly in both hands, his head dropping to study it. His effort gave the air a sudden sacerdotal poise. Alyce couldn't imagine what horror must have happened on the set.

He said, "I need to rehearse this scene for tomorrow." He looked directly at her for the first time since she'd joined him. He asked,

"Will you read with me?" He held the copy of the script out to her. "I haven't *quite* got the feel for this scene just yet." He said, "Here. Read her part."

He had never in their marriage shared a script with her, so her surprise was not unreasonable. But the instant threat she felt touched not just his self-doubt but hers. She said, "I don't think so, darling. I'm tired, and you must be exhausted." She waited a moment, then stood up. "Why don't you come? I'll lie down with you."

"Read with me," Billy repeated. "It will be fun." His voice was cloying. "The timing of this scene is quite delicate, quite *subtle*. I need to make sure I have it, or it won't be as funny . . . as it might be." She recognized his language as someone else's. Again he said, "Read with me."

Alyce took the script and looked at it. The page Billy had turned to was wrinkled and smudged. Coffee rings were stamped here and there.

"Wonderful," Billy said. "This will be great fun." He came to stand next to her and started to explain the kitchen scene. As he spoke, Alyce told herself that this would be all right. They would read the scene together. The very act of concentration would help to sober Billy up. Then, with luck, he'd go to bed and sleep through the night.

Billy said, "And while Elaine is making all these crashing sounds, Arthur prattles on about his Paris *at*—" He hiccuped. *"Atelier."* Billy smiled at Alyce. "You see, darling, it's a highly stylized scene. It's written to be played at a farcical level. I think of it as dialogue between myself and the pots and pans. Like . . . syncopated jazz."

He put his finger on the page and said, "Let's start here." He was showing Alyce the point at which Arthur turns to take in Elaine's chaos. Billy said, "You may have the script. I have my lines memorized. Just imagine all the bowls of food and such." He moved away from her and plopped down in a chair, as at the kitchen table in Elaine's apartment.

He nodded his head and began. "Oh, how thoughtful. You've made some canapes."

Alyce read, "Um, not exactly, Mister Demarest. Come here. I want to show you something."

Billy rose unsteadily and stood next to Alyce. "What is it?"

"What am I holding in my hand?" Alyce read. She paused. "In my *hand*, Mister Demarest. Please stop looking out the window. You will *not* find Paris out there, I assure you."

There was silence in the sun room. Alyce looked up at Billy. She saw his face wrinkling. He said, "What's my line?"

Alyce read, "You're holding a Dem—"

"Oh, yes," Billy said. He continued, "You're holding a Demarest Deluxe, of course, but I don't see—"

"Wrong!" Alyce read. "I'm holding the last hope for the survival of the Demarest Corporation." She paused and read, "I just thought of something, Mister Demarest. Have you ever used a Deluxe yourself? Have you ever even held an eggbeater in your hands?"

"Well," Billy said. He paused. "Well, I suppose not, come to—"

"That will have to change, Mister Demarest, beginning right now! How can you expect to run a company when you don't even know how your product works?"

"But of course I know how it *works*."

"Prove it!"

They read through the scene of increasing mayhem, as Arthur tries to get the egg beater under control. Billy's thick and overly careful enunciation remained but his voice began to sound slightly stronger.

Alyce imagined herself in an audience watching the scene on the screen. She couldn't tell if anyone was laughing. But she heard her arrhythmic delivery as she offered Elaine's lines. She heard her deadening emphases. She told herself that she was reading the scene for the first time. But even so, it seemed to her, standing in her sun room beside her sad and pretty husband, that here was the part, here was the disgrace, here was the grand humiliation unfolding.

The script's directions described food flying from the bowls; Arthur nearly bumping into a side-stepping Elaine; Arthur seemingly being pulled and tossed about the kitchen by the Demarest Deluxe as he madly churned its handle. The dialogue consisted of, "Look out," and "Duck!" and "Sort of works like a fishing reel, doesn't it," and "Oh dear, did that get you in the eye?"

Alyce heard Billy's Arthur say, "Oh, I'm so sorry. I'll certainly buy you a new dress." His sobering voice drew a witless monochrome, but Alyce heard its searching. She knew then that her dread was not only for herself. She heard in his voice just how lost her husband was and she felt the disgrace descending on them both.

There was an unscripted silence in the sun room and when Alyce looked at Billy she saw that he was weeping. She put her hand to her mouth. She thought his tears were for the fear she'd somehow just exposed. Reflexively, she said, "Don't pay attention to me, darling. I reacted much too strongly."

Through his sobs, Billy said, "I don't understand." He shook his head and repeated, "I don't understand."

Alyce came to him and touched his cheek. "What?" she asked. "What don't you understand?"

Billy's mouth was open wide. He forced it closed. "He's a fool," he whispered.

"Who's a fool?" Alyce asked.

"Arthur," Billy managed. He breathed. He breathed again. "Everyone mocks him. His brother. The members of the board. The sound man, all the workers on the set. I don't understand . . . he's laughable . . . how Elaine could love him."

Alyce stroked his other cheek. She pressed his tears with the backs of her hands. She held his wet face in her hands and felt it go slack. She knew his eyes were waiting for hers.

When she met them, he whispered, "Help me." He tried to smile. "Help me, darling."

Alyce took her hands away from Billy's face. She stepped back from him and looked away from his stare. She wanted to help him; she was certain she did. But she was made dizzy by the extent of his asking. It meant they'd moved to a realm of even more elaborate weakness. She felt her strength leaving her.

"Who is Elaine?" she heard Billy ask. "How could she love Arthur? People *laugh* at him."

Alyce began to shake her head. She said, "I can't."

Billy's head tilted slightly. "What?" he asked.

"I can't."

"You can't?"

She continued to shake her head. "I can't. I don't know."

"You can't what? You don't know what?"

"I can't help you. I don't know who Elaine is."

"Darling," Billy said, "why can't you? I need you. Tell me why she'd love him. Tell me who she is."

Alyce made a bawling sound. "I don't know who Elaine is! I don't know how she could love him!"

"Alyce, dar—"

"I can't help you!" She was hurrying toward the French doors.

"Alyce!"

"No!" She opened the doors and ran down the hallway. He heard her tennis shoes shrieking on the tiles. There was a pause, then the sounds of her running up the stairs. A moment later, he heard an upstairs door slam.

He'd not moved. He waited until the possibility of further sound had passed. Then he walked to the couch and sat down and crossed his legs. He reached for his cigarette case and lighter. His state of shock was advising his every breath. It whispered to him to sit calmly for as long as was necessary, whatever that meant, however long that was, perhaps forever. He lit his cigarette and exhaled. As was his habit, he picked a shred of tobacco from the tip of his tongue.

He watched the sky through the process of darkness. Fear was the strongest feeling in his heart; anger and mourning were equally the others. But they all seemed oddly self-contained, not simply connected to what had just occurred. What few thoughts he had were of original fears, moments from childhood when various terrors had been born. He remembered falling from a tree in his back yard in Santa Barbara and getting up to see his forearm sickeningly twisted. He remembered the nausea, not from pain but from the horror of the sight. He remembered his alcoholic mother coming drunk into his bedroom where he'd wakened from a nightmare, crying and calling for her. He remembered her leaning down, her whiskey breath engulfing him, and whispering that she hoped he'd like his next mother more. Such ruminations, his shock assured him, were the way to spend this time.

He sat alone in the sun room for nearly two hours. He drank nothing more and smoked half a pack of cigarettes. He was an unwavering figure of grace and dignity throughout.

When Alyce came back into the room, she saw his silhouette, rigid on the wicker couch. She made her way—she felt the need to tiptoe—and sat down next to him. She put her hand on his knee.

"I'm sorry, darling," she whispered. She had little voice left.

"Yes," Billy answered.

"Forgive me?"

"Of course. There's nothing to forgive." He placed his hand on top of hers.

They were quiet for some time. She said, "Shall we have a bite of supper? Can you eat? You must be starving."

"Supper?" he said. Finally, he turned to look at her. "All right."

Alyce stood and held out her hand. He took it and rose and followed her out.

They sat before plates of scrambled eggs and toast. Billy drank a bottle of rare white Burgundy in inattentive gulps. It affected him imperceptibly. Alyce drank nothing. She smoked four cigarettes, taking quick nervous drags, and ate a few bites of food. She listened to the scrape of knives and forks against their plates and heard the ticking of her parents' dining room clock.

The next morning, Billy was called at home before leaving for the set and asked to come to the studio for a meeting in Abe Zietman's office. When he arrived, he found MacKenzie Holmes there, too. Abe Zietman asked Billy to sit down and then he told him in a quiet, even voice that they'd decided, for the good of all concerned, that *You Can't Beat Love* should proceed without him. Zietman said the problem was a simple blameless mismatch of the character of Arthur with Billy's quite special qualities, something no one could have known when the picture had been cast. He observed that it only proved once again how unpredictable the business was, how inexact as craft. He said there were three or four or a half-dozen pictures currently in the scripting stages, any one of which would be perfect for Billy.

For his part, MacKenzie Holmes said that the decision was equally his, so that Billy, were he wishing to place blame, should give at least half of it to him. Then Holmes stood and offered his hand and said it had been an honor to work with so great a star. He looked into Billy's eyes as he gripped his hand and added that he truly meant what he'd just said.

You Can't Beat Love was rewritten to explain Arthur's abrupt disappearance. It seems that he'd suddenly risen from Elaine's kitchen table, stirred by the memories of Paris her apartment had called up. He'd hurried out, down the stairs, and sailed for France the next day. This left Elaine to convince the older brother, Lawrence, that greater profits could be his if he would keep the factory open. When Lawrence saw the genius of the improved Deluxe, he recognized not only great profits, but also Elaine's intelligence and beauty. Not much more than a moment later, he also realized his lifelong selfishness, so he changed his ways and asked Elaine to marry him.

Clearly, *You Can't Beat Love,* as offered to the public, was confused beyond rescue and the fact that it was seen to be even at the time is often used by film historians to help mark the sophisticated turn audiences were then taking. No longer were they content with the grand effect of sound, never mind a story that made any sense. No longer would they simply ride along on the energy of a goofy illogic, which MacKenzie Holmes, to his credit, somehow gave *You Can't Beat Love.* In this respect, as Billy's biographer suggests, these changing times in films were very different from our own.

18

"Good evening, my friends, my cherished listeners. Let me first take this opportunity to send out my hope that each one of you will enjoy, not merely a happy, but a bountiful and joyous New Year. I realize I'm just a little early in offering these wishes since it's but eight o'clock here in Del Rio. But no matter what the hour, what unites us all at this moment in our history is the faith and courage the country has demonstrated through the twelve hard months of nineteen thirty-four. For there can be no argument that it has been one of the most difficult years of any in this century, save those calamitous seasons of the Great War. And maybe it might do us all well to recollect briefly the fear and uncertainty that gripped us while the German monster raged across the sea, as that way we can put our current hardships in just a little bit of perspective, although Doctor Mathias would not diminish for a moment the suffering inflicted on so many of his listeners by this cruel Depression.

"But surely we have lived through the worst of it now. Surely we have weathered the meanest of the economic storms, have survived the most disastrous economic seas, have withstood the passing of the most violent economic winds carrying their dust and despondency all across our land. Surely, having endured, we are ready now to welcome calmer weather, quieter seas, gentler breezes free of dust in the new year ahead."

In Del Rio, South Main was already filled with people celebrating New Year's Eve. The night was crisp. There was a gibbous moon. Its light put a luster on the surfaces of the town, or rather, put a luster on the luster of the surfaces. For Del Rio's facades were as usual neat and clean. The windows of its shops appeared to have been just

washed. Against the grime and rotted desuetude of the world surrounding it, Del Rio's prosperity always seemed to people just arriving a sort of crystalline mirage. The several hoboes who came
through town every day appreciated Del Rio especially. They left the
freight cars of the International Great Northern and moved patiently
from house to house in search of food. They found the people neither
unusually generous nor discouraging. But they sensed Del Rio's life
and they saw its gleaming neatness and, compared to other towns,
they simply liked to be here. It inspired a feeling of harsh nostalgia
in them. Their thoughts were led back to a time when most every
place in America had something of a choice in whether or not it
wished to keep itself clean.

Moving among the celebrants were the customary number of new
patients, just arrived. Mostly they were older men, mostly unaccom-
panied. They wore lumpy suits of heavy tweed. They'd checked their
trunks wherever they were staying and determined when they were
scheduled for the Mathias Operation. They'd been encouraged to
relax and take a stroll around the town. Their preoperative fear
rendered them obedient. They'd said, Well, all right, if that's the
thing you think a person ought to do.

They inched along South Main. In their manner there was something both decorous and fugitive. The local people hurried past
them. If one stood close to them, the aura of loneliness they gave off
was overwhelming. They stopped to let a Mexican boy shine their
already gleaming dress boots for a nickel. One block later, they
stopped to let another one shine them again. They peered through
the windows at the boisterous goings-on inside the City Club and the
Val Verde Café. Farther down the street, at the Frontera Lounge,
they looked in and saw two women dancing on a tabletop. The
women seemed not so much uninhibited as casual. They seemed to
know the clefts and attitudes of each other's bodies.

"Now, because it is New Year's Eve, I've decided to extend my
broadcast tonight to one full hour, and also to include some special
surprises, some holiday gifts from Doctor Mathias, the first of which
you'll be receiving in just a few minutes.

"It seemed only fitting that I should pause to enjoy some addi-

tional time with you all tonight, since that is how I believe this
evening *should* be observed—quietly, with those friends we feel
most familiar with and most thankful to. That is certainly how I feel
tonight—so deeply thankful to each and every one of you who has
loyally supported the work of the Mathias Clinic through this year
and in years previous.

"I suppose, in part, I think New Year's Eves are best celebrated in
this quiet, simple way because I have such splendid memories of the
way my mother and father and myself watched the new year come
in when I was a boy growing up in the Panhandle. There were just the
three of us together through the fall and winter holidays, and as you
know we were very poor and had only an abundance of love to serve
as our gifts to each other. But of course what could be more in
keeping with our Creator's intentions than a family giving and receiving the kindness and concern of one another's love? And as
wonderful as Thanksgiving and Christmas always were, it's the memories of our New Year's Eves that have remained the most vivid.

"Every New Year's Eve my mother prepared the most delicious
supper, and we all sat down to eat it at eight o'clock, the very hour
at which I'm speaking to you right now. Other nights, we ate
promptly at six o'clock, after my father had washed up from his long
day outdoors. And most every other night, we were each of us so
ravenous after working hard all day that we ate our supper in less
time, or so it seems as I remember it, than it had taken my father to
say grace before we began.

"But somewhere along the line, my parents had decided to mark
the year's coming to its end with this special supper at this special
hour and I cannot adequately describe what a thrill there was in that
for me. Because I felt very grown up, don't you see? To be given
permission to sit around the supper table with my loving mother and
father at so late an hour! To be allowed to savor the heavenly tastes
of my mother's cooking! And then, while we all three were finishing
up our portions of warm apple pie, my father—who, though un-
schooled, was a man of eager intelligence, always trying to quench
his thirst for knowledge—he would say to my mother, 'Sarah Jane,
tell me what you've done this past year that you're the most proud
of. And after that, tell me how you want to improve in this new year
upcoming to make things better for yourself and for our family.'

"Now I should say that my father asked this in the most gentle, loving voice. He was simply encouraging my mother to think about her pilgrim's progress through this life, inviting her to consider how she might better herself. And after she had spoken, he would proceed to answer the same questions as they applied to himself. I must admit that I have no specific memory of what they said. Probably because I cannot, at this adult remove, imagine what either one of them might have offered in the way of criticizing themselves, for as far as I'm concerned, they were both of them perfect.

"But I know you see, my friends, as you listen to my little remembrance, that whatever particularly was said among us is not the point. What mattered was that my mother and father cared enough to pause in the course of their daily effort to think about what they could do to make life richer. Because they both of them realized that when a member of a family does something to improve himself, then he has also done it for his whole family's sake. They understood that when one family member thrives, so does everyone in his family. And on the other hand, when one member falters—and it's only logical that this would be especially true when that member is its head, the husband and the father—when he has for whatever reason become discouraged, maybe somehow weakened and lackluster, then his difficulties are ones which he is likewise imposing on his wife, certainly, and even on his children."

At the Del Rio depot, at the far north end of town, the sounds of shouting voices from the bars on South Main rose and fell like a wavering radio signal. The depot itself was dark and quiet. The day's last train had left the station minutes ago, having delivered two men and five enormous sacks of mail. Both the passengers and the mail were here because of Luther, the men for their surgeries, the mail to XALM.

The men had disembarked and scrutinized each other. Both of them guessed instantly why the other one was here, though they were oddly surprised, as Luther's patients often were, to see that someone else had come to Del Rio for the same purpose. As much as Luther emphasized the size of his audience and the vast population of satisfied patients, he also spoke of privacy and confidence. He promised anonymity and utmost secrecy. And he'd only gotten better at broadcasting the illusion that he was whispering into your ear and your ear alone. Consequently, the two men had felt embarrassed and found out. Standing on the platform, they'd worked heroically but not well to find a common root of conversation. They'd looked off toward South Main and the source of the sounds. They'd looked up into the sky, up and down the empty tracks. They'd looked everywhere but into each other's faces. Then, frightened and resigned, they'd headed off together.

The sacks were piled on an eight-foot flatbed handcart, waiting to be pulled down the street to one of the new warehouses. Perhaps half the letters were requests for Luther's pills. Others were orders for the sponsors' products. Kolorbak. Man-o-Ree. Luvolife. Peruna. Kormelu. Marmola. Crazy Water Crystals. The remainder of the mail expressed simple admiration.

Five women worked through the night to prepare a mail report which waited for Luther every morning. He studied it over breakfast. He noted trends and percentages and arcane ratios he'd devised over time. He observed, for example, that some XALM personalities inspired more fan mail than orders; others predictably produced the reverse. He wondered why. He was forever in search of the ideal match of sponsor and performer. He ran tests against control groups. All in all, he'd come to rely absolutely on statistics. Though he still held clear opinions of the talent of his performers, he refused to let his taste or instincts interfere. He was, as a result, often perplexed, even apart from the phenomenon of Cowboy Buck Winter.

He couldn't fathom, for instance, the very recent rise in popularity of Ma and Pa Lester, the rural humorists, whom he'd hired in the first place because they'd touched his pity and because, at the time, he'd been desperate for performers.

The Lesters had arrived without notice in Del Rio, having ridden the rails of the Missouri Pacific system. They'd labored up the steps of Luther's old second-story office and knocked on his door. He was alarmed by the appearance of the couple on his stairs. They were dirty and spine-bent and white as albinos. A ring-worm coil was stamped like a cattle brand above the man's right ear. The woman was rheumy-eyed. Luther had asked them to wait, he had some apples and milk and the last of a pot roast he could give them. No, the man said, that's not why they'd come. They were here in search of work, not charity. The woman nodded weakly. The man said they'd listened to XALM in Lone Valley, Virginia, and that as much as they loved every one of the programs, they'd detected a void of much-needed country humor.

"Country humor?" Luther asked.

"Country humor," said the man. "That which makes country people laugh." He asked permission to perform one of their routines.

Reluctantly, Luther let them in.

Once inside, the man turned immediately to the woman and asked, "Howdoo, Ma?"

"Howdoo, Pa?" the woman answered, nearly whispering.

"Say, Ma," the man said, "y'all will never believe what I just seen. I was walkin' through the barnyard a short while ago and I saw two sows dancin' with one another. They look to be right smitten. Now whatcha' think of that?"

"I'm a mite dizzy," the woman replied.

"Dizzy?" the man asked.

Dizzy? Luther thought. There's not a person alive who'd think that was humorous.

The woman whispered, "If I could maybe rest for . . . jist sit down . . ." and then she staggered through a clumsy pirouette. Luther caught her as she fell, having hurried to reach her when he realized her dizziness was not part of the routine.

"Doctor Mathias would ask you all to think about what I've just said: that it is nothing less than a man's responsibility, first to himself, and then to his wife, to keep himself strong and active and energetic in all ways, as is appropriate for his age. I know you'll consider that truest of truths, my friends, on this New Year's Eve, while you listen to my first special present to you tonight—the inspiring Gospel sounds of Brother James and His Two Sisters.

"And here I see them coming into my Desert Gardens study now, Brother James and his lovely sisters, Lonetta and Loretta, who've generously consented to spend some time with you all on New Year's Eve. Please, the three of you, take your places at the microphone and favor us with your uplifting Gospel message."

*   *   *

At the Del Rio depot, Ma and Pa Lester stepped from the shadows and scampered toward the mail sacks piled on the handcart. Ma carried a much smaller cloth sack of her own, which pendulously swung at her side as she ran. They reached the cart and stopped and looked around. Sensing all was quiet, Pa selected one of the mail sacks and tugged at its drawstring. When he'd loosened it, Ma pulled a fistful of envelopes from the cloth pouch she carried and reached into the opened mouth of the sack. She dropped her envelopes among the hundreds of others and mixed them in with a raking of her fingers. When she withdrew her arm, Pa pulled the drawstring tight and proceeded to the next sack.

In the studio in Villa Acuña, a transcription disk turned. The guitar and autoharp of Brother James and His Two Sisters marked a tempo that was quick and elated. The thread of wax coiled out from the turning table needle.

> *High in Heaven, Jesus watches us.*
> *Love and mercy in His blessed eye.*
> *I pray I'll join Him, looking down on Earth.*
> *The view from Heaven, our promise when we die.*

The Lesters worked in moonlight with coordinated haste, the efficiency people gain through repetitive work that means everything to them. They spoke not a word. They'd learned, having spied on the mail routine for weeks, that half an hour sometimes passed before a man named Ruddy Ruggles arrived to pull the handcart down the street to Luther's offices. But the Lesters had been performing their nightly misdemeanor for a month and by now needed less than five minutes to complete it. They'd also reduced to an hour and a half the time it took them to sit at their kitchen table and compose and address and stamp the C.O.D. orders for Kormelu, their sponsor, an alarmingly virulent depilatory cream. They'd come to enjoy creating the letters. They liked making up names and studying the map for odd-sounding towns all over the country. Most of all, they liked to think of new phrases to describe how hilarious Ma and Pa Lester were.

"He is calling me!" sang the Sisters, their metrical beat strict as a primer from the B. C. Stamps hymn catalog.

> *He is calling me.*
> *Sweet eternity. (I hear Him!)*
> *He is calling me!*

The Lesters had begun to talk about their scheme late one night, sitting in their kitchen after returning from Luther's grand open house. Pa Lester had listened to Luther's speech urging each of them to think of himself as a member of the Mathias family. The idea of being seen as one of such a family had caused Pa Lester's stomach to turn. He could not forget that the station's performers had cruelly dismissed him and Ma when they'd arrived from the mountains to start anew in Del Rio. When they'd gotten home after Luther's party, Pa had turned to Ma and asked what she'd thought of the speech. Ma had shaken her head. "It was mule poop," she'd said.

> *Sweet Eternity!*
> *He is calling me!*
> *Believe! And if you do (He loves us!),*
> *He'll be calling you!*

But the Lesters saw only the details of their scheme. They hadn't the wit to look up and cast their eyes to its horizon. It had not occurred to them, for instance, that the envelopes they added to the mail sacks every night showed no cancellations across their postage stamps. (It was their momentary good fortune that the women who opened them hadn't noticed this either.) And they'd not considered what would happen when their invented orders began to be returned undelivered to the Kormelu Company.

Were they more intelligent, they might have devised a sabotage similar to Blind Ronnie Truehart's. Measured by the volume of mail received, Blind Ronnie's program was the station's third most popular. He closely trailed Brother James and His Two Sisters, though he remained far behind Cowboy Buck Winter. Blind Ronnie held no hope of catching Cowboy Buck but he loved the idea of passing Brother James, of rising so impressively in his first year on the air. With the help of Betty Neal's careful inquiries, he'd found a woman on the staff who needed money badly. Her name was Wanda May Mullen. She had four children and her husband had run off almost a year ago, disappeared into Mexico without a trace. For fifty dollars a month, Wanda May Mullen had agreed to lose fan letters addressed to Brother James and His Two Sisters, whatever number was required to make sure that Blind Ronnie received more mail than they did. When she'd accepted her first month's pay from Betty Neal, Wanda May Mullen had solemnly replied, "It's for sure y'all can trust me. 'Cause I can keep a secret."

"I don't need to worry about that," said Betty Neal. "It ain't only me and Ronnie's secret now, Wanda May. From now on, it's your secret too. So y'all just better hope that y'all can trust your*self*. Otherwise, they'll fire your saggin' behind in less than no time flat."

"Thank you so much, James and Lonetta and Loretta, for stopping by and sharing your New Year's Eve with us. Good night now. Watch your head on your way out, James, when you walk underneath the holiday ornaments hanging there. That's it. Good. Good night and you enjoy the rest of the evening.

"Now friends, Doctor Mathias knows you don't need to be reminded—in the words of the gospel song we just heard—that if you do believe, then He'll be calling you. Doctor Mathias realizes very well, from the hundreds of letters he receives every day, that you regard your responsibilities to God as a basic part of your daily life, as natural as the sun's rising up to start the dawn.

"But I also know that it isn't always easy, especially these days, to pause from the struggle and remember that our duties to God take in all that we do. And when you get a bit forgetful, it seems to me the best thing you can do is go directly to the source, the Holy Bible, for a reminder of everything your responsibility to Him includes.

"It was one of my restored patients, returned to his grateful wife and bursting with interest and enthusiasm once again, who best pointed this out to me recently. This man wrote me a letter and near its end he said, 'You know, Doctor Mathias, when I had just got back home, I was feeling so thankful that I picked up the family Bible and began to look for a passage that might put into focus the gratitude I was carrying in my heart. And by chance I came across this verse from St. Matthew, which reminded me that I was not just acting for myself when I arrived on your doorstep. I was also following the wishes of our Lord, Who makes it very plain that to refuse the offer you extend to all men who are afflicted as I was is to ignore His master plan.'

"And then my good friend—who'd come to us, I well remember, in a condition of pathetic defeat: lethargic, resigned, prematurely gone to fat—he goes on to cite the passage from Matthew, chapter nineteen, verse twelve, in which Christ says to His Disciples, 'For there are some eunuchs, which were so born from their mother's womb: and there are some eunuchs, which were made eunuchs of men: and there be eunuchs'—and this is the third and final category—'which have made themselves eunuchs for the kingdom of Heaven's sake.'

"So here the Scriptures plainly tell us that these three kinds of eunuchs are the only ones which God approves of: Eunuchs naturally born; eunuchs made that way for some earthly reasons frankly mysterious to our own American ways, say to be opera singers or to guard royal harems; and finally religious eunuchs, that is, for instance, priestly celibates who take their vows of chastity. But all the rest of us, as this passage in St. Matthew makes so clear, we have a responsibility not to be eunuchs, to fulfill our sexually active roles according to the Lord's all-wise design.

"So it's only fitting that I put the question to you, on this New Year's Eve: Are you for all practical purposes a eunuch of the kind our Lord did not have in mind, and which He has not provided for in His hierarchy of the sanctioned sexless? Have you begun to violate God's clearly stated wishes on this matter? Have you—to speak plainly to you, friend—forgotten or ignored or become incapable of the sexual duties which He expects you to perform?

"In other words, if you've recognized yourself tonight in the de-

scription I just gave of my former patient—if your formerly free-
flowing brook of capability is now a dammed-up, stagnant pool—the
remedy for your troubles is as easy as it is required by the Lord's own
rules.

"Now I want you to ponder your no doubt frightening loss of
energy and its guaranteed solution, which awaits you in Del Rio,
where summer spends the winter, while I give everyone listening
tonight my second New Year's Eve present. I know that you'll all
accept it as a very special present indeed. Because I marvel every
day at the amount of mail and orders he receives for his songbook.
Yes, listeners, you know who I am talking about. Our own Warbling
Wrangler, Cowboy Buck Winter, has agreed to stop by my home to
wish you all a Happy New Year in the form of a few songs.

"So let me greet him right now, here he comes through the door.
Good evening, Buck."

"God damn!" laughed Haskell Albright, "an outstanding stack of
bullshit!" Albright was listening to Luther while sitting in his bedroom. He was drinking champagne at a low round walnut table that
was placed by a window overlooking a valley. The hills to the west
were the tawny shade of a lion's hide. Albright raised his glass in the
direction of the radio, then took a swallow. "Sling it, Cowboy!" he
shouted to the radio.

Albright had become accustomed to hearing Luther in this way—
that is, with a drink, seated at his bedroom window. He'd tried every
location in his sprawling new home and determined the bedroom
received the signal best.

From the station's inception, he'd approved of Luther's programming. It was just the sort of unseemly assemblage that Albright had
imagined it should be. He'd been left to conclude that Luther knew
what he was doing and the extent of Albright's comments, when he
talked to him, was that. Still, he'd felt no less required, for the sake
of his investment, to listen when he could.

But in recent months, he'd begun to listen more avidly. He some-
times rearranged his schedule so he'd be home for Luther's Medical
Question Box. Now and then, as he sat at his desk at the *Los Angeles
Times,* his long stockinged feet kneading his carpet, he glanced at

his watch and, noting the hour, asked himself who was on the air and who was his sponsor. Whatever the answer, it caused Albright to smile. For he heard every program on XALM as its particular rendition of broadest comedy. He was made delighted by the mere concept of Blind Ronnie Truehart, while the opening lines of a Buck Winter tune could send Albright into wild whooping laughter.

"Good evening to you all," said the transcribed voice of Cowboy Buck. "I'd like to sing some songs for you that I been hearing around the campfires since the last time we visited. And here's a little song I just recently wrote, which I surely hope you all enjoy." He started strumming his guitar.

> *An old cowpoke, my dear best friend,*
> *I saw him die the other day.*
> *'Twas in the midst of his herd, that his saddle broke,*
> *And he fell 'neath the hoofs of that Long Horned fray.*

His twang, for some reason, was especially adenoidal.

"Oh, my Christ!" Albright laughed. " 'Neath the hoofs of a Long Horned fray'!" He poured himself more champagne.

Still, as much as he enjoyed Cowboy Buck now and then, he thought Luther's Medical Question Box was predictably hilarious. And it seemed to Albright that Luther was growing as a performer, pushing himself and setting greater challenges as he envisioned some ultimate idea of what he could get people to believe. He thought he'd sensed in recent months a new lewd glow of personality in Luther's voice. He heard an even more confident abandon driving the appeal. It was not so much in Luther's language as in the complicated message of libidinal pharmacy he was coming ever closer to perfecting.

Albright remembered the day Luther came to see him with the idea to build the station. He remembered, it still amused him, Luther's initial gravity as he offered his lies. He remembered that

Luther had spoken of his "calling," and that he'd used the phrase "the unspeakable sadness of sexual weakness." So it never once occurred to Albright that Luther believed a thing he promised in his monologues.

> *Darlin', I fixed his worn leather,*
> *But your 'So long' ripped me apart.*
> *His saddle holds me high on my trusty steed*
> *My love for you is leakin' outa my busted heart.*

Albright stood and drained his champagne glass and walked to his bed, where his tuxedo had been laid out for him. He was in especially good humor despite the fact that he was about to celebrate the coming new year at a large dinner party at his older sister's house. Albright hated dinner parties and he hated his older sister. He couldn't believe he'd gotten trapped into an evening eating rich French food with her imbecilic friends. Worse, he couldn't recall having said he would. He suspected his secretary had accepted for him and simply written it in on his calendar. Ever since he'd left his wife, there'd been a conspiracy between his sister and his secretary to manage his social life. He let them do it. He had better things to think about. And he'd realized some time ago that, no matter what he said, neither one of them would believe that he was happy as a bachelor. In fact, he'd never been so happy. He loved his utter freedom. He loved the simple sense of clean, pure space he felt every time he walked into his new house and knew that neither his loathsome wife nor anything reminding him of her was there. He also loved screwing young women, the younger the better, teenagers best of all. Screwing teenagers did not give him the illusion that he was younger than he was. Instead, it made him feel entirely satisfied to be his age. It made him feel that if, at the age of sixty-two, he could screw teenagers, then he could look forward to screwing them for the rest of his life.

"Thank you so much, Buck. That was beautiful and I know how much every one of your many fans listening tonight appreciates your taking the time on New Year's Eve to visit with us.

"How's that? Why, thank you, Buck, and Happy New Year to you, too. Good night.

"Now friend, have you been considering, as I asked you to, those matters of affliction and cure? I suspect you have, because you surely know by now that a man is only as old as his glands. I repeat, a man is only as old as his sex glands, the crowned king of all the glands.

"In other words, friend, as you sit there in your easy chair on this New Year's Eve—knowing very well that I am talking directly to you, that I have diagnosed your debilitating loss of sexual appetite even on those occasions when the veritable banquet of invitation has been set before you for the tasting—will you choose to take action to put an end to your misery and to your good wife's silent suffering?

"Will you make a New Year's resolution to come to the Mathias Clinic? Will you accept the directive of our Lord—Matthew nineteen, verse twelve—on this issue and remove your name from His roll of unacceptable eunuchs? Or will you just continue to sit there in your chair, too tired to move, too defeated to care, too senile before your time even to remember those frolicsome days of eager pleasure which need not, need *not,* be consigned to your dust-covered sexual scrapbook?"

As Albright dressed to join his sister, he reflected on the year just ending and he knew it had been among the best years of his life. His newspaper was prospering and so, although more modestly, was his radio station. He'd also continued to acquire land surrounding the city at prices made as cheap, well, as dirt by the Depression. And his share of Luther's enterprise had proven profitable beyond his dreams.

All in all, in the final hours of 1934, Albright knew himself to be one of those rare men who understood how the world worked. He'd always believed he was but he felt even more certain of it now. How could he not? The evidence was plain. Even unwelcome events had deepened his self-confidence. He'd seen the establishment this year of the Federal Communications Commission, replacing the old, passive body that had never done much more than dole out licenses.

Albright had watched these new commissioners immediately begin a more vigorous supervision—assigning signals, limiting power, establishing the law and order of the air. This was precisely the fear he'd expressed to Luther on the country club veranda in 1928 and six years later his prediction had come true.

He moved to his dressing mirror, listening casually to Luther. He opened a drawer and searched for his shirt studs. His unlinked cuffs flapped at his wrists. The wings of his collar peaked up and jabbed his neck. He poured himself another glass of champagne and chuckled appreciatively at a line of Luther's . . .

". . . That place of ultimate shame—the disreputable dust heap of humiliated husbands.

"But I would not want you to think that I am deaf to your financial circumstances. I hear your voices, because I read your letters, and I certainly understand that the cost of the Mathias Operation is not insignificant. I know that five hundred dollars represents a great deal of money to you. And so, I am right now announcing my last and best New Year's gift to you. After discussions with my dedicated staff, I have decided to establish a new scientific medical procedure which will instantly bring an end to your suffering. And the best news for you is that I have found a way to offer this procedure at a fraction of the cost of the Mathias Operation.

"Now listen very closely. Maybe you should pull your chair up a little closer to the radio while I carefully explain what I'm offering to you and why.

"After much thought and months of experiments in the Mathias Laboratory, I've perfected a new nonsurgical procedure which will bring you immediate rejuvenative results and will cost you only two hundred dollars, a mere fraction of what must be charged for the Mathias Operation.

"Now you'll recall that the vital ingredient necessary to the success of the surgery is the macerated essence of *hamadryas* baboon gonads, and you'll also remember that the highest quality essence is found only in Africa and must therefore be imported, indirectly through France, at enormous expense.

"Well, that same essence will be used in the new Mathias Nonsurgical Treatment. You can rest assured that I would never skimp on the quality just to lower the cost. But what makes the cost so much less expensive is that I've discovered I can simply *inject* the essential fluid and obtain extremely satisfactory results. In other words, an injection of the macerated baboon essence in your hip, just as you might receive any other injection with which you're familiar, will have an immediate and profound effect.

"This makes the dramatically low expense possible for two reasons. First, the procedure itself is much less costly than surgery. And secondly, the simple injection can as easily be performed by my nurses as by me. Which means, as an added benefit, that I will have more time to meet the constantly increasing schedule of Mathias Operations.

"Now I can already hear what you're saying: If Doctor Mathias has developed the new Mathias Nonsurgical Treatment, why is there any further need for the more costly Mathias Operation? That's a natural question, and an intelligent one, and I'll answer it completely. Because I could not in good conscience offer the new Treatment if I thought you didn't understand every aspect of it, both its tremendous advantages and its possible, and I say again, its *possible* limitations.

"You see, although it's clear to me that the new Treatment will bring you instant results, it's also true that I cannot at this time completely guarantee that your rejuvenation will be permanent. I cannot say with total confidence that the sexual zeal restored to you by the Nonsurgical Treatment will last your whole lifetime, as is absolutely the case with the proven Mathias Operation.

"Certainly, it's possible—I would even say it's quite likely—but it is not a claim I can make tonight and it would be irresponsible of me to do so. Worse, it would violate your trust, which is the very foundation that binds all of you out there with all of us in Del Rio."

"Yes," Billy whispered, nodding to Alyce. "Yes, I like that. Now turn in a circle. All the way around." Billy was sitting on the blue velvet couch in his mirror-walled dressing room. He loosened the sash of his silk robe as he watched Alyce. She was naked, on her hands and knees. She began to turn slowly on the carpet. The palms of her

hands took oddly precise cross-over steps, the movements of a show
animal performing for her trainer. As she turned, the muscles in her
back defined themselves in quick, graceful flows. They suggested a
ready strength that had never been displayed. Billy watched her
before him and at the same time in his mirrors. He saw infinite and
unimaginably angled Alyces. She was turned directly away from him
now. He saw the pink soles of her feet. They seemed somehow the
most naked part of her. He watched her arch her back to present her
ass to him. It made a heart shape of sex.

"Yes," Billy whispered.

She lowered her elbows to the carpet, raising her ass higher, and
began to move it back and forth in a languorous sashay.

"Do that. Yes." He took off his robe and slid off the couch.

"So, now that the expense is no longer a hindrance, when are you
coming, friend? When can I expect you? When will you see that our
time on earth is brief, in accordance with God's plan, which makes
it vital that we experience to the fullest every day He gives us? When
will you understand that you have the choice? That you can decide
between the dark clouds of impotence or the bright sun of manhood?"

Alyce could see Billy in the mirrors, walking on his knees toward her.
His face was slack, past stupidity. His lips were parted. It was the
expression she'd come to recognize when they fucked. That was how
she thought of it now, they no longer made love, and her own
participation had become more foreign than she could have
dreamed from that former sense she'd loved of being eagerly used,
of being a beautiful vessel absolutely filled. For weeks, they'd been
descending into her steadily more degrading submission. She
couldn't have said just when or how it had begun and she hadn't
been able to imagine how Billy would respond if she were to ask why
he wanted it, needed it this way. So she'd asked herself and had soon
understood that they were seeking for her in sex some nether realm
of humiliation as low as the place where Billy lived continually now.

Billy reached her and placed his hands on her hips. From behind, he bent over her and whispered what he wanted her to say.

She said, "Yes. I'll do anything you want."

"Will you crawl on your stomach across the room to lick my cock?"

Alyce nodded. "Yes." She turned her head and looked back over her shoulder.

"Will you fuck yourself with your fingers while I watch?"

"Yes."

"Will you beg and weep while you're doing it and say, 'Oh, Billy, but it's not you. It's you I really want.'?"

"Yes."

"Keep moving your ass like that."

"In the dwindling minutes of nineteen thirty-four, I ask you: Will you continue, in the upcoming year of nineteen thirty-five, to belong to that category of eunuchs God has no time for? Or will it be out with the old and in with the new? Will you resemble, in the way you feel and move about, the stooped and white-bearded and used-up old man of nineteen thirty-four? Or will you be that fresh and frisky and confident newborn of nineteen thirty-five?"

In the mirrors, Alyce saw the many pairs of them surrounding her. Her eyes ignored Billy's subtly muscled body and watched only his face. She focused on his involuntary smile. In the mirrors, its dementia was multiple. She felt Billy's fingers, they had found her now, but it was almost as though she were hearing the sensation described, for she had moved fully into the cool calm of watching him. And in the mirrors, she saw confirmed what she'd been sensing: that in this role, in these poses of debased compliance, she held a horrible manipulative power over Billy.

As though to test this power, she arched her back more and heard Billy's instant gasp. She moved her ass across his stomach, its softness grazing his skin, and watched his mouth fall open in response: Through an idiot's O, he emitted an unearthly wail.

She saw in the mirrors that his eyes were closed. Enraged, ecstatic, whatever his passion, he had never been oblivious to his image in a mirror.

"Are you coming? Are you? Will Doctor Mathias be seeing you in nineteen thirty-five, either for the Operation or the inexpensive Treatment? Yes? You say you are? Oh, I'm greatly relieved your common sense has prevailed, that you've decided to throw off that mourning cape and end your premature sexual death."

Alyce lowered her head and laid her face against the carpet. There was something poignant and childlike, far from the moment of a beautiful woman offering her splayed ass, in the way she lightly nestled her head. Her yellow hair curled out onto the carpet like licks of a cool flame.

She closed her eyes. She smelled Billy's cologne, its scent mixing with his sweat. She heard the ragged unconsciousness of his voice, a tribal moan. She felt him moving against her, pitiable and ineffective, and she knew they would find no humiliation that would take her low enough.

"Good night to you all from Desert Gardens, and may God bless America in nineteen thirty-five."

BOOK FOUR

· · ·

1935

Chapter

19

*L*uther was in the act of firing Ma and Pa Lester the day word reached him that he'd been barred from Mexico. The Lesters lived in a tiny adobe less than half a mile from the Rio Grande. The house sat amidst chest-high *coriza* that effectively surrounded it like a moat. Indeed, everything about the place suggested inhospitability, which was the very aspect of it the Lesters found appealing. When they'd first seen the adobe they'd been reminded, as much as they could be by anything in southwest Texas, of their remote mountain shack in a field of wildflowers off a snaking dirt path in Lone Valley, Virginia.

Luther had gotten in his Packard and headed out to fire the Lesters immediately after leaving the bustling mail room on Strickland Street. There he'd asked the woman in charge to give him every envelope addressed to the Lesters and had seen canceled stamps on only two of twenty-four. He'd been inspired to check their mail after concluding a long-distance telephone conversation with the owner of the Kormelu Depilatory Cream company. The owner had complained that eighty-nine percent of the past month's orders, coded to show that the station was their origin, had been returned to the company, marked undeliverable.

Luther drove past the adobe three times before he spotted it. He leapt from the Packard and fought his way through the *coriza* like an enraged adventurer. He spit stirred-up insects from his mouth with every step. He hadn't noticed, to his left, the narrow path the Lesters used.

Barging in on them, he found the Lesters at the table composing that night's letters. They were so surprised, and they'd so come to enjoy their letter writing, that it took them fifteen seconds to emerge from their delighted daze and rid their lips of smiles.

Luther stood over them as they sat in kitchen chairs, reminding them, in case they'd forgotten, of the day he'd taken them in. Of how he'd caught the fainting Ma in his arms as she fell. The Lesters sat mute. What daylight there was, filtered through the *coriza* in front of the windows, caught the ring-worm scar above Pa's ear. Luther asked the Lesters how they'd thought they could sustain their scheme. He was allowing his sarcasm to slant as meanly as it wished. He wondered just how stupid they were. He asked them if they knew how many generations back the inbreeding of their families had actually begun. Then he heard a knock on their door and turned to see O'Malley peeking through the screen.

"Irish."

"Doctor M," O'Malley said. "Something's come up."

"What is it?" Luther asked. "This is important."

O'Malley nodded. "I brought you a piece of mail. My guess is, it is, too."

Luther looked at the Lesters and told them he'd be back, then stepped outside and led O'Malley away from the house. Single file, they beat their way back through the *coriza*. O'Malley, trailing, did not call to Luther and point out the Lesters' path.

When they reached the road where their automobiles were parked, O'Malley took the envelope from his glove compartment and handed it to Luther. Luther looked at its seal. It said "Departamento de Communicaciones." It had come from the National Palace in Mexico City. O'Malley told him it had been hand-delivered not an hour before by a fat *federale* from the regional governor's office in Villa Acuña.

Luther opened the envelope and scanned the letter in one sweep. Its tone, in English, was one of high formality. It explained that after considering a series of complaints against XALM, President Cárdenas had, with reluctance, ordered that Luther be denied further entrance into Mexico. The order was effective immediately, February 1, 1935.

Luther leaned back against the Packard to read the letter more slowly. As he did, he reached for his handkerchief and wiped his forehead and his mouth. He picked absently at burrs and stems clinging to his suit. The letter spoke of the station's violations of Mexican law and it cited the broadcast of dubious North American medical cures that were potentially harmful to the health of Mexicans.

Luther handed the letter to O'Malley to read. Still leaning against the Packard, he looked off toward the Rio Grande, five hundred yards away. There were still times, and this was one of them, when the river, as a border, seemed to him absurd. What the hell, he thought. They might as well have drawn a line in the desert with a stick. His thoughts grew historical. He considered that where he stood at the moment had once been Mexico and that, given the covetous impulse of power, more of what was Mexico would be America soon enough. Then where would the border be? What new muddy creek would they designate? It occurred to him that the barren hillside on which he'd built his station would likely be America in, say, twenty years and he'd have to move it to keep it free and lawless. He chuckled in his thoughts. The old *zona roja* would be some witless Texan's pasture.

He looked back at O'Malley, who'd finished the letter. He felt more hurt than angry and, most of all, inconvenienced. He glanced back over his shoulder at the Lesters' rusted roof above the *coriza*. He sighed and looked up at the vastly bleaching sun, which hadn't quite reached the top of the sky. His thought was that, so far, this had been an Old Testament day; a day of Jobian trials. He'd been betrayed and banished and it wasn't even noon.

O'Malley pointed to the signature of the minister at the bottom of the letter. He asked, "Is this the same fellow we've been paying all along?"

"No," Luther said. "Cárdenas appointed a new one. The price went up last year, as soon as this guy took over."

In 1928, as Luther was completing his station's financing, Haskell Albright had given him the name of someone high in the American embassy. The man, Albright had learned, was an assistant to Ambassador Morrow and by every account an efficient courier. And so each month since 1928, he'd been sent a monthly sum of cash to pass along. Over the years of the Calles government, word had now and then reached Luther that it would be to his advantage if the sum were raised. But the requests had been modest and they'd come infrequently.

Luther said, pointing at the letter, "That's surely all this is. The son of a bitch has decided he wants a bigger *mordida*."

O'Malley swatted at grasshoppers circling his face. He asked, "What are you going to do?"

"I'll have to call Haskell," Luther said. He could already hear Albright's lecture. It seemed to Luther that Albright had taken to inventing concerns. He'd come to hear Albright's tone as that of a father who's handed over his business to his incompetent son, although, as we know, Albright only felt himself a contented enthusiast offering his praise.

Luther said to O'Malley, nodding toward the Lesters' adobe, "Make sure they're packed and on a train as soon as possible."

O'Malley frowned. He didn't know why Luther had driven out to see them. "Ma and Pa are leaving?"

"They miss the mountains," Luther said.

Two weeks later, he sat in an enormous chair of forest-green damask outside the Minister of Communications' office. His eyes followed massive double doors upward. He observed the gilded ceiling. The chandelier overhead was the shape and the size of a pine tree. It appeared in this vastness a reasonably sized lamp. He suspected he'd be taking less note of the excess had he visited the capital before Cárdenas had been elected. He'd read of the new president's ascetic tastes. He'd heard of his refusal to live in Chapultepec. He knew that he'd closed the luxurious casinos and had turned the lavish clubs into schools and orphanages. He pictured sleeping orphans opening their eyes to see chandeliers suspended from gilded ceilings.

He withdrew his pocket watch and saw that he'd been kept waiting half an hour. This did not disturb him. It was what he did himself when people came, bearing gifts, to ask for his help. His mood remained as confident as it had been through the three-day train trip from Piedras Negras.

To his surprise, his conversation with Haskell Albright the day he got the letter had lifted his spirits. Having expected to be scolded, he'd received Albright's concern. When he'd finished reading Albright the letter, Luther offered his assessment that it amounted to an elaborate dunning notice. Then he waited through a pause before Albright replied, "Maybe, Cowboy. Maybe. But Cárdenas has been pulling shit like this since he took office. Raising hell about American companies and their corrupting influence. Talking all kinds of crap about the goddamn Mexican poor." But Luther and Albright agreed that no matter what had caused the letter to be sent, the obvious reply was the money required.

The double doors opened and a small, thin man in a dark blue suit emerged. Luther stood. *"Buenos días, señor,"* said the small man, shaking Luther's hand. "And how was your journey?" Luther said that his journey had been fine. The small man explained that he was the minister's administrative aide and would serve today as their interpreter. He motioned for Luther to follow him in.

Luther judged the minister's office to be the size of his Desert Gardens ballroom. Its walls were covered with panels of red silk in geometric gold brocade. Heavy fringed drapes of velvet hung from arches and flanked several oil paintings in massive gilded frames. Luther's eye caught a portrait that he guessed to be Zapata. The artist had painted the darkly brooding revolutionary looking up at distant mountains with a beatific gaze.

The minister sat behind a requisitely enormous walnut desk. Papers were stacked in neat piles. A large bowl of fruit sat to his left. Like his aide, the minister was small and thin. The few hairs on his head were combed exactly back and lay on his scalp in fine grease-stiffened rows. He wore a military uniform that was decoratively compatible with the splendor of the room. Gold buttons were arranged on his chest in the outline of a pentagon. Brushes of seemingly animate fringe sat on each of his shoulders like exotic and remarkably well-behaved pets.

He gave Luther a flicker of a smile and motioned for him to sit in an overstuffed chair. The aide sat on the minister's right. Luther observed that the aide had a certain impalpability about him. He reminded him of a man who'd worked for several summers as one of Ray White's most talented shills and was similarly somehow spectral, so that when he'd shouted from the crowd about the magic of the compound it was as though a sourceless storm of testimony were descending.

The minister began by apologizing for being attired in his military uniform. He said he hoped that Luther would not think it reflected a style typical of the Cárdenas administration. He routinely wore a simple business suit, he said, but he was due to visit his failing mother in an hour and she loved to see him in his uniform. It was her birthday, he explained; it was the least he could do. Luther received all this through the translation of the aide.

The minister reached for a memorandum and studied it in silence. When he looked up he told Luther it was his duty to inform him that his Mexican visa had been revoked. He said that there was concern about certain broadcasts on Luther's radio station offering medical cures that the government believed harmful to the health of Mexicans.

"Yes," Luther said. "Your letter mentioned all that. But, if I may speak frankly, I'm confused. I can't think what your government has in mind when you speak of harmful cures." Over the days of his trip, he'd planned what he would say about the surgery. He understood that, historically, Mexican medicine was not averse to all manner of animal sacrifice. So he'd prepared an explanation that emphasized the spiritual properties of baboon gonad essence. "If you could specify these concerns, I could speak to them better and satisfy them, I'm sure."

The minister looked again at his memorandum. He turned its top sheet and began to read more closely. His index finger moved down the page. "We are concerned, for example, about the claims for a product whose name is Luvolife? Which your broadcasts say that, by swallowing a pill, it will make the body more limber for living?" He looked at Luther, then down at the memorandum again. "Also, there is a potion which is named The Crazy Water Crystals, and we understand there is a man on your radio station who tells the people that they should put the Crazy Water Crystals in a glass of water and drink them so that the bowels will relax." The minister slowly shook his head.

"Also," he said, and Luther listened as the minister proceeded to describe nearly every sponsor. Marmolu, the fat reducer. Peruna cold tonic. Man-O-Ree, another laxative. Kormelu, the depilatory cream. On and on the minister read, and each time he offered a name, his aide immediately repeated it for Luther.

"Lash Lure," read the minister.

"Lash Lure," said his aide.

"Hamlin's Wizard Oil."

"Hamlin's Wizard Oil," said the aide, then translated the minister's summary of the way Hamlin's Oil claimed it relieved pain.

Listening, Luther seethed. As though he needed the translation! As though he didn't know the claims! It grew obvious to him that he was being subjected to a planned indignity. He imagined the minister and the aide rehearsing, working up this skit to mock the helpless Anglo.

"Sunway vitamins," read the minister.

"Sunway vitamins," said the aide.

"Willard's Tablets," read the minister.

"Willard's Tablets," said the aide.

Finally, Luther sensed the minister finishing his list and he realized, through the boil of his humiliation, there would be no mention of the surgery.

The minister ran his palm over his stiffened strands of hair. He said, "So, you see, Señor Mathias, these are the cures about which President Cárdenas is concerned."

Luther nodded and said he was thankful to have the information. "Because," he said, "with all respect, I assure you there is no reason for the president to be concerned. I think the root of the . . . confusion is simple and that it's just a matter of Americans understanding the way medicines work somewhat differently from the way your people do. For instance . . ." Luther paused. "Again, if I may speak frankly?"

The minister nodded.

"To take just a general example, it's common in Mexico, as I understand, for a *curendero* to make a brush of special herbs and use it to stroke the skin of someone suffering from . . ." He'd forgotten the word. "It's what you call the big fright, I think?"

"*Si,*" the minister's aide said, "*la susto.*"

"*Si, la susto,*" said the minister.

"The *susto,* yes," Luther said. "The *susto.* Now that's a natural practice in your country, and yet in America we would consider it strange. So I would simply ask you, and President Cárdenas, to think of the medicines on my radio station as those which our *curenderos* offer to our people for all their aches and *sustos.*" Luther ventured a smile and unfolded his crossed arms to offer the minister his opened palms.

The minister sat back in his chair. His head rested halfway up its cushioned back. The color of the cushion nearly matched his uniform's, so that his head above his high stiff collar appeared a tiny and suspended thing.

Luther said, "If I might make another point. Even if the president had reason to fear these cures, which again I assure you he does not, my radio towers aim their signal directly back into my country, so no one in Mexico even hears it. And since all of the programs are in English, very few of your people would know what's being said if they *could* hear it. Which they can't."

The minister closed his eyes and rubbed his head back and forth against his cushion in a lazy, feline gesture. Then he sat forward and spoke in English. "You do not speak Spanish yourself, Señor Mathias?"

Luther was taken aback by the minister's sudden shift of language. He felt once again he was being made a fool of. "No, I don't," he said. "A few phrases, nothing more."

The minister said, "It surprises me, Señor Mathias, that you do not speak Spanish. You have lived on the border for many years, I believe. Your radio station is located in Mexico."

Luther said, "The truth is, I've always loved the sound of your language. Maybe I've thought that if I ever understood it, I wouldn't be able to hear its beauty so well."

The minister smiled for the first time since Luther had sat down. He reached toward the bowl of fruit on the corner of his desk and selected a banana. "With respect, señor, that is a condescending attitude. It is like saying that you do not wish to know what a woman thinks inside because it would spoil her beautiful surface." He began to peel the banana with extraordinary care. Using the very tips of his thumb and forefinger, he lifted away its dry inner strings.

Luther flushed. "With respect, sir, I didn't mean it was something I consciously thought. I think I can say that condescension is the last thing I feel for your language, or your country."

"I am sure you think that you can say that," the minister said. "I am sure you think you can. But, of course, condescension is not necessarily conscious, is it?" He broke off a third of the banana and offered it to Luther. Luther gave no indication of accepting or declining. The minister asked, "A bite, Señor Mathias?"

Luther was working to keep his thoughts clear through his rage. So a few more seconds passed before he heard . . . *the bite*? And when at last he did, he thought, The bite! Good lord, the bite! I've had to sit through this lecture just to be signaled by a goddamn banana. The moment seemed suddenly hilarious to him. He wanted to say to the minister, You know, the irony of this moment is that I truly love bananas. Let me tell you the story of my first day in Del Rio, when I bought a whole stalk of bananas from a Mexican on South Main and in his gratitude he offered me a good price on his daughter. Luther wanted to say to the minister, Speaking of understanding each other's language, señor, how is that for understanding one another perfectly? He couldn't wait to tell it all to Haskell Albright. He could already hear Albright's soaring laughter.

Luther shook his head and allowed himself a smile, then reached inside his suit jacket and withdrew an envelope and half rose from his chair to set it on the desk. He was mindful that his movements not be strenuous, that he call no attention to them, while at the same time making sure the envelope lay within reach of the minister. But the desk top was enormous and the minister's arms were short, so it was difficult to give the moment its due subtlety.

He sat back in his chair and rearranged his suit jacket. He drew its sleeve down his arm again until it cut the middle of his torquoise cuff link. He said, "Please understand, Mister minister, that I am deeply sympathetic with your wishes, and those of the president, for a strong and culturally independent Mexico. As you well know, I've been supportive of the Cárdenas government since its inauguration, and I've come today to demonstrate that I want to be even more so in the future."

The minister had given no indication that he saw Luther placing the envelope on his desk. He gave none now that he saw it at his elbow. It sat, pregnant and parchment-toned, midway between the minister and his aide. It contained five thousand dollars. Among the three of them, only Luther gave in to a glance in its direction. His was inspired by a certain nostalgia. He was remembering the days when the envelope was thinner.

The minister had turned away from the envelope and now looked toward his windows. He appeared fairly attentive to something outside. He said, "I gather you are an extremely wealthy man, Señor Mathias."

Luther looked at the aide, whose impassivity, he had to admit, was a talent of a kind. He turned to the minister and said, "That's an awkward question to answer, in that the truth makes me risk sounding like a braggart. But notwithstanding that all things are relative, I would say, yes, sir, I was dirt poor as a child and I've become a wealthy man."

"I am not a wealthy man," the minister said. He continued to appear to be watching the world beyond his windows. "And I have never had the desire to be one. That too is the truth. And perhaps that too makes me sound like I am bragging."

Luther smiled. He said, "Well, if you're worried that it's bragging to call yourself poor, let me observe that a major portion of my entire house could fit inside this office."

The minister turned to look at Luther. His smile came and went away. He said, "You know, Mexicans believe that God smiles on the poor. We believe that in order to be intimate with God you must suffer. The poorer you are, the greater will be God's sympathy for you. The more He loves you. It is my observation that this is one of the many differences between our cultures, Señor Mathias. Americans, it seems to me, assume just the opposite." He looked away from the window and into Luther's face. "That is why I said I was bragging to present myself to you as a man with no interest in wealth. For a Mexican, it is the same thing as saying he is someone whose natural instincts God approves of."

Luther nodded. "In that case," he said, "God and I have known each other well since I was a boy. As I said, I grew up very poor."

"But you are no longer," the minister said. "And so it must be that God has turned away from you." He smiled again. "Or at least that is what the Mexican people would believe." He shook his head. "You must find it very odd to hear talk of God in the offices of a government whose laws prohibit the Church." He shrugged his shoulders. The brushes of his uniform stirred and settled. "But we are nothing if not a people of contradictions, Señor Mathias."

He nodded and spoke more crisply. "And now I must leave you. As to the question of your radio station, let me inform you that our laws require that any company located in Mexico be owned, in the majority, by Mexican citizens. And so President Cárdenas must regretfully insist that you reorganize your station's ownership to include a board of directors, more than half of whom are Mexicans. In the meantime, I will pass along to the president what you have told me today. Perhaps he will be persuaded by your comparison of your products with those treatments favored by *los curenderos.* But for now, while we are still considering the question of the harm of your broadcasts, I am afraid the revocation of your visa must continue. It would be foolish of you, señor, to try to enter Mexico, and especially to try to visit your radio station in Villa Acuña."

He pushed back his chair and rose and stood beside it. Luther and the minister's aide stood as well. The minister leaned forward and offered his hand. In doing so, he nearly brushed the envelope. "Thank you for coming all this way, Señor Mathias." He looked at his aide. "Carlos will show you out whenever you are ready and he will make sure your papers are properly marked so that you will have no trouble on your journey home. I hope you will forgive me for having to excuse myself, but my mother is eighty-one years old today and, as I said, unfortunately she is not well."

Luther watched the minister turn and stride away toward a rear door. The heels of his high boots were muffled on the rugs, then made quick clicks as they struck the wooden floor. He reached the far end of his office and opened the door and closed it soundlessly behind him. The resulting quiet began to spread and fill the room.

"Won't you sit for a moment, Señor Mathias?"

Luther turned to the aide. He could do barely more than blink.

"Please," the aide said.

The two of them sat. Luther looked at the aide and at the envelope on the desk. It appeared to him huge, to cover half the surface. It seemed to be reflecting the sunlight through the window.

The aide sighed. He offered Luther a cigarette and then lit one for himself. He said, "These are new and, as far as I am concerned, I will confess to you, Señor Mathias, very strange times in the history of our country. Things have changed so rapidly that some of us are not sure even now what our leaders might do from day to day. When I say 'some of us,' I refer to those very few like myself who have also served in previous administrations."

Luther was trying hard to shed his dumb distraction. He stared at the aide and finally asked, "You worked for Calles?"

The aide smiled. "I would not misrepresent my position by saying I worked *for* the president. But, yes, I was privileged to assist a secretary of his cabinet. Naturally, when President Cárdenas was elected he swept out all the Callistas and as a consequence, there are, as I say, a small number of us who are attempting to make the transition a harmonious one."

Luther was looking all this while at the envelope. He was asking himself what he should do about it. How could he smoothly retrieve it? By any chance, would it be wise to leave it? He was trying to imagine various consequences of that. He asked the aide, "How was it you survived?" His voice was flat. He had the idea to write a note to slip inside the envelope, designating his contribution to the orphanages of Mexico. But in order to do that, he'd have to tear its seal.

"I'm the minister's cousin," the aide replied.

This got Luther's attention. He looked at the aide and laughed. "His cousin! So family counts for something in the Cárdenas government."

"But of course it does." The aide smiled. He took a drag on his cigarette and threw his head back to exhale toward the gilded ceiling. He shrugged and smiled. "But also, I am here because my cousin believed my experience would be of benefit to him. He had never held such a position as this before. He has been a farmer all his life. He has known the president since they were friends as young boys growing up in Michoacán. He fought under the president's leadership in the revolution. So of course he has the complete trust of the president."

The aide tapped the ash of his cigarette and looked directly at Luther. "Most of all," he said, "the president knows that my cousin is an honest man who has no interest in wealth, just as he described himself to you today. Which is—I must be frank, Señor Mathias— why I was so very surprised by your . . . gesture."

The reference caused Luther to hold his neck stiff so that he would not appear, in the slightest, to sneak a look at the envelope.

The aide leaned forward in his chair to rub out his cigarette in an ashtray on the desk. "I remember well my cousin's rage, soon after his appointment, when contributions such as yours began arriving in this office. His own letters in response were so intemperate that after a while he asked me to draft a standard refusal." Luther watched the aide stand and walk around behind the desk. "He said to me, 'I become too angry when I think about these matters. They take too much of my energy. They only remind me of all the rancid history that's come before.' "

The aide smiled and shook his head and then Luther watched as he reached across the desk and, with a matador's élan, swept the envelope up and into his suit pocket. As though it were a continuation of the same smooth movement, he walked away from the desk toward the window and stopped to look out over the plaza.

He said, "I was very impressed with my cousin today. He has learned to hold his temper in the face of such gestures as yours. When I saw you place the envelope on his desk, I must admit that I held my breath for a moment. I feared that he might lose control and that things would become very ugly."

He laughed and took a step closer to the window. He lit another cigarette. He slowly exhaled. He said, "But you should understand, Señor Mathias, that I am not like my cousin. I see our country's history quite differently than he does. And so your visit today reminds *me* of a time in Mexico—not really so long ago at all, but seeming like another century—when your country's food and your soft drinks and your cigarettes were the height of fashion here. And when our wives played the card game of bridge, and asked us to buy them mink coats which they wore even in the summer heat. And when we all wished to own your Lincoln automobiles."

He left the window and came back toward Luther. His look was wistful. He reached the front of the minister's desk and sat sideways on its edge. His short legs dangled and yet he managed a perched elegance. He said, "I know that you are not a stupid man, Señor Mathias, although your behavior today has been extremely stupid. Perhaps it suggests a certain desperation. Or an overconfidence, if you thought that your personal presence would change the minister's policy. I do not know. I cannot say." He patted the chest of his suit jacket where the envelope rested in an inner pocket. "My point is that I realize you will not be so foolish as to try to persuade the minister again. So I accept your offering as a way of saying to you that it is always possible that the future of our country will be more like its past. And if so, I may be in a position to be of more efficient help to you. Who knows? Who can say?" He slid off the front of the desk and stood erect. "Until that time," he said, "I am very grateful to you for coming, Señor Mathias. Your visit has given me the chance to recall how things once were, and the boldness to hope that they might be that way again."

Luther was escorted from the minister's office and driven to the railroad station. His fury was so great he felt a contradictory numbness. As he rode, he noticed nothing of the street life of the capital. At the station, he moved dazedly through the cars, past the peasants crowded in on facing wooden benches. As the train started forward, Luther barely noted the coal dust from the engine drifting back through the windows and settling steadily on the peasants, many of whom carried cages holding goats and chickens. Inside their roofed and relatively spacious cages, the goats and chickens would enjoy a more comfortable ride.

We have already witnessed several train trips here and have spoken of how the hermetic nature of the travel affected those with something on their minds. To Luther's credit, he again used the time to his advantage. He didn't try to quiet his anger prematurely. It was as though he understood that he had three days ahead of him and there was plenty of time to let his temper behave naturally.

When it had receded enough to allow him to think, he cursed himself bitterly. He thought of how he'd sat in silence while the minister's cousin was offering his drivel and snatching up the envelope. He asked himself why he hadn't responded. Had he grown soft? Did he emanate a softness? Had he become so unused to encountering resistance that he seemed to others to have none in him? Why had the aide sensed that he could mock him? Why had Ma and Pa Lester, for God's sake, thought they could manipulate his mail order system? He made a note to have O'Malley investigate the mail room.

The train was in the mountains, the welcoming ridge of rising shelves. He felt it slow and strain as it climbed. He looked out. The day was darkening. The plateaus were cleanly demarcated: dusky blue to violet, violet to near-black.

He grew gradually more resigned and from within that frame of mind he began to realize that his behavior had been the best he could have managed. No sort of mayhem could have changed the outcome. It was better, in fact, that he'd remained silent. He started to see himself as having sat, remote and apparently unflappable, as blankly impassive as the minister's aide had been.

By the second afternoon, except for a flickering of rage now and then, he was no longer thinking about what had happened in the minister's office. He was anticipating O'Malley waiting for him at the station in Piedras Negras. He was hearing him say, "How'd it go, Doctor M?" He was imagining Haskell Albright's expectant impatience. "Did you screw the bastards, Cowboy?" he heard Haskell Albright ask.

The train moved through a desert basin. Cacti stood in scattered communities. Acacia and nopal rimmed the basin's edges. Vultures looped and circled overhead.

In his mind, he was explaining to O'Malley as they drove back to Del Rio that they'd need to find three citizens of Villa Acuña who'd serve on the station's board of directors. He was observing, "If we keep the money in Acuña, then we can keep our eye on it." He was telling O'Malley that Haskell Albright would agree with this philosophy. He was asking, "Have I ever told you how Albright goes on about why he loves real estate and hates the stock market?" Sitting next to O'Malley in the front seat, he was chuckling and shaking his head. "Jesus," he was saying, "when Haskell gets started, he could bore a tree."

That night the train was in mountains again. It eased its way around the twisting bends, its wheels metal-shrieking through their negotiations. In the rear cars, where the people and their animals slept, the humans' noises were the cruder of the two.

He was imagining his conversation with Haskell Albright. He'd begun to fashion the first anecdotes. The minister had shrunk inside his uniform. He was nervously waving a banana and then scurrying off to see his mother. The aide's movements were a rodent's as he snatched up the envelope. There were tears in the aide's eyes as he

recalled the days of Calles. He dried them on his sleeve, apologizing
for his lapse. Luther was hearing Albright's booming laugh and when
Albright paused, Luther was explaining the idea he'd worked out
with Travis Fenbow. Fenbow would begin the simple task of a telephone hook-up to carry Luther's voice from Del Rio to the station,
then north from the towers back into the country. "Haskell," he was
saying, "what those larcenous bastards fail to understand is that
there's no such thing as a border in the sky."

At dawn the train was passing through a vast plain of grasses.
Jackrabbits, big as dogs, raced here and there in herds. The rim of
mountains, pale and final in the south, was the turned-up edge of the
world.

When O'Malley greeted Luther's train in Piedras Negras, he informed Luther that *policia* from Villa Acuña were posted outside
the radio station around the clock. They'd taken up positions at the
edge of Luther's property. They alternated, two at a time, in six-hour
shifts. Though they were only local men, they were under the direction of the *federales* stationed in Villa Acuña. They checked everyone who came and went to make certain Luther wasn't trying to
visit. As O'Malley finished saying this, a wince crossed his face. He
was clearly expecting Luther to explode. But Luther only shook his
head and smiled. Then he laughed and said, "It's like a changing of
the palace guard!" And on the drive back north from Eagle Pass he
told O'Malley what had happened and what they were going to do.

The following afternoon, after he'd talked to Travis Fenbow, he at
last called Haskell Albright. He'd refused to take his three earlier
calls; he wanted everything in place before he spoke to him.

Albright said, "I don't like this board of directors shit. You know
how it goes, Cowboy. You invite them in to use your plumbing,
they'll pitch their tent right over it."

Luther said, "It's a hell of a lot better than sending money to
Mexico City so the minister's cousin can put it in his pocket." He
said, "That's what most confused me. When the minister refused
that envelope I thought, Why has he suddenly gotten honest on us?
Then his cousin swooped it up and I realized *he's* been taking it all
along."

"Uhn-uh," Albright said.

"Uhn-uh?" Luther said.

"That's not what's been happening."

"Then what has been happening? And how do you know?"

"I made some inquiries. I've been trying to let you know about it for two days. If you'd ever accept your goddamn telephone calls you'd find out what was going on."

"What *is* going on? I'm listening, Haskell. Tell me now what's going on."

"The money never left our embassy."

"The money never left our embassy? What do you mean? What do you mean, the money never left the embassy?"

"The son of a bitch in our embassy has been keeping it. He found out right away the new minister wasn't interested. Apparently, the new minister jumped right on top of him in his office. Scratched his face. Wrenched his neck. Beat the living shit out of him, apparently. Right there in his office. Told him he would kill him if he ever came back and tried to bribe him again. So he decided he just wouldn't bother telling us. You've been subsidizing the traitorous little shit all this time."

"How do you know this?" Luther asked.

"I told you, I made some inquiries. I got suspicious. Didn't I tell you I was suspicious the day you called and read me the letter? I had some people ask around. Apparently, the son of a bitch was bragging about it."

Luther was silent before he began to laugh.

"Why the hell are you laughing?"

"Because it's funny," Luther said. Then he said that it only proved his point. From now on, he told Albright, they'd need to spend less money. It would cost less to pay three local Acuñans than the sum he'd been blindly sending off to the capital. "Think of it, Haskell, as owning real estate you can drive past every day."

Travis Fenbow's telephone connection was finished by the end of the week and Luther began to broadcast from the comfort of his study. Not two weeks after that, O'Malley had assembled a board of directors, its charter filed with the regional governor, made up of Fenbow and himself and three Acuñans, including two former mayors. At the same time, O'Malley reported to Luther there was no further evidence of anyone interfering with the numbers in the mail room. And after a month had passed it was clear that the station was running more smoothly and profitably than ever before. Its employees had begun to enjoy the presence of the posted *policia*. They saluted as they walked past them toward the station. They said, "Y'all be at ease." One of the guards always kept a sober bearing but all the others smiled and showed their lightheartedness. Travis Fenbow had a simple roofed shelter built for them so they could escape the pitiless sun. Luther had the idea to buy them uniforms, which even the solemn guard accepted with delight.

*A*nd now Luther stood in fading daylight at the Comstock, Texas, depot, waiting for Alyce Rae's train to arrive. Again he'd received a telegram from Los Angeles and he was naturally brooding among several recollections. He remembered Billy's telegram, in 1927, announcing his journey to Del Rio to claim his Alyce. Then Billy's second, asking Luther to come and hear a proposition. He remembered his own, to Haskell Albright, prompting Albright's reply that he get his ass there instantly. Luther saw these telegrams as having signaled the steps of his success. And he felt certain, as he stood outside the weather-bleached shack that served as Comstock's station, that this most recent one, from Alyce, assured another extraordinary episode. He had no idea why she was coming. It was evidence enough just to know that she was.

He nervously fingered the sweatband of his fedora. He watched an old couple standing near the tracks, the only others waiting. They were dressed in faded clothes so clean and neatly pressed as to appear the costumes of people trying to look like farmers. The lines in their faces made a regular crosshatched weave. When Luther had arrived, they'd bid him a good evening and told him they were meeting the woman's younger sister. They said that she'd just buried her husband and was leaving California to come and live with them. They'd offered this information very much as a team, alternating their sentences. Then they'd seemed to tilt forward slightly as their expressions lifted, waiting for Luther to return their overture. When he made it clear he was going to give them nothing, their pouts and the hurt they betrayed were infantile.

He glanced up at the sky. It was a flat world-wall of late spring twilight. There were low, thin clouds and there were masses building higher. He judged the blend of hues pinking up from the horizon to be sufficiently impressive. He reasoned that it would be dark by the time they began the drive to Del Rio and full night, an hour later, when they arrived at Desert Gardens. He pictured the red and green and blue of the huge tiered fountain in his circular drive. The presence of clouds promised a starless darkness, which would make the fountain's lights especially spectacular. His concern was as though he were readying a room.

Luther's thoughts returned to that ferociously hot morning when he'd waited with Alyce and the nurse for Billy's train. He remembered standing just behind Alyce and tracing with his eyes the graceful line of her neck below her yellow hair. He'd watched a rivulet of sweat travel the length of her nape and disappear below the neckline of her dress. It had seemed to him a sight so intimate that his glimpsing it felt illicit.

Again he looked at the sky. Waiting, in Comstock, the sky was what there was to look at.

Peter O'Malley had brought Alyce's telegram to Luther's home at ten o'clock at night, a week ago. At the moment O'Malley knocked on the door, Luther was screwing Betty Neal on the floor in front of his massive pipe organ. Its construction had finally been completed just the day before. It hadn't yet been played. For the past three months or so, Betty Neal had been meeting Luther at his home after his nightly broadcast, leaving Ronnie Truehart to watch her sleeping daughter, Netty. Ronnie Truehart had complained that it was a task beneath his status. Betty Neal suggested that if he felt that way about it he should take it up with Luther. She'd recently been given her own radio program of fortune-telling and advice, on which she called herself Dawn O'Day.

When Luther opened the door, his face showed the particular lopsided incredulity of one who's been interrupted in the midst of sex. The tails of his white shirt hung below his belt. "Irish!" he said. He blinked and scowled.

By way of reply, O'Malley handed him the telegram. Luther opened it and scanned it and his irritated expression corrected itself.

"Luther Luther?" came Betty Neal's voice from inside. Her tone was the same singsongy caw she used when she called to Nettie Neal. Hearing it, O'Malley noted, not without some admiration, how successfully Betty was able to lower and smooth her voice as Dawn O'Day.

"Luther Luther?" Betty called.

Luther looked up from the telegram. He smiled and winked at O'Malley. "I'll see you in the morning, Irish," Luther said.

He shut the door and stood in the hallway and read Alyce's telegram again. It gave him a telephone number and asked him to call her there at one o'clock the next afternoon. "Do not contact me at home," the telegram said. "Will explain."

But she hadn't. The number she'd given him was the home of her friend, Larraine Evans, the former starlet whom Alyce had known since their days at Paramount. She asked Luther if he'd meet her train alone, somewhere outside Del Rio, and if he'd not tell anyone she was coming.

"Would you do that?" she'd asked.

"Of course," he'd said.

"Thank you," she'd said. "I'm very grateful." Her deep husky voice wavered noticeably.

He'd asked, "Are you all right?"

She'd said, "I'm sure I will be."

It was as though, in the spirit of her secretive arrival, her train was waiting out of sight until the last trace of daylight disappeared from the sky. For at just that instant, the whistle sounded down the tracks and a few seconds later the train eased in with its ritual offering of steam gusts and groans. Is there a more expectant pause than that created when a train has settled to a stop and we stand waiting for its doors to open?

Luther saw a woman ease herself down the steps. This was the widowed sister, he assumed. She did not look as old as he'd expected. He saw the couple start forward to meet her. A few more seconds passed, not so many really. But nevertheless Luther's fear that Alyce hadn't come was about to escape his emotional grip and fly around inside his heart.

Then he saw her. She was dressed in a severely tailored suit with a long skirt that seemed to Luther, as he studied her, a futile effort to disguise her sexuality. She wore a cream felt hat, its brim pulled comically low.

He held himself still as she stepped carefully down and over a set of tracks. She was carrying a small suitcase. He watched her look left and right. For a moment he felt his fate as vulnerable to the will of the stranger approaching as he'd sensed it that morning, a ten-year-old in Cliffside, when he'd stood at his mother's grave and watched Ray White's horse-drawn wagon coming toward him from the sun.

He raised his arm and Alyce caught its movement. She nodded and smiled. He walked forward and reached to take her suitcase.

"Welcome to Comstock."

Alyce smiled again, handing him her suitcase. Her eyes in the darkness were a near-black jade. She said, "When I didn't see you right away, I was afraid you hadn't come."

He said, "Why would you think such a thing?" He pointed toward his Packard, parked beneath a towering live oak.

Alyce shrugged. Her smile had held.

He said, "You're looking beautiful."

"Thank you," Alyce said, "even though you're lying. I'm exhausted from the trip and I absolutely look it."

In truth, her appearance seemed to Luther not so much unchanged as emphasized. Her beauty, the compelling elusiveness that was somehow almost a physical aspect of her—these features seemed stronger than he'd remembered.

They reached his Packard and Luther saw the old couple and the widowed sister. They stood beside an ancient Chevrolet parked nearby. The widow bore no resemblance to her sister and appeared arguably the least mournful of the three. They were all staring openly at Alyce. Luther's first thought was that they'd recognized her.

He sensed Alyce's discomfort and was surprised when she said suddenly to the widow, "Oh, there you are." Alyce looked up at Luther. "This is my brother, Luther." He felt Alyce's grip tighten on his arm. She said, "Luther, this poor woman has recently been widowed and she's moving from Los Angeles to live with her sister and brother-in-law. She told me all about it on the train." She said to the couple, "You're obviously very kind."

"Damn straight we are!" the old man croaked.

✳ ✳ ✳

In the Packard, Alyce smiled. "Thank you for being my brother. The poor woman started up before we'd even left Los Angeles, asking if I traveled often, asking where I was going. 'Comstock?' she said. 'What a coincidence, so am I!' I had to be rude just to try to keep her quiet. Finally, she said, 'I'm sorry. I used to be a woman of few words. It just goes to show you how grief can change a person.'" Alyce shook her head. "No: 'free up a person.' She said, 'It just goes to show you how grief can free up a person.'"

Luther smiled. He repeated, "How grief can free up a person." He thought suddenly of Ray White with a flash of perfect and impregnable resentment.

They drove southeast on a narrow road that paralleled the Rio Grande. Alyce heard the muffled power of the Packard's engine. She looked straight ahead at the dusty night-beige blankness that the headlights gave her.

A quiet came between them. Alyce sensed it as awkward. Inside the Packard, inside the overwhelming night, she began to feel as though she were sitting next to Luther in an intimate cave. She decided the moment was demanding she speak casually. She cleared her throat and said, "Billy sends his fond regards."

Luther nodded. "I appreciate it." After a moment, he asked, "So he knows you're here?"

"Oh, certainly," Alyce said. "Of course he does."

Luther said, "I only asked if he knew you'd come because of your . . . instructions."

"Of course," Alyce said.

"In your telegram, and then on the telephone."

"I understand."

Luther waited for her to say more. He glanced at her beside him. She had taken off her hat and run her fingers through her hair. The darkness made her silhouette almost a cameo. He was certain that she was lying about Billy, but he'd decided as he'd watched her stepping down from the train that the direction of their talk was hers to determine. The most he would do was try to nudge her toward divulgence.

He sneaked another glance in an attempt to judge her mood. As much as he could see it in the dark, her face showed the slack docility of someone deep in thought.

She said, "I didn't stop to think, until I was on the train, that it must have been terribly inconvenient for you to meet me."

"It wasn't at all," Luther said.

"But your radio program. Its schedule, I mean."

He paused and nodded. "I'm surprised you know when I'm on the radio." In some sense, this was true.

Alyce said, "*My* impression is, there are very few people in America who don't."

Again he waited while he quieted his delight. He said, "I recorded a transcription earlier today." He turned to her and smiled. "One of the things I've learned, since the last time you saw me, is how to be in two places at once." His smile broadened.

Alyce smiled in response. "Well, that is impressive." She looked straight ahead again. Her eyes tried to focus on the infinite strip of road, but what her mind saw was Luther's smile of a moment ago. It seemed to her not a smile he'd have shown her years before. She didn't sense it as fraudulent, but as reflecting a deep and unapologetic confidence. She was startled not only by the smile, but by the degree to which she'd felt its force. In her mind, she tried to place it on the face of Luther in 1927, the open and awestruck face she'd looked into when she'd wakened in the Val Verde County jail. She could not. She turned her head and briefly watched him as he drove. She tried to imagine him smiling this new smile as he'd suddenly stood in the guest cottage and put his hand to her chin and lifted her face to his. Again, she could not. What she'd felt in him that day was fear and will and a blade of anger. She'd felt his power, that is, and, yes, a sort of confidence. But she'd sensed him working to gather it, his effort almost palpable, while tonight it naturally lit his very smile. She suspected this was a change that mattered absolutely.

She said, "I *assume* you know your station reaches Los Angeles."

"Yes," Luther said. He nodded and kept his eyes on the road.

"Especially recently, people speak of hearing you."

He looked at her and raised his eyebrows. He said, "We increased the strength of the signal." He turned his attention back to the road. The Packard provided the sounds for a short while. Then he asked, "And what do people say?"

"What do people say?"

"In Los Angeles," Luther said. "When they speak of hearing me."

"Well," Alyce said, "they say . . . they say a range of things." She regretted having mentioned this. Her intention had been to move the talk away from Billy.

"A range?" Luther said.

She thought she heard his tone as playful. She said, "I only meant you've been the focus of some lively discussions."

Alyce was trying to close the subject, but what she said was true. Now that the station's signal more thoroughly covered Los Angeles, Luther had become something of a cult figure within the Hollywood community. Most saw his radio persona as deliberately broad camp, but his rejuvenation message had shown the power to divide. There were a few, Conrad Early and other aggressively virile leading men, who mocked Luther with profanity and not a note of humor. Others, the director William Lanham Allister's circle of intellectual homosexuals, found Luther exploitive of an already vulnerable population, while a much smaller number of more political homosexuals insisted that impotence was just another form of inherent sexuality. They denounced Luther for suggesting it could be, should be, altered.

But as we know, there were also in the country at this time many who proudly admitted to having had the surgery. They were quick to add, however, that their restorative procedures had been performed in Europe and that Luther was, at best, a clown, at worst an unctuous huckster.

"You've heard some lively discussions about me?" Luther persisted.

Alyce was feeling cornered. "We were at a cocktail party, for instance, where someone praised you."

"Is that right?"

"Yes."

You have no evidence of that! Billy had screamed.

"Oh, for Christ's sake, Billy," said the insufferable screenwriter, who'd been a New York drama critic. "He's a hick. He's a snake oil salesman. I grant you, he's amusing with his corn pone appeals, but if you've ever heard him, you can't be defending him."

Alyce had watched Billy's eyes narrow on the insufferable screenwriter. She'd cringed, moments before, when Luther's name was mentioned and someone turned to her and said, "I've been meaning to ask you, wasn't it Del Rio where Billy came to get you when you had that little *crise*?" Alyce had replied, Yes, it was, and, Yes, it was a coincidence, and, No, we never met this man, Mathias, and then she'd heard the insufferable screenwriter use the phrase "a *soupçon* of drollery." She turned her attention back to Billy. He screamed, "You pompous faggot!" As he stepped toward the screenwriter, Billy's eyes were lit with a recidivist's gleam that appeared in them these days at the slightest provocation. She watched him raise his fist and then she breathed, "Thank God," when two other guests grabbed Billy and pinned his arms to his side.

In Luther's Packard, she began to wonder where Billy might be at this moment. In recent weeks, each time she'd left the house, he'd asked when she'd be back. Each time she'd returned he'd said she was late. He'd become so dependent that she couldn't imagine him seeing or speaking to anyone in her absence. Surely then he was alone, wandering through their house. Sitting dumb with drink in the sun room, staring out. In this picture of Billy, she found the rueful consolation that at least he'd be safe with the servants watching him.

Luther said, "That must put Mr. Boswell in an awkward position."

Alyce started. "What must?" she said.

"When my name comes up at gatherings like that."

She turned and looked at Luther as closely as she could. In reply, or so it seemed, he turned and looked at her. As best she could tell he appeared to be sincere. So she said, "Yes. It puts him in a very awkward position." Then she shifted in her seat so that she faced the windshield squarely. "Where are we now?" she asked. "How much longer will it be?"

Half an hour, Luther said, and he suggested she try to relax as much as possible. He said he knew from his own experience how tiring the trip was and he went on from there, having got her blatant clue, to speak with an impressively sustained innocuousness. He described the landscape they couldn't see. He said the purple sage had capriciously flowered a few weeks back. He wondered if she knew that mistletoe was a mesquite parasite. He informed her that Mexico was ten miles to their right and that its scrub earth at the border was just the same as Texas, with a pale-gray rim of mountains in its spectral southern distance. He said the Mexicans had nicknamed the mountains *La Mujer Dormiendo,* because their peaks against the sky drew a sleekly graceful line, the curves of a lady sleeping on her side, and that The Sleeping Lady, according to legend, woke at midnight and shifted onto her back to receive the pleasure of her lover, *La Luna.*

Alyce recognized what Luther was doing and she was grateful to him. It suggested the thoughtfulness she'd remembered as his guiding quality, in the days after she'd opened her eyes in the Val Verde County jail and looked into his face. It seemed to her she'd already recognized some of what she'd suspected Luther had become and some of what she'd once imagined him to be. This left her, as had so much else these past months, to try to reconcile deeply warring emotions. She was beginning to feel less regretful that she'd come, while, further in, her guilt regarding Billy was moving wildly.

Dearest darling, she had written in the note she'd left for him. I need—I feel *we* need for me—to go away for a short while. I want to think about us, about the problems we've been trying to deny, and I know I can only do this if I'm alone. I know, too, that if I were to tell you where I've gone, you'd immediately come after me or at least attempt to reach me. Try as you would to honor my wishes, you'd not be able to resist. Please forgive me, darling, if that sounds patronizing.

It seems we've reached the point where my presence only irritates you, so perhaps, with me away, you can think things through in a calmer state of mind. My special hope is that you'll consider your decision very carefully, that you'll begin to see how you can put your disappointments behind you and think about how you can move *on,* instead of looking to the past as the source of your solutions. So in my absence, while it's quiet, please ask yourself what is the best way to start anew, and know that I will be asking myself how I can help you to do that.

Please, please, be assured that I will be back soon, very soon—in a week at most.

I am doing this, yes, for me, I admit that, but also for you, in the hope of saving us.

Alyce

Over and over, as they rode, Alyce rewrote her note to Billy while Luther spoke of things like weather and the Packard cleaved the night. In her mind, she replaced "saving us" with "helping us." She eliminated the "patronizing" sentence altogether.

Her worrying drew her more deeply down. She lost sense of the time. She paid no notice to the thickening dust beyond the windshield, which had begun to meet the headlights like a boiling red fog. Her fixated concern and the dust clouds in the headlights and the lush monotony of Luther's voice all combined to mesmerize her. A drowsiness slowly descended and she fled the sensation, as she drifted into sleep, of the claustral suffocation Billy's desperate need inflicted.

Out of the corner of his eye, Luther saw her head drop. He stopped whatever he was saying. He looked at Alyce, and as he did, her head rolled to one side so that it lay where her shoulder met the door of the Packard. His eyes followed the line of her jaw, the breadth of whitest skin beneath it, the reptilian length of her lovely neck. A quick sexual eagerness ran through him, a sensation somehow both charged and hushed. She began to breathe deeply. Luther smiled. An elation filled him. He was driving Alyce Rae through a reachless Texas night! Once again, the tented splendor of a reachless Texas night! Her return, her presence beside him, seemed composed of the past and of the moment and of the luminous future.

He drove more slowly through the dust. His eyes moved from Alyce to the road to Alyce. He was reminded again of coming upon her, asleep on the bench in the Val Verde County jail. Her lank hair had fallen loosely across her sunburned face. He'd leaned forward and moved it away from her eyes and softly tucked it behind her ear. He remembered expecting her to wake from his touch but that she'd continued to sleep.

He reached across the Packard's leather seat and slowly lowered his hand. With a delicacy his deftness could accomplish, the tips of his fingers touched her tautly offered neck. He felt her blood pulsing.

In his mind, they were in the guest cottage and he was easing her blouse's buttons free and kneeling before her and softly, sacramentally pressing his mouth to her breasts.

Alyce was still asleep when they reached the outskirts of Del Rio and when Luther drove them past the doors of the Mathias Clinic. She was asleep when they passed the new warehouses and when they turned into the white gravel drive of Desert Gardens. He slowed to a crawl as they passed beneath the palms but she was soundly asleep when they came to a stop and the alternating lights of the fountain failed to wake her.

He shut off the motor and looked over at Alyce. The red and blue and green of the fountain lit her face. His disappointment was enormous, as unruly as a child's. Indeed, his impulse to complain contained a tantrum's essence. And it was at this instant that Luther realized how much and for how long he'd wanted to show her what he'd done. He suddenly sensed that she'd been integral all along and this took him greatly by surprise. So, at least as much, did the nature of his sadness. It was deep and ancestral and it made him feel afraid.

Once more he turned and looked at her. He was unsure of how to wake her. Should he gently shake her shoulder? Should he loudly clear his throat? Finally he decided to whisper her name. "Alyce," he said softly. "Alyce, we're here." In response, a riffled snoring issued from her nose.

Consuela, Luther's maid, helped Alyce up the stairs. Alyce held the massive balustrade with one hand and leaned against Consuela like an invalid. Luther's initials were carved into the vertical face of each step. These were among the features of the house she didn't notice. When he'd finally wakened her and helped her from the Packard, she'd closed her eyes tight against the fountain's lights, making a pained and cranky expression. Inside, she'd barely been able to open her eyes. She'd mumbled her apologies and said they'd talk in the morning.

In the soft, narrow bed, Alyce lay on her left side and then on her right. The wrought-iron frame creaked when she turned. She sensed another kind of night-quiet from the one she was used to. Night hawks spoke somewhere outside her windows. She was not completely conscious and, in that lightest realm of sleep, Billy filled her mind.

He was pacing back and forth at the foot of their bed but his movements were eerily languid and precise. He smoked half a cigarette, put it out and lit another. He'd said not a word on the drive home from the cocktail party and he continued to say nothing. Alyce watched him from a chintz reading chair in a corner of the room. She felt his outburst at the party had signaled some further descent. He'd heard talk of Luther on other occasions and had been able to turn away from it.

But he'd been tuning in the program religiously for weeks, and at times, when she caught the sound of Luther's broadcast, she'd found herself drawn to listen, too. Sitting next to Billy, she'd watched him shake his head in response to something Luther said. At other times, she'd heard him whisper, "No." But it was just as likely that he would nod and seem to smile approvingly. She believed him to be trying, as she was for her own reasons, to match the young Luther Mathias they'd known with the preposterous salesman they were hearing on the air. When Alyce had stepped back in her mind and tried to see their troubles whole, it sometimes seemed to her that the return of Luther's voice at this hour in Billy's life was something akin to the devil's idea of grace.

In their bedroom, Billy had come to a stop and ground his cigarette into a silver ashtray. He'd seemed to scan the room in an attempt to find Alyce and when he'd spotted her he smiled mawkishly and said, "I've come to a decision."

She looked at him. "A decision? About what?"

"I'm going to get in touch with Doctor Mathias. I'm going to undergo his current surgery."

Alyce sat up in Luther's guest bed. She blinked. Her eyes began to be able to see the room. She could make out its heavy woodwork, its beamed ceiling and dark wood floor. She got out of bed and walked to a window and tried to raise the sash. It was stuck in its frame and she struggled and banged it three times with the heel of her hand before she finally forced it up.

She looked out over the grounds. The night remained starless. She saw the abstract shapes of trees. She listened for any sounds, within or without. The night hawks were continuing, but the house itself was still. A cool breeze came into the room. She looked out again and could see below her window the linked geometries of rose gardens.

She walked to a corner and sat down in a chair. There was no give in its cushions, as though no one had sat in it before. As it happened, no one had. She lifted the skirt of her long nightgown and crossed her legs.

She had heard Billy declare his intentions and she had tried to mask the depth of her alarm. As we know, she'd been skeptical from the first of what Luther had done to Billy and from her fear she'd fashioned an incurious shield. She'd gotten no details from Billy and she'd asked for none. She'd said pointedly to Luther that she didn't wish to know. Her feelings toward Luther had already been confusing—as much as he'd helped her, she'd intuitively sensed a harm he'd done to Billy—and she'd tried to will them to become no more so. But she was convinced, when she heard Billy's announcement, that what he wished would be disastrous. For him; for them; in ways she couldn't, needn't, specify to herself.

So she'd asked him, in their bedroom, to come and sit beside her. He'd lit two cigarettes and walked across the room and handed one to her. He'd sat down on the bed. As was often the case when he made a decision in a state of terror, a pacific jauntiness had immediately come over him. She'd smoked and cleared her throat, then taken his hand and said that she wanted him to know that so far as she was concerned the recent return of his . . . difficulties was nothing that worried her in the least. His grip tightened instantly and his jauntiness disappeared. He said that that was easy for her to say and that besides, he knew she was lying to appease him. She said that she was not, absolutely she was not, and that she was sure, anyway, the recurrence would be brief. She asked him if he didn't think that, whatever the problem, it most likely had to do with the tension he was feeling, the pressure he was under? That whatever its cause, it was surely in his head? So, he'd said, are you suggesting I'm mad? She'd answered that of course she was not saying that at all. But she was wondering what he thought Dr. Mathias could do for him now that he hadn't done before? And Billy had shaken his head and said she didn't understand the medical science of these matters. No, she said, of course I don't, but that doesn't answer the question I just asked. What, she repeated, do you think you could gain by going to see Dr. Mathias again? And Billy had smoked and looked away and then looked at Alyce and said that the operation Mathias offered presently was something much more advanced, more efficiently directed and therefore much more powerful than the surgery he'd performed almost ten years ago. He said this had become clear to him in listening to the broadcasts, no matter what the supercilious Europhiles of Hollywood might say. He said his faith in Luther Mathias was unshaken. He'd been helped by him twice and he was sure he could be helped a third and final time. If you were loyal, Billy told her, to what had aided you before, the focus of that loyalty would continue to reward you. He said he'd been thinking about loyalty quite a lot these days. Mutual loyalty, he'd realized, was a kind of miraculously compounded currency, the trading of which made both parties richer. He said he'd come to see the strong connection between one's well-being and the fostering of loyalty. He added, with bitterness, that he was all too conscious of the spread of disloyalty everywhere in Hollywood and that it was time to rise above it and become better in the process. When he'd finished, she didn't attempt to talk him out of anything, but she continued to speak encouragingly to him and she could see, as he grew exhausted, that he was listening to her. His air of sharp resentment faded and by the time the sun was rising he had no strength left and she got him to agree that he would wait one month before he contacted Luther, during which, he promised her, he would weigh the benefits against any likely hazards. Although, he'd said, and smiled, there truly were no hazards.

Alyce rose from Luther's stiff-cushioned chair and walked back to the windows. She looked out at the night again and what she saw in her mind, to her surprise, was the image of Luther's confident smile. It almost seemed to Alyce to be sitting in the sky like a thin receiving crescent of a moon. She closed her eyes and opened them and her mind traced once again the moments that comprised her own history with Luther. As always, her thoughts settled on the day she'd come to him in the guest cottage. As always, she thought, what an extraordinary thing, to have made love as they had, with such slow and needful pleasure. As always, she asked herself why she'd come and if she'd known and if she'd somewhere in her mind determined that they would.

And now she began to feel she understood some things. Or at least to feel she was beginning to understand. Surely her being again in Luther's presence, being again in Del Rio, was helping her remember how she'd opened her eyes in the Val Verde County jail and seen his face and sensed a kind of newborn's imprinted trust in him. For those days, as she'd returned, he'd seemed to her a source of innocent and enormous competence. And so, she thought, she must have come to him that day in the cottage not so much to learn of Billy, but to get once more from Luther all he'd offered her in Del Rio. Because, in spite of whatever she feared he'd done to Billy, he had to that point only been of help to her and, yes, he had, she'd also known, desired her. Then surely that was what she'd felt she needed in the first uncertain weeks of her resumed life with Billy.

And perhaps, as well, she'd made love to Luther that afternoon because she'd also felt his anger, sensed his crassness and his summoned confidence. At the window, she looked out on the rose gardens once more. And she wondered, as she stared down at the night-patterned quilt they made, if she'd come here now in part to feel all of that again. She'd told herself she was coming to Del Rio to confirm her sense of Luther, for Billy's sake; for *his*. But had she really just repeated the deception of her visit to the cottage? For whom had she come to see Luther this time?

In his bedroom down the hall, Luther drank brandy. He'd been roaming restlessly among his rooms for several hours. After watching Alyce and Consuela climb the stairs, he'd stood in the middle of his living room. Then he'd tiptoed to the foot of the stairs and walked perhaps a third of the way up, trying to listen to whatever sounds there were. He imagined the whisper of her skirt against her slip as it fell. He imagined the padding of her bare feet on the floor.

He moved into his study and pulled some loosely bound reports from the shelves. He read the minutes of the most recent meeting of the XALM board of directors. He was pleased but not surprised to see that O'Malley and Fenbow were firmly in control. He put that file away and tried to read some figures comparing the net profits of the new Mathias Nonsurgical Treatment with those of the full Mathias Operation. It seemed that, as he'd hoped, the Treatment was becoming so popular that he could devote less and less time to surgeries.

Then his concentration left him and he knew he could not retrieve it. He leaned back in his chair and tried to picture her asleep upstairs and he remembered the day he'd been asked to call on Billy in the third-floor suite of the St. Charles Hotel. He'd sat trying to listen to Billy but all he could think of was Alyce in the bedroom just beyond. He remembered wondering if she were sleeping while they talked or whether she was listening with her ear pressed to the door. He remembered nearly missing the start of Billy's confession. And sitting at his desk, with Alyce sleeping overhead, he felt suddenly just as curious, and as far from the chance of being any more than that, as he'd been that day in the suite at the St. Charles.

He got up and walked into the kitchen and made himself a turkey sandwich. When he'd finished eating it, he took a bottle of good brandy from the kitchen's liquor cabinet and moved into the living room. He'd plopped down on a couch in front of the fireplace. He looked to the opposite end of the room where the massive pipe organ stood. There seemed to him a symbiosis between the cold hearth and the silent organ. He'd poured some brandy and taken a large swallow but that hadn't helped to settle him. So he'd reached for the bottle and risen quickly from the couch and toured the house a final time.

Sitting in his bedroom, he'd drunk nearly half the bottle. He was virtually ordering himself to sit still. He couldn't resist reviewing the scale of emotions he'd experienced this evening. The ten-year-old's fear that had swept over him as he'd watched her walking from the train toward him. The great disappointment as she'd slept through his tour. His complicated sadness, and his alarm at feeling sadness, when he'd understood how near he had held her all along.

He took a sip of brandy. He thought about all those instances when he'd stood back to watch himself moving through a scene with skill and grace and in his mind had raised his gaze to where she was watching also. It was true that he'd been conscious of his folly in those moments but he'd always thought them rare. Now he suspected that he'd imagined her almost continually. He asked how he could have let himself be so unaware.

He looked toward the window. The sky was beginning to lighten. He was not at all tired but told himself he should sleep. He stood up and moved toward his bed. He undressed and climbed in and sat propped up against the pillows. He watched the infiltrating dawn.

Then he heard, he was certain, a window slam shut in Alyce's bedroom. And the startling sound, its resonance, was what he needed to begin to see how changed things were. He was not the bemused caller, summoned to the St. Charles. She had come to him. She was visiting him in his grand new home, its dimensions doubly those of Billy's Tudor outhouse. And he realized how fortunate he was to have understood his need for Alyce in time. Now that he knew it, now that she was here, he could do what was needed to make her see she wished to stay. Doubtless she'd come because Billy was in trouble, and if Billy was in trouble, then her life with Billy was.

He recalled the day in the St. Charles, before Billy had arrived, when she'd paused in the hallway at the door of her suite and in saying good-bye had mistakenly called him Douglas and held his hand with a fierceness he saw the truth of only now.

Billy, Billy, the pitiful bastard. How much, in the end, there would be to thank him for.

And yet, among the three of them, only Billy was sleeping soundly at this moment, although his sleep, if it could be called that, had been chemically induced.

Billy had drunk himself senseless for the third day in a row and passed out at sundown, sitting in a high wing chair before a roaring fire in his living room. He'd been more or less camped out there since he'd read Alyce's note. The note itself lay crumpled at his feet among a growing pile of papers and dirty glasses and unopened bottles of sleeping pills. He'd been insisting that a fire be kept going day and night. Its flames snapped and unfurled. He'd wrapped his legs and feet in blankets. These late spring days in Los Angeles were extraordinarily hot, but unfathomable winter raged in Billy's heart.

Elsewhere in the house, the maid and the cook and the butler sweated like pigs. They dressed as lightly as possible and kept all the windows open in the rooms where they worked. They prayed for a break in the heat, inside and out. Huddling in the kitchen, amidst electric fans, they spoke among themselves of what to do. They knew of Alyce's note. The second day she'd been gone, Michael the butler had crept up while Billy slept and picked it up off the floor. He'd whispered, "Oh, God!" as he read it. When he'd told the other servants, they'd said much the same.

They all felt that, were they Alyce, they might have done as she had. None of them thought she would be returning. But their shared belief was that Billy would need care; that he would soon become a patient. For they knew, having watched his dissipation over the past year, that as alarming as things had sometimes been before, they'd seen nothing so hysterical as what was apt to come. Among their tasks, as they saw them, was to keep from the world the news that she had left.

*　　*　　*

It was just past eight A.M. when Billy's doorbell rang. Through the humming in his head, he heard Michael hurrying from the kitchen. He felt time pass, during which the doorbell's ringing refused to leave his ears. He shook his head, trying to clear it, which made the ringing worse while rousing the day's pain. He blinked and looked into the fire. He was turning his head to call for Michael when he saw him entering the room. He was dressed in plaid Bermuda shorts and long black stockings. His fat white knees looked like unbaked dinner rolls.

"Mr. Boswell," he said, "there's someone named MacLemore to see you."

Billy blinked again and frowned. MacLemore? He looked at Michael and then back toward the fire. He drew his palms along his cheeks and felt his three-day beard.

Michael said, "He says he's sorry to be calling so early, but that you made it clear he should come immediately if he ever acquired any information." He handed Billy a business card. Billy took it and squinted and read what it said: McCoy and MacLemore. Discreet Investigations. A Nationwide Network at Your Service.

Billy looked away again. He smoothed his blankets and tucked them in around his legs. He said, "What day is it?"

"It's Saturday morning, Mr. Boswell." He watched Billy's face twitch. "Shall I ask him to come back?"

Billy shook his head. "Tell him to come in." He watched Michael turn and leave. He could feel his heart beginning to race. It was the first time in three days he'd felt anything physically other than cold. He was aware that the reason for his heartbeat was dread, but at this point dread seemed to him like a friend, or something, at least, he could still rely on.

"Good morning, Mr. Boswell."

Billy looked up at a tall, thin man. Ah, yes, he thought. MacLemore. Good Christ.

"Sit down," he said. His voice was a scrape. "Is Michael getting you some coffee?"

"None for me, Mr. Boswell. Thank you, anyway." MacLemore sat on the couch. With the palm of his hand he carefully smoothed his hair. It was the blue-black shade of a gun barrel and made a sharp widow's peak. He indicated no surprise at Billy's condition. He looked into the fire and tried less successfully to hide his alarm at the level of the heat. "That's a great idea, Mr. Boswell, a fire first thing in the morning!" He was taking a handkerchief from his pocket to wipe his sweating face. He had about him the cheerful bumptiousness of a graceless mortician. Billy was beginning to remember that it was one of the reasons he'd despised him from the start.

"When the weather turns warm like it has, a person's likely to forget about the pleasures of a fire."

"What are you doing here?" Billy said. The ringing in his ears had become like something sung. It had a stridently pious Gregorian quality. The pain behind his eyes and at his temples was percussive.

"Well, to start with, Mr. Boswell, I have to confess I owe you an apology."

"An apology?"

"Absolutely. For months now, I've been saying it was obvious to me there was just no reason for you to be retaining Miss McCoy and myself. I've been saying the same thing to Miss McCoy, 'You know,' I've been saying to her, 'we're just taking Mr. Boswell's money.' If you recall, I said to you when we last spoke that all my years in this business had led me to conclude that there was nothing Miss Rae was hiding from you. Now I know that made you angry and I remember you said—well, there's no need to repeat what you said as we sit here this morning enjoying this lovely fire."

Billy said, "That was at least two months ago. It was the day I fired you." He now heard his own words as the source of the ringing.

"Oh," said MacLemore. "Oh, dear, Mr. Boswell. Did I hear you correctly? Did you just say it was your intention to fire me?"

"I told you if you were standing naked in front of a full-length mirror it would take you three hours to find your d—"

"No need to repeat what you said, Mr. Boswell! We both remember what you said very well. But frankly, I received it as something offered in the frustration of the moment." MacLemore hooked his collar with his index finger and pulled it away from his neck. "The irony here is that because you gave us such a generous retainer, there was no need for me to get in touch with you before today. If I had, then I'd have known you'd actually intended to dismiss us." He shook his head. "Now I see that we really have just been taking your money for the last two months. Especially these past few days, since Miss McCoy's been piling up some hefty travel expenses. Here you intended to dismiss us and—"

"Jesus Christ, what is it! What! Why are you here?"

MacLemore's head snapped back slightly; this was the sum of his reaction. He nodded. "Yes, of course." He said, "I spoke with Miss McCoy late last night. She telephoned me long distance from Texas."

"Texas?"

"Near El Paso," MacLemore said. "She's been following Miss Rae, you see."

"Alyce is in El Paso?" Billy breathed deeply in an effort to calm his heart. He breathed deeply again to try and ease the chanting pain. For the first time in years he thought of Émile Coué.

"A little place called Comstock, actually. Ever heard of it?"

Billy shook his head.

"I hadn't either," MacLemore said. "Apparently it's tiny, just a dust speck. Right near the Mexican border. Very tiny, apparently." He'd pulled a notebook from his pocket and was consulting it as he spoke. "Apparently, Miss Rae boarded the train here in town Wednesday night, so Miss McCoy, since she was following her, had no choice but to get on, too. Once the train had pulled away, she— that is, Miss McCoy—managed to engage Miss Rae in conversation and learned she was traveling to this tiny little Comstock." Mac-Lemore looked up from his notebook and smiled. "Miss McCoy is extremely good at doing that: Engaging people in conversation and drawing them out." He looked down at his notes again. "When she found out where Miss Rae was going, she told her—this is how I understood it when I spoke to Miss McCoy—that she herself was a recent widow and by coincidence she was traveling to Comstock, too, where her sister was meeting her. At some point, when the train stopped, Miss McCoy had time to get off and wire ahead to some people we've worked with in San Antonio, and they drove over, posing as her relatives, and met Miss McCoy in Comstock."

He looked up again and nodded. "I have to say that Miss McCoy is a consummate professional. I feel I'm fortunate to be associated with her. I feel I learn from her every day. I am constantly amazed and impressed by her agility in these sit—"

"Shut up," Billy said. He shook his head. "I don't understand."

"You don't understand what, Mr. Boswell?"

"Why would Alyce take the train to some dust hole in Texas?"

"To see her brother."

"Her brother?"

"That's what she told Miss McCoy. She said she was traveling to meet her brother. And when they both got off in Comstock, Miss Rae introduced this man to Miss McCoy."

Billy straightened in his wing chair and scooted forward. In doing so, his blankets slipped off his lap. "A man met Alyce when she got off the train?" He paid no notice to the blankets. He was feverishly working to imagine himself sitting beside Alyce on a train somewhere in Texas so that he could turn to her and ask her simply, *Why?* In his mind, the question had the power of original curiosity. He said to MacLemore, "You're telling me that Alyce met a man in Texas?"

MacLemore nodded and flipped a page in his notebook. "She said his name was Luther."

"Luther?" Billy said.

"Luther. First name, Luther. 'My brother, Luther,' Miss Rae said."

"What . . ." Billy said, and then his voice went away. "What," he tried again, "what did he look like?"

"A big man," MacLemore read. "Maybe thirty-five to forty. But very big. Very tall and broad shouldered. Big, apparently. He was well-dressed. Well, well-dressed for *Texas*, Miss McCoy emphasizes." MacLemore chuckled. "Sometimes Miss McCoy is a bit too urbane for her own good." He read again from his notes. "It appears he's prosperous. He was driving a shining new Packard, according to Miss McCoy. Miss McCoy noticed that the initials 'LM' had been inscribed in gold on all the hubcaps." MacLemore chuckled again, looking up from his notes. "Miss McCoy made a comment here about the sophistication of this man Luther's tastes, but I'm sure you can guess the gist of what she said."

When Michael had passed back through the living room after showing MacLemore out, he'd sensed that the nature of Billy's distress had altered and he'd decided to chance letting the fire die. He had worked for Billy for fifteen years and he'd acquired an instinct for just which irrationalities Billy might choose to furnish a mood.

And as it happened, he'd been right. For the past half hour, Billy had no longer felt cold. Instead, as he sat and watched the embers, he sensed the burden of a harsh and focused clarity. He shifted in his chair and crossed his legs. This minimal movement caused him to realize that his body stank. He smacked his lips and caught the foulness of his breath. He looked down at his shirt and slacks. They were absurdly stained and wrinkled. Again he felt his stubble. He ran his hands through his greasy hair.

His curiosity, his wish to ask her *Why?* had been eclipsed by a sense of validation. It floated, cool and prideful, at the edge of what he'd learned. He sat in his chair and recalled almost affectionately his fears and suspicions of the recent past. He thought about those who'd told him he was wrong to think that others were destroying his career. He remembered the people who'd told him he was foolish for imagining that he was being shunned. He remembered the night in Ciro's when Chaplin had pretended not to see him. He thought about Abe Zietman, the studio chief, swearing on his mother's grave that he'd given no orders to keep scripts away from Billy.

But the thought he held was of Alyce's denials: That she hadn't been late; that she hadn't been gone; that she hadn't been anywhere but where she'd claimed to be. He remembered her displays of seeming bewilderment. Her flashes of anger and then her showering patience; her weeping and her apparent despair. He remembered her duplicitous sexual obeisance.

And now he saw that his rage had been his work and he felt it had come at last to fruition.

He decided he must take a bath. He reached down and picked up the mess around him, leaving only the dirty glasses for Michael to take out. Then he sat up again and stuffed everything he could into his pockets. He looked around the room and blinked to clear his head. Its pain had ebbed and his ears no longer rang. He edged forward and tried to stand up but got no higher than a squat before he fell back in the chair. He tried again and with a push he succeeded. Standing, he waited for the room to stop spinning. He risked a step, then another. He held on to the back of the couch as he made his way.

He reached the hallway and started up the stairs, pausing on each step. When he got to the top, he stopped and rested, then headed toward his dressing room. He placed one hand on the wall for support. His fingertips grazed its stucco surface with quick Braille flutters.

Among the mirrors, he walked directly to the double marble sinks. Leaning against them, he began to peel off his filthy clothes. He found the stench of his body both appalling and recuperative.

It was not until he was naked that he glanced up. What he saw did not surprise him, for what he saw were memories. Looking at the infinite angles of reflection, he saw Alyce and him. The things they'd done. The positions she'd assumed.

And next he saw himself, dressed in a blue silk robe, walking into this room as it had been transformed for surgery, where Luther waited with Charlotte, the zoo keeper–nurse.

Only then did he admit Luther's name. He said it aloud. "Luther Mathias." He said it again, this time as a question. Had it been going on ever since they'd met, how many years ago? How had they managed to see each other? Had his fleeting fear, that her amnesia had been staged, been true all along? Had she used it as the ruse to see him in Del Rio? Then how and where had they met originally? Where had . . . how had . . . when? "Luther Mathias," he said again. He looked into his mirrors and shook his head.

A wave of weakness came over him. He grabbed the edge of the marble top and cautiously lowered himself to the floor. Sitting, he worked to cross his legs until he'd managed the classic campfire pose. He panned back and forth, bobbing his head, and took in his images as they all bobbed their heads. It was as though he'd summoned the audience he had left. It was as though he'd convened everyone he could still trust. And he began to think aloud about the currency of loyalty.

*L*uther had already been up for two hours when Alyce came down from the guest bedroom. He rose from the dining room table as she entered and poured her a cup of coffee. Alyce apologized once more for her exhaustion the night before and Luther said no apology was necessary. He said again that he well remembered his own fatigue after the same trip eight years earlier. Alyce sipped her coffee and said how good it tasted.

Luther had asked Consuela to prepare shirred eggs for breakfast. He'd remembered an eight-year-old detail from the guest cottage: that Alyce had told him she was eating shirred eggs when she thought she'd glimpsed the cause of her amnesia. He remembered his anger at his sense of being teased and he understood that, as much as anything else, it had been that anger that had given him the courage to rise and walk to her. The idea of serving her shirred eggs had given him an impish satisfaction.

"I love shirred eggs," she said, finishing her plate.

"Really?" he said.

"And obviously I was famished."

"I'm glad to hear it," he said. He asked Consuela to bring them second helpings.

"Oh, no, I couldn't," Alyce said.

The surface of Luther's mahogany table appeared to float, wide as a raft, between them. They were tired from their sleepless nights and they were nervous. The light of morning had done away with whatever comfort they'd established on the drive home from Comstock and they were starting once again with the fact that she was here. Alyce understood that she must be the first to speak of it. She recognized as well that Luther was allowing her the time to do so. But after thinking that she was once more grateful to him, she began to wonder—a continuation, really, of her thoughts through the night—whether his patience reflected etiquette or a strategy toward some end she couldn't imagine.

After breakfast, they walked the grounds of Desert Gardens. The day was chilly. Alyce wore a cardigan sweater the shade of the late-April leaves and wide-legged slacks that matched it. Against this color, her eyes were opalescent and flashing nearly blue. In the morning light, her skin looked pale. Luther noticed this immediately. His instinct to protect her had been, from the first, among his strongest responses to the presence of Alyce.

He led her casually about. They crossed a footbridge over a creek. They wandered through the citrus groves. He pointed out the network of the irrigation system. As they moved between a row of grapefruit trees, he kept stopping to look back at his everlooming house. "It's so huge," she said finally. "Yes, just huge," she added, when he stopped still again.

He smiled and told himself she was comparing it to hers and Billy's.

Finally, they walked around to the lawns behind the house and Luther led her to the rose gardens. Alyce responded as he'd hoped she would. "They're magnificent," she said. "I thought, last night, that's what I was seeing, but it was too dark to make them out from my window." He thought to himself that he'd been right: He had heard the sound of her window slamming shut. He saw her standing in a shaft of moonlight angling in through the window like a ghostly buttress. She wore the pastel silk robe he often gave her to wear in his fantasies.

Alyce stood beneath a pergola and her eyes followed the vines up and over her head. "Simply beautiful," she said.

Luther nodded and smiled again. He imagined asking her if these gardens reminded her of anyone else's and her smiling coyly and saying, Yes, perhaps they did.

"Thank you for showing me around," Alyce said.

"Would you like another cup of coffee?" Luther asked. "Maybe something more to eat?"

Alyce laughed. "Good heavens, no." She touched her stomach. "I won't eat again for days."

They stood for a moment. Luther lowered his head and breathed the roses. He sensed that she was looking at him and he felt the pause as one he'd lost control of. He was sure that she was trying to change the mood and he realized he wasn't ready yet. His curiosity remained keen, even more so this morning, but he was finding it a thrilling thing to hold in his heart and he wished to satisfy it at his pace. He looked at her and said, "I'd like to take you for a drive. I think you'll be surprised to see how much the town has changed."

"Oh." Alyce hesitated. "You don't need to do that."

Luther smiled. "But you have to see your old haunts again."

"My old haunts?" she said.

"Good!" he said. "You'll enjoy it."

They turned and walked back toward the house. Luther's subtly rolling gait seemed somehow instructional.

Alyce said, "What is the name of that nice woman, the nurse, who stayed with me?"

"Mrs. Hurd?" Luther said.

"Yes. Mrs. Hurd," Alyce said. "How is she? Is she well?"

"Mrs. Hurd? My guess would be that she is. About a year ago, she was nursing a hobo back to health—he'd collapsed on her doorstep—and when he got better she ran off with him. No one's heard from her since."

"My God, how extraordinary."

"Her husband surely thought so."

Luther chose to drive them in his grand black Cadillac. Alyce wore her cream felt hat and again pulled its brim low. Luther saw her slouch down in her seat as they approached South Main. It amused him and it touched him, her renegade's pose.

He drove them past the new boarding houses and the pristine store fronts. He pointed out that the businesses took up five or six more blocks than they had when she'd been here. He asked if she remembered how the town had looked and she said she did, just vaguely. They passed the St. Charles, with its entrance newly roofed, but it was Luther who looked up to its third-story windows.

"There's your old office, isn't it?" Alyce said. "I do remember that. I remember looking over at the sign from my windows.''

"I actually kept it until recently," he said. "I used to be able to hide away up there and think.''

The Cadillac moved along at processional speed. Its sharp-domed silver hubcaps shone like Prussian helmets. Its tires' white-walled bands were unblemished and voluptuous. People stopped to notice; others looked up from benches. Many of them smiled. These smiles were all the same, varying slightly in degree, and in truth they were vestigial of the smile of sorrow and wonder.

Alyce watched the peering faces float slowly past. The Cadillac's crawling speed made them seem to become splayed and emolliative as they crossed her window. She especially noticed a tiny man and woman with a young daughter in tow. He was blind, with dark glasses and cane. She was dressed like a twenties flapper and stared boldly into the car. Her lips were tightly pressed and her expression was choleric. Alyce slid farther down in her seat. She wanted to tell Luther to hurry along but when she looked at him he seemed to be paying no attention to the peoples' notice.

In the next block, he said, ''There's the Princess.'' He pointed to the theater, on Alyce's right.

She read the marquee. It said, ''Wrestling Matches'' and, beneath it, gave dates. The sight of the theater stirred an embarrassment in Alyce. Her face grew hot.

"Who appears in *Wrestling Matches*?" she managed. "Somehow, I've never heard of it.''

"No," Luther laughed, "it's not a motion picture. They sometimes stage wrestling matches at the Princess now, maybe half a dozen times a year. They build a ring up on the stage and they get a big crowd.'' He laughed again. ''Especially the women. They love to come and watch the hairy brutes.''

Alyce stared at the Princess in her door's rearview mirror. Its marquee jutted out to the street, appearing to her as displaced as a prow. Then Luther turned left onto Garfield Street.

He pointed out more buildings. The new post office was nearing completion. Its handsome stone, locally quarried, was the shade of light caramel. To the left, on the corner, stood an addition to the high school. Luther's name in beveled letters ran across its front.

Alyce was hearing his voice, but his words were filtered through her lingering unease at seeing the Princess. It was as though she'd been turning the pages of an album and come across a photograph she'd thought she'd destroyed. She saw herself standing stupid and disheveled in the theater's lobby.

"Is anything wrong?"

"What?" She saw Luther glancing back and forth at her as he drove.

"You look worried," he said.

"Oh, no. Just . . . I'm still a little tired, I suppose."

"You didn't sleep all that long. You should take a nap when we get back."

He made a right turn onto Strickland. On one side, small houses stood in yards of deep shade. Some were adobe, an equal number frame. Shallow porches fronted most of them. "Over there," Luther said, nodding to the other side, "are some new offices and the warehouses we've built." Alyce turned to see three light-brick buildings, two of them squat and flat-faced, the third smaller and trimmed with wooden filigree.

"And this," Luther said, turning right again onto Griner, "is new since you were here." She held her look on Luther's face for a moment and then shifted in her seat and saw the clinic. It was built of the signature light brick, rose four stories high, and was set back from Griner by a strip of grass and neatly barbered chinaberries and vines of queen's wreath that climbed a low wrought-iron fence. THE MATHIAS CLINIC, again in beveled letters, ran across the front just below the roof.

Alyce studied the clinic for the length of its block. She'd had no particular idea what it might look like. She hadn't, in fact, given it a thought. But the clinic appeared to her as purposeful as a sanitarium, as welcoming as a hotel. She found herself struggling to reject the sense of legitimacy it gave off.

She sensed Luther looking at her. Again she felt, as when he'd waited for her to praise his mansion, that he was prolonging the instant. But when they reached the end of Griner, her attention was caught by a small corner park across the street from the clinic where perhaps as many as two dozen men were milling about or sitting on benches.

"Who are they?" she asked.

"What?" Luther asked. Then he saw where she was looking. "Oh," he said. "Patients. Waiting to check in."

Alyce sat up, more alert. The men were dressed as Luther's patients always seemed to be, in old heavy suits, frayed-edged shirts, high-topped polished shoes. In the months since he had introduced the cheaper treatment, many of the suits had become even older, the shirts beneath them a bit more frayed.

Squinting to see the patients' faces, Alyce imagined Billy waiting in their midst. She saw him pacing the walk paths, incongruously fashionable in an elegant suit. She saw him smoking and smiling and taking deep breaths. Even in fantasy, she could feel his terror.

They'd turned the corner and she realized that Luther was speaking. She heard him say "lunch" and "Consuela's special tortillas." They were driving down a quiet street paralleling South Main. "I try to stay off of South Main as much as possible," he said. "Especially on weekends, with so many people out. The attention gets to be a fairly serious inconvenience."

She heard no boasting in his tone. He seemed simply to be offering a fact. "Yes," she said. "I could see."

"I drove it today because I wanted to make sure you saw everything you might remember."

"Thank you," she said. "I'm pleased you did." And this was true. For she was feeling, at last, no uncertainty, and if she'd lain in bleak confusion through the hours of last night, what she'd just now seen and imagined had lifted her doubts about the worth of having come.

For as long as Alyce had known Billy Boswell, she'd thought she loved him at those times when he felt strong and could present to the world his surface of grace. But suddenly she'd sensed, as she'd imagined him standing among the waiting patients, that his besetting fear was the thing that made him human, his flailing from its depths the thing that made him fine. And she felt sure, as she rode along with Luther, that she would never have known this so well, would not have seen the nobility of her husband's tremulousness toward life, if she hadn't sensed it here in Del Rio against the grandness that Luther's certainty had achieved.

"Oh, shit," Luther said. "Excuse me. I apologize."

"What is it?" Alyce asked. She looked to the sidewalk where Luther was pointing and she saw the tiny blind man and the flapper and the child. The woman looked, if anything, even angrier than before. "Oh, yes, I saw them earlier," she said.

"I know," Luther said. "They've been following us all over town." As the Buick passed Ronnie and Betty and Nettie, Luther said, "They work for me. We had a little disagreement a few days ago." In truth, when Luther had told Betty not to come by at ten o'clock until she'd heard from him, she'd performed, in her high heels, a flamenco of rage across his polished wood floors.

"Who are they?" Alyce asked.

"Have you heard of Blind Ronnie Truehart?" Luther asked.

"No," Alyce said.

So he told her of Ronnie's arrival in Del Rio, although he failed to mention that Ronnie wasn't blind. But he gave the story all its comedy, for he'd become concerned that Alyce was more than merely tired. He suspected she was distracted by whatever was troubling her.

As he described Blind Ronnie's audition and his imponderable success, Alyce's expression seemed to relax. Watching her, delighted he'd been able to cut through her brooding, he remembered his decision, years before, that his time with her should be left in the past where its delicate perfection would be preserved. And he thought how foolish, even cowardly, he had been.

As Luther parked and walked around to open Alyce's door, he noticed O'Malley's Chrysler at the far end of the driveway. He assumed he'd come to practice the organ. Luther had asked him to be ready to play for them as they sat with drinks in the evening before dinner. O'Malley had been thrilled. "How long will she be here?" he'd asked. Luther had winked and said, "That depends on how well you play."

"My assistant is here," he said to Alyce as she stepped out.

"Your assistant?"

"He supervises almost everything for me. I couldn't breathe without him."

"Does he know I'm here?" Alyce said.

"He's completely trustworthy. But I suspect he's just here now to practice the organ."

"To practice the organ?" She shook her head. He thought she smiled but he couldn't read its meaning.

Opening the door, Luther was surprised to hear silence. "Irish?" he called.

He heard O'Malley's answering "Hello!"

Alyce stood in the vestibule while she removed her hat and combed her hair before the mirror. Luther stepped into the living room and saw O'Malley approaching. O'Malley waved and nodded, a motion stiff as a salute, which Luther had come to know meant something needed tending.

Luther said, "I thought you'd be practicing."

"I was," O'Malley said.

Then Alyce entered and Luther introduced them. O'Malley's smile was shy. Luther saw that he was blushing. O'Malley told Alyce he'd been a fan of hers. Alyce said that was the most charming lie she'd heard in years.

"No, I *was*," O'Malley insisted.

"He *was*," Luther agreed. "He has old silent-picture magazines with photographs of you."

As proof, O'Malley cited three of Alyce's pictures, including *Blue Sky, Blue Sea,* in which she was one in a crowd pointing up into the air.

Alyce laughed. "It was my best performance, don't you think? Didn't I point fetchingly?"

O'Malley said it was an honor to meet her and then, with hesitation, he turned to Luther and said he needed to speak with him.

Luther scowled. "We're getting ready to eat lunch."

"I see that," O'Malley said. "I'm sorry."

Luther glanced at Alyce. He thought he saw her face fall. He asked O'Malley, "How long will it take?"

"I'm not sure," O'Malley said. "Maybe not too long."

"Go on, please," Alyce said, but Luther heard a resignation in her tone.

Luther said, "You should go ahead and have some lunch."

She said, "I'm still full from breakfast. I'll go upstairs and lie down for a bit."

"We'll eat later then. I'll tell Consuela."

She said good-bye to O'Malley. Luther felt a frustration as he watched her move toward the stairs. He'd heard her disappointment and seen it on her face. He assumed that, like him, she was annoyed

by this interruption. But his thought that she might have been eager
to talk was less than fleeting, since he'd decided in his own mind it
should all be said tonight.

"What the hell is it, Irish?"

"Haskell."

"Haskell?

"He's telephoned twice and he's extremely upset."

"What about?"

"He wouldn't say, but he insisted you place a call to him as soon
as you got back."

"You didn't tell him Alyce was here."

"Of course not," O'Malley said.

"Haskell, Haskell," Luther said. He shook his head.

"Sorry, Doctor M."

Luther said, "Stick around, in case Alyce needs anything." As an
afterthought, he said, "Maybe I'll want you to play for us before we
eat." He was trying to think of how to make her cheerful once again.

In his study, on the telephone, he heard Haskell Albright say, "He
says he'll talk to Cárdenas personally. He says he knows Cárdenas
would see him, that Cárdenas owes him one. He claims he did him
a favor in his guerrilla days."

"Is he telling the truth?" Luther asked.

"The truth? What is the truth, Luther? I can't remember when I
heard it. I don't know how it sounds. Tell me something true, Cowboy. Go ahead."

No sooner had Luther said, "Hello, Haskell," than Albright had
launched into an account of a visit he'd received from the American
embassy assistant in Mexico City. The assistant, Albright said, told
him he was in Los Angeles to see his in-laws and thought he'd take
the opportunity to stop in. And then he'd made it clear that he was
upset by the turn of events two months before. He said he'd gotten
quite used to the monthly sum of money and he was there to tell
Albright that it would be best for everyone if he started receiving it
again. Albright had asked him why he thought he should, since he'd
been keeping it for himself for more than a year and had performed
no service, so far as anyone could see. The assistant said he wasn't
so sure. It seemed to him he'd done everyone a favor by not trying
to pass along the money and thereby risking the minister's rage.

Who knows, the assistant said, what sort of action the minister might have taken then? Albright said to Luther that he'd pointed out that the same thing could have been accomplished if the assistant had simply sent back the money. Yes, well, the assistant said, but wasn't it finally a waste of time to split hairs about the past? He was there to discuss the present and the future. Then, Albright said to Luther, the assistant's expression became serious and he announced that unless the payments resumed at a higher figure, he'd make it known that Albright had had a hand in bribing him on behalf of Dr. Luther Mathias. After saying that, he'd smiled and said he was sure Albright wished to keep his name as far from Dr. Mathias's as possible.

Luther's anger instantly rose. He'd grown extremely tired of the preciousness of Albright's reputation, of Albright's insistence that he must not be traced to Luther. But he was also surprised by the alarm in Albright's voice and he found himself trying to calm Albright down.

"You know there's nothing on paper. No record of any money being sent."

"Yes, I do know that," Albright said.

"He's just calling your bluff."

"Maybe so."

"When you settle down you'll see there's nothing to worry about."

Albright said more quietly, "He said he'd spread rumors."

"Who will people believe, Haskell, you or him?"

"You know how I loathe the idea of every goddamn drooling slope-brow in this town gossiping about me."

"I'm sure they won't be, Haskell."

"He said he'd start the rumor that I've had your surgery."

Luther paused. He felt both the impulse to laugh and the wish that Albright were in the room with him so that he could do him great physical harm. He felt these things equally. Finally he said, "So is that what this is all about, Haskell?"

"He knows people here. He's married to somebody, I don't know."

"Just what are you afraid of, Haskell?'

"That's the kind of thing he wouldn't even *need* to take public. That's why it would fit the asshole's purposes perfectly. The whole power of a rumor like that is that it *isn't* made public but as many people hear it as if it *had been*."

"Are you afraid you won't get to screw your teenagers anymore?"

"*Everyone* will hear it."

"Are you afraid they'll think you're just an old man who needs to rest his shriveled peter in a sling?"

"And do you know what, Cowboy? They'll believe it. And *why* will they believe it? Precisely because it *is* a rumor. Precisely because it *hasn't* been made public."

"Jesus, Haskell. Pay the money or don't. It's up to you. It's your good name we're worried about, after all."

"That's why they're so insidious, rumors. They're like goddamn aphids."

"Aphids?"

"Rumors are the goddamn aphids on the leaves of social intercourse, Cowboy. You don't know how they get started. You can't see them. You only know they've done their work when they've eaten all the leaves. That's me, Cowboy. I'm the goddamn leaves and the rumors are the aphids. God*damn* it, I hate them."

"Haskell?"

"What?"

"I speak for everyone at the Clinic when I say we're proud to have you on our honor roll of patients."

"Cowboy, listen."

"Good-bye, Haskell."

Luther sat on one of his leather couches by the fire, waiting for Alyce to come down for their late lunch. He'd changed into a brown Western-cut suit with yoked lapels, custom made in San Antonio. He wore a starched white shirt and floral-patterned silk tie. He withdrew his pocketwatch. It was after three o'clock.

At the far end of the room, O'Malley played the new organ. He was offering a simple medley that did not call attention to itself. He was learning the touch of the keyboard and the play of the pedals. He was nervous and excited and a moment before, as he'd sat down and laid his fingers on the keys, he'd been struck with the thought that Luther had accomplished exactly what he'd outlined the night they'd sat together in the old St. Charles bar. "Irish," Luther had said, "I want y'all to come and work for me," and O'Malley had dismissed it at the time as one of Luther's drunken dreams.

But he'd built the house he'd said he would build. He'd laid out the rose gardens he'd described that night in such tedious detail. And now, as a kind of finishing detail, he'd had installed the massive organ, its pipes rising through his walls. It seemed to O'Malley, as he saw himself about to play for the beautiful Alyce Rae, that his meeting Luther placed him among the world's fortunate men.

Luther was thinking about his conversation with Haskell Albright. It had left him, more than anything, amused. After he'd hung up the telephone, he'd recalled the day they'd met, when Albright had announced his state of cuckoldry on the country club veranda and spoken of how he normally loathed the spread of rumor. Luther saw a kind of thematic symmetry in the particular scare the embassy assistant had put into him.

He listened to O'Malley's organ chords and watched the fire. He judged the yellow of the peaking flames, just before they vapored beyond their states of visibility, to be close to the color of Alyce's hair in evening light.

He heard the sound of heels on the stairs and looked up to see Alyce descending. She was wearing the severely tailored suit she'd traveled in. He stood and walked toward her.

O'Malley had looked back over his shoulder when he'd heard Alyce's steps and he unconsciously raised the volume of his playing. Alyce recognized this and laughed as she reached the foot of the stairs. "How impressive," she said to Luther. "I feel I've been announced. Do you do that for all your guests?"

"Only those who deserve it," Luther said.

Alyce called, "Hello again, Mr. O'Malley!"

O'Malley looked over his shoulder and smiled and nodded.

"Would you like a drink?" Luther asked. She said she would, a weak highball, and Luther motioned her to the couch while he moved to the bar. As he filled her glass he remembered the day he'd been summoned to the St. Charles and Billy Boswell, resplendent in white linen, had poured exact amounts of whiskey from his silver traveling flask into cloudy hotel glasses which he held in one hand.

He returned to Alyce and handed her her drink and sat down on the matching couch facing her. A low walnut table sat between them.

She said, "Did you resolve your crisis?"

He said, "Everything's fine." He raised his glass. "To your being here."

She blanched and gave Luther a flickering smile.

They sipped their drinks while O'Malley played the organ. Luther told her how he'd used to listen to O'Malley at the Princess. How he'd liked to arrive an hour before the picture started so he'd be sure to hear the medley. As he spoke, he was taken with the sense that he was describing a time very long ago, when his days were so unformed that he had hours to spend in a motion picture theater.

She smiled. "So that's why he's such a fan of silent pictures." She thought to herself that he was no doubt playing the night she'd wandered into the lobby of the Princess.

Luther said, "I thought we'd take a drive tomorrow. If the weather's warmer I'll have Consuela pack a picnic. There's a spot, some bluffs along the river south of here—"

"Luther," Alyce said. "Maybe you know already, if you *still* go to pictures and give any thought at all . . . maybe you know that Billy's career has not been going well." Her voice was calm and even, though her face was flushed. "These past few years have been very frustrating for him."

And so, here it is, he thought. He knew he couldn't ask her to wait any longer and he now realized he didn't wish her to. He was surprised by the suddenness of emotion that took him. It was giddiness, really, or something close to giddiness. "No, I didn't know," he said. "I haven't been to a picture in, I can't even remember." He thought: She said "these past few years." He felt a thickness of regret at that much time lost.

Alyce said, "Yes, well, I doubted that you had any sense of how things were. And why would you?"

"In any case, I'm sorry. I'm sorry for Mr. Boswell. But isn't that the nature of your business? Aren't there times when actors are working, and times when they're not? Obviously, I don't know. That's only my impression."

Alyce merely nodded. She reached into the pocket of her suit jacket and removed her silver cigarette case. Luther took her matching lighter and lit the cigarette. She exhaled and said, "I think you know Billy well enough, you've seen him at his most fragile, so you'll understand when I say that his unhappiness has . . . has affected him . . . completely."

Oh, he understood! And hearing her, his mind was instantly taken back to the day when he and Billy were circling the baboon in its cage and Billy spoke with the same touching need for euphemism. "Well," Luther said to Alyce, remembering some of Billy's language, "I understand that he's an unusually sensitive man. That he has a highly strung temperament, as his work requires."

Alyce appeared to grimace at these words. She looked at Luther with a sudden impatience. She said, "I need to know just what you did to Billy."

"What I *did*?" he said. It sounded to him as though she thought it was his fault. It sounded like the question of an angry mother asking on behalf of her bullied child.

Alyce took a deep drag on her cigarette. "I know how deliberately I've avoided all this, but now it's important that I understand."

From the organ bench, O'Malley glanced back over his shoulder and he was instantly reminded of his days at the Princess, when he'd looked up at the silent action and his playing emphasized the emotions on the screen. But watching Luther and Alyce at the far end of the room was far more compelling and titillatingly strange. They were, after all, alive, their behavior unpredictable, and he sensed that his music needed a larger purpose than mere embellishment. It required an anticipatory wisdom. He hurried through the end of "Stardust" and moved into "Night and Day," but in his haste he let the organ's power get loose so that it sounded momentarily like a Purcell processional.

Luther heard this and it increased his irritation. He shot a look at O'Malley's back and waited until the organ quieted again before he spoke. "Do you really think Mr. Boswell would want you to know?"

"I don't know," Alyce said. Then she shook her head. "No, that's not true. I know he wouldn't. But I'm asking you to tell me anyway."

Luther looked away again and drained his glass. He was trying to think through where this might lead. What words would satisfy her. He was unsure. His thoughts were hampered by his expanding fear.

He said, "You put me in an impossible position."

"Why?"

"I promised Mr. Boswell I would never say a word."

"You said you'd never tell me? Well, I suppose that stands to reason."

"No, it's more than that. I took an oath not to tell anyone. I signed a document. So it's even beyond the issue of confidence between a doctor and his patient. It's a written contract."

Alyce exhaled and watched her smoke plume. She heard O'Malley playing "Night and Day." She leaned toward the table to tap the ash of her cigarette into a tray. She sat up, her spine erect, and said calmly, "At least tell me that it's worthless. At least tell me that."

Luther smiled; he felt relieved. "For you to pursue this?" he said. "Yes, it truly is." His wish to comfort her was instantly called up. "I'm glad you see that I—"

"No." Alyce was shaking her head. He was surprised by the sad smile that crossed her face. "You misunderstand. I mean, what you *do*: that *it's* worthless."

"Worthless?" Luther's head seemed to snap back. Then he too came slowly forward on the couch. What part of his immediate heat was anger, what part alarm, what part a haunting echo was impossible to measure, but they all were moving in him. He met Alyce's look and said, "It absolutely is not."

"No?"

"I'm amazed, after all you saw this morning . . ." He said sadly, "Worthless?" He heard, *Worthless is one thing, and harmful's something else.* "I have a letter from you," he said. "I've never shown it to anyone, of course. Do you remember what you wrote in that letter? How grateful to me you said you were?"

"I *was* grateful. When I wrote that to you, Billy was feeling absolutely jubilant. Why wouldn't I be grateful?"

O'Malley had heard their more urgent voices and glanced back at them again. He saw that they'd inched forward on their couches and sensed the shift of mood. He assumed it to be one of rising passion. He felt as much participant as voyeur, in that the sympathy of his playing could influence the events.

Luther said, "How can you remember the change in Mr. Boswell, that very jubilation, and still call what I 'did to him' worthless?" He shook his head. "It sounds as though you think I set out to harm him."

O'Malley began, with elaborate sentiment, a song he believed would encourage things along. It was a slow blues of loosely spiraling persistence which he'd heard years ago in St. Louis. It was the blues, as he'd remembered it, in its unmannered infancy. It had been repeating and expanding in his head recently and he was sure it would evoke for Luther the florid heat of Memphis.

Alyce smoked and thought a moment. She said, "Well, it seems to me you *did* harm him. Not 'set out to,' perhaps, but, yes, I sense you've harmed him."

"I gave him years of a revitalized life." Luther's frustration was at its margin and somewhere within it was the vague recognition that O'Malley was playing some morose Negro dirge. "And you see that as my inflicting harm?"

She said, "However you took advantage of him, that's, yes, I think that's harmful."

He felt an urge to lash out. He was tempted to say that maybe Billy's lust was such that she couldn't really tell when he'd lost his ability to perform. But he held himself in. He was grasping the idea that her impertinence would pass. They would soon enough resume and he mustn't say something they'd have to work to overcome. He said, "Why would thousands of patients, you surely have no idea how *many* thousands, why would they have come to me if what I did was worthless, never mind harmful? It's really that simple, Alyce. If the surgery was worthless, people wouldn't come. It's—" He paused. ". . . Yes, I'll risk saying this: It's the same in my profession as it is in Mr. Boswell's. If people haven't been coming to his pictures, then perhaps, perhaps there's . . . a validity in their not coming." He waited for her expression to show reaction, but it didn't. He said, "Come with me. Let me show you letters I have in our files. Let me show you the figures, the *number* who've come."

Alyce smoked. She was aware of O'Malley's funereal undersong beneath Luther's words. And she began to suspect that Luther might, at least in part, believe what he was saying. Such was the earnestness he seemed to her to be displaying. She thought perhaps the steady flood of patients had over time persuaded him. Perhaps his wealth had convinced him. Perhaps, on the other hand, he'd believed from the beginning. Perhaps he'd believed in 1927.

She heard him say, "It was *him,* after all, who asked for *me.*"

Alyce put out her cigarette and took another one from her case. She looked to the fire. It had gotten low; its flames displayed a lassitude. She said, "I realize that." She turned and looked at Luther. "And he wants to again."

Luther frowned. "He wants to what?"

"He wants to come to you again."

"He does?"

"He wants you to operate on him again."

"He wants a second surgery?"

"He thinks there's something better about what you do now than whatever you did to him in Los Angeles."

"Does he want to come here? Does he want me to come there?"

She ran her fingers through her hair to comb it back off her forehead. Luther watched her do this and, despite everything, thought for a moment only of the beauty of her hair.

She looked at Luther and said, "I don't know. What does it matter? The point is, I want you to refuse him." Before he could respond she said, "Billy's extremely weak right now, he's confused, and it would be very cruel to confuse him even more. I know that for certain. Believe me, I do." She waited a moment and then said, "Luther, if it makes *any* difference, I'm asking you to refuse him as a favor to me."

Luther sensed all at once that Alyce was too close. Her beauty and the color of her hair and what she'd said and what she wanted, all of it was circling and pressing in on him. He sat back on the couch and almost pushed against its cushions. He looked up at his ceiling beams. He heard O'Malley's slow sepulchral strides and he wanted to get up and walk the length of the room and kick his ass off the bench.

When he lowered his look he saw, over Alyce's shoulder, Consuela coming toward them. He shook his head and was preparing to say that they'd be in soon. But Consuela said, "Doctor Luther. Someone is calling on the telephone."

"The telephone?" He hadn't heard it ring.

Consuela said, "It is the long distance."

He thought, Jesus Christ, Haskell! He said, "I'll return it later."

"But, no, Doctor Luther. It is calling for Miss Rae."

"For *me*?" Alyce said. Her head snapped around.

"Yes, and do you wish me to say—"

"No, I'll take it, please." She was already standing. "Show me where, if you would, Consuela."

Luther was watching her. She turned to him and said, "I'm sure I should take it."

He said, "Yes," and started to stand, but she was already following Consuela from the room. She disappeared through the doorway and he was left with the dying fire and his frustration—Who could it be but Billy? Why had she left this number?—the fire, his frustration, and O'Malley's organ playing.

He looked down the room toward O'Malley and shouted, "Irish!"

O'Malley jumped and turned around.

"Can you play something that's not *quite* so goddamn depressing? Is this the anniversary of the day your mother died?"

O'Malley was shaken and he was surprised to see Luther sitting by himself. He cleared his throat and said, "What would you like to hear then?"

"I don't give a damn. Play 'Night and Day' or 'Begin the Beguine.' Christ, anything." O'Malley started to say that he'd already played them, but Luther said, "Better yet, *don't* play anything. Go get something to eat and leave us alone."

Consuela led Alyce through the dining room toward the kitchen. Alyce's vision was peripherally dim and her mind, as it raced, was forming questions similar to Luther's. She was asking herself how Billy had found her. She was already searching for the words that might calm him. She would ask him to hold himself together until she'd returned and could explain. She followed Consuela through the kitchen to a small alcove where the telephone sat on a wooden stand. Its receiver lay beside it. It seemed separately black. Alyce saw it through a watery blur.

Consuela turned and Alyce heard her say something before she stepped away and closed the door after her. Alyce wiped her tears with the back of her hand. She was shocked to feel the heat of her cheeks. Then her lips formed a smile as she lifted the receiver and said, "Hello? Is this you, darling?"

The emotionless operator asked if she were Alyce Rae. She said she was and then again said, "Hello, darling?" There was a silence before a woman's voice said, "Alyce?"

"Yes?" Alyce said.

"Alyce, it's Larraine."

In the living room, Luther paced. He heard the room's immense and vaulted quiet. He paused by the fire, reached for the bellows, and bent down to give it air. Its embers pulsed, small flames licked up, and he laid new kindling on them. When they'd caught, he set a pyramid of three thin logs.

His being suddenly alone, while Alyce talked to Billy, was hardly an aspect of the day he had planned. But he realized it was giving him the chance to think and he'd already come to understand that it would be to his advantage to honor Alyce's wishes. He'd readied what he'd say to her when she returned: that of course she knew what was best for Billy and that was all that mattered. In doing so, he'd win her gratitude, and Billy's weakness would only continue.

The fire's heat was building. Luther loosened his tie. He walked to the bar. He was remembering the night of his open house, when he'd particularly imagined Alyce watching him throughout the evening. Filling his glass, he felt more sharply than ever that his need for her had been in everything he'd done, her presence subtly threaded through all of his ambition. He took a swallow of whiskey. He took a smaller sip and smiled.

Thinking this, he realized he could best ease her suspicions by speaking of the day she'd come to him in the guest cottage. His voice would find a measured fever in which to describe it to her, as though she'd not only been a participant but was today also a listener to whom he'd present a fable, as he had to listeners all his life. Here, he would say, is the quality of the light as it came through the window. And here is how it fell on the curve of your hip. This is how the whiteness of your skin felt to me. And this is how your heart felt when your finger traced the scar on my thigh, so now you can feel how you were also thrilled.

She had come to him before, had come to him again, and she would wish to come to him from now on. He would convince her of this, not just because he could, but because he needed to. He had finished this thought when he heard her coming back into the room.

Odd as it may seem, her paleness was the second thing he noticed, after he'd experienced a moment of fresh disappointment that she was wearing the severely tailored suit, its style so incongruous with the feelings he'd just summoned. Because her paleness was astonishing and, for Luther, had a precedent. Its limpid absence was his mother's final paleness. But then he did see it and set his glass on the mantel. But before he could speak she looked away and whispered, "Billy . . ."

"Yes," he said, hurrying toward her, thinking she was saying that she'd been speaking with him. He reached her and looked into her face. He held her shoulders and felt her body trembling. And he was certain that, whatever it was, she would let him lift her free of it.

Chapter

23

Michael the butler had been pleased to see that Billy was finally out of his chair. He'd heard water running through the pipes and recognized the sound of a bath being drawn. Passing through the downstairs hallway, he'd heard Billy's voice on the telephone speaking loudly but not angrily. He'd pictured Billy sitting in his dressing room and talking over the rush of water as it filled the nearby tub. These activities—his leaving his chair; his taking a bath; his speaking once again with the outside world—seemed hopeful signs to Michael.

So he'd listened for further sounds of Billy overhead. As he'd swept the fireplace, he'd cocked his ear toward the ceiling. He'd once thought perhaps Billy had called his name, but heard nothing further when he hurried into the hallway. After that, he'd gone to the foot of the stairs three times more. But each time there was silence and there were no more sounds from upstairs through the hot afternoon.

It was nearly five o'clock and Michael was once more in the front hall, straightening a closet, when the doorbell rang. He opened the door to find Leland Wheelock, Billy's pear-shaped asthmatic press agent. Wheelock was patting his face with a handkerchief. Large beads of sweat clung to his chin like a cluster of translucent warts. He stepped inside and Michael waited as Wheelock gathered his breath and complained about the heat. Michael nodded barely, reluctant to ally himself with the despicable Wheelock on even so immaterial an issue as the weather. Wheelock glanced at his wristwatch in a show of impatience and asked where Billy was. He said he had only a few minutes. Over the past few years, as Billy's popularity had fallen and he'd become impossible to satisfy, Wheelock had decided his career was beyond rescue. He'd stopped spending any promotional imagination on Billy and he answered his requests when nothing else was pressing. He was waiting for the day when Billy became so angry he would fire him at last.

Michael said Billy was upstairs and asked Wheelock if he had an appointment. Wheelock said he sure as hell did, in Santa Monica in forty-five minutes. Then he saw that Michael was confused and explained that Billy had telephoned him that morning and asked him to come over. He said he'd been busy and couldn't break away till now.

Michael asked him to wait in the living room while he went upstairs for Billy. When he'd reached the top, he stopped and wiped his brow.

The door to Billy's dressing room was open and Michael, pausing in the hall and looking in, saw him there, lying on the blue velvet couch. He was unable to decide whether to call to him again or to tiptoe in and wake him. He'd normally have had no second thoughts about entering the room but, although he was not a particularly spiritual man, he sensed even from the doorway a penumbral privacy protecting Billy. "Mr. Boswell?" he called. "Mr. Wheelock's here to see you." He waited a moment and repeated, "Mr. Boswell?"

It always startled Michael when he walked into the dressing room and saw the crowd of his images moving with him in the mirrors. He was aware of them as he crossed the room toward Billy, despite the sensation of his heart moving up in his chest and into his throat.

When he reached Billy he looked down and thought, No. He glanced around the dressing room. It felt orderly beyond measure. He seized the idea that a scene of breathtaking slovenliness was somehow requisite. But there Billy lay in his meticulous room, just bathed and freshly shaved. He'd chosen a magnificent gray silk double-breasted suit. His silk tie was maroon, his white shirt crisply starched. He wore black hand-made English oxfords on his slender feet. His arms were folded on his chest, his right hand holding an envelope. Michael reached down to take the envelope and in doing so brushed Billy's hand and the touch of his skin, cool in death and free of sweat on a torrid late spring day, also suggested to Michael nothing so much as a last impeccability.

He'd blinked his eyes to clear them and read the words "For Leland Wheelock" on the back of the envelope. His instinct had been to hide it but before he could put it in his pocket, he'd heard wheezing sounds behind him. "Jesus Christ!" cried Wheelock, who'd grown impatient waiting downstairs. He'd trudged up the stairs and walked across the dressing room to stand next to Michael and, noticing the envelope in his hand, had asked, "What's that?"

Wheelock had to hurry to prepare his office for the press conference. He ordered his assistant to rummage through the storage room for Boswell memorabilia. He himself looked through the files. Each of them had luck and as a result, by seven o'clock, Wheelock's walls were hung with posters advertising some of Billy's silent classics. *The City Sheik*, with Clara Bow. *Darkest Before Dawn*, in which he'd introduced the controversial back-of-hand-to-brow fainting gesture. *Two Dirty Sweethearts*, his most profitable picture ever. Noticeably absent was *Lasting Impressions*, where he and Alyce had met. On the wall behind Wheelock's desk was a large, darkly lit photograph of Billy. The line of his splendid nose was highlighted. The left side of his face was deeply shaded. The cleft in his chin was subtly apparent. Wheelock had framed the photograph in mourning crape.

The news of Billy's death from an overdose of sleeping pills had been released only an hour before and reporters and photographers were packed tight inside the office. The windows were wide open. Electric fans whirred in vain. Wheelock stood behind his desk and asked for quiet. Several photographers aimed their cameras, their flashbulbs set in concave disks as big as plates. One of them asked Wheelock to take a step to his left so that the photograph of Billy could be seen over his shoulder. Wheelock did, then put on his reading glasses and filled his lungs. He said he was going to read a statement and show some documents, as Billy's final note had instructed him to do. Tributaries of sweat ran down his cheeks and his glasses began to slide forward on his nose. He asked the reporters and photographers for their cooperation. Without it, he doubted he could maintain his composure. A reporter at the back, whether perverse or confused, took this as an invitation to ask where Alyce was. Wheelock shook his head and said he himself didn't know for sure. What he did know, all he knew, was what he was about to read and show to them. Then he reached into the envelope and withdrew a piece of paper.

Billy's statement accused Luther of violating his trust both professionally and personally. It divulged the first treatment in Del Rio and, after that, the surgery in Los Angeles, and it said that the latter had not only failed to cure Billy's impotence but had also made him sterile. It said that although it was too late for him, Billy hoped that by making his plight public knowledge he might save others from the same tragic mistake he'd made.

Wheelock paused and looked up. He appeared to be fighting back tears. Bulbs flashed. He said he hoped the reporters would make clear in their accounts the altruism and the courage of Billy's final statement. Some of the reporters nodded as they wrote, their straw hats bobbing.

Wheelock warned that the second part of the statement was even more painful to hear, but that Billy's final instructions insisted he release it. Resuming, he read Billy's claim that Luther had kept him impotent in order to steal Alyce Rae from him. Wheelock read the chronology of Alyce and Luther's secret life, as Billy had imagined it. He read Billy's admission that he didn't know how or where they'd met, that he'd learned of their treachery this very day and that the two of them were together even now. He gave the name of the detective, MacLemore. Finally, the statement said that he was making all this known not so much to hurt Alyce as to warn the world of the calculated cruelty of which Luther Mathias was routinely capable.

Wheelock looked up again and took off his glasses. While he wiped his face, the reporters began to shout questions. They wanted to know how Wheelock had obtained Billy's statement. They demanded proof of its legitimacy. They seemed strangely to react as though they were themselves accused. Their voices sounded defensive.

Wheelock nodded and waited through their shouting. He asked for calm and said he'd expected that such a dramatic last statement would be greeted skeptically, though he reminded them that Billy's reputation had always been above reproach. A few of the reporters looked at one another. Had it? they whispered. They'd forgotten that. Then Wheelock reached into the envelope again and withdrew the document that Billy had written in 1928, verifying the surgery and binding both Luther and himself to secrecy. "I'll place this on the desk here," Wheelock said, "so that you can all inspect it and note the signatures."

The photographers shouted, "Hold it up! Hold it up!" Wheelock's mouth pursed. He held up his hand instead. He said that if they'd wait a moment more he had a final piece of evidence that spoke to their suspicions. He reached once again into the envelope and produced a crumpled page of stationery that had been smoothed out as much as possible. "You'll see," he said, "that in this last note to him, Alyce addresses Billy's difficulties, even as she tries to present her absence as a sacrifice." He said he had to confess that, when he'd read this letter, he'd found the depth of her heartlessness absolutely shocking.

While Leland Wheelock conducted his press conference, Alyce was flying back to Los Angeles in a Lockheed Orion low-wing monoplane that Luther had chartered. From the moment she'd gotten the news of Billy's death, she'd behaved with sure purpose from inside her state of shock. Having walked back into his living room to tell Luther what she'd learned, she'd asked him how she could return most quickly. She'd refused to hear any expressions of comfort or remorse or disbelief. Not from Luther, not from the summoned O'Malley. She'd said there was no time for that. There was no time for anything but to arrange her departure. Though her manner had been anything but officious, it had seemed that of someone who was used to command. She'd paced and smoked and it had been clear she was incapable of sitting down. Her color did not improve and her expression remained stunned. In parting, she'd broken free from Consuela's attempted embrace, explaining to her that there simply wasn't time.

"*T*o those *thousands* of you who've written letters over the years saying there was no way you could thank Doctor Mathias enough, please listen carefully: There *is* a way, and the time is *now*. Because the forces conspiring against Doctor Mathias continue to gather as ominously as the November storm clouds that have been massing in our desert skies this past week. As I speak to you from my study this evening, I glance to my left where a stack of letters lies on my desk. I would judge it to be at least two feet high, and yet it represents the smallest fraction of response, a grain of sand plucked from the shoreline of your testimonials over the years. Letter after letter, and I'm thumbing randomly through the pile, speaks of youth recovered, of pain and suffering ended, either as a result of a pilgrimage to the Clinic, or after experiencing the benefits of one or another of the medicines developed in the Mathias Laboratories.

"Here, for instance, is a letter from the wife of a former patient, who writes from Missouri, 'You have done so much for us that we can never repay you. But I want you to know that we keep your picture on our mantel.'

"I could read on and on, as every one of you brave and independent-thinking listeners who've remained loyal to me knows. And yet despite the evidence of our good works, I come increasingly under attack from every quarter. Which is why I say to the good housewife in Missouri: 'Yes, you *can* repay Doctor Mathias, and now is your chance to do so!' It's fine for all of you out there to keep Doctor Mathias's picture on your mantel, but now you must do more than pay homage. If you want the work of the Clinic to continue, direct your letters and your energy not to us here in Del Rio. Write instead to the envy-ridden butchers of the American Medical Association and insist that they stop telling their craven lies about Doctor

Mathias. And write to your congressman and your senators and order them to put all due pressure on the feckless boobs of the Federal Communications Commission who are threatening even now to silence the many voices on XALM. Tell your elected representatives to stop these spineless commissioners who don't have the courage to think for themselves and yet would presume to legislate the ether! Who act as if they own the very air!"

Luther was wandering through his house after Alyce's departure, holding a bottle of whiskey by its neck, when the telephone calls from the reporters reached him. He was alone, having insisted to O'Malley that he wished to be and asking him to drive Consuela to her relatives in Villa Acuña. His own entranced behavior was a version of Alyce's as she'd prepared to leave. He made no sounds, not a mutter, not a curse, but the worlds of his mind and his heart were raucous. He moved from room to room, pausing at each threshold to peer in. He leaned against the doorways, drinking whiskey from the bottle. It was as though his interest in the rooms was ulterior, as though he might find the answers to why things had gone so wrong in the way the draperies were hung or in the way the chairs were set. He stood and appeared to conduct his inspections and grew enraged that his pain was as successful as a child's. No, even more than that: It was the same, it *was* that pain. He studied the polished wood of his ballroom floor as though he might see in its reflection the answer to why his mother had died. He heard, *I'll go as soon as y'all close up that hole in your belly,* and it seemed to him the words of her delirium held some vital hidden meaning if only he could listen patiently enough. He stood next to the living room mantel and looked toward the massive pipe organ and heard it play his Aunt June's coughing and heard it counter with a chord of his own unearthly cry that had drifted down through the near-gleaming heat of Pampa.

When the telephone rang, he thought first that it was Alyce, even though he knew her flight had barely had time to take off. Then, hurrying into his study to answer it, he imagined it was news that her plane had crashed. It seemed at that instant the day's inevitable end.

When the reporter from Los Angeles identified himself, Luther was amazed that he had his private number. He asked him how he'd gotten it and heard a snickering in response. The reporter then asked Luther whether Alyce Rae was with him.

The question seemed to Luther to surround him. He said that of course Alyce Rae wasn't there. He worked to sound as though he were trying to place the name.

The reporter asked if she'd been with him this past week and Luther said he hadn't seen Alyce Rae since she'd suffered amnesia in Del Rio years ago.

How then, the reporter asked, do you explain the report of a private investigator who claims you met Miss Rae's train two nights ago in Comstock, Texas? And how do you respond to Billy Boswell's charges—the *late* Billy Boswell, I should say, I'm sure you've heard—that you made him sterile to take Miss Rae from him?

As the boldness of the questions increased, Luther stopped hearing them specifically and the flow of his denial became rhythmically sustained—It's ridiculous, preposterous, a lie, absurd—while he thought to himself that he couldn't warn Alyce. He held the image of her flying home, completely unaware of what she'd face when she arrived. He could do nothing about it. He thought of telephoning her servants, but realized they already knew what he did. He'd stopped listening to the reporter altogether and hung up the phone in the middle of a question.

No sooner had he done so than the telephone rang again. He hung it up a second time and when it rang a third, he lifted the receiver and laid it on his desk.

"Speaking of the letters written to me over the years, I'm going to read portions of one very significant letter, a letter from an especially pleased and grateful patient which I received in 1928. Many of you who listen devotedly know that this letter has itself become controversial and has only aggravated the swirling climate of attacks and accusations. But I have persisted in reading from it because I believe it's vital that as many right-thinking Americans as possible know what it says. It's also my hope that some of my accusers in high places might be listening tonight and will come to realize, after they've actually heard the letter, that the hysteria building up over these past several months must be quieted. They should finally accept it as their duty and their responsibility to set the record straight. And they should publicly admit what's behind their orchestrated plots is nothing more than low human jealousy! 'Jealousy is cruel as the grave,' the Bible tells us in the Song of Solomon, chapter eight, verse six, and how right that is. It's as 'cruel as the grave: the coals thereof are the coals of fire, which hath a most vehement flame.'

"A *most* vehement flame, Doctor Mathias can assure you."

By the time he finally spoke to Alyce on the telephone, the newspaper stories had blanketed the nation. SUICIDE NOTE CHARGES BOSWELL WIDOW AND REJUVENATION DOCTOR IN SECRET TRYST said *The New York Times*. BILLY GETS REVENGE FROM BEYOND THE GRAVE! said the *Chicago Tribune*. The coverage of the story in Haskell Albright's *Los Angeles Times* was exhaustive and openly caustic in its opinion of Luther's surgery and medicines. It was written by Wally Jacobson, the reporter who'd ridden with Billy to Del Rio.

Luther had placed countless calls to her. He'd been told she was indisposed or out of the house for no one knew how long or in no condition to speak with anyone. And then one afternoon, after the voice of Michael the butler had asked him to wait, he suddenly heard her say, "Hello." He was stunned for a moment and couldn't reply.

"How are you?" he asked finally. "How are you doing?"

"Actually," she said, "not very well."

"Have you been able to sleep?"

"Sleep?" she said. "Yes, I suppose. Off and on, an hour or so here and there." Her voice gave off an odd carelessness, that uniquely casual tone that bitterness produces.

"What can I do to help you?" Luther asked.

There was a pause that made him think she was considering the question. "Nothing," she said. "There's really nothing." Then she added, "Thank you, though."

Luther said, "I wanted you to know I haven't answered any more questions from anyone. What would you like me to say? What would help you most?" His denials the first night had of course been exposed.

Again she was silent. He could hear her breathing shallowly. "I don't care," she said. "I don't plan to say anything further. I will not speak about any of it again. I tried, at first, I actually tried to say why I'd . . . what I'd done. I said to a reporter, 'If you honestly want to know what happened, sit down and listen, because it will take a long time to explain. But as soon as I began he started interrupting and asking the most unbelievably brazen questions, asking them very naturally, very casually, as though he were asking if by chance I could recall how the weather had been on a certain day, and I saw that it was futile. So nothing you can say will make the slightest difference."

Hearing her, Luther shook his head but held his tongue. He wanted to explain to her the reach of his power and the way he could influence what would ultimately be thought. But he could tell he'd have to wait until a later time to say this, when she was able to listen and to hear him. He said, "I'll telephone again soon."

"No."

"And in the meantime, if you think of any— . . . What?"

"No. Please don't telephone again."

"You're saying—"

"Please."

"Alyce, I understand. When you—"

"Please."

"I—"

"Please, Luther. Don't telephone. Don't try to speak with me again. If you want to help me, that's what you can do."

"I'll read the pertinent portions of this letter, written to me by the late Billy Boswell, whose confidentiality as a former patient I had of course considered inviolable until he himself broke it. I also want to make it clear that I do not so much blame Mr. Boswell for the libelous horrors I've been subjected to since his death. No, the blame must fall squarely on the shoulders of the immoral cowards who've taken up his sad charges and are now using them to try to destroy me. How, after all, could I find fault with Mr. Boswell, whose mind was obviously confused and unstable at the end, in contrast with the calm,

clear-headed intelligence he'd always shown me and which this letter exhibits?

" 'Dear Doctor Mathias,' he wrote, in the summer of 1928, 'My
mood is one of enormous relief and joy and is the cause that compels
me to write this note to you. For I simply had to tell you that my life
is once again full, in that most vital and treasured way, indeed it is
optimally full, more so than I could have possibly imagined.

" 'It is clearly all your doing, the result of your research, which
you've artfully translated into surgical acumen. I can only express
my immeasurable gratitude.

" 'I now resume my days at a pinnacle of energy and commitment.
And so it is in a spirit of trust and admiration that I once again and
finally emphasize my heart and my soul's debt to you. I remain,
forever thankful and, yours sincerely, B. Boswell.' "

He'd revealed the existence of Billy's letter when it had become
apparent that the clamor was not quieting. The newspaper stories
were becoming speculative, the headlines above them ever more
shrill. A kind of chronicler's curiosity, like a spirited new fad, had
started up across the country. It was similar to Billy's own mind in
his last hours, when he'd wondered how Alyce and Luther had first
met; whether Alyce's amnesia had been a ruse. These questions and
others like them were being offered by reporters in their daily dispatches.

Immediately after Luther first read Billy's letter on his broadcast,
he received dozens of requests to examine it and he felt confident he
was about to offer the evidence that would quiet the reporters and
turn their sympathies. They came from newspapers in New York and
Chicago. They came from Detroit, Kansas City, and Baltimore. Naturally, they came from San Antonio and Houston and Dallas and
Austin. They brought photographers with them and, to Luther's
surprise, several were accompanied by handwriting experts, humorless and bespectacled men whose spines had been shaped in libraries
and dark studies. They examined Billy's letter in variously prayerful
attitudes.

When the reporters were finished interviewing Luther, they

walked around town and questioned local people and talked to the willing waiting patients they could find, after which they filed atmospheric stories whose tone alternated between condescension and incredulity and which made heavy use of the word *bizarre*. In their subsequent accounts that pertained to Billy's letter, the reporters used Luther's words sparingly, while the handwriting experts were quoted at length. To a man, they suspected that the letter had been forged. They explained that, while Billy's childlike scrawl might seem easy to copy, there were a few identifying details—for example, the way Billy's double l's always leaned like inebriates against each other—missing in the alleged letter to Luther. Finally, they pointed out that the paper on which the letter was written was a common page of pulp tablet and Billy had never been known to use anything but his engraved stationery.

A month or so after Billy's death, three young men, the first volunteers of Billy's Brigade, appeared in Del Rio and began to circulate among arriving patients. They greeted the men as they stepped down from the trains and handed them pamphlets that advised against their being there. They asked them what they knew about Billy Boswell's suicide.

This was several weeks before the American Medical Association began to call for Luther's censure, to speak of what it termed his "charlatan empire." It was also before a legal representative of the Federal Communications Commission journeyed to Mexico City to meet with members of the Cárdenas administration.

"Doctor Mathias invites *you* to judge whether or not that letter is authentic. To answer the question in your *own* minds, and not meekly accept the biased judgment of others. And as you do, to ask yourselves who has the most to lose in this argument. Is it Doctor Mathias, whose pioneering science has rejuvenated the health and appetites of thousands? Or is it the shamed hypocrites of the American Medical Association who cower beneath their vaunted sheepskins, those worn and faded diplomas which only guarantee that whoever holds one subscribes to the old, timid methods which have proven inadequate through all the years of human suffering?

"You know, Doctor Mathias believes that a man should be judged by the results of his efforts and by the stature of his allies. And I say tonight, my friends, that Saint Luke, the greatest healer ever to walk among men, with the exception of course of the miraculous divine hand of Christ himself, Saint Luke was not a member of the AMA. There was no framed sheepskin hanging from Saint Luke's office wall. Saint Luke's compassionate care and strength-restoring medicines were not approved by the AMA. So, given the choice, Doctor Mathias is proud to stand in the towering company of Luke and against the weaklings of the AMA.''

When Luther had first heard about the three young men stopping patients at the depot, he'd had Del Rio's sheriff question them and put them on a departing train. From the sheriff, Luther learned that they'd come from Los Angeles and that they'd boasted of a long dislike of him. In fact, they were members of the outspoken homosexual community in Hollywood, that same group that had never been willing to dismiss Luther simply as a figure of high camp.

A few weeks later, they returned in larger numbers and this time employed sophisticated guerrilla strategies. They copied the plain rural dress and the brutish swaying walk that were characteristic of Luther's patients. They were thereby able to move indistinguishably among them at the depot, in the park.

They also began to board the trains destined for Del Rio at their penultimate stops, moving through the cars, looking for men in rustic dress with frightened eyes. In the frequent interviews they gave, the Brigade described the confusion and anxiety of those who would be patients and likened their emotional states to Billy's own at the end. In truth, few of the volunteers had known or even met Billy, but they were genuine in their view that Luther's work was evil.

Against them, Luther employed a sizable number of detectives who watched the depot and patrolled the boardinghouse hallways. They were often able to spot an imposter by his worn scuffed shoes, which the volunteers wrongly thought consistent with the old tweed suits and the frayed shirt collars. Luther instructed the detectives only to threaten anyone they caught, but sometimes they forgot or didn't stop with mere threats. This was effective against some of the Brigade, but many others had themselves photographed with their blackened eyes and sent the pictures off to newspapers along with lurid descriptions of their being beaten up.

Historians continue to debate the true effectiveness of Billy's Brigade, especially its role in encouraging the former patients who'd begun to come forward and announce that, like Billy, they'd been surgically brutalized and were planning to sue. Those who discount the volunteers' success say that the turmoil and all the resulting official action were inspired by the melodrama of Billy's suicide itself; his status in the culture; the extraordinary note and Leland Wheelock's press conference; the implication of Alyce Rae and Luther. They speak of its being a decade that was unusually susceptible to feverish publicity. They point to the nation's attention being held for two weeks while it read dispatches from rural Kentucky and waited to see if a man named Floyd Collins would be rescued from a cave. They cite the phenomenon of interest in the Dionne quintuplets.

Regardless of who caused what to happen, it's well documented that a faction within the FCC had been longing for years to take steps against Luther and had had little luck finding sympathetic attitudes in Mexico City while Plutarco Calles ruled. But as Luther had learned, the ambitions of Lázaro Cárdenas differed fundamentally from Mexican presidents of the past, and on a day in early June 1935, Cárdenas's courtly minister of communications, more typically dressed in a plain dark suit, had risen from behind his enormous desk to welcome a lawyer from the FCC and say how pleased he was that he had come.

The lawyer himself had felt deeply pleased to be there. For he was someone who was zealous in his wish to silence Luther and at times almost alone had kept the idea active within the bureaucratic warrens of the young agency. The lawyer was a solitary man of inflexible habits. He worked long hours and had no social life. His recreational pleasure was the radio. He so loved listening to it that he'd decided, in gratitude, to apply his legal talents to the regulatory tedium of the FCC. For years, he'd come home late from his office every night and prepared a simple supper and sat down to listen to *Amos 'n' Andy* while he ate. It had never occurred to him to vary this routine. Why should it have? How can one imagine beyond sublimity? And then one night he'd set his dish of stew and cup of black coffee on the table and turned on his Philco console. And he'd instantly recoiled as he heard the voice of Luther Mathias, rather than the Kingfish's buffoonish profundo. He'd been unable to tune in *Amos 'n' Andy* after that night, the first evening of Luther's doubly amplified broadcast.

"People have asked me—friends here in Del Rio and from all across the country who've written to express their concern—they've asked, 'Doctor Mathias, how is it you've been able to maintain your strength and continue to do the Clinic's work?' And my answer has always been the same: When you understand the motives of your attackers and see behind their pure-sounding words to the base and scurrilous inspiration for their actions, then it's not difficult to survive.

"Of course, my other source of strength, as always, has been the unrivaled wisdom of the Scriptures. There is no misfortune that cannot be made understandable through Christ's teachings and nothing has made my enemies' motivations so clear to me as the story, as chronicled in the gospel of John, of Jesus curing the impotent man and the wrath that ensued among the Jews as a result because He did His healing work on their sabbath day. Because, in other words, He didn't follow *their* rules, never mind that He healed a man who'd been sick for thirty-eight years and couldn't even crawl down the hillside to get to the holy waters in the pool of Bethesda. No, never mind that. And also never mind, by the way, that not once in all those thirty-eight years did one of them think to pick the poor man up and carry him down the hill to the healing pool. For all the Jews could think about was that Jesus hadn't followed the *rules*. 'And therefore,' John tells us, 'did the Jews persecute Jesus, and sought to slay him, because he had done these things on the sabbath day.' "

When he'd dwelt upon events of the past months, he'd begun to view their narrative not as linear but circular, as the Latin sensibility perceives the shape and run of time. The sheer number of threats and setbacks encouraged this thinking and so, just as much, did the swiftness with which they'd spread. Sometimes, he relived the hour after Alyce had left and he'd walked through his house, staring in at

every room, feeling the undiluted power of a child's pain and sus-
pecting, as a child does, that all he'd done, all he'd accomplished and
acquired, had been illusory. If not, he'd reasoned then, how could he
be feeling such simply defined pain? How could it be moving so wild
and unchecked in him?

Otherwise, his thoughts of Alyce seldom placed her in particular.
Instead, she had moved, almost diffused, into his history, darkening
it still more and deepening its teachings of inevitable betrayal. Most
often, that is, Alyce was less a figure than an enlivening new ingredient and in this understanding of his past as some reach of malevolent
harmony, Luther was refashioning a frame of feeling much like that
of the first years after Pampa. Then as now, his anger ranked no
distinctions. Then as now, he reacted primarily to his sense of recurrence, his rage in response to a merciless consistency that could still
astonish him.

And whenever he did think of Alyce within an instance, he found
it was not her visit to Del Rio, filled with her lies and her withdrawal
of what she'd promised. He thought instead of their afternoon in the
guest cottage and the question he still asked was why she'd come to
him that day, if not to commence an intricate revenge? And then,
very often, late at night when he was drunk, it seemed to him this
was the question he could ask of anyone who'd ever tried to get him
to believe them. It seemed he could have asked it of his mother and
his aunt. He could have asked it of his uncle, who'd sent him away
twice. He could have asked it of his father, as he was mounting his
horse to return to the huge cattle ranch near the Oklahoma border.
Why, he could have asked him, did you come for me in Cliffside, if
not to commence some intricate revenge?

"And so, like all of you listening tonight, I find wisdom in His lessons,
I take solace in His word, and I see the model for my own healing
conduct in His example." Luther leaned forward in his chair for the
bottle of whiskey on his desk. As he refilled the glass beside him, he
instinctively considered how well he was performing. His old habit of
self-assessment was deep within him and even now he could pause
and critically step back in his mind. Tonight he was interested simply in making clear that he'd been wronged and consequently had

achieved, indeed had invented, something like a state of feisty martyrdom. He heard the echoing sum of his words so far tonight and deemed that he was close to the pure pitch and cadence of distress.

He said into the telephone, "If the Son of God, that Criminal for Good, saw fit to violate some meaningless laws once in a while, then how can I possibly worry if a few witless lawyers, desperate and jealous as the Jews of Jerusalem, accuse me of breaking *their* silly rules?"

His other telephone began to ring beside him and he jumped slightly. Anyone who had the number knew he was broadcasting at this hour. He took a swallow as it rang a second time. He asked himself where the hell O'Malley was. It rang again and he squinted, as though trying to see the sound. He was very drunk; lately, he tried to be when he broadcast. He felt it kept his rage new-seeming and his sentences rode on his rage. It was becoming harder to get drunk enough, but he'd been drinking all day and had gotten so tonight. And though liquor might send him stumbling up the stairs, it conversely perfected his pained enunciation.

"But even though my faith assures me that everything will be all right in the end, that doesn't mean any one of us, not you and not me, has to live with our suffering in the meantime if we can find a way to put an end to it." The telephone stopped ringing. "We all know that Job's faith kept him going but we also know he endured an awful lot of pain he could have done without. Not that he should have denounced God, of course. I'm not saying that." The study door opened and Luther looked up to see O'Malley hurrying in. He moved toward the desk. Luther shook his head and frowned, his concentration threatened. O'Malley stood directly in front of him. His outline shimmered and blurred in Luther's vision. Luther said into the telephone, "But I don't think the Lord would have minded if Job's friends had lobbied some on his behalf . . ."

O'Malley was moving his lips with great exaggeration, mouthing words that Luther couldn't possibly read. Luther shook his head again. His eyes widened and closed and widened again. O'Malley made several pantomimic gestures, then his arms rose and fell in a frustrated flapping motion.

" . . . if they'd told the Lord that Job's faith had not faltered for a moment, and *would* not falter in their opinion, but that it seemed to them he was suffering more than necessary."

O'Malley reached for a piece of paper on the desk and began to scribble frantically.

"After all, isn't that the other lesson for us in the example of Job?" Luther leaned forward and craned his neck, trying to read O'Malley's writing upside down. "Isn't it suggested that the Lord was a little disgusted that Job just sat there, at a loss, pouting and feeling sorry for himself, since the Bible tells us again and again that the Lord has no sympathy for the timid acceptance of misfortune?"

O'Malley held up the piece of paper and Luther leaned forward and squinted at it. It read, "That telephone is dead! Your *voice* is off the air!" Luther said nothing for some seconds, then looked up at O'Malley, his expression completely bemused. He took the telephone away from his mouth and glared at it.

O'Malley said, "It's dead! They cut the line!"

Luther said, "Who did?"

"*Federales!*" O'Malley said. "They're at the station. Fenbow's on the other telephone. He called. That was him calling. He called to tell you."

"I haven't been broadcasting all this time?"

"You were until just before the telephone rang."

"Jesus Christ!" Luther shouted. "Jesus, Irish! Why the hell'd you tiptoe in here, using all that goddamn sign language if I wasn't even on the air?"

O'Malley shrugged. "What difference does it make?" He pointed to the other telephone. "Talk to Travis."

"Jesus Christ!" Luther shouted again as he reached for the telephone. "Jesus *Christ!*" He picked up the receiver and said, "Travis! What the hell is going on?"

"Quite a lot, Doctor M," he heard Fenbow say. "I'd reckon there's twenty, two dozen *federales* here. They just all of a sudden appeared like Injuns on the horizon. Then one of those local *policia* that's been guardin' the door all these months, he comes in with this order that says the station's Mexico's now. It says y'all been ignorin' Mexican guidelines, Doctor M."

"Son of a bitch," Luther said. He held up his whiskey bottle to show O'Malley it was empty and O'Malley went to an armoire by the door. "Those son of a *bitches*," Luther repeated. He asked, "So then they cut the line?"

"Not right away," Fenbow said. "Excuse me, Doctor M, I'm getting ahead of my story. The *federales*—y'all will appreciate this—they got held up from comin' inside by the two *policia*. We heard this ruckus outside, that's how we knew they's here in the first place. We looked out and all the regular crowd camped outside to watch the light show was packin' up and hurryin' back down the hill and everbody's yellin', and it's dark acourse, but maybe half the *federales* got big flaming torches so we can see they got their rifles pointed at the *policia* and the *policia* got theirs pointed back at the *federales*. The local boys were guardin' the station for y'all, Doctor M, how 'bout that? They's brave little bastards, too, you think about it. Just the two of them to the others' maybe twenty." Fenbow laughed. "Bill Loomis here, he looks out and says, 'We got us another Alamo.' "

Luther took the bottle from O'Malley. With the telephone at his ear, he reached behind him to the top of a low cabinet. He got a second glass and filled it for O'Malley. He heard Fenbow say, "When one of the *policia* came in to hand us this order, he said he's on our side 'cause we built that guardhouse for them and y'all bought them their new uniforms. He says that's more than anybody in Mexico ever done."

Luther lifted the bottle by its neck and took a swig. He heard Fenbow's low chuckling. He was struggling through his dumbness to gain some sense of the scene. He said, "If there's a standoff, how'd the *federales* cut the line?"

"That was before," Fenbow said.

"*What* was before?" Luther said. "Before *what*?"

"The standoff was before. There ain't no standoff now." Fenbow's voice was suddenly more somber. "What happened was, about ten additional *federales* come up the hill, including that fat sumbitch that's stationed permanent in Villa Acuña? They's all walkin' up the hill in a kind of huddle and when they got to the locals, they started yellin' and the locals started yellin' back and it was gettin' highly agitated out there, Doctor M, and then somebody fired his rifle in the air and things all of a sudden got real quiet. I figure the locals, by that time they could see the numbers they was facin' and, well, they's loyal, Doctor M, but they can count. So they put their rifles down and stepped aside. And that's when the *federales* came in and cut the line.''

Luther pushed his chair back and stood up. He rose too quickly and staggered. He bumped into his desk. Finally he said, "Then the *federales* are inside now?"

"They are, for a fact," Fenbow said. "They's yellin' at everbody over and over that the station belongs to the people of Mexico. I'd say they's pretty worked up after their triumph over the locals. It ain't at all clear what's gonna happen next. I doubt we'll be arrested, but, hell, you never know. I would say a good portion, maybe half of them, is sober. I'm a little worried they might destroy the transmitter and such." Fenbow chuckled again, "Acourse if it belongs to the people of Mexico now, I don't guess they'd wanna do that."

"How much longer are they going to let you talk to me?"

"They don't know I am yet. I'm back here with the transmitter and they's all still swarmin' around out in the studio, shoutin' at Bill Loomis and some others, Betty Neal." Fenbow laughed. "Betty Neal's givin' it right back, by the way. It's kind of an interesting scene, actually."

While he listened to Fenbow, Luther paced back and forth behind his chair and drank whiskey from the bottle. Between gulps, he looked at O'Malley. O'Malley continued to stand in front of the desk, hearing Luther's end of the conversation. When Luther grimaced, so did he. They nodded and shook their heads almost in unison.

Luther asked Fenbow, "Tell me what, exactly what does the government order say?"

"I left it out front," Fenbow said. "Let me think. It says, oh yeah, that the board of the directors that runs the station is, I forget the word, but essentially that it ain't what they had in mind. And what else? That y'all have ignored their askin' for half the programs in Spanish, which they say they been tellin' you to do for months. And then—is that true, by the way, Doctor M?"

"Jesus!" Luther snapped. "Who the hell are you, their lawyer?"

"I's just curious. Anyway, that's the gist of it, and then they's still harpin' on that whole business about the products being dangerous to—oh, shit.''

"What's wrong?" He stopped his pacing.

Fenbow whispered, "A couple of 'em just walked in." Luther could faintly hear Fenbow greeting the *federales* and, more faintly still, their Spanish in response. He could hear Fenbow breathing harshly into the speaker and then he heard him whisper something unintelligible. He heard a door slamming, the scrape of a chair across the floor.

"Travis?" Luther hissed. "What's going on?" He paused. "Travis?" he said. And then this line too went dead.

"Shit!" Luther shouted. He held the telephone away from him and studied it. It seemed to him like the lifeless extension of a limb.

"What?" O'Malley asked.

Luther looked at him but said nothing. He looked back at the dead telephone with apparent fascination. Finally he said, "How could this happen?" His voice was soft and sounded sincere.

"*What* happened?" O'Malley asked.

Luther answered by throwing the telephone across the room. He stared fully at O'Malley. He appeared just to have heard some ultimate irrelevance. He put the bottle to his lips and leaned his head back. When he'd finished swallowing, he wiped his mouth with the back of his hand. He began to pace behind his desk again, cursing unimaginatively. His voice rose and fell and rose again as he relayed to O'Malley what Fenbow had described. O'Malley's eyes followed Luther back and forth, unconsciously providing the accompanist's punctuating murmurs and obscenities.

Luther heard himself say, "That's all Travis told me. I don't know what else is happening." He said, "I imagine—but I don't know, Travis didn't—I don't think he said that." As he listened to these admissions he felt them emphasized and when he'd finished saying, "And then the second line went dead," he was so furious about the ignorance he'd been forced to confess that his vision was briefly a pulsing light.

He started around from behind his desk.

"Where are you going?" asked O'Malley.

"Call Haskell," Luther said.

"Haskell?" O'Malley said. His surprise had good foundation. Luther hadn't spoken to Albright in months, though he'd continued to send him his share of the declining profits.

"I know," Luther said. "Call him anyway. Tell him what's happened and see if he can get anyone in Mexico City. If he thinks we're losing the station, what the hell, he might help." He handed the bottle of whiskey to O'Malley. "Here," he said.

"Where are you going?" O'Malley asked again.

"Oh," Luther said, as though he thought he'd already told him. "To the station."

"You're barred from entering the country," O'Malley said.

"What the hell does that have to do with it? They're trying to take my station."

"You can't do anything by yourself. *I'll* go. I'll come back and let you know."

"They're trying to take my goddamn station, Irish!"

"You're drunk," O'Malley said.

"If I was sober," he said, "they'd still be trying to take it." He crossed the room, his fumbling fingers laboring to button his vest as he went, as though he were preparing to greet a ballroom filled with guests. He paused at the door and looked back at O'Malley. "Call Haskell," he said again. "Make it sound like things are desperate." He opened the door and disappeared behind it. O'Malley heard his arrhythmic step strike the ballroom floor.

O'Malley shook his head and thought, Make it *sound* like things are desperate?

Outside, Luther moved toward his Packard. Rain had been falling for the past several nights and he could see it falling now in fine slants through the lights of the fountain. The gravel was slickly polished. The rain had given the surfaces of the Packard a false sheen.

He climbed in and took a deep breath. Then he started the engine. He turned the headlights on and reached for the knob that started the windshield wipers. He leaned forward and squinted through their delta patterns on the glass. He saw the front entrance of Desert Gardens and tried to focus his eyes on the heavy wooden door. It wavered in his vision until he blinked. He stared at the door through the rain for several moments. He blinked again and saw that the door was still there. This encouraged him. The door, its size and weight, its scrolled and beveled recesses, was indisputably real and if it was, then so must be everything it opened to reveal.

After some effort, he managed to put the Packard in gear and slowly guided it around the circular drive. When he reached the road he turned left toward the river.

"Hello, Mr. Albright."

"Mr. O'Malley," Haskell Albright said. "It's been a long time."

"Yes, it has," O'Malley said. "Let me tell you why I'm calling," and he began to describe what had happened at the station.

Haskell Albright listened quietly, so much so that O'Malley paused at one point to ask if he were still there.

"I'm here," Albright said.

O'Malley thought he heard a certain merriment.

For the past several months, Albright had been paying the embassy assistant to keep his mouth shut. He'd given some thought to having him killed, but he'd decided the idea was extreme as a first step. So he'd agreed to meet the assistant's price and, especially since the day he'd heard the news of Billy's suicide, he'd regarded it as among the soundest investments of his life. For even now, the thought that he might have been included in the sordidness filled Albright with a dread he had to work to quiet.

He still dreamed a dream now and then, one of punitive verisimilitude. In it, he was sitting on his country club veranda while all those around him, beneath the gay umbrellas, were openly asking one another if they'd heard he'd had the surgery. They were laughing uproariously. Their voices rose. Their laughter shrieked and redoubled. They leaned back in their chairs and raised their hands to shield their eyes from the sun and sighted across the veranda, shouting his name from table to table. Did you hear about Haskell!? Did you hear? Did you hear? And all the while, he sat visibly in their midst, inexplicably voiceless and unable to move. It was not as though the crowd didn't know that he was there. No, much worse than that, they knew and didn't care.

He'd had this dream perhaps half a dozen times, always waking at a point where he tried to stand up and fell back in his chair.

"So anything you might be able to do, Mr. Albright, anyone you could talk to right away, even as soon as tonight, Luther would be extremely grateful to you."

Albright said after a moment, "Where's the Cowboy now?"

"He's on his way to the station," O'Malley said.

"But he's barred," Albright said.

"Yes he is," O'Malley said. "I tried to tell him not to go."

Albright had also decided some months before that Luther's end was imminent and in his mind he'd abandoned him, cut his losses and moved on. He'd turned his energies to investigating profitable possibilities in ever more forlorn tracts of desert real estate. And since the time he'd made his judgment, everything Albright had heard and seen regarding Luther—the FCC investigation; the AMA attacks; the growing number of lawsuits brought by former patients; most of all, his own steadily lessening returns—had confirmed for Albright that, yet again in his life, he'd been remarkably astute.

"You know, Mr. O'Malley," Albright said, "when I called him some time back to warn him there was trouble, he was so interested, as I realized when I eventually figured out the chronology of it all, he was so interested in trying to tickle Alyce Rae's tonsils with his big hick weiner that he didn't even know my name. So you can tell him this for me when he gets back, *if* he gets back. Tell the son of a bitch to go screw a cow."

He slowed the Packard even more as he approached the Rio Grande bridge. It appeared in the night behind the drape of rain. Squinting toward it, Luther felt a surprising stir of fond recollection cutting through his sense of insult and outrage. He'd not been near the bridge since he'd been barred from Mexico and now, a quarter mile away, he felt intensely drawn toward it, impelled by the store of pleasure and meaning he'd compiled through the years of moving back and forth across it.

As he'd driven the distance from his home, his emotions had narrowed to a push of vehemence. It was immensely whiskey-driven. Its simple insistence was that he get to the bridge and only now, as he inched forward in his automobile, did he suddenly realize that of course he had no plan. It was the sight of the bridge itself, standing now perhaps fifty yards away, that served to make him see there was no chance he could cross.

He was aware of headlights behind him. It occurred to him that they'd been there for some time. His drunkenness had been accepting them as though they were a natural feature of the night. He moved the Packard to the side of the road and watched the automobile pass and continue its way toward the bridge. He braked the Packard and shut off the engine. The rain appeared suddenly heavier; did it seem so just because he'd come to a stop? He looked again toward the bridge. Besides the one that had just passed him, two other automobiles were waiting to cross. He watched one of them move forward and the other two start up and come again to a stop. Their taillights blinked brightly as they braked. Luther filled his lungs with air and loudly exhaled. He peered through the rain and thought he could make out a border guard stepping out from his shack and looking in through their windows. He thought he saw the guard's long poncho. It appeared that some car doors were opening and shutting, but the rain and his dim apprehension made it impossible for Luther to know whether this was what he was seeing.

The last of the cars passed through into Mexico and the bridge stood suddenly empty in the rain. Staring at it, Luther felt himself inside a thickly intimate moment. It felt as though the bridge were inviting him to come. He shook his head and smiled. He saw how foolish he'd been to have driven to this spot. He supposed that it would have been better if he'd tried to make his way on foot through prohibitive terrain and swim across at any of a hundred other places. But rage and habit had made his drunken dumbness perfect and brought him to the bridge. And now that he was here, he felt himself growing excited. It seemed fitting that he figure out a way to cross where the challenge was greatest and his history resided.

He thought suddenly again that they were trying to take his station. A bilious curiosity rose in him. His mind filled with images that were racist clichés. He saw *federales* roaming through the studio and breaking things just for the sport of doing so.

He cursed and climbed out of the Packard. He shut the door and started unsteadily through the rain along the side of the road. Drunk as he was, he felt things, and his sensation was of being effortlessly powered. At the core of his eagerness was a proprietor's indignation and there was something impetuous and unmanageable surrounding it. His urge was also moving to, being moved by, that.

Marshes of *coriza* flanked the road on both sides. The rain was steady. He pulled the collar of his suit coat up around his neck. He was less than twenty yards from the bridge. Suddenly, he was sure he heard the voice of the border guard floating back to reach him and he took it as his signal to head into the reeds. It's clear that he was moving to that instinct of his youth, when his pulse had been anger and fine arrogance and he'd thoughtlessly left one place for the next, sure only of the fact that whatever came next was unknown and was possible.

He parted the reeds and entered. In the marsh, the ground was soft and tried to hold his heavy feet. He felt the land sloping immediately toward the river. He was distantly aware that flies were biting his flesh and that mosquitoes were drawing his blood. The *coriza* was his height and he was entirely inside the rustling noise he made. He could hear nothing else. He couldn't hear the rain's softer rustling as it struck. He lifted his feet and set them down and he suddenly wondered if he might come upon a nest of hoboes; dozens and dozens of them now lived in the reeds. This somehow reminded him not to think of snakes. Consequently, he began to.

The slope of the marsh dipped steeply and he stumbled and fell to his knees. He knelt there for a moment, small as a child, and felt the suddenly tree-tall reeds closing over him. He struggled to his feet. The bridge was above him on his right. He was soaking wet. He started forward again, the reeds and thorns tearing at his face and hands. Again, he tried not to think of snakes. He was unaware that his trousers were being ripped. He squinted up through the reeds at the bridge's ribbed underbelly. He worried that the guard would hear his noise. He saw the *federales* setting fire to his station.

At last the marsh thinned, then ended, and a brief flat of sand began. As he stepped free of the reeds, he bent over and placed his hands on his knees. He was exhausted. He spent several moments taking breaths. He could hear, in front of him, the river's movement and over it he heard the guard's voice again. He was surprised and impressed by the distance it carried through the rain. Then he heard it once more and heard another answering it and as he began to form the suspicion that these voices could not possibly be reaching him, he heard the same rustling sounds he'd made through the reeds. He stood up and looked around and saw two guards crashing through the marsh toward him.

"*El Doctor!*" they cried.

Luther turned and started running away from the bridge.

The guards emerged from the marsh and released *vaquero* yelps. They raised their rifles and fired into the air. Luther stumbled and caught himself. He was squinting fiercely toward the river on his right, trying to sight across it for any limbs, anything that would be in his way. He saw wet night.

The guards fired their rifles into the air a second time. Luther felt himself moving with an agonizing slowness, the wet dead-weight of his clothes, the sand accepting every step, and yet the guards sounded no closer. He risked a backward glance and it appeared that he was right. They were running at a speed that seemed intent on keeping pace, less interested in catching him than herding him along. He tried to increase his distance from them, struggling to shed his jacket and his vest as he ran. He sensed the course of his path weaving wildly over the sand.

They each fired again, one a beat after the other, and Luther saw the sand ahead spray up in small explosions. He swerved toward the river and met the water in four strides and waded out in a kind of frantic shuffle. It was maddeningly shallow, giving him no cover, and then at last the bed dropped away and the water reached his chest. He dove down and duck-walked below the water, managing to pull off his shoes and then his stockings.

He worked to keep himself below the surface. But he was badly winded from running and drink and had nothing in his lungs. He felt his air going, then it was gone and he tried to come up to the river's sounds.

He blinked his eyes several times and squinted hard toward the shore. Nothing was moving. He saw nothing in the darkness. The river sloshed up into his face. He spit. He heard only the river and the rain. He saw the rain pocking the surface of the water as it struck. He filled his lungs as best he could and turned. He gauged himself a quarter of the way across. He told himself it was an easy swim; it was such a meager river. But he of course had no true measure of just how drunk he was.

He gathered himself to push off, then came slowly out of his crouch and lengthened in the water. With his second stroke he heard the guards' *vaquero* shouts, which broke into syllables over half an octave. He extended his arms and pulled toward Mexico. The guards fired a fourth round and a fifth.

He swam in clumsy frenzy, his palms slapping the water, and suddenly he imagined a line running midway with the river, a border through the border where the Rio Grande touched the Rio Bravo but was itself neither one place nor the other. He lifted his head to gasp for breath and that was when he saw the far shore come alive with light. Lights dotted the hillside and were moving down toward the shore. He stopped his stroke and his body swung under him and he sat in the river, watching more lights appear.

Through the rain, he could tell that they were torches. He was close enough to hear voices behind them. He breathed and spit and paddled in the river. He could vaguely feel his strength leaving his limbs.

Two rifle shots were fired and behind him, from Texas, a rifle answered them.

He bobbed below the water and came up again and watched the torches moving closer to the shore. He guessed twenty, thirty, just as Fenbow had said; no, probably fewer; some of them would have stayed behind to guard the station. It all seemed to Luther no more orchestrated than some perfect randomness inspired by the rain, and in the coming weeks both countries' governments would insist they'd not agreed on any sort of plan and that they were nothing other than dismayed by the way the night had senselessly transpired.

He saw the torches. In his mind, he saw his station in flames. He felt a sense of terror rising in his heart that thrilled him utterly. It was the terror he had carried the day he'd fled from Pampa. It was what he'd used to hurry through the fog away from Memphis. In it were the exaltation of his love for whores, that amber decadence, and the sense of revenge he'd take on everyone who'd asked him to come near. He gathered the breath he had and used much of it to give a thin shout of delight, a peculiar trill of language, at the thought that he would follow the line that halved the river out of danger. He'd follow it exactly until he could cross, all the way to river's end if that's what he must do. He kicked and reached and as he lifted his head he heard the agitative lilt of the lovely Spanish voices and saw the torches arranging themselves along the shore. He thought, *The bush burned with fire, and the bush was not consumed.*

DOUGLAS BAUER has published *Prairie City, Iowa,* a nonfiction book about a year of reunion in his hometown, and a highly acclaimed novel, *Dexterity.* He lives in Boston with his wife and is at work on a new novel.